MW00563453

DAVID EBSWORTH is the pen name of
negotiator and workers' representati
General Workers' Union. He was bor
Wrexham, North Wales, with his wife Ann since 1981.

Following his retirement, Dave began to write historical fiction
in 2009 and has subsequently published nine novels: political thrillers
set against the history of the 1745 Jacobite rebellion, the 1879 Anglo-
Zulu War, the Battle of Waterloo, warlord rivalry in sixth century
Britain, and the Spanish Civil War. His sixth book, *Until the Curtain
Falls* returned to that same Spanish conflict, following the story of
journalist Jack Telford, and is published in Spanish under the title
Hasta Que Caiga el Telón. Jack Telford, as it happens, is also the main
protagonist in a separate novella, *The Lisbon Labyrinth*.

Each of Dave's novels has been critically acclaimed by the
Historical Novel Society and been awarded the coveted B.R.A.G.
Medallion for independent authors.

This ninth novel, *Wicked Mistress Yale, The Parting Glass*, is the
third in a trilogy about the life of nabob, philanthropist (and slave-
trader) Elihu Yale, who gave his name to Yale University, but told
through the eyes of his much-maligned and largely forgotten wife,
Catherine.

For more information on the author and his work, visit his
website at www.davidebsworth.com.

Also by David Ebsworth

The Jacobites' Apprentice
A story of the 1745 Rebellion. Finalist in the Historical Novel Society's
2014 Indie Award

The Jack Telford Series
Political thrillers set towards the end of the Spanish Civil War. The first
of these is *The Assassin's Mark*. "This is not a novel you will be able to
put down." (Rachel Malone, Historical Novel Society). The sequel is
the much-acclaimed *Until the Curtain Falls*, published in Spanish as *Hasta
Que Caiga el Telón*. Telford also features in the e-book novella, *The Lisbon
Labyrinth*, which follows Jack's later misadventures during the Portuguese
Revolution of April 1974.

The Kraals of Ulundi: A Novel of the Zulu War
Picks up the story of the Zulu War where Michael Caine left off. "An
accomplished, rich, beautifully produced and very rewarding read that
brings a lesser-known era of history to life." (Cristoph Fischer, Historical
Novel Society)

The Last Campaign of Marianne Tambour: A Novel of Waterloo
Action and intrigue based on the real-life exploits of two women who
fought, in their own right, within Napoleon's army. "Superb! David
Ebsworth has really brought these dramatic events to life. His description
of the fighting is particularly vivid and compelling." (Andrew W. Field,
author of *Waterloo: The French Perspective*)

The Song-Sayer's Lament
"A rich, glorious, intricate tapestry of the time we know of as the Dark
Ages, with echoes of Rosemary Sutcliff's magnificent *Sword at Sunset* and
Mary Stewart's, *Crystal Cave* series. It's steeped in authenticity and heart. I
loved it!" (Manda Scott, author of the bestselling *Boudica* series and
Into the Fire)

The Doubtful Diaries of Wicked Mistress Yale
Mistress Yale's Diaries, The Glorious Return
Parts One and Two of the Yale Trilogy

Wicked
Mistress
YALE
The
Parting
Glass

DAVID EBSWORTH

SilverWood

Published in 2020 by SilverWood Books

SilverWood Books Ltd
14 Small Street, Bristol, BS1 1DE, United Kingdom
www.silverwoodbooks.co.uk

ISBN 978-1-78132-999-3 (paperback)
ISBN 978-1-80042-000-7 (ebook)

British Library Cataloguing in Publication Data
A CIP catalogue record for this book is
available from the British Library

Page design and typesetting by SilverWood Books

Dedicated to all women who've been swept from the pages of history

Author's Note

As I said in the introduction to the preceding parts of the trilogy – these are, of course, works of fiction, though very firmly rooted in history and, for the period in question, this throws up a particular issue about the dating of Catherine Yale's diary entries, which are written as they would have been at the time. Under the old Julian Calendar, then in use, the new year officially began in April of one year and ended in March of the next (although the 'calendar year' still began on 1st January, of course), so that February would, for example be dated as 1674/5, while May three months later would simply be dated as 1675.

Second, there are a lot of real-life characters to be recalled from Parts One and Two, so here is a quick summary of some significant family and related members...

Catherine Hynmers Yale (née Elford), born 1651
Joseph Hynmers, Catherine's first husband, born 1641, died 1680
And their children...
Joseph Hynmers Junior, born 1670
Richard Hynmers, born 1672
Walter Hynmers (probably fictional), born and died 1674
Elford Hynmers, born 1676
Benjamin Hynmers, born 1678

Elihu Yale, Catherine's second husband (married 1680), born 1649
And their children...
David Yale, born 1684, died 1687
Katherine (Katie) Yale, born 1685
Anne (Nan) Yale, born 1687
Ursula (Ursi) Yale, born 1689

Katherine Nicks (née Barker), Yale's alleged mistress at Fort St. George, Madras
John Nicks, her husband

Winifred Bridger, Jewish-Portuguese treacherous friend of Catherine's from Madras

Jeronima de Paiva, Yale's "other" mistress at Fort St. George
Carlos Almanza Yale (Don Carlos), her illegitimate son

Streynsham Master, a former governor of Fort St. George
Sir William Langhorn, another former governor

And the main fictional characters:
Matthew Parrish, diplomat, spy and poet
Vincent Seaton, the now deceased Jacobite assassin
Colonel John Porter, a Jacobite traitor

Volume Five

Monday 1st January 1700

I knew from the bitterness of the sauce that it should end in disaster, a gravy in which I feared we might all stew.

'Then let us raise a glass,' said my husband Elihu. 'A parting glass. An end to separations and our families united in harmony. A stirrup cup to that tired old century and the beginning of a new journey.'

Locket's may no longer quite live up to its former reputation but I truly would not know for certain since I never before had the privilege of crossing its threshold.

'Does the mathematicks not show, sir,' said my son Benjamin, who had already consumed far too much of the wine, waving his cup about and spilling some of the contents, 'that the new century, our eighteenth century, should not begin until this day *next* year?'

He had the bearing of a young billy goat, lowering its head to challenge the old ram – almost his permanent manner whenever he is in Elihu's presence. And Elihu, I saw, took a pace back from the table as if to accept the combat from his stepson.

'Yet our natural instinct, my boy,' Sir Stephen Evance tried to pacify Benjamin, 'declares that this is a wondrous new age. The seventeen hundreds, sirrah, must begin here and now. Every letter we write, every contract we sign, must surely shout the logic of the thing.'

And every journal entry, I thought, as I picked over my kickshaw of chicken.

Sir Stephen – though he hates me styling him so – was master of today's feast. He has done business with my husband over these past ten years and some of it, I collect, not strictly within the rules permitted by John Company. He is a prodigiously foppish beau, of course, his emerald silk suit making a sparrow even of Elihu, though I cannot help but like him. And, goodness, did ever a fellow rise so far, so fast. By the age of twenty-five, one of England's foremost goldsmiths and bankers, now Jeweller to the King.

'England behind the rest of the world, I fear,' Benjamin told him. 'As always. We live in the past, do we not?'

The rest of Protestant Europe – most of it anyway – has intelligently opted to change the way we calculate our calendar, to use the system devised by Pope Gregory. A century ago? I think so. It will bring us into conformity with most of our major trading partners.

'Nothing wrong with our calendar,' Elihu roared. 'For heaven's sake, great Julius Caesar gave it to us. May hell freeze over before we have some German, Dane, Butter-box or Swede tell us how to measure our years. You do not support the thing, Catherine? This Popish iniquity?'

'Well said, sirrah.' A redcoat major at the table alongside our own. 'Well said. A pox on the pope and his Jacobite banditti.' Well, that is complicated. I know it is complicated. Many of the Jacobites may indeed be papists, though all papists – and probably not Pope Innocent either, as it happens – support exiled James Stuart and his followers. But I was more concerned with some of the ribald comments from several of his fellow-officers, one of whom seemed unable to take his licentious eyes from my Katie.

'There you have it, husband,' I said. 'So many evil things to be confronted in this world.' I held the gaze of that particular lecherous cove, a captain, I think. 'But whether our calendar is fashioned by a Romish pope or an ancient Romish dictator hardly signifies.'

I turned my attention to Katie. Fifteen this year, pretty in her way, pretty in her primrose-yellow skirts, and just old enough to have betrayed me. The last thing I should have expected.

'Stap my vitals,' said Evance. 'You have a pretty turn of phrase, Catherine. And where, gentlemen,' he shouted to the redcoats over the general hubbub of the dining room, 'might you be posted to root out those rascals?'

A young subaltern at their table sniggered into his ragout, made some murmured mockery of Stephen's manner of speech. I had heard them bandy the word sodomite several times already and I wondered whether they should be so free with their offence had they understood Evance's proximity to the king.

2

'To Ireland,' laughed the major. 'Brewer's Regiment, at your service. We shall "woot out those wascals" over there.' Hilarity and table thumping. 'I suppose you have never served His Majesty, sirrah?'

'Allow me to name Sir Stephen Evance, Major,' said my husband, tugging imperiously at the edges of his mustard waistcoat. 'He serves His Majesty every day, sir, in more ways than you might imagine. In a most personal capacity.' More sniggering from the soldiers. 'And I, too. Recently returned from India and our Presidency at Fort St. George.'

He has been home four months after our ten years apart. The first few weeks were tolerable enough and I counted myself fortunate that we continued to enjoy separate bedchambers. But then his melancholy began. A demonic black dog. He became morose and only seemed to rise occasionally from his dark humours, most frequently when he had been at his writing desk. Missive after missive to Mistress Nicks back in Madras until, late in October, I had ventured into his room when he was absent from the house and read the draft on which he had been working. I should not have done so. I know I should not. But espionage seems to have become so rooted in my essence that it was impossible to resist.

My dearest friend, he had begun. Well, if the things Katherine Nicks had told me before she left were true, they had been much more than dear friends. And now here he was, spilling his sorrow and despondency all across the page. So sorrowful, he thought he should die. *And should you hear of my demise*, he said, *I prithee dispose of my house on Middle Street* – his house, damn him, that was *my* house – *my godowns, the garden house and my various gems and jewels, and gift the proceeds to your youngest.* The youngest, two of them anyway, the two girls, now also here in England with their father – though actually at boarding school in Hackney. Those that Mistress Nicks had sworn to me were not Elihu's. Simply their godfather, she had said. And I had believed her. Yet now? *Your good man*, he continued, *seems to fare well enough, though the girls suffer somewhat for their lack of English.* You can hear the accent, of course, in their mother's speech.

The Nicks girls have been raised almost entirely by her aunt, back there in Madras Patnam, an aunt who speaks a word of almost nothing but her native Portuguese. And then this: *You must pay my respects to Madam Paiva, and to young Don Carlos, naturally.* His mistress and his by-blow. His son and heir. *For though I am with my family here in England, all is unsettled and sadness. You understand this, that I am married in India too. Married in India, married to India, yet always too far from your thoughts.*

I had confronted him when he returned. A furious rencounter after which he had stormed out. Gone to stay with one of his London associates. To my astonishment, Katie had insisted on going with him. Just like that. Almost worse than any of my bereavements. Oh, so many bereavements. Betrayal. Still, she is presently back with me at Broad Street and I have chosen to forgive her. Elihu is returned there too, though I know not for how long. He has a plan, he says, the foundation upon which, I now understand, had stood his toasting of an end to separations, of united families, there in Locket's dining room.

'And how long, my friends,' Evance was saying to the scarlet-coated officers of Brewer's Regiment, 'before your masters have no scruple but to send you to France?'

The war clouds gathering again. Charles the Second of Spain, and also Holy Roman Emperor is ailing and without an heir. The vacant throne is certain to be contended by the Catholic Bourbons and the Austrian Habsburgs – the latter bound to seek a Protestant succession. As usual, the rest of us in Europe will take sides, and how long before we bathe the fields of Flanders with the ritual blood of our young men as we seem to do with such monotonous frequency?

'Oh,' said the major, 'I doubt we shall now be moved from Ireland.'

'My dear sir,' Evance scratched at his bar-wig and his usually buffle-headed blather settled to a different tone entirely, 'you may be certain I shall make it my business to ensure that His Majesty dispatches you good gentleman there for the very first volley.'

The first volley? I know what this will mean. That as soon as we are at war with France once more, the Jacobite rabble will be back out of the woodwork. I shall have none of it. Not this time. I am done with spying.

'The king?' Ursula piped up as the soldiers chewed on Evance's menacing promise. 'Tell them how you met the king, Papa.'

It had been in that golden few weeks after his return. His father's will probated, settled in the Prerogative Court. His inheritance of

4

Plas Grono secured. Northern Wales. And I had arranged with Sir William Cavendish that Elihu might have an audience. It seemed the very least the Duke of Devonshire could do, after all, given that I had saved his life, and I thought it might help. Indeed, His Majesty had been pleased to spend a half-hour being appraised of the latest developments in Indian affairs. From somewhere, Elihu had drawn an assumption – something must have been said, I suppose – that a knighthood may follow. A Patent for a Baron Knight, Elihu claimed. But then, nothing. And, as the melancholy grew, so the tale was transformed. This more subdued Governor Yale, it seems, is satisfied simply to be so esteemed by His Majesty and his Ministers of State that they should seek his opinion.

"'*I think the King*,'" Elihu quoted with great solemnity to poor Ursula, '"*is but a man, as I am.*" Have I not told you that before, little one? Still, I expect he shall settle the debt he now owes me in due course.'

Ursi wrinkled her milk-pale face in confusion while Annie, at her side, rolled her eyes, pushed her coulis of stewed and mashed vegetables about her small bowl.

'All a matter of *actori incumbit onus probation*, I suppose,' said Benjamin. 'The burden of proof falls upon the claimant. For each of us to make our case in relation to the debts owed us.'

There it was. Benjamin's obsession with the legal claim he was preparing to pursue against my husband for his rightful inheritance. A claim about which Elihu as yet remained blissfully unaware.

'Yes, I know the law, young man,' Elihu snapped, his veneer of good humour slipping fast. 'I inherited from Governor Langhorn…' He stopped, set down his fork and set a hand to his forehead, and I know that each mention of Langhorn's name brings back the recollection of my story – the story he had insisted that Sir William himself should verify: Vincent Seaton's true nature, the years he had spent as a papist intelligencer and a tool of the Jacobites; the parts that myself and Katherine Nicks had played, deliberately or inadvertently, in his downfall and death; the harm this had inflicted upon poor Ursula; and the awful injury suffered by Mistress Nicks herself, an injury, he had convinced himself, that must have occasioned her mysterious return to Madras. 'Governor Langhorn…' my husband repeated.

'A pity about the knighthood, though,' said Benjamin, toying with his white neck cloth. 'They say that peers of the realm may get away with murder.'

The jibe seemed hardly to register. Elihu remained somewhere else entirely, oblivious to the reference, the fact that he had been tacitly accused himself of murdering the witnesses against him in those charges of corruption back in Madras, three of the four mysteriously dead.

'Perish the thought,' he replied, as though only then collecting where he was, 'that I should ever have designs upon a life at Court. Besides, your Mama now moves in circles of society sufficient for us all. The Duke of Devonshire. The Czar of Muscovy. Whereas I...'

And was that not where the melancholy had begun? Not with sorrow for Katherine Nicks and her sufferings, nor even her loss – for in our confrontation he had admitted that yes, he hoped one day to follow her back to Madras – but the realisation that, upon the Coromandel Coast, he had been a very large golden fish in a modest pond, the world apparently revolving around him. The realisation that, meanwhile, world events had actually seen myself and Mistress Nicks at their heart, at least for a few brief hours. The realisation that, here in London, he would never again be at the centre of global affairs. All that and the longing for India too, a longing that still tears at my own heart these ten years after I, myself, sailed back aboard the *Rochester*.

'Whereas you, my dear fellow,' Evance beamed at him, 'have brought back such riches and wealth that would make even His Majesty blush. Why, he told me so himself. And shall you not share your news with us?'

Stephen had been playing some word game with Anne and little Ursi, while Benjamin, seemingly tired of trying to bait his stepfather, was deep in conversation with Kate. He has always been gentle with the girls but I have noted that, of late, he has begun to treat Katie with a great deal of respect. He is much older than her, of course, and I have on occasion had cause to wonder whether he might be paying her just a little too much attention. Whenever she has the opportunity, I have noted that her attentions turn always to Evance. Still, I suppose I should be grateful for any evidence of resins that might help to bind my family – or perhaps I should say families – together at last.

'News,' said Elihu. 'News, of course.'

At that moment, Edward Locket himself appeared at the table, stained apron, asked if we should favour some dessert. Red fruit pudding was duly ordered, and Parmesan cheese, of course. More wine, too. And was everything to our satisfaction? he asked. Indeed, sirrah, we all replied.

'Though not as good as in his father's day,' murmured Evance as the proprietor moved away to take payment from our now more subdued neighbours. 'Well, Elihu, your news?'

I saw a smile return to my husband's rubicund face, and I wondered what this might presage. But he merely leaned back in his chair, patted his belly in contentment, smiled inanely at each of us around the table.

'Now,' I said at last, 'for pity's sake, Elihu, this news.'

To be honest, I was filled with dread as he stood, cheeks aglow, raised his glass again.

'Well, it is this,' he beamed. 'New beginnings, as I have said. And what finer way to begin again than with a new property. I have found one, my dear. Much more commodious than our present abode. Yet not far away, neither. Austin Friars, sirrah. Austin Friars. What say you, Catherine?'

I tried my best to smile, to feign delight while, inside, my stomach churned. The house on Broad Street may not be ideal, but it is my own, part of my independence. And to sacrifice that independence once more, is that a price I am prepared to pay for the sake of my making us a single family again? Shall it help protect me from whatever ravages the feuds in my life might throw at me? From the ravages of war that we all see on the horizon? I have no idea just yet.

Though while I contemplated all this in the moment before I must reply, it was my dear friend Matthew Parrish who was uppermost in my mind. For he has written to me recently from France where he still serves as a diplomat. He has written and enclosed a new poem. It is simply entitled *My English Chains*, and there is this brace of couplets:

Oh, wondrous Spy, that watches all yet fathoms naught,
Who's set to catch the Traitor, then by Traitor caught –
But shall the Spy not recognise the Traitor's Art?
For ne'er was worse a Traitor than this true Friend's Heart.

What is this? Some profession of his own sentiments? Or do I read too much into these few simple lines? For this is one of Matthew's longer works, twenty stanzas and, taken in context of the rest, innocuous enough. These couplets keep repeating themselves to me. The spy he mentions could, of course, merely be himself. But I think not that simple. He still sees me as active in his espionage network, I collect, and though I long to be reunited with Parrish, know not what the future may hold in that direction of our friendship, I shall refuse to be drawn into that world of espionage again. Ever.

'What I say, husband, is that if Austin Friars was good enough for Great Henry's Thomas Cromwell...' Cromwell's palace there may have been lost in the Great Fire but it is still remarked as one of London's old wonders...'then I am sure it will suit us very well also.'

As I looked from one face to another, my husband's ruddy jowls, my son Benjamin's pinched cheeks, and the rouged lips of our associate Sir Stephen Evance, I saw that the words, which I had intended to seem so positive, had produced nothing but frowns. For, of course, Thomas Cromwell's story did not end well either. And nor would this one.

'Prime!' Elihu declared. 'And a new home deserves a new broom, do you not agree, my dear?' I must have looked confused. 'Why,' he went on, 'our household shall be considerably larger, requires a steadier hand to manage our affairs than poor Ellen.'

My housekeeper. I knew she vexed him by her loyalty to me alone.

'You have somebody in mind,' I said, suddenly afraid that I already knew the answer.

'Naturally,' he smiled, and lifted his glass once more. 'To Mistress Bridger,' he said.

Like a cold claw gripping my innards. Winifred Bridger, who had returned with him from Madras Patnam, the Jewish Portuguese widow of John Bridger, long dead at Fort St. George – and likely by my own hand. Yes, the bitterness of that sauce and the sour taste it has left in my mouth.

'I will not stay a moment longer under the same roof as that old scoundrel, Mama, and nor should you.'

'Joseph, my dearest, you are only just come home.'

And such a joyous surprise it had been. After all this time. My first-born in my arms once more. Three weeks past. He had sailed from Fort St. George on board the *Neptune* before Christmas, having finally resigned his position, latterly as Provisional Mintmaster for John Company, and now determined to become an independent trader, a gentleman merchant as he already described himself.

His welcome by Elihu had been tepid.

'Must he stay here, my dear?' he had complained, flapping the folds of his old brown banyan in a fit of pure petulance. 'It is like having the ghost of Hynmers haunting my home.'

There is an uncanny resemblance, I must admit, and it tears my heart asunder.

'Or is it,' I said, 'simply uncomfortable to have somebody beneath your roof who so recently bore witness to your various infidelities? Does he, perhaps, remind you instead of those other lives, your other families?'

Whether Elihu wanted it or not, Joseph Junior had brought word of them to me, at least. Jeronima de Paiva suffered one distemper after another, he said, though her business – I suppose, truly, the business of her questionable brother, Joseph Almanza – still flourished. But White Town's prittle-prattles seemed convinced she would soon be here in London, word on the street claiming she had made no secret of Governor Yale's letters to her, inviting her to join him. Don Carlos too, of course. Elihu's by-blow, though Joseph Junior accounts him a handsome yet wayward boy. Eleven now, I collect. Well, I shall write to sweet Jeronima by the first available ship this coming winter.

And Katherine Nicks? Joseph says he was astonished to see the extent of her disfigurement when she returned to Madras Patnam and I had to explain the story to him several times before he finally accepted that the affair with Seaton had been no mere flight of the fantastical. Joseph brings his own strange tale of her too, rumours that she has employed surveyors at that worthless shaft in the gravel-clay pits near Kollur village, and sent a message for me. *The most empty of caverns, the deepest of echoes.* It is, I collect, a line from one of Matthew Parrish's poems and I fear its significance may bring me some regret, yet I must confess to missing the damn'd woman.

But Joseph Junior. I must get this down. The first night of his homecoming, after he finally tracked us to this boastful brashness on Austin Friars, a supper fraught with tensions and, after I retired, hoping to take up my journal again after a lengthy period of neglect, Joseph Junior knocked upon my door.

'Too weary to talk, Mama?' he enquired and I told him of course I was not. How could I be, having endured his absence so long? I lit a second candle, settled him upon the monstrous divan that occupies almost an entire side of my equally monstrous bedchamber. 'Great heavens,' he said. 'These rooms, each of them a veritable godown.'

'Both in size and purpose,' I replied, easing myself onto the stool of my dresser.

'How do you tolerate this, living in Mister Yale's warehouse?'

'He offered to buy Broad Street from me, to house still more of his collection, though I refused him. Sold it myself. And that besides his three properties on King Street. Oh, and the actual godown formerly in the hands of Mistress Nicks. Every inch filled with furniture, textiles, crates, paintings, statuary, weapons. Not an inch of room to spare anywhere. Even here, in this – this...'

I gestured around the green frame-filled walls, at the rich clutter that was almost none of my own. And it devoured me, this loss of the independence I had valued for ten years. My capital is secure enough, invested with care, though it seems to count for so little against this cruel and unaccountable sense of imprisonment that now dominates my life.

'Well, God be praised that you are safe, Mama. After your ordeals. But Ursula,' he had said. 'Is there no cure for what ails her?'

'Dear boy,' I told him, 'how many times have I wished, when each of you was young, that you might grow no more, that you should remain forever in that state of joyous grace you enjoyed when you were small, that time itself should stand still. And now, with Ursi...'

'She will be forever child-like and you wish it otherwise. Yet to so put yourself in harm's way, Mama. And Ursula. Mistress Nicks even.'

'There is a great deal of blood on my hands, Joseph.'

I lifted them before my face, could almost see the gore upon them.

'Seaton's hands, surely.'

'I once thought so. I cling fast to your grandmama's words. That simply being on the right side, to be self-righteous, is never enough. That only the actions we take in defence of right stand to our true credit.' That, as Sathiri would have reminded me, is *karma*. 'But those Jacobite traitors, my dear. Had I been ignorant of their murderous intent, perhaps I could have stood aside, allowed their evil doctrines to triumph, watched impassionately as they cursed our land with more bloody war, left others to intercede against them. But the Almighty, it seems, had other plans for me. I take comfort from the fact that He must have considered all the hurt to be part of His scheme. He is done with me now, I do believe.'

'Sir William certainly holds you in great esteem, Mama. The Duke of Devonshire and Czar Peter of Muscovy both indebted to you for their lives, he says. And is that the piece?'

He crossed the room, carefully picked up the geographical clock from my dresser. Well that, at least, I still possessed.

'You see?' I said. 'It kept time for you both. That dial set for the hour at Madras. This one for Smryna.'

'There was a letter waiting for me from Elford. Did you know? Conferring power of attorney upon me.'

'Must you, Joseph?'

'After tonight? Mama, of course we must. That patronising wretch. I wonder that you tolerate him.'

'He is, after all, still my husband. The father of my girls. Your sisters.'

'He buys their affections, does he not? Sets them against you?'

The supper, and Elihu boasting that he had already been approached by a broker interested in seeking suitable matches for Kate and Nan – gentlemen of substance, he stressed.

'A status,' he had said to Joseph Junior and to Benjamin, 'to which I hope you shall both aspire.'

'You think we lack substance, sir?' Joseph snapped back at him, his face crimson with rage. 'I can assure you…'

'Bah,' Elihu scoffed, 'I do not consider substance to commence at less than two thousand pounds per annum, young man. Any sum of income less than this is mere entertainment.'

'Perhaps,' said Benjamin, 'we should possess more substance if our creditors could be brought to settle their debts with us.'

'A man who cannot call in his debts, Benjamin, is no man at all. And here you are, slaving away for old Sir William Williams and still without even the means to seek your own redress.' I thought my youngest would choke upon his mutton pie, but Elihu allowed him no time to respond. 'Oh, but good news. To save you from this conundrum, I made arrangements on Friday last for the bank to pay you the eight hundred pounds I have kept safe for you.'

It was now Joseph Junior's turn to restrain his brother.

'Not now,' he said. 'Not just now.'

'Not now?' said Elihu. 'You have something to tell me? No, I should think not. For this should be an evening of joy. Joseph home with us.' Hypocrite, I thought. 'My duty to Benjamin discharged.' Miser, I screamed inwardly. 'And for you, my dears,' he turned to the girls, 'a prince's ransom set aside for each of your dowries. And that, you may all wish to collect, is the true meaning of substance.'

Later, in my bedchamber with Joseph Junior, I recalled every word, picked at the amber threads of my coverlet.

'Changed, is he not?' I said.

'Once master of all he surveyed at Fort St. George, now governor of naught but the auction house. I have seen such before, Mama. Humiliation that creates a thirst for domination of the smaller world men like your husband are now forced to occupy. The delusion of greatness now replacing the true power he once enjoyed. Either that, or it drives them to their cups. This alters nothing. We are set upon the thing now. Myself, Elford and Benjamin. Especially Benji. Tomorrow we take our claim to the Equity Court. Chancery,

Mama. We set down our pleadings at the Six Clerks' Office, then we shall see.'

'How much?'

'The claim? The third of Papa's estate divided between myself, Rich – God bless his memory – and Elford was calculated at eight hundred pounds a-piece. Our attorney believes he can now show that the sum was badly under-estimated. If so, there will be interest to factor. And Benjamin's own eight hundred pounds has sat in your husband's accompts all these years, earning him this substance of which he boasts.'

I thought about the papers I had brought back with me from Madras, many of which still showed the true extent of Elihu's income as Governor. And I wonder, now, what I should do with them, those that I had not already gifted to our allies among the Company's Directors. The real ones, not those with my forged signature.

'In total?' I said.

'We claim interest and principal amounting to five thousand pounds.'

'I fear,' I told him, 'that Mister Yale would kill to protect a lesser sum.'

'It is like sitting upon a powder keg,' I said, sipping at a pewter saucer of brother Richard's finest chocolate.

'And all this subterfuge,' Matthew smiled, though needing to shout above the gaggle of Turkey merchants haggling across the coffee house floor. 'Like old times, my dear.'

'Do not make jest of it, sirrah. You cannot imagine what it is like.'

Yesterday, my private booth at Richard's place, having used the pretext that my brother was fallen ill and needed me, clandestine messages dispatched with old Fletchley. He is the only one of the servants left me – Nanny Green now gone too – and, even then, Fletchley was likely to be followed. For my every movement is presently subject to Elihu's scrutiny.

'You are the very essence of resilience, my dear.' He took a long pull on his pipe before continuing. 'Must you needs tolerate this form of despotism when you have stood against so much else?'

'My children,' I said, setting down the rose-patterned dish and licking a remnant of the chocolate from my lips. 'I feel them all slipping away from me, day by day, and each effort I make to counter the influences upon them seems to simply cast them further adrift. I caution the boys against Chancery and they say I betray their father's memory. And the girls. Can you believe it? Kate asked me, only two days ago, whether it was true that, when she was young, I had almost poisoned her. I demanded to know the source of such nonsense, and she told me it was Winifred Bridger. The damn'd woman denied it, naturally, claimed some crossed understanding. Her Portuguese tongue, perhaps. And it would be a foolish example were it not that there is something of this ilk every day. Or Elihu lavishing money upon Kate and Anne, filling their heads with nonsense about their royal Welsh blood.'

I left it unspoken, of course, that this mention of poison by Winifred Bridger might have some deeper significance.

'Dismiss her?'

A tendril of tawny smoke curled around his suggestion.

'I am no longer mistress of my own household, Matthew. And resilience? Any I may once have possessed is long exhausted. Me too. Great heavens, you cannot imagine what I might give for a dose of Sathiri's wisdom and a few drops of her *soma*.'

A shadow passed across his eyes and I reached over, set my fingers upon the crimson silk of his sleeve.

'Such a long time ago,' he said. 'And yet…'

'She would be proud of you, Matthew. All set for Parliament, great heavens.'

I caught one of the Turkey merchants peering at us and I drew my hand back, perhaps too quickly, for I saw the rogue exchange some knowing remark with his fellows.

'There will be an election,' said Parrish, oblivious to their glances, 'that much is certain. January, most likely. And I am persuaded to stand. By poor Langhorn, of course. The old Company is set upon contesting no fewer than eighty-six constituencies. Seeking to increase their influence. They shall not have them. Indeed, the scheme is set to explode in their faces. Hoisted upon their own petard.'

Yes, poor Sir William. Wed less than a year before his wife died so tragically. February last. Even so, the marriage made him the richest man in all England, they say.

'Is that the extent of your political ambition, Mister Parrish? To score a few points for the Directors of the new Company?'

I called for Richard's boy to replenish our saucers.

'You know me better than that, Catherine. Yet before we begin to change the world, we must first secure nomination. And for that I need the sponsorship of those who favour our faction.'

'I fear I cannot assist, my dear.'

'In that direction, no. All resolved. I must confess it hinges upon the second reason I was so delighted to receive your note. A more modest task, perhaps, though one that might still help immeasurably.'

'I have told you, Matthew, I am done with spying.'

The lad brought a pot from the hearth, though Parrish declined a second dish.

'Truly?' he said. 'You think the country is out of danger. But this news of Princess Anne's child...'

The Protestant line of succession had seemed so secure. After William, Queen Mary's sister, Anne. After Anne, her son, William Duke of Gloucester. Now young William is dead at the tender age of eleven. You can almost hear the Jacobites back about their treacherous business.

'All the same, I am done with it. The politicks.'

'This hardly does justice to the term. But your husband seems to have developed an interest in the contest for the Denbigh Boroughs.'

I stabbed the dish towards him.

'Matthew, I shall not do it. I shall not. And it would be impossible. I am too much under scrutiny. A limit to how many times I can depend upon poor Fletchley. Secret notes to Matthew Parrish, of all things. It would simply not answer, sirrah, if we were discovered.'

He ran a finger along the parting of his full auburn peruke.

'He still harbours suspicions about us?'

'It is simply that I cannot be certain he did not read the lines you wrote me. Whatever possessed you?'

'I am no love-struck loon, Catherine. No callow boy neither, scribbling nonsense to his coy mistress.'

'No, you are not. You are a spymaster, sirrah, and even when you profess affection, you cannot help yourself. "Oh, wondrous spy." Was that not how you addressed me?'

'Catherine, we are no longer young. And you, forced to live as a virtual prisoner. I cannot brook it.'

'And you propose what, precisely?' I had not intended to raise my voice so, knew I sounded like a shrew. 'What future could there be for us? Our positions in society afford us none of the impropriety that those of higher station so routinely enjoy. Still, it is another couplet that has been troubling me. A message that my son brought back from Katherine Nicks.' I told him about that too. 'What do you think she means?'

'That the Kollur mine may not have been as dry as you imagined. Would it trouble you so much if she had, after all, found some residual deposits there?'

'Residual? I suppose not. I was certain... Still, this profession of your sentiments. It was foolish to write thus.'

I could not look at him, turned my face to the whitewashed wall.

'I agree,' he said. 'But I have a solution. Literally, a solution. For both of us.' He reached into the deep side pocket of his topcoat, drew out a small corked ochre pot.

'*Soma*?' I said, and offered him my brightest smile though, inside, I was all a-tremble. When he sent me the poem, other notes from him in the past, I have been riddled with doubt. I know he cares for me, as I care for him in my turn. That closeness is born of long and comfortable acquaintance, of shared joys and tragedies – adventure even. But beyond that? I do not feel it, doubt he feels it either. And I am cautious that neither of us should mistake our respective loneliness for something else.

'Far more potent, my dear.' He glanced about as though to ascertain we were not overheard. 'Artichoke juice. We may each perhaps use it. Innocent missive in plain ink on one side of the page, our deepest secrets written in juice on the other. It only becomes visible once the sheet is warmed. Hence, I may keep about my frustrated affections. And you may furnish me with anything you might overhear about the Denbigh Boroughs.'

'I shall not do it, sirrah. You know I may not. But you, Matthew,' I smiled, somewhat beguiled by him, 'tell me more – about what you would write.'

'Why, perhaps an offer to take you away from all this.'

'Husband, the geographical clock, where is it?'

I had dressed for dinner, my silver-threaded grey brocade,

noticed that the timepiece was no longer in its customary place. Indeed, I could not recall having seen it there last night either. And now, as I entered the dining hall, it was plain we were on the verge of still another *contretemps*. How I have come to dread them. They cast such oppression upon the entire house, despite its sombre splendour, and upon each Sunday without fail.

'Perhaps some other time, wife. Some other *time*.'

Our midday meal set upon the side boards, yet the atmosphere thick as the russet meat sauce in its earthenware serving jug. The girls and my two sons seated on opposite sides of the manorial table in their now customary and respective battle lines, Ursula a little apart from them all, busy at the psalter that, of late, is her constant companion. I took my chair beside her, but Elihu stood in his outdoor clothes, greenish-blue topcoat, fingering at the food as though this were some *piquenique*. Except, at such a social gathering, he might have seemed happier whereas, here, he was flushed, simmering like a lidded pot beneath another new full-bodied peruke.

'Is that intended as a clench?' I said, with contempt. 'You are going somewhere?'

'Do we eat, or do we not?' said Joseph, and Elihu rewarded him with a glance of pure contempt.

The air in the room was still and cloying too, the open windows at the farther end of the room allowing nothing but yet more stifling August heat, a stench of decay from outside and the peel of bells from St. Peter-le-Poor around on Broad Street where we had passed the morning in a hypocritical pretense at family piety.

'I thought,' my husband said, 'I should go and visit my dear brother-in-law, Richard. At death's door, is he not? No less than my family duty to see if I might comfort him.'

So, he knew. And if he had been informed about the coffee house he must also be aware of my liaison with Matthew.

'Oh, I found him much improved,' I said, 'though I am sure he would be pleased to see you. He relishes your company so much.' Benjamin and Joseph Junior barely repressed snorts of ironic laughter. 'But the geographical clock – you were saying?'

'Evance, if you must know. He admired the thing. I had intended it for another auction at Garraway's but...'

When his cargo had finally been unloaded from the *Martha* –

half the entire cargo belonged to Elihu – the value of his oriental furniture of red and black lacquer, his curiosities, his woodwind and brass musical instruments, his spices, his jewels, his paintings, his opium, his decorative weapons, his fabrics – varieties of long-cloth, chintz, gingham and taffeta – amounted to more than twenty thousand pounds. And that without the bulses of blue-hued Golconda diamonds, which totalled at least a further five thousand. All this just a small portion of his wealth and possessions. The proceeds from the sale of his four ships.

'My gift,' I stammered. I was astonished, almost speechless. 'The Czar…'

Though does he suspect, I have often wondered – the profit gained by myself and Sir William Langhorn from the assurance contract we arranged, knowing of his imminent return? A contract ostensibly in the name of others though, in practice, our own signatures below the agreement to guarantee the sums involved – and our generous premium paid into Hoare's Bank after the successful passage.

'A house so grand as this deserves an equally grand design, my dear. Not such Muscovite playthings. And Mistress Bridger has managed the whole business admirably, despite your tiresome and interminable complaints. Anyway, it seemed the least I could do.'

We had barely affected the move before Winifred Bridger assumed command and, since Elihu is paying her so handsomely, she has no doubts about where her allegiance lies. Ellen is already dismissed – some nonsense about missing silver against which I was, to my humiliation, unable to defend her.

'The least you could do,' I said, 'because…?'

'Perhaps you should ask your sons.'

I was determined that I should not and, instead, pulled the yellow-fringed bell sash to summon Mistress Bridger, who appeared immediately in the doorway. For a housekeeper, her turquoise mantua, her matching coif, her ringlets, seemed somewhat excessive.

'Arrange for us to be served,' I said. It was more imperious than I had intended, but she ignored me in any case, simply turning to my husband for instruction.

'*Senhor?*'

'You may serve my daughters,' said Elihu. 'But not these ingrates. They have soaked me long enough.'

'You speak in riddles, sir,' said Joseph Junior, with some annoyance.

'I do?' Elihu snapped. 'You skulk off to the Equity Court without even the courtesy of discussing the matter with me. Then you add cowardice to calumny by including a joinder against my dear friend Sir Stephen Evance in your suit. Outrageous. The King's Jeweller, for pity's sake. Outrageous, I say.'

'Say this is not so, Joseph,' I said. 'Sir Stephen is a friend. And Winifred...' She paused, all insolence, in the process of plating the potatoes. 'You *shall* serve dinner to Master Joseph and Master Benjamin.'

'A friend,' Benjamin replied, 'who retains a considerable amount of your husband's fortune within his coffers. My own inheritance, it seems, held in some form of trust by him.'

'I notice, wife, that you show no surprise at this action against me, and that your only concern is for young Evance.'

I could not deny it.

'Our attorney's advice, Mama,' Joseph Junior insisted, his face like thunder as Winifred fussed over the girls' bowls, my instruction entirely ignored. Indeed, she almost slammed down my own portion of pie, some of the pickled cucumber and quince cream splashing onto the table.

'And does this, husband, warrant the theft of my personal possessions?'

'Personal, my dear? Can there be property of the wife that does not naturally fall to the husband? You should perhaps consult your youngest son, for did he not have designs to be called to the bar?'

'As I still do,' said Benjamin.

'Truly?' Elihu laughed at him. 'The senior of your Chambers now dead and young Sir William Williams more biddable than I could have hoped. I think you can rest assured your legal career is ended.'

Benjamin rose from the table, his mouth gaping open and, I think, a tear gathering in the corner of his eye. All that study, the time he has spent honing his legal skills. Surely Elihu's reach cannot be so long.

'Mama...' he said.

'Will that stop his lies, Pa?' said Kate in her most waspish voice.

'Lies?' I said, pushing some of the cucumber around my plate.

'I have been schooling my daughters,' said Elihu, his own mouth stuffed with piecrust, 'in the ways that these Hynmers boys have concocted their fabrications against me, falsely accused me of denying their birthright. After all I've done for them.'

Bridger had taken up a position at the side boards, hands folded across her ample belly, and a vixen's grin upon her lips.

'You cannot mean it,' I said. 'About Benjamin's vocation. And Elihu, please instruct our housekeeper to serve my boys.'

He was about to respond, though Joseph Junior cut across him, standing now beside his brother.

'And were you so honest, Mister Yale,' he said, 'about the birthright of their sundry brothers and sisters, both those back in Fort St. George and the others here at Islington?'

A shocked silence that fell upon the room was ruptured by Elihu's spluttering, almost choking on the pie. He had made no secret of the Nicks girls, Betty and that other Ursula, now being at boarding school in Islington, and at his own expense. But this open attack upon his morality he had plainly not expected.

'I am not without influence of my own, Benjamin,' I said. 'Do not rise to this bait. And please, both of you, sit down. Mistress Bridger,' I almost screamed the words, 'the food…'

Benjamin did indeed sit, though he pushed back his chair from the table, settling like a coiled spring, barely able to restrain himself, while Joseph merely turned to the fireplace behind him, took a pipe from the rack and began to fill it, though with difficulty for he was shaking in anger.

'You see?' Elihu said to the girls. 'How they try to blacken your father's character.'

I watched him catch Winifred's eye, shake his head at her, and she offering him the most polite of curtsies, a smile, damn her. I seethed, more at my own impotence than anything else. Mistress Bridger, for her part, seemed to plant her feet even firmer upon the spot she'd chosen for her stand against me.

'You warned us, Papa,' Annie murmured, though she was herself on the verge of weeping. 'So you did.'

'And your papa forgets,' said Joseph, 'that I have seen them with my own eyes. His son, the little Jewish boy, Charles de Paiva. And that youngest boy of Mistress Nicks. Another Elihu. Coincidence perhaps. But I tell you, stepfather, that the lad favours neither Mister Nicks nor poor Mistress Katherine. Whereas…'

Stepfather. Yes, my marriage to Elihu had indeed conferred upon him the responsibility for my orphaned boys, but Joseph could throw the word back at him as though it were the worst of insults.

'Joseph!' I cried. 'This is not for the girls' ears. Nor for this Lord's Day. Pray heaven…'

'You see,' said Elihu to his daughters, 'how meddlesome things are become here, my dears? Bad enough that some cove dishonestly pursues me in court on a claim that I have rooked him on the price he paid for my diamonds, but now your mama's own sons. You see why it should have been better had I not returned at all?'

It is endless. Barely a week going by without some new legal entanglement; without his groaning about ingratitude from one or other of his indebted associates; without some belly-ache about the unhappiness of his life in London; without some complaint written to Governor Pitt at the inadequacy of income from the sale of his horses, his property, his coaches, his palanquins back in Madras; without his assertion that these things, collectively, all serve to impoverish him.

'Say it is not so, Papa,' said Kate, a tear dripping from her chin. 'Say you will stay with us.'

'Well,' he told her, 'I am here. And I shall ensure your futures at least. There is considerable interest in you both.'

I chewed on a piece of my own pie, smothered it in the quince cream – though I had little appetite for it – and saw Annie lean over to nudge her older sister's saffron-sleeved elbow.

'Oh, I wonder who that could be,' she goaded her, teasing, and I wondered whether Kate might still harbour an affection for Stephen Evance. If so, she will be sorely disappointed.

'And me, Papa?' said Ursula, glancing up from her psalms. But oh, how I wish I could dissuade her from such affection for widows' weeds.

'Ah, little dumpling. No, I fear you are – well, too young. But never doubt. There is a plan for you too, despite everything. You shall join the Nicks children at boarding school. An excellent…'

'She shall not!' I cried. 'You cannot make such a decision.'

I threw a protective arm around her shoulders.

'It is made, wife. Settled. The fees paid. She begins in September.'

I felt myself drowning as I have done so often recently. Bridger undermines me with the girls at every opportunity, as she had done when Nanny Green left us. 'Gone,' I had overheard her tell them. '*A bruxa velha* poisoning us all.' Nanny Green, an old witch? Is that what she has been teaching them. And then this: '*Vossa mãe*, she know all about those things.' Their mother does, indeed, know a fair amount about poisons. And Mistress Bridger should therefore be more careful with her tongue. She remained standing by the door, that supercilious smirk upon her face.

'Well?' I said to her, releasing Ursula from my embrace. It was plain that I was never going to win this battle for my sons' sustenance. 'You have done here, I think.'

I stood too, promising myself that there would be another day, another chance to make her obey me. But she merely turned again to Elihu, who nodded his agreement that she might leave us. And she did.

Typical. For whenever I seek to assert myself again in the girls' affections, or to counter Bridger's influence, Elihu literally purchases their diversion, rewards each of their insolences towards me. But the bitterest blow falls when the boys fail to heed me also. Great heavens, Joseph is thirty now. Thirty. And while he may possess his dear father's looks, he lacks his other qualities in so many regards.

'This is beyond toleration,' I heard Joseph saying now, as he lit the pipe. 'Come, brother, we shall eat elsewhere. And there are folk I would meet at the chophouse. To speed my departure from this damn'd prison as soon as I'm able.'

'Aspirations to become a gentleman merchant?' Elihu sneered, wiping the grease from his fingers into his kerchief. 'I fear you may find the prospect more difficult than you imagine. I have written to those friends who still remain to me within the Company. They are happy to make it known that your service in India was less than satisfactory. Issues of trust, perhaps. And difficult, don't you know, to establish oneself as an independent trader where there are questions of trust.'

'My service has been exemplary,' Joseph replied, jabbing the pipe's long clay stem towards Elihu like a rapier's thrust. 'Governor Pitt will vouch for it.'

'He may have a view on the matter,' my husband parried, 'but I count him a reliable friend also. And by the time missives pass to and fro – well, such delays will not aid your case, I fear.'

'All this,' I said, 'because you will not honour your full debt to Benjamin? Or make an equitable settlement with Joseph and Elford?'

'Settlement?' he replied. 'Was it not you, my dear, who agreed the figure of eight hundred pounds as a fair portion for Benjamin? And does that not mean that the same amount for your other boys was not also fixed at an equitable level?'

'Settlement,' Joseph repeated. 'What is this, Mama?'

I left the question hanging in the air, ignored his look of exaggerated consternation.

'So far as Benjamin is concerned, husband, it was also agreed that the sum should be subject to interest being taken until his coming of age, or until the payment might be discharged. You still have your copy, I collect. For evidence is all, I have often heard you say.'

'Then perhaps you should have taken more care,' said Elihu, 'to also settle the rate of interest itself. Yet you did not. And this Chancery claim, it is frivolous in the extreme. Eight hundred pounds was their portion, eight hundred pounds precisely the amount they received. Or perhaps you would now wish to amend other clauses of our Marriage Settlement?'

'Amendment? No, though perhaps a re-affirmation of the clause in which you agreed to treat them as your own sons.'

'An agreement I might have honoured if you had similarly observed your promise to keep them under control. And this, Catherine,' he gestured towards the boys, 'does not answer.'

There was a great deal of shouting, back and forth – Kate screaming that Benjamin had no right to speak falsely of her papa, and all trace of the respect that had once grown between them now entirely disappeared; Joseph Junior reminding her that she was little more than a child and could know nothing of these things; Annie repeating her father's assertion that Benjamin was an ingrate; Benjamin insisting that they were all here, under these fine gilded ceilings, for no better reason than the wealth *their* papa had gained from his own father's death; and Ursula, poor Ursi, with her hands pressed against her ears and loudly reciting the Evening Prayer from her psalter, her favourite, through her incessant weeping.

I, on the other hand, sat heavily again upon my chair, tried to recall happier days. Elihu in the kitchen at Middle Gate Street. Easter, and his instruction to the younger boys in the gold-leaf decoration of Pace Eggs. Another vision. Elihu dangling Dormouse Davy on his knee in the small hours of the morning after we had been kept awake all night by the little one's croup, and my husband crooning some pat-a-cake rhyme to soothe him. Where had that fellow gone? For I think I might have learned to love that particular Elihu. Then these recollections swept aside by Joseph's words earlier. About young Elihu Nicks. Had he spoken merely out of spite? That point about the boy favouring neither of his parents? The implication that, perhaps, he more closely favoured my husband? Katherine Nicks had sworn to me...

'Control?' I spoke quietly enough into the chaos of raised voices and finger-pointing, yet still loud enough for Elihu to hear me. 'I asked you once why you thought Katherine might have married John Nicks so swiftly after our own marriage.'

He sighed, turned to stare out of the window.

'Perhaps they were enamoured,' he murmured. 'Would that not be strange?' He glanced back at my sons, our daughters, saw that they were all – apart from Ursi – at each other's throats, felt secure enough to continue. 'But us, Catherine? Neither admiration nor affection was part of our own marriage portion. Were those not your own words, wife? Any wonder I may have sought those precious gifts elsewhere? As you have done with that wretch Parrish.'

I slammed my hand on the table, though the clatter went unnoticed, I think, amid that background cacophony.

'If you believe that, husband, you are more the bubble than I could ever have imagined.'

I was upon the cusp of repeating Katherine's revelation to me, pregnant with Elihu's child when he and I were wed but the babe lost almost immediately after her hasty marriage to John Nicks. I held back – and received only his bitter scowl by way of reward.

'Secret assignations? Amorous poetry?' he said, and sent what was left of his pie skittering across the table towards me. I prodded the thing with my knife, thinking that I had rarely seen him in such an evil humour.

'Those,' I said, 'who eavesdrop to confirm their suspicions hear only that which justifies their own self-deception. You should be careful, Elihu, when you set Mistress Bridger to act the insinuating pickthank. Lest you hear your servant cursing you instead.'

'Ecclesiastes,' he blustered, buttoning his coat. 'You quote Ecclesiastes. Sir William Langhorn confirms your own abilities as a spy, wife. So what is Parrish now? Paramour or spymaster? Or both?'

'Your question is beyond contempt, sir. But learn this at least. You make threats against my sons and their futures yet know that you shall be answered tip for tap. You think you may interfere in the Denbigh Boroughs with impunity?' I saw him pale, ball his fists in anger, the muscles of his cheeks twitching. 'I want it back, Elihu,' I said. 'The geographical clock.'

'Or you will spy on me? Report to Parrish?'

'Among others, yes.'

He ignored me for the nonce, turned to the table once more.

'For pity's sake,' he yelled. 'Can we have an end to this menagerie? And you, sir,' he said to Joseph, 'did you not say you intended to eat elsewhere? God's hooks, sirrah, I should be pleased if you were now gone.'

I should have spoken up, but Joseph Junior tossed the pipe into the wide fireplace, its shattered pieces exploding onto the hearth. And I thought for an instant there might be violence, for there was a look in his eyes I have never seen before.

'Gladly,' he barked, and grabbed Benjamin by the arm, almost hauled him out into the hallway, with no word of farewell from either of them.

'They are my boys,' I said, at last. 'You cannot simply dismiss them from my side.'

'I believe I have just done so,' he said. 'And now I have business of my own to attend elsewhere.'

I heard the front door slam, while Elihu fussed over the girls, promised them all manner of rewards for their goodness in having to endure such intolerable behaviour, and I made my way to the open window, looked out upon Austin Friars, the midden that had somehow appeared along the lane towards Broad Street, saw my boys skirting the Dutch Church, which is now almost all that remains of the old priory, and I felt my heart sink into a despair more profound than anything I have ever experienced outside the loss of my children and poor Joseph. I knew I should not have said anything to Elihu about the Denbigh Boroughs, that it had achieved nothing except to confirm his suspicions towards Matthew, and I was filled with a desire for peace, turned to make some attempt at apology, at concession. But, by then, he too was gone, the dining hall door closing behind him, and the moment lost.

'The geographical clock,' I cried, uselessly. 'I shall have it back, sirrah.'

As I try to script this epitaph to my family's disintegration, all this grief and torment – feeling myself sinking lower with every sentence, with each tear shed – the Maysmore below mourns the demise of midnight. Another gift, of course. From Mister Edisbury, and I am surprised Elihu has not sold that piece at auction too. Midnight, and two hours since Joseph came here to my room, greeted me with his still angry assertion that he would not stay another night under this roof.

'I did not hear you at the door,' I said when he had calmed himself a little.

'You're busy, Mama.'

'My household accompts,' I lied. 'I do not entirely trust Bridger's method of accounting, I find.'

'We woke Maria,' he told me. It was terse, humourless. Maria Bridger, Winifred's eldest, occupied one of the rooms at the rear of the house, with her sister Beatriz, on the lower ground floor next to the kitchens. And she almost swooned like a love-struck loon each time she was in Joseph's company. 'I am truly not here for long. Truly. Though Benji is safe in his bed. Somewhat mauled, I fear. He does not handle confrontation well, does he? Would never have made a barrister, Mama. So perhaps your dear husband has done him a favour, after all. I suspect they will now simply keep out of each other's way. Me, I'll go to Uncle Dick's for the nonce. After that...'

He shrugged.

'Benjamin, I am certain, will have his day, but you – you will sail away and leave me again.'

'What would keep me, Mama? It might have helped if you had told me earlier about this damn'd settlement you reached with Mister Yale. Before we filed our claim with the Six Clerks' Office at least. Is there more I should know?'

I should have been angry but at that moment I could see his father standing before me.

'My marriage settlement,' I said. 'Not exactly a normal nuptial arrangement. I had hoped you might understand that.'

He kneaded those slender fingertips into the furrows of his brow.

'How could I? I was already dismissed from your affections.'

My own generation seems to have learned how to take the blows, the disappointments, the inevitable deficiencies inherited from our childhoods. Gracious, look at Elihu himself, just to do him some small justice for a moment. His experiences at St. Paul's school, the horror of which I can only surmise. But our children? Resentments at every turn, each failure in their own lives always the fault of another – and usually their parents to blame. It sometimes seems to me that the easier the childhood, the more deluded, the more distanced from reality, the life that follows. That realisation does not make the distance between parent and child any less oppressive, crippling.

'Oh, how deep the ague of old resentments can bury itself in our souls,' I said, fixing him with my sternest gaze. 'Yet I am certain your attorney will confirm that its clauses can have no bearing on your own claim at all. Your father's will was clear, Joseph. One third of his estate to be shared equally between yourself, Richard and Elford. At the time, our accompt-keepers calculated that amount at eight hundred pounds each. But if there is evidence, as you say, that the figure was under-stated, the Equity Court must surely find in your favour. And Benjamin? His case is different. You know it. Yes, I foolishly agreed the eight hundred pounds as a fixed settlement for him, though he has never received it, nor the significant interest Chancery must recognise he is owed. So why, precisely, this antagonism towards your mama? You are a man grown, sirrah, for heaven's sake.'

'Why? My father barely cold in his grave and you were in Yale's bed.'

I threw down my pen, splattered ink all across the paragraphs I had already entered in this journal and have now had to recreate so painfully afresh.

'In his bed? You dare speak to me this way? The sacrifices I made were all for you boys. Each of you, Joseph. And it was your father's wish that you be taken from me, not mine. Never mine.'

I could feel the walls closing upon me, something dragging me down into a pit of despair.

27

'If I had not been sent away...' he said, lifting his hands in exasperation.

'What? You would still be having nightmares about the death your father suffered, boy. So better indeed that you go now. As you say, what is there to keep you? I barely hear from Smyrna, from Elford. Kate and Annie, it seems, are lost to me. Ursula too, very soon. Benjamin will keep chasing rainbows. And between my husband and Mistress Bridger, my life no longer my own.'

He picked up a small blue-glazed pot I keep on the mantle shelf, turned it over in his hands.

'And how much of it brought upon your own head, Mama? Maria still remembers being forced from their home by your friend, Parrish.' He spat the word "friend" with a firm degree of sarcasm.

'You've spoken to that chit of a girl about this? About our family's affairs? She would not know, of course, that they were forced from their home by the foolishness of her papa. Nor that Matthew was working under instruction from your stepfather.'

I thought for a moment he might smash the pot, as he had earlier done with the pipe, but he set it down again. More composed now.

'As much as I despise the old witch, that hardly explains why Bridger should treat your husband as though he were a saint, and you as the devil incarnate. It often seems that she is the mistress and you the servant. Demeaning. Why should you permit it?'

'How in the name of Sweet Jesu can you understand so little of the world, Joseph? I am too exhausted to explain it to you.'

And so I was. Or perhaps nearer the truth that I do not entirely know how to explain it myself. My age, perhaps. I have reached that point in a woman's life, as I approach my fiftieth year, about which my mother warned me so often. The former enthusiasms now dimmed, my humours more frequently dark than light, and the darks much deeper than in my younger days. I have accepted Elihu's domination as the price for my family's unity, his insinuation of Winifred Bridger into our household for the same reason, believing that, at some point of my choosing, should it prove necessary, I could assert myself afresh, never thinking that the result would dim my spirit to this extent.

'Exhausted?' said Joseph. 'Or is it simply too much trouble? I see I am dismissed yet again.'

I stood then, at last, went to him and held his arms.

'If you wish, yes. I swear that my children will force me to an early grave.'

'You?' he snapped. 'I think you shall outlive us all, Mama. For what was it the serpent said to Eve? *"Woman, ye shall not surely die."* Were those not the words of Genesis? Choose the wicked path and live forever.'

And with that he pushed me aside and was gone. It was a warm evening but something in his words sent a chill down my spine.

A holy day, one that I had hoped would serve my own resurrection, a return to some semblance of light after these six months of blackness, a day that would see me capable of a first attempt to set down here the unspeakable, though I dread the thought. And besides, there has been so much more to record of this Easter Sunday.

It began quietly enough. This echoing cavern of a house so still with the creature himself gone to Wrexham, taking the three girls, and Benjamin now spending far more time in the company of my brother Richard than ever he does with me.

You would think these absences might restore some freedom to my movement, liberate me from the disapproval with which Mister Yale berates me whenever I suggest the need to see my family, to renew my acquaintance with Sir William Langhorn, with Streynsham Master or so many of my own associates. From Matthew I have heard nothing since long before his election as the Honourable Member for East Grinstead in January, before the sorry affair of which I now try to write. I am isolated from them all. Not that I might have known what to say, how to hide my shame – as I shall later make plain – should we have met in the meanwhile. But I accept that I have brought this near imprisonment down upon my own head.

So there, I have arrived at the thing sooner than I had intended, and the nib trembles in my hand, the pale parchment already splattered with the purple-black ink, with its iron aroma of blood.

It was last October and Elihu had fulfilled his promise to take poor Ursula from my care. How would boarding school cope with her difficulties, her tardiness of wit? But he would have none of it, she was gone to Mistress Freeman's in Islington, and I had set myself on the path of spiteful revenge. There had been talk of knighthood again and I had been pondering how to employ those papers I brought back from Fort St. George – those that provided evidence of his fiduciary improprieties in Madras. I could, I suppose, have chosen a dozen ways to thwart his ambition, to pay him back for his actions against my sons, but I chose to entrust the documents to Benjamin, to be delivered to His Grace, the Duke of Devonshire still Lord Steward to King William.

The following night I had retired early, preparing to work on this precious journal and about to retrieve it by candlelight from the false bottom of the strongbox when the door to my shadow-strewn bedchamber burst open.

'Is that where you kept them hidden?' Elihu yelled, a sombre and malevolent shape, waving a sheaf of correspondence in his thick fingers, and I did not need to see them to know Benjamin must have betrayed me.

'What price did my Judas extract from you?' I said. 'Arrangement for him to be called to the bar after all?'

He wore a dark banyan over his night gown, the grease stains glimmering in the tallow-glow, and a turban upon his head, though all askew – a comical figure, even in silhouette, bating the menace blazing in his eye, piercing the gloom, fired by the excess of wine that he had plainly consumed.

'Oh, that your son possessed the acumen to barter thus,' he said, swaying like the serpent that haunts my nightmare thoughts. 'The sad truth is that I found him fumbling and bumbling with them out in the hallway and when I saw their direction merely relieved him of the burden.'

I pitied myself, more guilt, for the level to which I have sunk. As though Benjamin, of all people…

'I have come to expect no more of you,' I said, 'than my private correspondence opened. Or the torment you inflict upon me whenever I wish to see my family. The purchasing by stealth of my daughters' affections. Your hideous objections even when I seek no more than to hang Joseph's drawings upon the walls.'

'I've told you Catherine. There is no "private" between husband and wife. And this!' He thrust towards me the covering letter I had written. 'This note for the attention of His Grace. *My husband a long and close associate of the traitor Vincent Seaton.* God's hooks, you name me in conjunction with the very fellow who tried to kill him. It is enough to see me hanged.'

'You try to ruin my sons and wonder that you might be paid in kind.'

'I punish your sons for the wickedness they practise upon me. This Chancery case. To add to the claims already being pursued against my person in the Equity Court. This too?' He held up a page from his old private ledgers, one that I had appended within the package, along with the sheet from his more official accounts, showing the disparity between his true earnings and those he had declared for the purpose of his returns to the Company. 'When I was charged by the Directors – had you...?'

Indeed I had. Shared them with Sir William Langhorn, though he had not required me to bear witness in person. His sworn word to entirely impeccable evidence, a sheaf of similar documents, it had been enough.

'Again,' I said, 'you thought you could parade your concubines around Fort St. George with impunity?'

He was raging now, and I wondered how much greater his fury if he had known about the denunciations sent to Governor Pitt against him. Or would it? Those original documents had, after all, driven him from office, disrupted his ability to create wealth, while the denunciations written in my name had simply been a device, if needed, to drive him back to England.

'Was it not enough that you dishonestly persuaded so many to invest in a mine that proved worthless? The ignominy your misdeeds heaped upon my head. Even without this treachery.' He shook the ledger sheet at me. 'Oh, how I repent of ever having left India. And how fortunate for John Nicks that he will, by now, have returned there. But what is the point of giving account to my disappointments, my afflictions? They are too many.'

'I expect you find the time to recount them fully in your letters to Jeronima though, or to Mistress Nicks.'

He took a step backwards, steadied himself against the door frame, while I rose from the strongbox, closed the studded lid upon which I set the candlestick, stood with arms folded across my breast to stop them from shaking.

'That poor sweet girl,' he muttered. 'So disfigured now, they say. And you – you have been reading them? My letters?'

'I have no need, Elihu. You make your feelings known so often. So tediously often. A day-to-day accompt of your own woes, of how much Katherine's clever girls serve as your only consolation. Have you told that to Katie? To Anne? And to Ursi? I wonder.'

'Consolation? Affection, I should say. For I find none here, you cold and miserable creature. I can almost hear the laughter when I am abroad on the street. Ah, there goes Governor Yale. In India wed, and there he thrived, though now condemned to misery in London by his shrew of a wife.'

He flung the documents across the carpet, staggered forward, then slammed the door shut at his back, leaning against it, his face puce with rage. And I feared him then, as I had never done before.

'If you must go about the streets of London dressed like a Gentue,' I howled, 'I am hardly surprised at the mockery that follows you.'

I was screeching like a harridan. I know I was. That was the fear too. But in this house I also knew there was nobody else close enough to hear our quarrel. I had chosen my bedchamber so, for my own seclusion, though now I began to believe that my isolation would be my undoing.

'Yet Parrish,' he said, 'you would, I suppose, commend for his rakish vivacity.'

'This again. Does he truly make you feel so much less a man, sirrah?'

'Now I am the lesser man?'

I know that he saw himself that way, diminished by his reduced position back here in England. It ate at him every day. He still harboured that suspicion about Matthew and myself, too.'

'If you say so, Elihu. Any cove would see that this invention you have concocted against Parrish is no more than a device to help justify your own infidelity.'

'If I am so deficient a man, then perhaps we should visit your marriage settlement afresh.'

It might have been six months ago but I can still hear the tone of his voice coming at me through the echoes of this dark time, some sweet syrup that spoke, rather, of bitterness and evil intent. But then there was still some vestige of resilience, defiance in me that is now entirely spent, stolen from me that night by Elihu Yale, perhaps forever.

'Settle Benjamin's claim, you mean?' I said. 'Bring peace to our household. Or do you intend, rather, to make allowance for your by-blow brats – the entire brood of them?'

He advanced upon me then and I recoiled against the wall, stumbled against the bedside table, spilling inkpot and pens upon the floor.

'Katherine's girls? Your witch's tongue shall not name them so.'

'She denied it, of course,' I said. 'That they are your own. The girls and young Elihu. And like a fool I believed her. But at least she was more honest about the babe she was carrying when we wed, husband.'

He shook his head, confused.

'Babe?' he said. 'What babe?'

'The reason she married Nicks so quickly. You fool. Though she lost it just after. You should ask her, next time you write.'

'What I should give for a scold's bridle at this moment, Catherine. Such evil artifice. As though my dear friend would not have shared that news with me.'

'Believe it or believe it not. It is no concern of mine. And the settlement? I should only visit that cursed document again for the purpose of tearing it apart – of annulling this pretense at marriage.'

He laughed. Angry, maniacal laughter.

'To leave me? You did that once already, wife, and shall never do so again. Not without me willing it, at least. Duty, my dear. Marital duty. Duty imposed on you by our Lord God Almighty.' I knew then that I should never be free of him, that my big mistake had been surrendering the Broad Street house, trapping myself at his side. 'And I see now the true product of your retiring early each night. The pretense at needlework. Well, there shall be no more poisonous penmanship. Tomorrow you shall surrender the contents of your box to Mistress Bridger. Parchment, quill and ink. Sealing wax. Everything. That damn'd writing slope even.'

'Marital duty,' I repeated. 'Is it marital duty that drives you to the whores of Covent Garden each night, now that you have none under your own roof? I am surprised you have not purchased yourself a garden house here in London too, for that very purpose. Well, I hope they have pox'd you, sirrah.'

'Is that it?' he murmured, seized me by the shoulders and threw me against the wall. His breath was acrid with stale wine, his breathing laboured, and that foolish turban now almost entirely undone. 'That without Parrish to service your pleasures, you are envious of my own? Well, we could correct that, my dear.'

That false accusation, that slur upon my good name, deserved a response, but his fingers were groping for the ribbons at my neck and I needed to slip from his grasp, succeeded, made for the door, thinking that the wine would slow his reactions. I was wrong, felt his arm around my waist, lifting me from the floor, dragging me towards the bed.

'For pity's sake, Elihu,' I screamed. 'You cannot mean…'

And then I remember that he almost squeezed the breath from my body, whispered in my ear, almost with tenderness.

'Marriage is a covenant, Catherine. A sacred bond between man and wife. *"Therefore a man shall cleave unto his wife: and they shall be one flesh."* Cleave, my dear. What do you think?'

Of that which followed, why can I not write the words? Because others might one day see them, observe the pale linen of my shame torn aside and my intimacy naked before their eyes? Because the words would reveal the twisting, writhing struggle of my soul in a contest I could never win? Because some other person would share the thrusting, rutting desiccated discomfort of my indignity? Because the very act of such inconsequential scribbling would offend fragile minds? No, it is none of those. Simply that I cannot find words that might be adequate to the horror.

I have prayed every day since that despicable evening for the Almighty's deliverance from my consternation, just as I prayed today upon my pew in St. Peter-le-Poor. Is it possible that a husband can violate his own wife? Foolishly, in all my fifty years, I have never given the matter any thought. Why should I? At Fort St. George, where I was more often in the close companionship of other women, there were always half-spoken tales over our chatter-broth of whispered things. Sins that have no name. Here was one that I cannot recall ever being bandied abroad.

Perhaps I am now close to understanding the reason. The self-devouring shame and guilt. The bereavement too. As if the Elihu

I had married, with all his flaws, with all our open warfare, is also now dead. Dead to me, at least. How this offends against all that holy scripture has ever taught me: that the husband is the head of the wife, even as Christ is the head of the church; and that, just as our Lord Jesus is the saviour of the body collective, so is the husband the saviour of my body personal. Yet Papa, in his gentle Dissenter way, taught us that Ephesians must be tempered by Colossians, the exhortation that husbands must love their wives, and not be harsh with them. Love. Harsh. How those two words now grate against my sensibilities.

For how has Mister Yale's behaviour changed during these six months past? In private, not at all. Still the same draconian control of my every waking movement. Almost. And though Mistress Bridger indeed obeyed his command to strip me of my writing materials, she still had no idea about the false floor of the strongbox, these journals, and the quantities of spare pen and ink that it protected. He still blames me, though, for the lack of any further nod towards his knighthood, wrongly convinced that the doing must be mine, some method I have for secret communication with those in high places, which warrants ever more stringent observation of my actions. In public? He is almost joyous, friendly, telling everybody who will listen how happy is his household, how clever is his wife – her suggestion that he should perhaps purchase a garden house for our pleasure, at the very edge of London itself. To be honest, I am no longer certain which is worse, the private Elihu Yale or the public.

Consternation. The spring flowers scattered about the tiny church at least helped to somewhat dispel its normal musty odours and the children's choir pressed around the altar was paying discordant tribute to Mister Purcell's *Sound The Trumpet*. Poor Purcell. Dead these six years. Barely thirty-five, though his music has touched my life so many times. But, as I prayed, I was conscious of being, even here, a prisoner. Alone, not a single one of my children for company, but Bridger's girls, Maria and Beatriz, across the aisle. Not Bridger herself, naturally. For she, I suspect, still clings to her Portuguese Jewish faith, while the daughters have been raised, so far as I can discern, in the High Church beliefs of their now deceased father.

So my sons were in my mind as Reverend Hoadly's sexton, Lame Landry, sprinkled us liberally with the holy water.

'May the God of love and power,' Hoadly intoned, 'forgive you and free you from your sins, heal and strengthen you by His Spirit, and raise you to new life in Christ our Lord.'

Forgive my sins. Free me from the wicked path that Joseph Junior somehow thinks I have taken. *"Woman, you shall not surely die."* Only the briefest of notes from him, now lodging in Portsmouth where, I assume, he believes himself sufficiently distant from Yale's reach to succeed in his wish to become a gentleman merchant – though, so far, he seems to have only secured work as a supercargo on a single passage to Lisbon.

Reverend Hoadly scrutinised his parishioners before announcing the parting hymn – *The Lamentation*, little Ursi's favourite – and gave some final instruction to his sexton, while I felt something gently touch my left sleeve. I turned quickly to the column that rose behind me, and from its dark shadows I found the face of Matthew Parrish staring back at me.

'Alone, my dear?' he murmured.

I span around, fearful that I might be observed. But the Bridger girls were no longer in their seats.

'Alone, yes. And wish to remain so.'

O Lord in Thee is all my trust.
Give ear unto my woeful cry:
Refuse me not that am unjust
But cast on me Thy heavenly eye.

Alone. No word at all from Elford in Smyrna. And Benjamin gone to stay with my brother Richard, for Mister Yale had generously shared with him my hasty assumption that he had betrayed me, named him a Judas. Alone, I pressed my way along the pew, hoping that, despite the paucity of congregation, I might be able to mingle with my old Broad Street neighbours, avoid Parrish and whatever foolishness had brought him here. There were greetings, of course. From those who, a year before, would have seen me at market, at the shops, at some festivity or social gathering. Those who now only saw me here at St. Peter's. Had I been ill? I looked ill, they said. Must take better care of myself. And my husband, Governor Yale – he was well, they trusted?

'Go with God, my dear,' said Reverend Hoadly, with a certain edge to his voice, as we filed past him in the narrow vestibule, though he seemed to be paying more attention to those who followed behind. I bowed my head just enough to pay the limited respect I have for the fellow. A friend and close confidant of that same Reverend John Evans who had been our chief chaplain for the Bay of Bengal, the pecksniff who had made such profit – along with many others, including my damn'd husband – from the trade in human bondage. But at least I had refused to have Evans officiate at my wedding with Elihu. And now? Evans too was back from India, serving as rector in some remote corner of Wales.

'It would be a poor substitute,' said Matthew, catching me as I stepped up into the street, 'but perhaps you might go with me instead?'

'I want no company.'

'I believe, Catherine, that you presently want for a great deal. What has become of you?'

'Sirrah, I could not be more content.' I turned and caught the knowing looks of those old neighbours as Parrish fell in alongside me, swinging his walking cane and gazing up at the gathering rain clouds.

'Nor me, my dear.' And he launched into an almost boyish account of his first months as the Member for East Grinstead. 'The election a great success. Sixty-seven fresh supporters for the new Company. Sixty-seven. And, great heavens, this fellow Walpole. Have you seen how the broadsheets laud him? No? You were always so… Anyway, I still tend towards the Whigs, of course, but these days I find myself more often in agreement with other factions, those like Mackworth, who seek to bolster the power of the Commons, urging greater transparency on the part of the King and Lords in their dealings with the House. After all, it is the very reason we have fought our civil wars.'

The irony of the age, that the Tories seem so often to have stolen our clothes.

'Truly, Mister Parrish, none of this interests me anymore. And see, we are at Austin Friars. I should prefer to continue on my own.'

We had arrived at the end of our lane, the ancient gatehouse that once marked an entrance to the old friary, and the tavern at the corner known as Old Tom's.

'Is it a matter of finance, my dear? Does the devil starve you of money?'

The house on Broad Street had not been the best of investments, and I had been forced to sell too rapidly. There is no doubt that my wealth is diminished but, worse, I have banked the balance with Sir Stephen Evance and, though I suppose it is safe enough, I am far from certain that my husband's influence over him might not place barriers to my accessing those funds. Besides, my recent lack of engagement with Sir William Langhorn has plainly resulted in a cessation of our joint enterprises in providing assurance for ship owners – and hence a further detriment to my independence. Yet I had no intention of sharing this with Matthew Parrish.

'My husband?' I snapped. 'You are impertinent, sir. And now...'

And now I intended to leave him there, fearful that even this brief encounter might be reported to Mister Yale, bring down further retribution upon my head. But then I noticed two fellows emerging from the tavern door, something familiar about them, and each of those hackums producing a wicked-looking cudgel from within his coat. 'Matthew!' I cried, and he needed no further warning, span upon his heel and crouched low, the first of his assailants' weapons finding nothing but thin air, Matthew's cane smashing against the rogue's knee. That one went down, as the second attacker folded over, the tip of the cane thrust into his midriff, another blow catching the side of his head. Parrish took a step back, readying himself for any renewal of violence, but there was none.

The scoundrels had suffered enough, satisfied themselves with a few profanities as they recovered their cudgels and helped each other to hobble away, forcing a passage through the onlookers who were already screaming for the constables.

'Well,' said Matthew, straightening his periwig and his fine beaver hat, 'it seems your husband keeps you on a tighter rein than I had imagined.' Then he grimaced, rubbed at his right arm. 'Never been the same,' he said, 'since...'

Since the wound he took at Deptford from Seaton's rapier, of course. He was correct. I was almost certain. The Bridger girls slipping away from St. Peter's just ahead of us. The two ruffians. Coincidence that they were here at Old Tom's? I think not. But nor did I consider any of it a reason to give Matthew Parrish even a crumb of encouragement.

'I believe,' I told him, 'that it is your own tongue, sirrah, which requires a bridle.'

'You are mistaken, *senhora*,' said Mistress Bridger, as I shuffled out of my cape. 'My girls, they speak to nobody. And what do you accuse?'

What, indeed? Could it be correct that my husband had paid a pair of ruffians to no other purpose except to wait at Old Tom's on the offchance that Matthew Parrish might somehow happen along? No, surely more likely that the rogues were using the tavern to seek out likely marks for daylight robbery – a danger we all seem to face with monotonous regularity as the city's population multiplies.

'We were attacked,' I told her. 'See? I cannot stop my hands from shaking.'

No, I could not. Was it the attack? Or was it my consternation at having left Parrish standing there on the corner, calling my name just that once as I disappeared from his view.

'We?' said Bridger.

I was fairly certain she was wearing a tawny bodice that once belonged to Ellen. The skirts and apron familiar too.

'Never mind,' I said. 'Shall you bring me tea?' It was hardly an instruction, more a subservient plea of the sort I now so frequently adopt in dealings with my housekeeper-cum-gaoler. And I despised myself afresh as I settled in the smaller of the withdrawing rooms, on the green Turkish divan, imagined the incident over and over, until she appeared with a tray, my best China porcelain, a small glass and a small stone bottle. 'What is that?' I asked.

'To help. With shaking.'

I lifted the brown bottle with its stopper and studied the words printed in blue beneath the glaze. *Elixir Salutis. Tinctura Opii Crocata.* Then I pulled the cork, sniffed the bittersweet scent of its contents.

'Sydenham's Laudanum?' I said. 'I have used it but once. A bout of the flux. I have heard tales...'

It took me back to Madras Patnam, of course. Elihu had made great profit in the opium trade, Apothecary Sydenham having been keen to purchase every ounce for his proprietary elixir.

'*Melhor que soma, senhora.*'

Better than *soma*? But was it more or less addictive than that blessed beverage? If it possesses the same properties, helps me deal with this darkness in my soul. I filled the glass, saw in its reddish-brown depths so many reasons why I should trust neither the contents nor Bridger, then decided I did not care and threw back the liquid, the sweetness of sherry but a bitter after-taste.

'You may leave the tray,' I said, but then as she made to leave I was taken by the urge to confront her. 'No, Winifred. A moment of your time?'

She turned back to face me, a twitch of her shoulders as though to say that it was of no concern to her whether she left or stayed. Her dark eyes were triumphant.

'*Senhora?*'

'You say that word as though it were a curse. Some resentment you feel towards me, perhaps? I did not seek the changes made by Mister Yale to my household, your position here, though I understand he must have felt some obligation to you. But there is more, is there not?'

She closed the door behind her, leaned against it as though she owned the place.

'Your husband, he is a good man. At first we blame him for John's trouble. But when John, he is sick, your husband explain me it was not his fault. That it was your friend, *senhor* Parrish.'

My friend, I thought. So, by implication, my fault too. Elihu exonerated, despite the obvious evidence to the contrary. And I could feel the elixir loosening my tongue. To be honest, I felt somehow elated, as I had done so often under the *soma*'s influence. It caused me to stand, determined to defeat her, yet my legs felt suddenly unsteady.

'And Seaton?' I said.

'*Senhor* Seaton say me the same. How your husband gave orders but, *de verdade*, word comes from your friend Parrish. From Parrish to Directors. From Directors to Governor Yale.'

'Oh, I think he said a lot more to you than that, Mistress Bridger. Did he not? Threatened to tell the world about your Jewish blood, perhaps?'

She froze for a moment, but then she found her defiance afresh.

'*Senhora*, I am *conversa*.'

I found myself sitting back upon the divan, my legs no longer supporting me.

'A convert? To what, Winifred? But at Fort St. George that would have availed you little, I fear. No Jews within White Town unless authorised by John Company. Like Jacques de Paiva. Do you know what Seaton told *me*? That you were his ears and eyes. The ears and eyes of a man we now know was a Jacobite traitor. The ears and eyes that spied upon me. Clever, Winifred. To work out the secrets I was garnering over the chatter-broth that would hurt those same Jacobites. To work out the secrets and relay them to Seaton. And Seaton used those things to menace me. To menace my whole family. It made me a target, Winifred. Do you not understand? The Roundsmen pirates. Sathiri's death.'

Oh, how I hated her for Sathiri. In turn, of course, I had betrayed Jacques de Paiva. Caused his demise, I am certain. I saw that she regarded me with contempt, or perhaps confusion. No, I thought, she does not understand, and I filled the glass afresh from the laudanum bottle.

'And my husband,' she said. 'He die too.'

I find I am still not certain – whether John Bridger's death was my fault or not. I had put the Poison Nut powder in Winifred's drink, to avenge myself for her betrayal of me. But she had plainly not supped from the poisoned chalice. Had John, by mistake? I know not. Though, unless she is a great dissembler, I can trace no hint that she herself holds me accountable. Simply her continued belief that I may have been implicated, along with Parrish, in her husband's financial downfall.

'Yes,' I said, 'John died too. But I fear this tincture tires me, causes me to swoon.'

'There is more,' she smiled. She seemed satisfied with herself on a task well done. 'More, when you want.'

She left me wondering whether she meant more of the laudanum, or more to discuss. Perhaps both. But I was drowsy. And as the elixir began to soothe my humours, to clear my thoughts, I returned to the assault on Parrish.

It struck me that every inn and alehouse along Broad Street – and Sweet Jesu knows they are plentiful enough – must have its share of bravos like those who had attacked us, each simply waiting for the slightest of opportunities to cut a purse. Yet a robbery? Why pick on somebody of such obvious military bearing as Parrish? Great heavens, there are enough of the old, the weak, the vulnerable on the streets each Sunday morning. But if the assault had been targeted at Matthew, how had it been triggered? By whom? Was it even connected to me? After all, Parrish makes enemies easily enough and this could, I supposed, equally have had something to do with his activities in Parliament. Though I began to wonder at those final instructions whispered by Reverend Hoadly to his half-crippled sexton. Hoadly would know Parrish, of course. But had he received some form of *pishcash* from Elihu to watch out for him, then identified Parrish among his parishioners? It would not surprise me. And how easy for Lame Landry to slip away, find a couple of biddable thugs who could be paid to do the deed?

Do I care? Perhaps not. So, one more sip of the elixir and then to bed.

September 1701

Yes, I believe it must be September.

How is this? My bedchamber, always far too grand for my taste, has grown larger still. I cannot even see the farther end at all now. Shrouded in some amber fug, which itself emanates from those distant wall hangings. I swear they once conveyed pastoral scenes, upland meadows and grazing beasts, gently swaying trees. But somebody has changed them. Elihu? Bridger? I know not, though it is certain they now portray less peaceful images, the demons of my life's sad conflicts, breathing fire to torment me always with this intolerable heat, the stench of brimstone in my nostrils, the screams of the dying to fill my ears, and the clouds of war to dim my vision, all pouring from my furnishings.

And when did this happen? Twenty years ago, perhaps. Somewhere back in that infinite tunnel of time beginning with the pyramid tomb of my sweet Joseph and poor little Dormouse Davy, leading me here to this cavernous room, and ending – where *does* it end? Anywhere? If infinite, of course it cannot.

Though I shall record them. My duty to record them. At least each of the lesser scenes playing themselves out across the nearer portions of my walls. Those that hold less horror. So, where to start? Maybe on that day when news of the diamond arrived.

Sir Stephen Evance is being served light refreshments in the library and I have made my grand entrance, against Elihu's wishes, arranged myself so delicately on the window seat and, from there, I have drifted into such sweet slumber. But not so deep that I do not hear him, my husband's monstrous voice.

'I find I must apologise for her, Stephen,' he says. 'The bottle again, I fear.'

Ah, you apology for a husband. And the bottle, my sweet elixir of life? There is nothing to fear from my bottle.

'You have the patience of a saint, sirrah,' Evance murmurs.

I snore a little, for emphasis. For irony. I watch them through half-closed eyelids. Like my bedchamber, they seem to have grown to monstrous proportion, shrouded in a green fug.

'I am stayed, as always, by word from Madras,' says Elihu. 'Mistress Nicks tells me they are all hale and hearty. John Nicks finds work abroad. And the two companies seem to be coming together. There in India, at least. God's hooks, if they continue to do so I may yet agree to work on their behalf. Though not otherwise. And they should be grateful I consider even that much. Great heavens, how they must need me. Above all, this diamond of Pitt's.'

Through veiled eyelids I see him stuff his face with apple pie. He is unkempt, still in his banyan and turban.

'A wondrous thing,' Stephen Evance replies. 'Forty-five carats. It rivals anything I've ever seen.'

That is some commendation from the King's Jeweller, is it not?

'And from the very mine,' Elihu says, and helps himself to a glass of ruby wine, 'that my evil-minded wife foisted upon poor Katherine and so many of my associates. Well, she is bit in her turn now, though too insensible to know it. Look at her.'

Yes, just look. But is it true? The mine? Did we blunder so badly, Antonio do Porto and myself, in those gravel-clay pits we thought entirely barren. Or did he simply betray me as so many others have done?

'Mistress Nicks must have a fine nose,' says Evance. 'She will receive an excellent price from Pitt when it sells, and you say there is more to be garnered from this seam she's found.'

God damn her. And, to think, I had even missed her. A little. But there had been those rumours, that she had employed surveyors for the Kollur mine. Sent me that message too. *The most empty of caverns, the deepest of echoes.* That drab whore.

'Confident, Stephen. She is confident. And Governor Pitt has set a substantial value on the diamond if you, my friend, can find a buyer. Meanwhile, you shall profit from its care and sale. It all serves to raise my spirit from the depths, at least.'

'You are too much confined to your house, Elihu,' Evance tells him. 'Become too much the recluse.'

'How can I not, sirrah? Look at her. Incapable. Mistress Bridger does her best, but there is the household to be managed. My properties. My collections. The girls and their private tuition. Beautiful Betty and Ursi Nicks to be provided for at Freeman's. My own Ursula boarding too. Though why I should trouble about her I do not know. So plain and plump, so lacking in wits that I shall never find a match for her. Were we papists, I suppose it would be the nunnery for her.'

I almost rise to confront him. To confront the pair of them with some home truths about beautiful Betty and her by-blow sister – to remind them that Seaton would never have been free to damage my own baby girl had this bubble of a husband dealt with him at Fort St. George. Yet, somehow, my limbs will not answer, cannot shift me from this perch.

'Perhaps some young curate?' says Evance. 'And the boy? Have you word?'

'From Jeronima, nothing. But Mistress Nicks keeps me in touch with him. Don Carlos, she names him. He will be eleven by now. God bless him.'

His son and heir. This prime ambition of his. God bless him indeed. Though disingenuous of me, this feigned concern about Jeronima's son. For had I not almost wished the child upon her – and Elihu too, of course? The most suitable punishment I could conceive for her. If Jeronima did not provide him with an heir, I had told her, as though it were a witch's curse, then there was unlikely ever to be one. Nor has there been another so far as I know. Though perhaps he has sired an entirely different beneficiary.

'And God bless your efforts, Elihu,' said Evance, 'at resolving your differences with John Company.'

'Oh, I am certain of it. I have written already to the Directors, demanding redress for the grief they caused me, the money they owe. The charges against me dropped, though my good name not entirely cleared. No verdict of innocence. After all, I now have two allies working on my behalf. Governor Pitt at Fort St. George for the Old Company, and his brother, Jack, governor at Fort St. David for the New. They are coming together, my dear. When they do so, as they must, they shall need me afresh. And, at that juncture, I hope there shall be no further obfuscation against my becoming a baron knight. What think you, wife?'

I am almost forced to laugh. Oh, dear Elihu, I am as certain of your knighthood as I am about the Company redressing your grievances.

There is great commotion. I hear it from my window and it comes from Broad Street. Some raucous procession. So I determine to see what is afoot. I have my nightgown, my modesty cap upon my head. A vision of respectability. Nobody to prevent me either, Elihu away from home once more and Mistress Bridger gone to market, I think. Or perhaps to purchase a fresh supply of the Sydenham's. The cobbles are cool beneath my naked feet, pleasant, yet revellers stare at me with impudence, a hint of mockery, and I mock them in my turn, dare them to say to my face whatever is in the minds. But they do not, content to mutter about mad women and the rest.

'What passes?' I call out as I reach the corner at Old Tom's.

'He's dead,' somebody shouts back. 'Catholic James Stuart is dead.'

And there he is, borne aloft in the midst of a drunken crowd pressing down the centre of the road. Borne aloft in effigy, at least, those round about singing a bawdy ballad concerning the exiled king's codpiece and other intimacies, the manikin they carry unmistakably with James Stuart's features.

'Apoplexy and bleeding in the brain,' says a fellow at my side. He has copies of the *Gazette* for sale. 'And the old bastard – begging your pardon, Mistress – all over the place, you might say.'

I ask his meaning and it seems the defective brain itself has gone to some college in Paris; his heart in a silver locket to a convent elsewhere; his entrails divided equally between a church and a Jesuit seminary. The rest on display at a French papist chapel with lights burning all around the coffin.

'Mistress,' says the fellow's companion, 'are you quite well?'

'How could I not be well, with this enemy of my faith dead?'

He laughs.

'The enemy of us all, madam. One less with which to contend in our war with France.'

'We are at war?' I say.

'These many months past, ma'am. Are you sure we cannot assist you?'

There is a voice from behind me. Benjamin.

'I thank you, sirrah, but I shall care for her now.' And he takes me by the arm, begins to lead me back into Austin Friars.

'No,' I cry. 'I must see more. Look!'

Some old men in the uniforms of times past, a marching band with pipe and tabor, shawm and crumhorn. Behind them, a prancing pony bearing a cove in the guise of King William, but a gasp from the crowd as the cavorting beast slips on a generous heap of dung and spills its rider onto the cobbles.

'Better to come home, Mama,' says Benjamin. I see there is a tear in his eye and I wonder at his concern for this clown's antics.

'Shall you come home too, my son? Leave your Uncle Dick's and come home?'

'Mama, I have not been at Uncle Dick's since June. Do you not collect?'

Suddenly I fear for him, the things I have heard slowly coalescing in my fuddled mind.

'But not in the war?'

'Not in the war, no. Though I follow its progress closely enough. I have given you reports. For I knew you should want to be informed. You showed great interest, when I told you we must stop the papists uniting the thrones of Spain and France under a single Catholic Bourbon king. I read the news to you.'

But no, I do not recall.

'I think I mis-spoke, Benji. About you. Did I not?'

I am also unable to recall whatever that might have been.

'It is of no matter, Mama,' he says. 'None.'

'I hate it here, Benjamin,' I tell him, as some footman I do not recognise opens the door to us. 'I hate it.'

Monday 20th July 1702

It has cost me dear. The simple act of climbing from my bed at this ungodly hour – the Maysmore tells me it is three hours past midnight – on these desperately unsteady legs and then, with treacherous fingers, fumbling the steel, stone and tinder to light my candle. Next, to retrieve this jaundice-tinted journal, my porcupine quill and nib, my inks, from their compartment beneath the strongbox. I had wished to do so days ago, after Annie came to speak with me, but then I had known that, while I might have the strength to collect them, it would not sustain me long enough to set down my thoughts and also see my treasures returned safely to their hiding place once more. And I could not risk their discovery.

Annie tells me I have been two months a-bed. Two months from a time when, she says, I must have made a decision to renounce Sydenham's cursed laudanum – though I have no memory of setting myself upon that course. It seems more as though it was some other woman, writhing in my miry slough, this dungeon of despair. And I am the sinner awakened about my lost condition, beset by fear and doubt, the torture chamber of my torments, struggling to strike off those chains. Though they still bind me. The fever. The shaking that makes this writing so difficult – almost illegible, I fear – and the pounding in my brain, the flux that grips my innards. Worse, the constant voice, whispering to me that the one certain cure for all my ills is the elixir itself. Perhaps the smallest of doses. Just one. To see me through the night. Though I shall not. Shall not! Shall not!

She came to me with a question, or rather a sequence of questions, another leather-bound book clutched to her breast, having ascertained that I was at least reasonably lucid, eating again and free, for a while, from many of the afflictions Elihu's opium has piled upon me. She came to me while I was still lying in my filth, still contemplating the impossible task of rising, and she stood at the farther bedpost.

'Is it true, Mama – that you cannot love me? Papa says it is so. That you blame me somehow for my brother's death.'

With her free hand she held a kerchief to her nose. A whiff of rosemary, which served simply to heighten the stale sweat odours of my own body. I struggled to sit upright, hoping she might come nearer. But she did not.

'My dear, several of my childbirths were difficult. My old companion, Sathiri, at Fort St. George…'

'Papa has spoken of her too. A heathen Gentue, was she not? The harlot of your friend, Mister Parrish.'

Elihu the hypocrite, I thought, but noted that the room had, at last, shrunk to its more regular proportions once more. And she had angered me. I looked towards the travel chest in the corner, which still carried the personal possessions I had brought back from Madras – including that elegant *saree* in which I had been wed to Elihu.

'Sathiri and Matthew were as close to being wed as any couple I have ever known,' I shouted. 'And you have a short memory, Nan. Our *ayah*, Tanani, who cared for you so generously was a Gentue also. But heathen? You would do well to be more cautious with your words.'

She took the kerchief from her nose, studied me a moment.

'You have never called me that before. Not Nan. Not ever. It is Papa's special name for me.'

'If I have not, it is a lapse I regret.'

'A regret too little, too late, perhaps.'

'Do you say so? You have become so replete with worldly wisdom of a sudden? You should add this to your knowledge, my girl. That, when you were little, my mind was often clouded. Much as the elixir has done the same. Yet there was reason. Sathiri taught me that, in giving birth, the babe can sometimes draw from the mother's body some elements without which we are pitched into profound melancholy.'

'So, the blame lies with me for that, too.'

Imperfections in the window glass caused joyous beams of evening-pink sunlight to dance upon the ceiling. Tomorrow would be a fine day.

'I did not say so. And more than mere melancholy. Almost a measure of madness. And so it was when I gave you light, sweet girl. It was coincidence, nothing more, that David fell ill so soon afterwards. But in my ramblings, and for a long time later, that madness caused me to believe you were stealing from him his own life's essence.'

'You believed it was the truth. Papa was right. How could you have loved me?'

'The truth? It was probably more my fault than anything else. That my own weakened state perhaps made me less the mother for him than I should have been. I am sorry Annie, that you may have suffered for it. But you must believe that I can indeed love you – and do so very deeply.'

Outside on the street there were the noises of an altercation, two men arguing about the ownership of a horse as they passed below. It sparked a recollection. My belly huge with her, and Davy bringing each of his wooden animals to me, pressed each in turn against Annie's bulge. 'This is mine,' he had said gently, his infant's voice explaining ownership rights to his still unborn sister. 'And this is mine too.' His father, I think would have been proud.

'Kate is convinced you love none of us. She is gone, did you know?' I did not. 'Papa has a new house. Queen Square. Very elegant and Katie gone to live with him.'

'Mistress Bridger?'

I vaguely recalled a confrontation with her, she insisting I should continue to imbibe the elixir. Physician's orders, she had claimed. But I had resisted. Yes, resisted.

'Still here. Benjamin too. Though you should not flatter yourself. True, he feels he has a duty. I think it is more an excuse to be near young Beatriz.'

'He came to me. On the street, I think. Or perhaps...'

'For pity's sake, it was almost a year ago, Mama. Upon Broad Street in naught but your nightgown. Papa swore you should be sent to the Bethlem Hospital, but Benji made some legal threat against him.'

'He succeeded in being called to the bar?'

'He will tell you himself but his attorney says that when he wins this dreadful claim in Chancery against my papa he will not have to worry about gainful employment ever more. For pity's sake, how can he boast of such a thing? Spends so many of his days there.'

'And there will be many to come if I know anything about the Equity Courts. Do not judge him too harshly though. He feels he has just cause.' She waved the kerchief in front of her face, as though to dismiss my foolishness. Or my complicity. So, to change the subject. 'But Ursi, is there word?'

'Still boarding. Still unhappy. Still at her prayers. But good that you remember her name, though you have not spoken it in a long while.'

'I must bring her home. As soon as I am able. Will you help me, Nan?'

'You know Papa will not allow it. And he forbids us now to call this home at all. Queen Square, and Plas Grono – those are the only homes for us, he says.'

'Then how...?'

'Am I here?' She gave a small laugh. 'Mister Smedley refuses to journey all the way to Queen Square for the purpose of my lessons in mathematicks. And I refuse tuition from anybody else. So I am permitted here each Monday, in company of a footman. The fellow is much taken by Mistress Bridger so I take advantage some weeks, at the end of my lesson, to see...'

'Your Mama.'

'To see whether you still live. My curiosity.'

'I suppose I should be grateful for so much. And do I smell as ripe as I imagine?'

'Overpowering. Unpleasant. Mistress Bridger's girls do their best for you. Benjamin makes sure of that. For now.'

'I have missed so much.'

'You missed my birthing day.' I looked in her stubborn face and I saw, staring back at me, the Catherine Elford of that same age. Before sweet Joseph. Not the hag reflected so often now in my glass. Fifteen already. I apologised again. 'And that very morning a package arrived for you. With the Queen Square direction. She must have assumed – well, here!' She passed me the book she carried. A copy of Margaret Fox's *Women's Speaking Justified*.

'George Fox and Mistress Fox were great friends of my father,' I explained. 'But why the book?'

'There was a note,' Annie explained, 'though Papa destroyed it. But I remember it, more or less. A bequest, she wrote. In honour of that friendship between her husband and Walter Elford. *"To his daughter."* That's what it said. *"May this give her comfort."* I think that was it.'

'She is dead too, then,' I said. I never knew her in person, Margaret Fox – Margaret Fell as she had once been when she came to prominence among the Quakers. But here it was, the kindness of strangers, a message from the grave to stiffen my resolve. Everything for which she stood, highlighting those sections of holy scripture that speak in favour of women's ministry, her belief that God created men and women alike, that we are all equal in His sight and, therefore, as capable of preaching the gospel as receiving its light.

'Dead at the end of April, I think,' Annie told me.

I held it in my hand, studied the title page a moment.

'This is a valuable gift, Nan,' I told her. 'But I believe it more properly belongs to you than me.' She demurred politely, but I knew she had already begun exploring its depths and, in the end, she accepted, clasped the volume to her bosom once more. 'But fair exchange,' I said. 'Have I missed much more?'

'Things I suspect you would not wish to hear. The king. You know nothing of that?' Of course, I did not, and she curtly unravelled the strange tale of King William's death, the fall from his horse after it stumbled on a molehill. Yet, when she told me, it all sounded so familiar, until I recalled that procession, the cavorting pony and the spill taken by the buffoon masquerading in the king's clothes. But, in this version, there was William's actual death, two weeks later, the coronation of Protestant Anne Stuart, Princess of Denmark, in April.

'And after Anne,' I said. 'What then?'

'It is decided. The Succession. Last month. There were great protests. And the Scots furious. But it is done. If Queen Anne dies, the crown passes to Sophia, the Electress of Hanover. And thence to Sophia's descendants.'

'Sophia?' I said.

'It seems she is a granddaughter to James the First.'

'I should have remembered that.'

My brain struggled to digest all this. A strange way to restore the fabric of the Stuart line of succession – but the Protestant weft to counter the Catholic warp. Clever. Pulls the weave knots, I imagine, of those who must now be clamouring for a Jacobite solution.

'According to the broadsheets, there is a pretender to the throne. The son of Catholic James Stuart. James Francis Edward. French Louis has already recognised his claim, names him James the Third.'

That same boy who, thirteen years ago, we had believed – I still believe – had been substituted for the child stillborn to Mary of Modena. Yes, praise God, I remembered that much.

'Well,' I said, 'once I should have cared more about all this. But now, dear Annie, I wish nothing more than my children back with me again.'

'Papa shall not permit it. Can you blame him? He is entirely occupied with his brokerage of matches for each of us.'

I saw something in her face, began to understand.

'Is that what brings you to me, Nan? What is he planning?'

'He says Sir Stephen Evance has shown great interest in me.'

'Evance? He must be…'

I stopped myself, recalling the difference in age between Joseph and me.

'Twelve years, yes.'

'He has wealth and position, I suppose.'

'But I believe his interest in me stems only from Papa's insistence. I fear it would be something of a parody.'

Oh, Annie, I thought. You have grown so much. I could see her intent plainly now. I have always liked Evance, but there is a quality in his character that makes me certain he would marry for no other reason than to protect his own reputation. There are cruel names for men like Sir Stephen Evance that I would not repeat here, though I recall that day in Locket's, two years ago, the soldiers bandying about the word sodomite.

'Our lives are full of little parodies, my dear. Nothing may come of this yet. And Katie, is there a match for her too?'

'A whole parade of them. For Betty and Ursula as well.'

'You mean Betty and Ursula Nicks?'

'Papa is much taken with them both. He commissioned pictures to be drawn, sent them to their mother in Madras. He says it is your fault he is burdened with them, besides his own children.'

'I suppose, in a way, that is true enough. And news of Mistress Nicks herself?'

'He says he expects her return to London. The rest of her children too. And Madam Paiva also, though I know she had suffered some form of injury. Papa sent me to purchase Epsom Salts that he might dispatch them to her.' I studied her face again. Was she attempting to goad me? 'Oh, I know what you are thinking, Mama. I suppose you share the scandalous stories that your sons spread abroad. But Papa has warned us we must not heed their nonsense.'

Nonsense? Katherine Nicks and Jeronima de Paiva coming to London? And Queen Square, I supposed, providing him the garden house he needed for his harlots and his by-blows.

'Then, perhaps for the first time, I may see some purpose in being here, in Austin Friars.'

A voice from somewhere else in the house, a man's voice calling her name. Mistress Anne. She started at the sound.

'I must go,' she said. 'It would not answer... But, Mama, do you not know? About the house?'

I did not, and she explained that the place was already sold. I suppose I was not surprised. Nor greatly troubled to be rid of this pile.

'Then no more Mister Smedley. No more secret visits to your Mama.' That elicited at least a nervous smile. 'Yet you might do me a service, Annie. Can you do that?' She looked hesitant, glanced towards the door. 'No, wait,' I pressed her. 'Sir Stephen Evance holds all my investments, and I must access them very quickly, my dear. Perhaps a note appointing Benjamin to act as my agent a while. Is he biddable, d'you think? Sir Stephen?'

That voice calling her again. And now Mistress Bridger's voice added to the hue and cry.

'Perhaps,' she said, 'though I must be circumspect, satisfy myself there is no betrayal of my father in this.' There was no parting kiss, no word even of farewell. But she paused at the door. 'This may give you comfort, Mama. Sir Stephen has already gifted me a token of his affections, parody or otherwise. Your wondrous geographical clock. I have it now and shall guard it for you.'

'I trust you to do so, my dear.'

'And Sir Stephen, Mama? Yes, I will do as you ask if you will promise me one thing in return.'

'Anything in my power, sweet Annie.'

'Simply promise me I shall never have to marry him.'

*

There is light coming through the drapes, the Maysmore chiming six o' the clock. My letters all written and, later this morning, I shall try to get the most important of them to Benjamin, give him power of attorney to act on my behalf. For, if Elihu has sold the house, and I cannot access resources of my own, I dread to think where I shall end. On King Street, perhaps, along with the rest of his collectibles.

Meanwhile, I must get these things back to their seclusion. I pray that I have the strength, can still the shaking limbs, sweeten the foul taste upon my tongue – and silence, too, that voice of temptation. Just one small dose perhaps. Just one.

Volume Six

Sunday 28th March 1702/3

Easter Sunday, and I have been in this place seven months now. Betrayed. Betrayed again. Then betrayed a third time.

The first? That morning, when I had ventured unsteadily down the stairs to look for Benjamin, found him gone once more to Chancery. Mistress Bridger was also absent, or so I thought at the time. But I had bid Maria and Beatriz Bridger begin the arduous task with as many other servants as could be mustered of fetching water from the conduit, commencing to boil the pots and pans, prepare a tub that I might begin my restoration, despite the dangers such immersion might entail. And once the process was begun, fresh linen selected for me, I returned to the bedchamber only to find the letter for Benjamin disappeared from my writing slope. How could I have been so foolish? My only excuse, now, is that the laudanum continued to dull my wits, would continue to do so in ways far worse.

The second, when I had survived the bathing, dressed afresh in my plainest grey linsey-woolsey and Benjamin was returned to the house some hours later. He was anxious to tell me his news from the Equity Court but I did not afford him the opportunity, being by then almost hysterical with worry about the letter's disappearance. I took him aside, explained its content.

'If the letter finds its way to Mister Yale's hands,' I said, 'I fear how he might react. That it may precipitate some scheme on his part to thwart my own.'

'I would doubt, Mama, that such a letter would confer any sustainable legal status upon me in any case. But be not fretful. I shall go down and ascertain what might have happened.'

A quarter-hour or more went by, while I paced the floor and Benjamin did not return. I could hear Winifred Bridger below again, however, yet only the older of her girls appeared in my room.

'Forgive me, madam,' she said, 'but Mister Benjamin bade me bring you this.'

It was a posset, hot milk and liquor in a cup of royal blue, heavily spiced. It was delicious, soothed me almost instantly, though it took me just too long to recognise the bitter after-taste.

So, the third? It is all still so vague but I remember being back upon my bed, head swimming, and Winifred Bridger pouring the laudanum down my throat, drop by spluttering drop, until they came for me that same afternoon.

It is the shortest possible carriage ride from Austin Friars to the Bethlem Hospital for Lunaticks, though I do not recall the journey. They must have put me in restraints, for that seems the usual practice with new patients here, but I cannot be certain of that either. Simply another fug, an amber miasma.

There is a recollection: of being hauled from the closed conveyance, a looming gateway, grotesque gargoyles gaping down at me from their lofty pediment; of being half-carried through ill-lit corridors to an even darker cell, where I was put to the manacles upon an iron bedstead with straw-filled palliasse. Then swarming faces, at times with the features of Mistress Bridger, though I now recognise them as those of Matron Nurse Wood.

After that, another indeterminate period of quaking delirium, the screaming nightmare visions, the disgusting visitations by Vincent Seaton, the depths of melancholy, the retching – until, at last, there came the day when I was seemingly no longer considered a danger to myself or my new keepers, the manacles removed, the hospital's physician finally treating the weeping sores they had left, and I was escorted, in my now permanent state of protest, to my admission interrogation.

Matron Nurse Wood was stiff as her name implied, any human personality she might possess hidden carefully behind a thicket of formality, a sibilant veneer of Kentish drawl wrapped in charcoal skirts and cloak as she drummed her fingers upon the table.

'Was you simply a sot, Mistress Yale, in the grip of liquor or similar intoxicant, the governors would not 'ave accepted your 'usband's petition. 'Cos why? 'Cos our charitable duty 'ere is to restore the poor insane to their wits.'

My reasoning words – that I was no lunatic but merely the victim of laudanum fed to me against my will – hung unheeded among the sunshine motes of the Matron's office, the light from her well-appointed windows hurting my troglodyte eyes. No place for me to sit, so I stood – as best I could, for the manacles had left their mark in various ways – while, at the door, a keeper slouched against the wall, finger delving up to the first knuckle in her pig-like nostril.

'I am not poor,' I murmured, though I found I was wringing my hands like some mendicant pauper. 'I have means. Independent means.'

'We makes exception. At times. Where petitioners be charitable benefactors of the 'ospital.'

'My husband?'

'Says...' She picked up a letter from the office table. 'Le'me see – yes, 'ere. "*My wife is also much distracted in 'er mind, a danger to 'er children and 'erself.*" Cites examples too.'

'Danger...'

There was a twitch at the side of her eye, I noticed.

'Incident,' she said, 'in which your youngest daughter were injured. Permanently, it seems. And – wandering the streets in your nightgown. Lots more, there be. You seems lucid enough at present, though. That be 'elpful.'

'To classify me?' I said, wondering whether she would list me, on the one hand, as merely idiotic, mischievous, simple, addle-pated, foolish. Or, on the other, as maniacal, furious, evil, lunatic. Oh, I knew a little about this place.

'You enjoys such lucid intervals frequently, my dear? Temporary remission, as you might say?'

'There is a thin line, is there not,' I said, 'between lunacy and a sot's stupefaction? Were I simply a drunken sot, you would be obliged to release me, yes?'

I turned, as though I might simply walk out of the place, but the keeper span me around again, pushed me back towards the table.

'Possible to be both,' said Matron Nurse Wood. 'In the opinion of the President, the Steward and our physician, Mister Tyson, you falls into that category, Mistress Yale. Your 'usband's opinion too, and that be important, do ye not think?'

When I was a child, the old Bethlem Hospital at Bishopsgate was the stuff of legend. Unpleasant legend. The treatment of Bedlamites barbarous, primeval. But that place is long gone now, built anew here as an example of modern medicine upon the Moor Fields.

'Have I received visitors?' I asked, glancing about as though they might be there, waiting for me.

'Many,' she replied. 'That not so, Agnes?'

'Oh yes, Matron,' said the keeper, and curtsied as she spoke. 'We 'as no other gentlewomen on the gallery. So she be quite the thing.'

Yes, that memory too. As though a dream. The raucous presence of those crowds who paid a penny for the pleasure of gazing upon us in our cells, the constant opening and slamming of the wicket window of my door.

'I meant my children.'

'There be instructions, Mistress Yale. From your 'usband.'

Benjamin, I thought. Where are you? And what has become of my strongbox, my precious journals?

I write these recollections upon the paper that, with my changed status now, I am entitled to receive, on the strict understanding that all my words are subjected to scrutiny by the Steward, Mister Yates, or by the porter, Mister Wood – Matron's husband. And I hope that, one day, I may either transcribe them or keep them as a separate volume.

'But my son. You cannot keep my own son from me.'

'Mistress Yale,' she said, with a deal of condescension, 'we may do whatever your 'usband instructs if we is collectively agreed it be for your own good. I'm 'appy to move you, though. One of the more cosy rooms?'

'Cells,' I said, and caused Matron Nurse Wood to grasp the edge of her table, pull herself closer towards me.

'Cells, if ye prefer,' she said. 'And you shall now 'ave the freedom of the women's gallery, unless at meal times or when there be visitors about.'

'How gracious.'

She frowned at my insolence, but pressed on regardless.

'And ye shall, of course, be permitted visits from your obligors.'

A spark of hope. Who had Elihu appointed to provide me with essentials? Though the optimism was quickly extinguished. 'They be...' Another piece of paper, a more formal, contractual document. 'Mistress Bridger. An' Reverend Hoadly.'

My heart sank.

'I shall have neither,' I said. 'I am no lunatick, to be subjected to such imprisonment.'

'Are ye not?' she replied. 'You be an ingrate, madam. Without food, clothes an' other essentials from yer obligors, you thinks your treatment should be sustained by charity alone? Agnes, take Mistress Yale back to 'er leg-locks 'til she discovers that such 'aughty behaviour will not serve 'er interests in this 'ere establishment.'

And so it was done. Though I hasten to add, for the benefit of Mister Yates and Mister Wood, that I fully support the wisdom of her decision. Of course I do!

July and part of August had, I now know, passed with me in manacles while I sweated out the worst of the addiction, the rest of August and the first two weeks in September in those same leg irons while I learned humility. That was the instruction I received, from Agnes and the other keepers, each time food was brought me. Dishwater gruel at first light and then the meagre rations at dinner and supper. I wept, of course, for much of those two weeks, during the interminable hours of darkness: desperate for my children; for the chance of contracting any of the evil distempers that seem to so abound here; for my freedom; for my want of revenge against Bridger and the addiction she had inflicted on me; for the injustice of my captivity here; for the laws that allow my husband to so confine me; for my lost journals; for the vermin I hear scratching, squealing and scampering beneath the bed. And when not weeping, I prayed endlessly for our Sweet Lord Jesu to provide the strength with which to endure, to overcome. Or consoled myself by trying to recall each page of the volumes – my Donne, my Bunyan and many others – I had previously taken so much for granted. Yes, humility. And strength. Those were the qualities I tried to draw for myself.

During the hours of barely discernible daylight I demanded, variously, that word should be sent to my son, care of Elford's Coffee House, or to my daughter Anne at Queen Square – for surely they must have no idea of my confinement, my predicament; that something should be done about the bugs, which bite me with such avid enthusiasm; that I should be allowed access to the governors, or at least to that same Mister Yates, the hospital's Steward, so they might see I have no place here; that I should be allowed to pen appeals for assistance – to Sir William Langhorn, to the Duke of Devonshire, to my friend Matthew Parrish in Parliament, to the Czar of Muscovy. Yet all of these, each refused, seemed to elicit naught but confirmation of my madness, some unwelcome reprisal from the keepers, most usually their refusal to empty the stinking contents of my chamber-pot for days on end.

Maybe it was the stench that meant I saw neither of my obligors during this time but I knew they must have visited simply because Agnes would occasionally bring me fresh linen and, of course, the meals continued to arrive each day at their allotted hours. I could see by peering through the wicket that my diet was precisely the same as for everybody else in that section of the upper gallery in which I was confined. The women's section, separated from the men's cells by an iron grille and gate. But, wherever I looked, the view was all the same, a uniform shadow-strewn deep grey, making it almost impossible to distinguish between floor or wall or ceiling, either within my own cell or without. But I can assure both Mister Yates and Mister Wood that, yes, I perfectly understand this total and deliberate lack of colour to be efficacious in our treatment, avoiding the undesirable excitement that some garish decoration may incite. Similarly, the limitations of the food, the keepers reminding us constantly that a healthy hunger will also speed our cure. Of course, it shall!

The open wicket was both curse and comfort in equal measure. We needed no mechanical piece, nor the church bells' chime beyond the walls – which at least helped momentarily deaden the cries of the most insane – to track our time, for at precisely nine each morning, every day except Sundays and holy days, the outer doors were thrown open to admit those who had queued for admittance as visitors. Visitors? Theatregoers, rather, who would pay their penny-piece on leaving, satisfied with the entertainment they had enjoyed. The stream of this perambulating audience would flow almost without remission until seven in the evening. And I recalled a handbill I had once seen that announced a grotesque show outside the very gates of this place, the penny admission price including the chance to view the other sad grotesques within Bethlem itself. So here I am now, one of those same grotesques.

A penny for the poor box. Perhaps a penny for the porter's purse might be more accurate – though I expect Mister Wood may force me to delete that sentence in due course – while those with greater garnish to distribute might pay considerably more to be taken aloft, to the upper level, the Checkers, where the most dangerous, the most incurable of my fellow-maniacs are held permanently in restraint.

The open wicket was a curse, too, for the light it shone upon the condition of other patients. Maudlin Mary, for example, from the cell opposite, who cavorts about the gallery, convinced she is William's dead queen. Yet dressed only in the sombre blue smock of subservience issued to those maintained by the hospital's Wardrobe Fund alone. That poor creature, who soils herself so often she has no bedstead at all, no palliasse, and naught but a bale of yellow straw on which to lay her head whenever our Lord Jesus allows her that luxury. Otherwise she is mocked and baited by those penny-peepers, sometimes even spat upon – though most often our keepers will prevent such extremes whenever they can spare an eye to turn upon the malefactors. And at the beginning I would feel obliged to speak out too.

'Do you laugh at God's creations, sirrah?' I cried on that memorable occasion when the gentleman offender, painted harlot upon his arm, rewarded me with a precisely aimed riposte of his walking cane that almost took out my eye, left me half-blinded for weeks.

I can more easily forgive the poor and uneducated who venture upon the Bedlam Round, those young homespun fellows who come here a-courting in their leisure hours, as they would to a country fair, the cheapest possible source by which to amuse their sweethearts. But the others, the silk and satin gentle-folk who I might have expected to know better, the rich devotees of the bear pit, the cockfight, the bull baiting, the public pillory, the whipping post – for those I reserve my greatest scorn. The wretches who see us simply as wild animals. Sometimes as objects of their lust, those who will slip the right keeper a guinea or more to have their desires sated. And when not inflicting their wantonness upon the patients themselves, then using the place as a resort for their lecherous assignations, as they would in many another public place. Oh, the world is full of dark and secret corners within which miscreants like these may practise their carnality.

Mister Yates and Mister Wood remind me that such folk are a minority, that most of our visitors venture here for the correctional benefits offered by the hospital – the purpose of allowing access to the galleries more in tune with enlightening the public, illustrating the wages of vice, indulgence and disobedience. For observation, they each tell me, is the gateway to enlightenment, turning the mirror of madness on society itself, the chance to contemplate humanity at its nadir. Personally, I think it would be equally effective, and less cruel, to simply pay the entrance fee for a performance of Master Shakespeare's *Lear*. *"O! Let me not be mad, not mad, sweet heaven."* But of course I must still be mad, for how, otherwise, could I not see, as Mister Yates and Mister Wood do so plainly, that only a minority of our visitors are venal and debauched?

And the comfort of the open wicket? To at least bring me a modicum of news from the world outside. From that Frenchman last week, for instance – a Protestant Huguenot who had fled papist persecution in Paris, settling in Amsterdam. I had watched him for several moments as he was jostled in the women's gallery, a pamphlet in his hand, seeming somewhat lost. He saw me looking out at him and approached my door, leaned a little to address me through the open hatch.

'Forgive me, *madame*,' he said. 'Can you help? I am not wishing to offend but here, you see?'

His accent was pleasant, his English perfect, and he showed me the broadside. *An Eminent Guide to the Attractions of London*. And there we were, listed just after the lions at the Tower of London menagerie and the still unfinished splendour of St. Paul's.

> *The Bethlem Hospital at Moor Fields invites you to enjoy the tomfoolery of our patients and, at the same instant, to learn about the most modern treatments of insanity.*

'Tomfoolery,' I said. 'Is that what you seek here, *monsieur?*'

'I was told there is a lady who crows like a cockerel. Another who parades about believing herself the Empress of Rome.'

'And have you no better purpose for being in London, sirrah?'

'*Mais oui.* I am here to do business with *Monsieur* Pontac, of Lombard Street.'

'Oh, I have eaten there.' I almost choked upon the words, recalling that other life. That lost existence. 'But I fear your informant may be somewhat outdated. The poor creature yonder,' I pointed across the gallery to Maudlin Mary's cell, 'is almost certainly the only entertainment of that sort you will find in this corner of the hospital. You should take care though, for she threw a full piss pot at the last Frenchman who came a-visiting.' He recoiled somewhat at my choice of words. 'For, believing herself Queen Mary, she shows a certain animosity to those who may be enemies of the Crown.'

He laughed, then told me his story.

'But you, *madame*,' he said, full of incredulity, 'what tragedy brings you here, to such a parlous place?'

I told him my own tale. Of course, he did not believe me. I could see it in his eyes. But at least he brought me word from beyond the walls, the military successes of that one-time Jacobite, then favourite of the Court, John Churchill, now made Duke of Marlborough, it seems, by Queen Anne. The Frenchman tired of that too, however, in due course, glanced anxiously and often at his pamphlet, keen to move on and perhaps find a London attraction more readily satisfying to his curiosity.

'Yet *monsieur*,' I said, 'if you are bound for Lombard Street, you will be no more than a step or two from the George Yard, and there you will find Elford's Coffee House. Might I trouble you, sirrah, to simply convey word to my brother, Richard Elford, or to my son, Benjamin Hynmers, that you have seen me here?'

I almost soiled myself with excitement as he carefully repeated their names, promised that he would do so. For while he may have brought me news of England's fortunes at home and abroad, he could never have brought me that which I most craved – word of my children and, at least, some understanding of how, for pity's sake, they thought their mama could possibly have vanished so thoroughly. The girls, I suppose, may have been told something approaching the truth. But Benjamin? If he had even an inkling of my whereabouts, I know he should have shifted heaven and earth to reach me. He would, would he not? I prayed anyway that it might be so and here, with this Frenchman, I finally had the chance to let my sons know my fate – though the condescension in the fellow's *adieu* and *bonne chance* gave me to understand that he had no intention of carrying out my request. A fool's errand, I suppose he thought. For there is no greater fool than he who takes instruction from the insane.

"*'The secret to happiness,'*" my father used to tell me, quoting Thucydides, "*'is freedom. And the secret to freedom is courage.'*" It was a subject he understood well after the time he had spent in prison. He has, once again, become something of a comfort to me. Kindred spirits, I suppose.

And at least I am now at liberty to leave my cell, to draw my own water from the cistern here upon our gallery. Liberated too from the tyranny and tortures of my chamber pot, having access to the easement seats in the noisome jakes, outside in the women's yard at this western end of the building.

Yes, outside, fresh summer air. Stretching my legs. Thirty paces from one extremity of the yard to the other. Thirty paces of coarse grass, rampant dandelion and crackling gravel. Back and forth, as long as I am able. The caged beast, now released to its cramped enclosure, happy with its limited perambulations until that limitation itself becomes a new and more subtle torment, for now I can see the palatial rear façade of the Bethlem Hospital in all its glory – glorious despite the meagre cell windows that adorn this side only – wonder how its interior can be so at odds with this splendour. Beyond the building itself, and here on the northern edge of the airing grounds, the perimeter walls that are the reality of our imprisonment.

Somewhere beyond the wall lies my life. My children, who now all seem so lost to me, careless of my plight. It has been the hardest of my lessons here, that the practice of dutiful motherhood itself is plainly not enough to secure reciprocal affection from our children. It seems to me simply a matter of *karma* whether a parent's love is returned, or whether it is thrown back in our face.

But I ramble, as I rambled on that other occasion, a month ago, enjoying one of the first of my excursions out into the yard and then not knowing how fragile a freedom can be. At least today, I had thought, it being a Sunday also, we would be spared the visitors. Yet, when the keepers instructed us to return to our upper gallery, a familiar figure was waiting for me.

'Mistress Yale,' said Reverend Hoadly, 'I hope we find you well.'

One of the rare occasions in my life when I could think of no suitable words with which to reply.

'My obligor,' I said, simply, and he acknowledged my greeting by sweeping the broad-brimmed black hat from atop his peruke.

'Indeed,' he beamed. 'And I trust myself and Mistress Bridger have been adequately obliging your needs.' I really wanted to ask him about that other Sunday when Matthew Parrish had been attacked after leaving St. Peter's. But that intimate recollection of Matthew and how badly I had left him merely brought me to tears, trying to hide them, lowering my eyes and smoothing the folds of my broadcloth skirts. 'There, there,' my dear,' he said. 'It must be moving to see a friendly face after all this time. And the porter warned me you are still prone to profound melancholy on occasion.'

He touched my sleeve, stroked my arm, and I looked up at his spittle-smeared lips, took a step back from his presence.

'Why are you here at all, sirrah? Might you report to my husband, help him gloat upon the paucity of my existence here?'

'Gloat, madam? Your husband cares for nothing but your...your condition, Mistress. Might we not sit in your room, perhaps? Discuss matters in some privacy? Governor Yale, after all, desires to merely see you restored – well, to your senses.'

'My room?' I laughed. 'And I have no condition except that which Winifred Bridger inflicted upon me. An addiction to Sydenham's Elixir. To laudanum, sir. To opium. But that was driven from my system eight months ago.' Ah, how I wish that were true, but the cravings have never quite deserted me. 'Longer,' I said. 'The physicians here with their bleeding, purging and blistering. Cured. Yet I am still here.'

'Not entirely cured though, they tell me. But please, is there nowhere...?'

'Who tells you?'

'Matron Nurse Wood. The porter. The steward.'

'And what, prithee, do they say?'

One of the keepers – that same Agnes who had attended my admission interrogation – had been watching our exchange from her perch at the bar gate.

'If ye needs some quiet, Reverend,' she called, 'ye may use yonder Warmin' Room. The fires be not lit, but Yale will show thee.'

I was reluctant to be alone with him, but I knew better than to defy the keepers, so I led him along the gallery to the gloomy chamber where, in winter months, those at liberty to wander might gather round a miserably inadequate blaze in the wide fireplace.

'Well?' I said again, once we were inside. 'What are you told?'

'Why, that you exhibit strong signs of errant faith. It is the reason I have come. To give instruction, both to yourself and any of these poor creatures you may have infected.'

'My faith is all that has sustained me here, Reverend. Did you think it was this?' I plucked at the broadcloth, uncertain whether it was himself who had brought the skirt among the packages of fresh clothes that occasionally arrived for me, or whether it had been Bridger, though not really caring very much either way. 'Or the food you deliver to the kitchens? The food that neither I nor any of these other poor women ever see? The food that goes straight to the officers and their families while we are left with the gruel.'

Another sentence I expect to see expunged from this parchment very soon.

'They assure me, madam...'

'They tell you precisely what you want to hear, sirrah. The truth? That the clothes, the food, the garnish – my husband's wealth – they are the only things that imprison me here. Without those, the hospital's charity would not permit me to remain, and I should be set free upon the streets. My instruction would be the last thing the governors would consider.'

'I fear you are wrong, Mistress Yale. The governors – and I know several of them personally – take a direct interest in your presence here. And they are concerned, madam. Concerned that you so often rant like a Quaker, preaching the gospel of the antichrist as though it were holy scripture. Consider it a significant part of your illness.'

I wanted to laugh, though bit upon my tongue.

'I am prone to reciting verses from Master John Donne when I am minded to do so, and some of the other women frequently ask me to speak the words aloud. They comfort them, I think. And why should I care, Reverend Hoadly?'

'Oh, but you should. Life could, after all, be so much more comfortable here. Promotion to a better cell. Even to a room within the Steward's house. All such things are possible, and I am instructed to secure such improvements for you, should you be agreeable – should you cooperate. Should you allow me to be both friend and confessor.'

'It seems to me that would defeat the object. For is not the keeping of lunaticks in our kennels the best way to our cure?'

Yes, kennels. Good word. Even here, this poor excuse for a withdrawing room, the same small windows that grace our cells, the openings fitted with iron bars, with wire grilles, with wooden shutters barely capable of keeping out the elements in winter, of providing relief in summer.

'A better way might, perhaps, be to receive word of your girls from time to time.'

'Where are they?'

'Gone north with their father for the summer.'

'Even Ursula?'

'Of course.'

'My sons?'

'I have not seen them. Nor heard any word. I fear they may have forgotten you, madam.'

I dreaded the same, though I should never admit this to Hoadly.

'Word could be sent. To my son Benjamin at Elford's Coffee House.'

'A den of iniquity I could not possibly visit. Though my sexton might, I suppose, be persuaded.'

'The price?'

At Bethlem Hospital there is a price to be paid for everything. And this was precisely as I had expected. He closed the gap between us once more, set his simian fingers upon my sleeve again.

'I have said.' Those damp lips formed a fevered smile. 'You must learn to conform, madam.'

Sweet Jesus help me, for I almost complied, lifted a hand to my mouth, thought about my predicament. But then I used one of the skills taught me by my fellow-patients and spat in his eye.

Agnes and two of the male keepers were summoned hurriedly from beyond the iron gate. And I imagined I could still hear his curses when they held me naked in the laundry tub so long, immersed in the ice-filled waters until I was fully subdued, numb with cold and easily conveyed to the Dark Room, where they have kept me in black confinement these weeks gone by.

Well, it gave me time to contemplate Hoadly's words, I suppose. The governors' personal interest in me? Have I missed something here? And when I was returned to my own cell, I was pleasantly amazed to find I am not required to be manacled – that my parchment and pens are still here, not confiscated. Yes, a Sunday, and my papa's spirit is strong with me as I write.

The Warming Room again, the fire lit but making barely a degree of difference to those of us huddled about the hearth: myself; the tallow chandler Mistress Bingley; two of the vagrant women, Judith and Dutch Dolly; and the young maidservant, Sukie. I have grown accustomed to them now, to their twitching and dribbling, to their snot-smeared cheeks and stammering chatter, to their desire for sometimes cowering in corners or to their occasional clamourings for attention, to their unpredictable bouts of screaming and to their unexpected affectionate embraces. I have come to love each of them, each much younger than me, my surrogate daughters, even Sukie, who has only recently joined us from the women's Checker above – and from whence somebody in authority must have deemed she no longer poses sufficient danger to require further restraint among those terrifying denizens of the hospital's topmost storey. Well, I hope they are right.

In any case, I had made some remark that today was plainly too cold to entice any visitors, for it was already late in the forenoon and not a single alien being had passed along the gallery. I must have spoken so loudly I had not even heard the door, simply caught Sukie's hungry glance in that direction and turned to see one of the other women keepers, Meg, holding the thing ajar. Beyond her, the face of the young man who had caught Sukie's eye so intently.

Benjamin, enveloped in a heavy blue cape, and unwrapping a scarf of brown wool from around his neck and broad-brimmed hat.

'Yale,' said the keeper. 'Visitor for thee. Ye may use the Keepers' Closet.'

I found myself incapable of moving, all manner of emotions screaming in my brain.

'I'll go with 'im if you don't wants, Mistress,' Sukie leered at him.

My son returned her gaze, then stared at the other women, finally at me. Then he turned away, buried his face in both hands, his shoulders heaving. And I ran to him, steeled myself against a similar show of tears, acknowledged the keeper with a nod of thanks, and took Benjamin's elbow, began to lead him along the gallery, past the cells, the gawping, slack-mouthed curiosity of those constrained to the beds either by their own will or their blackened leg-irons.

'Those creatures,' he sobbed, as we reached the bar gate.

'God's creatures, Benjamin,' I murmured, and waited for Agnes to open access onto the landing and the keepers' own accommodation there. 'Meg said...' I began explaining to her, though there was no need for she waved us through, pointed to their room. A pair of wooden truckle beds, table and two chairs. Smut-stained glass in the windows.

'I could never have imagined,' he said, still sobbing uncontrollably. 'Mama...'

I wished to console him. Truly, I did. I ached to do so. Yet I knew that a moment of weakness would unravel all the fortifications I had built for myself. Instead I reached into the pocket of my skirt, passed him my kerchief.

'Dry your eyes,' I said, repressing the wild waves of crashing sentiments that threatened to overwhelm me. 'I gave up shedding tears for this place long ago. Almost gave up hope. Thought you had abandoned me.'

He sat at the table, wiped his face, and I settled myself on the other chair. I knew I was shaking but I could not so readily control that physical embodiment of my internal turmoil.

'How could you think so? Annie sent me a note. Dear Nan. Hospital, she said, though your damn'd husband would not tell her which. An affliction of the soul, he said. I went to Austin Friars, found the place all closed. Sold. Then to Queen Square, though he would not see me. So we tried them all, Uncle Dick and I. This one last. Last because – well, we could not imagine it. Bedlam itself. And then I came every day. But I made the mistake of announcing myself to the porter.'

'Mister Wood. He would have had his orders, I am sure. But no letter? Did you try?'

'Of course. Many times. You didn't receive them?'

'Not one. But you are here now, my dear.'

'By some miracle. This correspondence to the coffee house.' He delved in his own pockets, pulled out several folded documents, selected the one he sought, let me read the words. From the Steward, Thomas Yates. And if you read this, Mister Yates, then God bless you for your kindness. An authorisation to visit. Yet very precise. This date, the exact time. Why? 'It seemed bizarre,' Benjamin went on. 'All those times I came to the gate, saw every sort of harlot and huckster London possesses, all admitted, but your own son refused. Uncle Dick too.'

'The rules here are only to be understood by those mad enough to be affected by them.' I tried to lighten his mood, desperate to avoid this turning into some maudlin deathbed visit, though I could see it had little effect. 'And if there were no harlots, hucksters and heft-purses among the crowd, it would be the strangest thing, would it not? It would make this Bedlam unique in all London.'

'By what rule are you kept in this hell, Mama?'

'Hell?' I said, and looked about me. 'I can assure you there are worse places, Benjamin. And I am here by rule of my husband. His legal right by marriage. The dictatorship ensured by the *pishcash* he pays to the hospital for precisely this purpose. His reciprocal duty only to name obligors who might keep up a supply of food and clothing, that I might not be a drain on their resources.'

'You have grown so thin, Mama. I barely recognised you.'

'A medical conviction that lack of food will aid our melancholy, our dark humours.'

Easy to make light of all this, I thought. But the reality? My joints are always stiff now, as though I am grown old, aged by twenty years. He can see it in my face too. In my greying hair. I know he can.

'How long has he planned this, your husband?'

A good question. One I have had plenty of time to ponder.

'My husband, Bridger, the governors here. I know not whom else he has embroiled in his schemes. But a long while, I think.' I watched him clench his fists, rage replacing his distress. 'You must not involve yourself, Benji. I will deal with this in my own way. My own time. Yet you are here. And news, sweet boy. You have news? If so, you must dole it out slowly, gently.'

I felt as though I had been starved almost to the point of death, but still sufficiently aware to know that if I broke my fast too swiftly, devoured too much of the life-giving food finally set before me, it should cause me untold damage.

'Then perhaps read these later,' he said. 'At your leisure.' He handed me the rest of the folded letters, one by one. 'This from Joseph, though he wrote it last spring. And this from him too. He is due to sail as a supercargo again, but he is bound for Batavia and, at last, able to establish himself as a gentleman merchant.'

'An interloper.'

'I think he prefers the word independent.'

'And these?' I accepted the remaining documents, shuffled them between my hands, while Benjamin blew upon his fingers, and I think I must have grown accustomed to the chill in here, almost pay it no heed any more.

'Both from Elford.' I almost wept. I have not seen him for six years now. 'Still with Sir Richard Levett. And now responsible not only for the factory at Smyrna, but also at Aleppo. Constantinople too. He says they are trading strongly in Turkish opium.'

He looked away and I guessed he was unsure whether he should have told me.

'Oh, the irony,' I said, setting down the precious letters before me with reverence, as though they might be sacred objects – as, of course, they are. 'But listen, there is a crucial task you must undertake for me. Crucial, do you understand?'

'Tell me,' he said.

'No,' I corrected myself. 'Not one task but two. The first, to deliver a message to my friend and associate, Matthew Parrish.'

'Mama, he has been here too. Also refused entrance. Yet I wondered whether he has somehow used his position to secure my own summons here from Mister Yates. But yes, I will tell him I have now seen you. The second?'

'Indeed, tell Parrish precisely that. And your second task? If the house is closed, you must discover what happened to my personal possessions. One in particular. My strongbox. Knowing Mister Yale, it may already have been sold at auction. Camphor wood, brass mounted, gilt handle on each side. A gift from Governor Langhorn when I first arrived at Madras Patnam. A house-warming gift, he said. It is precious. I must have it back.'

I could feel the blood pounding in my veins as I spoke, my hands still trembling, my voice beginning to quake.

'You must not distress yourself, Mama,' he said, wrapped both arms tightly about himself. 'Be calm. If I cannot find it, I shall buy you a replacement.'

'No, you do not understand,' I yelled. 'For pity's sake, listen to me. It is precious.'

Benjamin stood from his chair, placed his hands upon my shoulders.

'Mama, I hear you. I will enlist Annie to help me.'

I tried to breathe more deeply, remembered some of the instruction that Sathiri had given me all that time ago.

'Can you trust her?' I said, as he sat once more. 'Yes, of course you can. But Kate? And Ursi? Do you have word from them too? Reverend Hoadly told me they had spent the summer at Plas Grono.'

'Hoadly? He was here?' I told him yes, though without the details.

'But I do not expect to see him again. And nor, I think, shall he be well placed to see me.'

He threw up his hands in rage.

'Why, the pecksniff. The rogue. We went to him but he denied all knowledge.'

'Never mind that now,' I said. 'You will do as I ask – the strongbox?'

'Of course. But if you need your jewels, money to buy your way out of here...'

'Whatever we offered, I fear, Elihu would simply raise the bid. And it is not my jewels that worry me. Not greatly. They will be in the care of Evance, I imagine. But we shall worry about those in due course. That is, if your Chancery claim has not ruined the fellow.' He grimaced and I knew it must still be grinding its way through the courts.

'And if I discover the whereabouts of the chest, but your husband has sequestered it somewhere?'

'Then you may need to find another old friend. Parrish will know. Wadham the thief-taker.'

Easter Sunday 16th April 1704

For every right there must be a remedy. That was the thought with which Benjamin had left me, a legal case recently decided in the Court of King's Bench. Something to do with Aylesbury. Voting rights. But my son seemed to think it had some bearing on my case. Remedial justice. My right to freedom.

'There has to be some legal process by which you may be got out of here, Mama,' he had said. And I encouraged him to think he must be correct, though I had no faith that any such legal remedy existed.

No, I must be patient, settle upon reading these precious letters before me. The two from Elford with many unexpected endearments, his ambition to soon be back in England, his fortune now made, not only in Turkish tobacco and opium but also in Damascus raisins, the soft leathers he calls maroquins, in carpets and in soda ash. Then these from Joseph, each from Portsmouth, before he boarded the *Toddington*, bound for Batavia, full of sorrows for the distress he must have caused me, but also replete with excitement. He had agreed to undertake some scientific work on behalf of Captain Bowrey, an old friend and business partner of my father's family. But he had also been entrusted with some valuable packages on behalf of Sir Hans Sloane – the famous Doctor Sloane, no less, that most eminent of physicians.

Yet the most precious of my growing correspondence must be this. A letter penned by dear Annie and delivered – through Benjamin, I suppose – just less than two weeks ago, on the occasion of my fifty-third birthing day. How I wept upon its arrival. Her longing to be with me once more. Her confederacy with Benjamin. Desires that her words would find me well and in recovery. The illnesses, agues and a flux, that have afflicted each of the girls in turn. Ursula's irritation of her father by constantly wishing to be united with me once more. News of their summer spent at Plas Grono. Elihu's apparent vexation with them, with his life in general, the only exception when he speaks of news from India, the wedding of an older daughter of Mistress Nicks, the cleverness of the Nicks girls here in London. And, finally, this cutting piece of news – Kate's tentative betrothal to a fellow Nan describes simply as Master Dudley. My own daughter's betrothal and her mama not even featured in the process. Oh, I am cast aside indeed, and it made me so very, very low.

I found solace in studying each phrase of every note until I had virtually worn the ink from all the pages, clutched these tear-soaked letters to my breast, knowing in fact that our Lord Jesus had heard my prayers, that He was slowly returning my children to me. I prayed too that the others remained contented in His care – Walt and Davy. Richie, of course. And I prayed that Parrish would, indeed, also find some way into this place. And so he did, this Monday gone.

'Do they always allow you this liberty?' he said, as we walked the airing grounds, a blackbird singing somewhere out of sight. Our greetings had been difficult, somewhat formal, for I think we each struggled to control our feelings. He had almost failed to recognise me, had visibly recoiled when he finally knew me, and he still seemed less than comfortable in my presence.

'Matthew,' I replied, 'we should move away from the walls.'

He had brought two valued gifts. A woollen shawl now wrapped about my shoulders, and a copy of one of his poems, recently penned, held tightly in my fingers within the shawl's folds.

'Lest we be overheard?' he said, glancing at the other patients let loose out there and several other visitors who had presumably paid extra to see this part of the hospital – just as they often bribed the keepers for a frightening glance inside the Checkers.

'No, my dear. Simply that some of my fellows here are wont to hurl their excrement through the wires of those windows. And you must also steer clear of those guilty feelings I see written on your face.'

He looked up at the windows above, quickly sidestepped to safer ground, grimacing before he replied.

'Such a place for you to be, Catherine. But did I give you to believe I am burdened by remorse?'

'Your whole demeanour screams contrition, sirrah,' I said. 'And pity. I shall have no pity. It is fruitless.'

'All this time you have languished here. And your many friends incapable of coming to your rescue.'

'There is no gain in arguing with a lunatick – and only another lunatick would think to do so. You have already said. With all the power of our associates, you could still not secure my release. How could you not feel guilt?'

Over at the northern wall, Dutch Dolly was making a fine display of baying at the moon, plainly visible in the clear afternoon sky.

'Is that her regular affliction?' Matthew asked.

'Dutch Dolly? Gracious no. She shares the gallery with me. Enjoys playing to it, I think. And the visitors often reward her performances with coin or cheesecake, sometimes small beer.'

'It is your husband, I think, who should be incarcerated here. Such a creditable fellow to the outside world, but a maniac in truth. The mean-spirited dog.'

He had already told me some of the story: his own quest to find me, never thinking I would be here, in Bedlam itself; his encounters with Benjamin; and Matthew's own efforts to visit, the attempts to use his position as a Member of Parliament, his connections, but all serving to make refusal of access to me that much easier. Then weeks and months of patient investigation, seeking weaknesses in the walls of conspiracy with which I had been surrounded. Yes, conspiracy, he had insisted.

'At least Mister Yates proved biddable,' I said. 'We should be grateful for small mercies.'

'Thank heavens for Mister Yates indeed. And the President's illness too.'

The second part of the story. For the hospital – along with the neighbouring Bridewell – is, of course, officially managed by the Board of Governors, though it is a Governors' Court, their inner circle, that makes or ratifies all the important decisions. And within that inner circle, it is the President and a very small number indeed who truly rule the roost. The President? Why, none other than Sir Robert Geffrey, a former director of John Company and well known to my husband. Subject to Elihu's influence. But he has seemingly been ill of late, things somewhat askew, and thus the date and time of Benjamin's visit to me, and Matthew's own, set to coincide with meetings of the Governors' Court, over at the Bridewell, when it could be guaranteed they would all have their attention turned far away from us here.

'I wonder, Matthew, that Mister Yates should so trust the porter and his keepers with such discretion.'

'Oh, we have provided sufficient *pishcash*, I think. We can be reasonably confident of their silence.'

Yes, discretion. Whatever else may happen, neither Mister Wood nor Mister Yates himself shall see this particular entry, for I now have some excellent new hiding places for those things I wish to keep private. Along with this parchment poem, of course. *A Penitent's Address to the Duke of Devonshire*, he has titled the thing.

'And His Grace,' I said. 'Was this ode the wisest way to appraise him of my plight?'

'It was the one that gave me the most pleasure, my dear.' He smiled for the first time since he had met me here. 'And besides, as I recall, Lady Mary is wont to bristle at mention of your name or in your presence, is she not? I thought it best not to be overly direct in naming you.'

We had reached the far end of the yard, near the stinking red brick latrines and Matthew was still glancing back to where Dutch Dolly was now cavorting about in some parody of a country-dance. But I had caught a glimpse of young Sukie rutting against the wall of the jakes with an old lecher, breeches about his knees.

'I fear that Lady Mary is wont to bristle at mention of any woman with whom His Grace is acquainted,' I argued, turning him swiftly in the opposite direction and apologising for the stench. 'Yet I believe his roving eye,' I said, 'would pass me by completely now, do you not think?'

He quite correctly ignored this pathetic display of self-pity.

'His Grace will read between the lines and secure a place of greater safety for you, I am certain. But we shall have a second plan, I think. In case of delay. For you should be free as soon as possible, Catherine. There is much afoot. Do you remember the artichoke juice I gave you?' How could I not? Still hidden within that secret compartment of the chest I had set Benjamin to recover. 'Well, I shall write to you. Formal. Naught of importance. But if you warm the blank reverse side...'

I shook my head in dismay, astonished that he should have made such a crass attempt to draw me back into his other life, his clandestine world, but we enjoyed a pleasant enough sojourn, back towards the bars separating us from the men's airing ground, from the bawdy cries, the disgusting hand gestures, the rank odours that seem to permeate these fellows even when they are outside.

But news from home and abroad, at least, to distract me. From India, he said, word that our old adversary, the Mughal Emperor, had laid siege to Fort St. George for a full three months. And oh, how I hoped that Mistress Nicks had suffered in the process – all my old animosities towards her kindled afresh. But Governor Pitt had seemingly sued for peace while, elsewhere, the son of our other former enemy, and occasional ally, Shivaji, had died and one of the widows of the Maratha Chatrapati was now ruling his lands as regent and leading the Gentue armies. I thrilled at the story, drew strength from it, I think.

'And Queen Anne,' I said. 'You have met her?'

It occurred to me that I knew very little of our new monarch, apart from the news that my own Nan had brought me when I was recovering from that earlier bout of my addiction.

'Several times,' Matthew replied. 'A keen sense of her duty as a monarch, I feel. A great patron of theatre and poetry too, God bless her. Though tragic eyes, Catherine.' Ah, that much I knew. The daughters lost to smallpox. The untimely death of her young son. The still-borns. The mis-births. These were all things with which I could discern the woman beneath the crown. 'But she has several times,' he went on, 'thwarted the ambition of the High Church Tories. The other side of that coin? Her obsession with rooting out any sort of religious non-conformism or dissent from the established Anglican Church.' This was disappointing news indeed, but Matthew ignored the grimace I gave him in response and simply pressed on. 'I have never seen her in Cabinet meetings, of course, but I'm told she stands her ground with the best. And that despite her fevers, her awful gout. Did you know she had to be carried to her coronation on a chair?'

'I did not. But there was a Frenchman here. A Huguenot. He brought me some news, about her elevating John Churchill to become Duke of Marlborough. Does she trust him so much, to make him a favourite of the Court?'

I saw that my words stung him, waited for an explanation and, after a moment, it was forthcoming.

'I was less than honest with you, I fear. My inability to gain admission here. Attempting to use my influence, my dear, when in fact I no longer have any.'

Sukie came sauntering past, adjusting her skirts of hospital blue. There was no sign of her lecher but she flashed a silver shilling at me, winked and gave Matthew an appraising glance.

'No longer in Parliament?' I said, and stopped to admire some common Cat's-Ear growing upon the path, its sunshine yellow a joy to me in all its simplicity.

'Technically, yes. But no longer in the public eye. I made the mistake in my last audience with Her Majesty of cautioning her about Churchill. His earlier Jacobite tendencies. She was less than pleased. Churchill's wife, Sarah, has her ear. It was a piece of crass stupidity. And make no mistake, if you ever want to see how the world works in practice, forget the policies, the ebb and flow of factions, it is all about the influence of personality. He or she who has the Queen's ear determines the taxes we will pay, the wars we will wage. Those who shall be forced almost into retirement.'

He stooped to pick the false dandelion for me. It was kind, though I was rather sad to see it plucked so from its home.

'You, Matthew?' I said.

'At this moment as well, of all things. I told you, Catherine, matters are afoot. The Jacobite rabble parading openly on the streets. The songs that celebrate William's death. Willie Winkie. Willie the Wag. They mock him. I feasted three days ago at a tavern where a brace of rogues openly toasted the little gentleman in black velvet – the damn'd mole, of course, that caused the King's death.'

He presented me with the flower, and I curtsied my thanks before we moved off again along the path.

'No longer my concern, Mister Parrish. I appreciate the poem, your efforts on my behalf with His Grace. But, in truth, I should rather you used your undoubted talents to fetch me intelligence about this blade apparently betrothed to my daughter Kate – this Master Dudley.'

'Is that all we have? It is very little, but I shall do my best. Not your concern, my dear? The Jacobite banditti?'

'Certainly not.'

He laughed.

'You think it is simply your husband's wealth that keeps you here, then? You could not be more wrong, Catherine. Among the governors of this fine establishment are several whose roots run much deeper than simple garnish. High Church fellows. Sir Gabriel Roberts, for instance. The old Turkey merchant just back himself from Fort St. George where he was Second to Pitt. He has certain allegiances of his own. And Sir Jeffrey Jeffreys, a French sympathiser, if ever I saw one. Three others happy to argue in public that, after Anne, the crown should pass back to the rogue they openly call James the Third. The King Over The Water, as they name him. A hotbed of Jacobites, my dear. And they will know who you are. Will know, I am certain, about Seaton. They have their own scores to settle, Mistress Yale.'

The notes began to arrive. Simple things, from invented correspondents, names Parrish knew I should recognise. Father Ephraim. Major Puckle. Others. And since now permitted light in my cell – tallow candle – I was able to apply the necessary warmth to the blank side of those otherwise meaningless missives, reveal the messages themselves.

Plans afoot. Be patient. Timing crucial. Your daughter betrothed to Dudley North.

A week later, this one.

Governor Yale made High Sheriff of Denbighshire. Now at Plas Grono. Opportunity soon.

High Sheriff indeed. What were they thinking? Then nothing for several weeks though, to my joy, another visit from Benjamin, a se'nnight ago. We sat in the Warming Room, the fire unlit on that stifling summer morning, but at least it gave some respite from the day's many visitors. He was less strained than on the previous occasion, though only a little. And where he had then been afflicted by the chill, now it was the heat that troubled him, for he fanned his face continuously with his hat and begged leave to d'off his peruke.

'Another invitation from Mister Yates?' I said.

'Indeed. And once again very precise about time and date.'

The Governors' Court meeting once more then, I thought, while he gave me the news, limited though it might be. No sign of my precious strongbox – and, God's hooks, I had been certain he might at least have located the thing. Nothing further from Joseph or Elford either. Benjamin's lawsuit proceeding a-pace – or so he said – in the Chancery Court. Another encounter with Annie, Ursula still missing me greatly, but Kate…

'Betrothed to a young man,' I said, and shocked him into silence. 'Dudley North. But what do we know of him?'

'You have other sources of intelligence, Mama? Then you should know he is *Sir* Dudley North.'

'The son of the Turkey merchant?'

'Kate did not say so.'

I should have associated the name from Matthew's brief mention but I had been so dispirited by confirmation that she was indeed promised without any reference to her mother that I had not thought too deeply on the possible connection. This young man I did not know, of course. But the father? Some notoriety, I recalled, from his association with the late and entirely unlamented Catholic James Stuart. Sir Dudley's father dead too now, of course. Yet that did not bridle my suspicions. For Parrish's words ate at me every day. Jacobites among the Bethlem governors? Was he right? My incarceration here also a political reprisal? Some link between Elihu, the governorship and the family of young Sir Dudley? Or was my imagination running away with me?

'Is that the limit of your knowledge, sirrah?' I snapped, and instantly regretted my tone.

'Only that he is cousin to Lord North and Grey. The very fellow who so distinguished himself at Blenheim. Lost a hand there.'

'Blenheim?'

'Great heavens, Mama. What a strange place this must be. All London is alive with it. John Churchill. A great victory against the French. More than a week past.'

He was right, naturally. Those who came to visit at Bethlem, or the keepers who controlled our lives, seemed entirely apart from the wide world beyond our walls, their interests all centred upon the lunacy within, rather than the madness without.

'There must be a great deal I need to learn,' I said. I was beginning to feel the heat myself. Or was that something else? Anyway, I began to waft my hand in front of my face to gain a little relief. 'Once I am free. And a great deal of influence to recover.'

Benjamin studied my face, perhaps saw some excitement in my eyes, some sense of anticipation.

'You have heard something,' he insisted in a whisper. 'About release.'

'No nothing,' I told him honestly. 'But I hope to do so soon. And meanwhile you must find out more about Sir Dudley and his family. Search harder for my strongbox. For now, what else did you learn from Nan?'

There was apparently more rancour against the children of Mistress Nicks, her own and Ursula's belief that Elihu cared far more for them than the daughters under his own roof. A certain cruel satisfaction in the smallpox that had afflicted Betty, Elihu no longer quite so ebullient about the girl's great beauty now that her face was left pitted and scarred. And her star fallen still further, her importance to him diminished, with the arrival in London of that other Elihu, Katherine's youngest. My husband's latest by-blow? I still have no idea. And, worse, Annie had heard her father boasting to Kate that he fully expected another old friend from Madras – Madam Paiva and her own son, Charles.

'Mama, is that the boy...?'

'Indeed, my dear. Can you imagine what a huge and happy family we shall all become?'

This day began as notably as it would end. An early journey to the jakes, a cold rinse from the water buckets at the cistern, then back to my cell for the thin gruel before the first of the paying visitors began to flock through the galleries. A Saturday, and a few more than usual perhaps. And many of them more noteworthy than might be customary too.

First, an old fellow in purple summer satin, with not one harlot upon his arm but three. It was early, yet all seemed badly cupped, one of the white-faced wenches constantly toying with the guard of her paramour's rapier, running her fingers down the silk baldrick from which it hung.

'You, woman,' he yelled at me as he drew abreast of my open cell door. 'You must have been a handsome drab when you was young. Shall you not show us your glories, madam? I shall make it worth a sixpence.'

I should wish to say that such propositions were a rarity or even that they still had the power to shock me. But I merely dismissed him with a few of the sailors' expletives I had learned so dutifully from Sukie and the others. Indeed, it was Sukie who answered him in kind, while I planted myself firmly in the doorway, hands upon my hips and menace in my eyes.

'Look 'ere,' Sukie yelled from across the gallery and hefted the skirts of her blue smock up above the bulbous waist. 'Gotta be worth more than a sixpenny bit though, mister, don't thee think?'

Matron Nurse Wood was making her rounds, stopped to censure poor Sukie, threaten her with icy immersion if she could not herself cool those ardours.

'Ah, Matron,' said the fellow, as though he knew her, and flicking Sukie the sixpence for her display, 'they tell me you has some choice flesh up in the Checker. Do ye think…?'

Matron looked around quickly, urged him to lower his voice and led him and his party to the bar gate, through onto the landing while, back at the cells, yet another group of borrachios. All-night revellers, I supposed. Three young men this time, all silver buckles and lace-trimmed beavers, raucous and stinking of cheap liquor.

'Great heavens,' I said to Keeper Agnes, who had perched herself next to Sukie's cell, 'standards are slipping, even for here.'

'An' on this 'ere day of all days,' she replied. 'No respect, that's what.'

In her Kentish drawl she explained that the hospital's president, Sir Robert Geffrey, had died during the week. Funeral this very morning and most of the officers in attendance. But great consternation at his passing, the place all a-turmoil. It is always thus, I suppose, when the titular head of an institution like the Bethlem Hospital – especially one who has held that position as long as Sir Robert – is suddenly no more. Uncertainty abounds. What changes might follow? What opportunities arise? But I had no time to dwell on Agnes and her preoccupations for there were more newcomers and, this time, I believed I might recognise one of them.

'Forgive me,' I said, stepping into their path, 'but are you not – well, the player, Mister Cibber?'

He had a face that could easily have qualified him for treatment here, the head making small darting movements like a bird, the eyelids constantly a-flicker, the mouth unnaturally wide and fixed in a permanent fool's grin.

'You are one of the keepers here, madam?' he replied in a stentorian voice entirely unsuited to his jester-like features.

'I saw you, sir. At the Theatre Royal. Oh, ten years ago or more. Congreve. *The Old Bachelor*, I collect.'

Impossible though it seemed, the smile widened still further.

'Did you enjoy the performance,' he boomed, 'then you must remember this lady also. For she played alongside me in that very production. Allow me to name Mistress Anne Bracegirdle.'

The name indeed struck a chord. Had Elford not scolded me because I did not recognise her then either? Younger than me. Twenty years younger, perhaps. Though her face was painted to seem older. Much older. But even without that, she would have been no beauty. Yet a presence, she certainly possessed presence.

'You must forgive me but I only recall Mistress Bracegirdle slightly, though I am delighted to make your acquaintance, madam. And no, sirrah, I did not enjoy the play. A foolish confection, I thought.'

'You, Yale!' shouted Agnes. 'Leave that gen'leman be, if ye knows what's good for thee.'

And, to my surprise, Mistress Bracegirdle winked at me while, back at the bar gate, Matron Nurse Wood was returning with that insulting rogue and his trio of whores. But all was not well, for one of the women had backed straight into the young borrachios, who had been amusing themselves with taunting Dutch Dolly.

'You clumsy oaf,' the whore scolded the young gentleman with whom she had collided. But he simply laughed, caught her about the shoulders and began to press his lips against hers.

'Saucy wench,' cried one of the other inebriates.

'You will unhand my daughter, sirrah,' shouted the woman's companion. Daughter? I thought. Surely a jest but, to my horror, I saw him reach for the sword, the practised way in which he drew out the naked blade. After that, pandemonium. One of the drunkards wielding his own rapier, though without the old degenerate's finesse, Agnes somehow embroiled with the other two women, Matron Nurse Wood trapped on the farther side of the bar gate, screaming for assistance from the keepers along in the men's gallery.

'Mister Parrish sends regards, ma'am,' Mistress Bracegirdle murmured and she, Colley Cibber too, pressed me into my own cell. At first, I thought, for my safety but soon realised this was more than simple concern. Much more.

Outside, steel rang upon steel, women screamed or shouted profanities while, within, Cibber began to empty his pockets, small pots of grease paint and powders, the actress quickly divesting me of my own clothes, swapping them for her own. Theatrical attire, I now realised, simple fasteners allowing costumes to be changed in mere moments. And in those moments my features, my hair, were transformed into a rough approximation of Mistress Bracegirdle's, her own into a likeness of mine. The glass she carried was tiny, but sufficient for me to see the artistry with which they had worked.

'How?' I asked, and 'Where?' But Cibber began to push me back out through the door, into the gallery where the fracas still raged. 'No, wait,' I said, returned to my old bedstead, pulled apart that section of the frame in which I had hidden my papers.

'We must go,' he insisted, as I triumphantly waved the pages at him. Then he gently placed my hand upon his arm, exactly the same pose as I had originally seen when he made his grand entrance to the galleries, and he sedately led me forth. 'Just play the part, Mistress Yale,' he whispered in my ear as we pushed our way past the commotion, Cibber feigning disgust at that unseemly spectacle and doing his very best to shield his companion from any possible harm. 'Just play the part. For I understand you can be an accomplished player too, when you choose.'

Cibber handed me up into the carriage with still barely a further word spoken between us, despite my many backward glances and my innumerable questions, my terror that, at any moment, we should be apprehended. But he maintained his slow, theatrical composure all along that extensive pathway through Bethlem's front gardens to the main gate.

And there my conveyance to liberty awaited me. By then I was convinced I must find Matthew waiting there too, though the figure seated in the shadows was not he, but rather my other old friend, Streynsham Master. I knew he was weeping but, through the tears, he managed to thank the actor, promised him he would not be forgotten for this service.

'Drive on,' he yelled.

'Parrish?' I said.

'Needed elsewhere this day, I fear. But he made all the arrangements.'

It was so like him, that confidence in his own planning.

'But Streynsham,' I said, trying to catch my breath, to still my agitated heart, to hold back the flood I knew should engulf me too if I allowed it. 'Mistress Bracegirdle. How...?'

'You must not fret, sweet lady. Dear, dear Catherine. How you have been wronged! But they shall not detain her once they discover her identity. Why should they? The hospital made to look foolish. In any case, she does not qualify as insane among the poor. And I doubt your husband will wish to continue paying them for another's upkeep.'

'The others,' I smiled, settled myself back on the seat, brushed my fingers over the expensive velvet, breathed in the coachwork's beeswax, gazed at Streynsham's fine silk. 'All part of Cibber's troupe?'

'Naturally,' he said.

'I cannot believe it, sir. Am I dreaming all this? But he will pursue me, surely? My husband.'

'It may be one thing to have you sequestered while all hugger-mugger and defenceless, while under the influence of opium, my dear, and for him then to argue that treatment in Bethlem Hospital was the only feasible solution – for him to apply restrictions and conditions in line with his legal rights as your husband. But once you are free, capable of assessment both by the most eminent physician in the land...'

'Sir Hans Sloane,' I said. 'My son, Joseph, is undertaking duties on his behalf.'

'And was therefore able to interest Doctor Sloane in your situation. If necessary, he will speak to your case. But, that aside, your simple return to normal society shall, in itself, demonstrate the state of your mind. Besides all that, His Grace the Duke of Devonshire has consented to put you under his personal protection. Under his own roof, so to speak.'

'Roof? But there you have it. I no longer have a roof.'

'Well, it is not perfect, though it shall suffice for the nonce. His Grace insisted. An apartment at old Devonshire House. You shall have to tolerate my mother-in-law, old Madam Legh, of course. But the arrangement shall, I am sure, only be temporary.'

And in that apartment I spend my first night of freedom, writing upon the parchment so kindly provided to me by the old lady herself.

When I am able, I shall visit Mister Northcott at the printer's shop in George Yard, have him bind my scribblings from the hospital into a single volume, purchase a new journal for my new beginnings.

Volume Seven

How strange, that I should fetch up here. Devonshire Street. And from my bedchamber window, to the left, I can see that modest dwelling I had purchased in Governor Yale's name to accommodate Katherine Nicks after I secured her service – twelve years ago now – so she might spy for us on this very house.

A glance across to the far right shows me the distant green hills of Hampstead and Highgate but, just yards away, the new-built glories of Queen Square, where Elihu has set up home with my girls. Oh, if I had Sukie's expectoration skills I could almost spit upon the place from this casement. And spit upon it, or at least some of its occupants, Mistress Bridger and Governor Yale himself, I undoubtedly shall.

In this house, old Madam Legh's son Peter had hosted gatherings of his Jacobite associates and among them had been the same Colonel Porter – that arch villain – who had conspired with Vincent Seaton in their plot to assassinate both the Duke of Devonshire himself as well as Czar Peter of Muscovy. Madam Legh had once accused me of having a sharp tongue, upbraided me for having ideas above my station, only being daughter to a coffee house proprietor and, in her eyes, a coffee house being nothing more than a den of iniquity. But she has now, I think, a better opinion of me. And me? A different perspective of Madam Legh too.

'Strange,' I had said to Matthew when he first came to visit me here, after my escape, full of apology for having to send Streynsham in his stead to receive me from the hands of Colley Cibber. 'But, when I first met her, she seemed so ancient, understandable that the world knew her as "old" Madam Legh. Yet she is only ten years my senior. And now...'

'The years catch up with us all, my dear. But you will be safe here. Fitting refuge too, I think, given the part you played in eradicating the schemes once hatched within these walls.'

The place had truly been purged, naturally: young Peter Legh brought firmly to heal; Streynsham now married to the older sister, Elizabeth; several of those involved in the worst of the Jacobites' schemes gone to the gallows, a few with my help; and Seaton dead at the hands of Katherine Nicks. But Porter had escaped, back to France, they said, to serve the Stuart Pretenders in their exile.

Purged, and tonight the setting for a glittering occasion. Music filled the air throughout, from the onyx front door, to the mirror-lined entertaining hall in which the Society of Friends still hold their gatherings on occasion – one of the terms within Madam Legh's lease – and out into the stone-walled gardens at the rear, where a voluminous pavilion had been unfurled. Inside this marquee roseate lanthorns hung in every topiary tree, sculptured shrub and beautified box bush, so that the effect was as one might imagine some faerie festivity. Music, and dancing, upon the wooden flooring laid for just this purpose.

'More wealth here in perukes and periwigs,' I said to Parrish, who was once again my companion as we watched the triple measure minuet unfold, 'in silks and brocades, than in all my modest fortune still held by Evance.'

Benjamin was playing happily nearby beneath the rounded foliage of a yew tree with two of Madam Legh's many dappled lapdogs.

'It should not have taken this long,' Matthew replied. 'But I believe tonight will see an end to that particular problem.'

'If Evance makes an appearance at all,' I said, sipping at my wine. 'And if he does, it might be best to keep Benjamin out of the way. I fear how he would react.'

As if he had heard his name, my son looked up from scruffing one of the dogs' necks and waved at me.

'Oh, Evance shall come. I have made sure of it,' said Matthew, brushing at the green velvet of his sleeve. 'Though I cannot say I feel especially comfortable in this company.'

A voice behind us caused him to start. Myself also. Almost jumped out of my skin.

'Present company excluded, I trust?' Streynsham, his mouth crammed with mutton pie. 'God's hooks, Parrish, you always kept a closer guard upon your tongue.' He was dressed in the very latest mode, his coat a shade of cherry red, the skirts flared, the neck cloth excessively long.

'Ah,' Matthew laughed, 'but nobody pays heed to my utterances any more, sirrah. Though that would not stop some of those rogues finding a pretext to house me in the Tower.'

'A success for Her Majesty,' said Streynsham, 'certainly seems to be cause for celebration on all sides of the divide, does it not?'

The *Courant* has carried the story daily. Victory for our forces besieged all this time at Gibraltar. Having seized the town and its fortifications from the Spanish, they have successfully repelled all efforts by our enemies to take it back, the siege abandoned. Our enemies – the Bourbon Spanish and French, the latter including that legion of exiled Irishmen still loyal to the Stuart *prétendants*.

'All sides?' I said and raised my glass to him. 'Really?'

'Well, perhaps that one to watch,' said Streynsham, gesturing towards a fellow, not yet forty, I guessed. Auburn wig down to his waist, suit of sky-blue silk. 'Despite his family connections to Cavendish. What say you Catherine? Did your friend Mistress Nicks ever mention Ormonde?'

Nephew to the Duke of Devonshire's wife, Lady Mary, I knew. But no, Katherine had never mentioned him, I was certain. I would have remembered.

'I do not recall,' I told him, 'and this is less than subtle if you seek to embroil me again in your machinations. I have had enough of Bedlam. And is it not time you returned to your wife?'

He glanced around to see where Elizabeth might be, but she was safely engaged in conversation with her mother's closest friends. I was rescued from this particular envelopment by another reminder of my former role. Mister Penn, forsooth.

'Mistress Yale,' he exclaimed, always jolly, rotund, regardless of whatever might be afflicting him. 'Give you joy of this fine celebration, ma'am.'

'Friend William,' I said, setting down my glass upon an occasional table. 'A glittering occasion indeed. But so many dead in the fighting, I should not have thought it a matter for elation within the Society.'

'We simply thank the Almighty for the ending of the siege, my dear. And perhaps that there was so little loss of life among our own forces.' He was right, of course. Casualties among the besieging forces had been frightful, according to the *Daily Courant*. 'Though if I might be permitted the liberty, I have to say it also warms my heart to see you so in looks.'

I had tried. I have been trying. To turn back the ravages from my cell on the galleries. My face painted to recapture lost years, my hair dyed to the natural shade of my youth and piled high in a commode fan of Mechlin lace.

'Not the same creature we rescued...' Streynsham began, but I cut him short.

'I need no reminder, sirrah.'

I took Penn's arm, led him off to survey the dancers, the others in tow behind.

'Well,' said Penn, 'it is a contrast to the condition in which I found Governor Yale.' I was less than certain whether he knew we are estranged – a generous word to describe our situation but the only way in which I might express the thing. Though I need not have troubled. 'And might I say, Friend Catherine, how much I admire your forbearance of all that has befallen you. Your husband, however – oh dear, what shall I say? I found him in a most pitiable state. Middle of the afternoon and still attired in a grease-stained nightgown. At least, so far as I could see. So much tobacco fug, ma'am. So much smoke.'

'You went to see him?'

'This very day. I should not have wished to trouble him but I have been bilked very badly. You may have heard. The rogue who was supposed to be my financial advisor. Dead now, and may the devil take him. But his widow saying she has claim on Pennsylvania itself. I fear I shall be ruined, thought that some assistance might be forthcoming from Governor Yale...'

'Financial assistance?' said Matthew. 'From Elihu Yale? Great heavens, sir, that might be the fastest possible way to find yourself in the Marshalsea.'

The musicians were playing a saucy little chaconne. *Fairy Dance*, if I remember correctly, and I found myself inadvertently skipping a step or two.

'And did you perchance see any of my daughters there?' I asked.

'I fear not,' Penn replied. 'And I thank you, sir,' he said to Parrish, 'for that cautionary note. Yet I may certainly see the inside of the debtors' prison with or without the Governor's help. Still, he brightened somewhat when I told him about Madam Legh's festivity. Perhaps he might venture forth to join our celebration.'

I was not sure whether I should take myself to hide within my apartment for, in truth, I did not believe I could cope with confronting Elihu. I had not seen him for three years. And however difficult may have been our preceding time together, that violation of my person and these past three years had left fearful scars beyond my comprehension.

'Surely Mister Penn is jesting,' said Benjamin, his face crimson with rage and setting down the dog he had been fondling. 'He would not dare show his face. Not here.'

'Elihu Yale knows no shame,' I reminded him, and bent to scratch the pup's ears. 'You should collect that.'

'If he does...'

I stood again, set a hand upon his chest.

'Stop shouting, Benjamin. Please. If he does appear, you have my permission to avoid him – and nothing more. I am a guest in this house and under the protection of His Grace.' The Duke of Devonshire was at that moment engaged in a lively jig with a gay young drab with heaving bosom, only a third of his age though with whom he was displaying the most amorous attentions while Lady Mary laughed loudly at the food tables, trying her best to ignore her husband's outrageous behaviour. 'He never changes,' I said. 'And that young man.' At Lady Mary's side, a fellow with intelligent eyes. 'Great heavens, can that be young James?' Their son. Yes, I was certain, even though I had not been in his company since Streynsham's wedding, not long after my return from Madras Patnam. But I had followed his exploits from time to time.

'I know not,' said Benjamin, his ire still not entirely abated. 'Though I see Doctor Sloane has his ear.'

Streynsham had taken the trouble to introduce us. A privilege, for Sir Hans is a great man, a true gentleman, enquired politely after my condition, said it gave him joy to see me so plainly restored to full health.

'In a foolish way, it pleased me greatly. His certainty that Joseph would look after his interests with dedication.'

We had received a letter from Joseph too. He reached Amoy safely, described the terrible famine he had witnessed in India on his journey out, then a little of that strange Chinese land, the trade in which he is engaged as an interloper between local merchants and the Spanish who control the fort and island, he says, from where they supply their ports on the Pacific coast of Mexico. I would read it again later but, for the nonce, Matthew was back at our side, bringing fresh glasses of wine. At the same moment, a commotion of new arrivals at the double doors from the house into the marquee.

'Now,' said Parrish, 'there is a guest who should interest you.' An unexceptional young man in dusky blue, on the arm of an older matron, presumably his mother.

'Dudley North?' I suggested. A shot in the dark, as they say, but it was the obvious thing with which he may have hoped to shock me.

'In heaven's name, how did you know?' he said behind his hand. 'But yes, the very same. What say you, Benjamin? That fellow is soon to be your brother-in-law.'

The jibe cut me, reminded me of the distance grown between myself and Kate, my totally forced segregation from the betrothal arrangements for my eldest daughter.

'If Mister Yale has brokered the arrangement,' Benjamin scoffed, 'I can only assume the gentleman has wealth. Yet you would hardly know it.'

He gazed at Dudley North with some bemusement.

'His father's death provided amply for the boy,' said Matthew. 'He inherits Glemham Hall too – and I must assume that will become your sister's new home. A shame about his connections though.'

We had made the full circuit of the dance floor, found ourselves at the salon arranged for the card players, just back within the house itself. Some at Five Fingers. Others at Lanterloo.

'Benjamin,' I said, 'once told me he is cousin to Lord North and Grey. And that gentleman a hero of the war, is he not?'

'A Jacobite, to be sure. And young Sir Dudley? His father thick as thieves with Catholic James Stuart.' Ah, yes, I vaguely recalled it then. 'The boy,' Matthew went on, 'not so distinguished as his cousin but already worth three thousand pounds per annum, they say.'

But I was barely listening for, as we emerged again from the card tables, there was my daughter Kate herself, upon Elihu's arm. And, following them, Annie escorted by Sir Stephen Evance. Then two other girls I did not recognise, but seemingly also in Elihu's company, the older of the pair with a thin yellow veil hiding her face, the younger swarthy-skinned and surely as much the homely Joan as her mama.

'You see?' I said to Benjamin. 'No shame. To bring the daughters of his mistress so openly into our society.'

I almost said, "As though they were his own." But, of course, despite the denials of Katherine Nicks about that same younger girl – Ursula, I assumed – about her young son too, the other Elihu, I could no longer be certain one way or the other of their origins. Still, if I was correct, the girl with the veil must be Betty and she must at least have the same mettle as her mother to be here abroad and thus masking the disfiguring scars of her smallpox.

'Are you quite well, Catherine?' Parrish was saying, while Benjamin stood wordless, though with venom in his eyes. But Matthew's voice seemed to come from a great distance. 'You are grown quite pale, my dear.'

I thought I must swoon, though I collected that other allies were gathering on my flanks.

'God's hooks,' said the Duke. 'I never thought to see that rogue in my company again.' I had at times thought to share with him those papers I brought back from Madras, though they were no longer in my possession, of course. The strongbox. To share them with His Grace. But instead I had taken the opportunity to put a word in the ear of this Lord Steward for the royal household, about those rumours, those four who had made allegations of impropriety against Elihu – and three of them almost immediately dead. No, no, I had demurred, no evidence that Governor Yale had been responsible for their demise, but... 'Great heavens,' the Duke murmured now, 'and to think I arranged an audience for him with the king.'

The musicians had changed to a foot-stamping canary.

'I cannot believe,' said Streynsham, who had also joined our ranks, 'that Madam Legh would have invited him.'

'I rather think,' I replied, 'that Mister Penn might have mentioned the celebration and, in his normal fashion, Elihu would have taken the invitation as tacit.'

Friend William himself no longer with us, gone to seek assistance from more reputable sources that Matthew had suggested.

'Evance would undoubtedly have been invited more formally,' said James Cavendish, His Grace's younger son. 'Would he not, Papa? But who is that enchanting creature on his arm?'

'Personally,' the Duke snorted, 'I'd not spare her a second glance.'

'My daughter Annie, Your Grace.'

He harrumphed loudly, offered a polite apology while Elihu made show of noticing me for the first time, handed Katie to the arm of Sir Dudley North, motioned for Evance to escort Anne onto the dance floor and, though Nan did indeed allow herself to be led away, she did so almost without taking her loving eyes from me. Kate, on the other hand, kept her nose in the air, refused to look in my direction, as her father straightened the silken mustard edges of his expensive summer coat and sauntered towards me, master of all he surveyed.

'I shall have him thrown onto the street,' the Duke growled. And I almost begged him to do so. I was trembling inside, every step taken by my husband reminding me of my time in the Bethlem Hospital. Yet I knew it would not answer.

'I believe I need to speak with him, gentlemen. Prithee, if you might allow me?'

They drifted away like roiling storm clouds, protesting that they would not be far away if needed, protesting in general.

'What? Am I some leper now?' said Elihu, glowering at their departing backs. His coat may once have been very fine, though at close quarters there were subtle stains, signs of neglect. And his tawny periwig, I realised, had been neither curled nor cleaned in some while. Overall, he had about him the air of decay.

'They are my friends,' I said. 'What did you expect, sirrah?'

'It was my duty as your husband,' he murmured, and led me back out to a more private corner of the covered garden. 'To seek treatment for your affliction.'

I pulled up the ruffled cream sleeves of my chemise as far as the cuffed elbows of my mantua, showed him my wrists.

'You see?' I said. 'The scars still there. The manacles with which they treated me.'

'Always so prone to exaggeration, Catherine. I am assured you received naught but the kindest of behaviours.'

I tried with difficulty to quell my rage, sat myself down upon the nearest stone bench.

'And the girls, my friends, the steps you took to ensure I should receive no visitors?'

'Our daughters? I could not wish them to see you any longer in that condition.'

'You mean you could not wish them to see the conditions in which you had me incarcerated. But my son? My friends?'

'I took careful advice. From the hospital's physician, Mister Tyson. From the President. From several of the governors. They were right. Your assault on poor Reverend Hoadly. He had a warrant issued.'

Yes, decay. I rolled the sleeves back into place. There was no mistaking the smell as he leaned closer to me. I lifted my scented kerchief to my nostrils, as delicately as I was able. For his odour reminded me of that despicable act he had committed against me.

'Because I spat in his eye?' I said. 'Yet neither you nor he can send me back. Not now. And the governors? The Jacobite governors, I suppose you intend.'

'You see? Not fully cured. They warned me. This obsession you have. Feelings of persecution. It must stop.'

The music carried me back, helped quell my trembling dudgeon. The torch-lit grounds of our own garden house beyond the walls of Madras Patnam, the one that once had belonged to the Bridgers. Then, as now, the musicians performing the moderate steps of an allemande, that one we always call *The Runaway*. The first time I was threatened by that other devil.

'Was Seaton an obsession, sirrah?' I said. 'How long did I warn you about the churl and you were too blind to see the truth before you. Or chose not to do so.'

'Ancient history, madam.'

'You say so? There was an element to the story I never told you. About the first time Seaton defiled my household. Yes, the occasion when he attacked Susannah, then struck dear Ursi. It was not the first. There was a terrible night, some time before, when the devil had dug up the body of an infant.' I watched the colour drain from his jowls. 'Sounds familiar, does it not? And he left the poor mite's mortal remains in my bedchamber. A warning perhaps. But to revive the memory of little Walter too, of course. To plunge me into despair. A memory that only you, sirrah, could have shared with him.'

'It is…' he stammered. 'Well, possible. I had so few friends at Fort St. George. And that night – terrible for me too, Catherine.'

'You swore an oath.'

'As did you, wife. To honour and obey. You saw fit to pen denunciations against my character. Oh, do not deny it. Tom Pitt is my friend. I was happy to accept the inducement he offered, to return with my fortune intact. But he was honest enough to share with me the papers you wrote. Wicked. No less than wicked.' I could have told him my signature had been forged but it would neither have persuaded him nor made the slightest difference. 'And then I began to ponder the parliamentary investigation into the Company's affairs. Pitt tells me they took affidavit evidence. Anonymous, though verified. Two and two makes four, my dear. It suddenly became clear to me. My own wife, at the bottom of it all.'

'And thus you had me incarcerated.'

'It seemed the most fitting place. After all, did you not once threaten dear Katherine Nicks with Bedlam if she ever again appeared at your door unbidden?'

I must find time to read my journals afresh, if I am ever lucky enough to retrieve them.

'Your whore,' I spat. I never married him for affection, that much is certain. There had been some depth between us. The portions we shared almost as equals for a while, rather than rivals: nine years together; the three girls; Davy and his sad death; and even that night with Walter and the serpent. All vanished now. Killed by his own brutal actions.

'And you did, in any case,' he said, 'put yourself and our daughters in harm's way. Playing at politicks with that scrub, Parrish. It was these that brought you to Bethlem Hospital. Do you not understand?'

'I understand precisely how I came to be incarcerated, my possessions sequestered. Where are they? My Maysmore. The strongbox. My precious books. Joseph's portraits of my boys. Great heavens, Elihu – even my clothes.'

At least I did not worry about the geographical clock, for Annie had been as good as her word. I had innocently suggested she might seek Mistress Bridger's assistance in the arrangements to have it sent to me here at Devonshire House. It has not yet arrived, of course, but that troubles me not in the slightest. At least I now know it is safe. Safe and useful.

'Safely in storage,' said Elihu, as though he read my mind. 'No more than a hundred yards from here. King Street. And they shall be returned to you. So long as you agree one simple condition – that you shall do nothing to interfere with the arrangements made for Kate's betrothal. Great heavens, the time they have taken. Brokers, don't you know? Sir Dudley's father a Turkey merchant, Catherine, like your own papa. Why, I have his *Discourses Upon Trade*. Almost my second bible, if that is not a blasphemy. Member for Banbury to boot.'

My relief at knowing the strongbox, my journals, were safe almost overwhelmed me, but there would be time to revel in that glory a little later. For now, I had resolved simply one of the issues that caused me to suffer his presence. There was much more I needed to spew upon him, as Sukie might have said.

'Was the father,' I said, 'not called to account for his dubious dealings on behalf of James Stuart?'

Some acquaintances of Elihu's from Queen Square came to introduce themselves and I greeted them politely enough.

'Great heavens,' he said when they had moved on, 'that was fifteen years ago. Must it always be politicks with you, my dear? You see what I mean?'

'He died, I collect, before he could be held to account.'

'As it may be. But that is no reflection upon the son.'

'No reflection either, I suppose, on your own gain from the arrangement. Not to mention the fortune that will come your way through the furnishing of Glemham Hall, I assume.'

I had not intended to be so loud, saw heads turned in our direction.

'How…?'

I stopped him. Another shot in the dark, though I saw I must be correct. I have never seen Glemham Hall, though I know it by repute. One of Suffolk's finest houses and I could almost hear him whispering in Katie's ear that she should, as a minimum, insist on replacing all of its previous effects. Where better as a source of her new comforts and chattels than her father's own collections? And yes, the prices abated somewhat. Naturally. Though still a handsome profit for her generous papa – who, I noted, was looking over my shoulder, his features set like stone.

'If this wretch has the temerity to accost me,' he snarled, 'I shall call him out.'

I span around, Parrish attracted by my foolishly raised voice, I assumed.

'All is well, Mistress Yale?' he said.

'You have the decency to address my wife so formally, Parrish,' said Elihu, 'so I would ask you to observe the courtesy of allowing us some privacy.'

'You lost the right to any courtesy on my part, Governor, when you committed your wife to that hellhole. And it was your wife I was addressing, if you recall.'

'If you seek satisfaction, sir…' my husband began, and I saw Matthew's eyes assume that aspect I had seen once or twice in the past. He had been a soldier, after all, competent at arms. But Elihu? I had no idea. He had undertaken weapons practice often enough at Fort St. George. But a duel with Matthew Parrish? Might that solve one or more of my dilemmas? I shook the thought away before Matthew could answer him.

'I thank you for your concern, Mister Parrish,' I said in haste. 'But I am perfectly well. And more than capable of concluding this negotiation with Governor Yale.'

For a moment I thought he might accept Elihu's challenge regardless of my wishes, but he merely dismissed my husband with a shake of his head and turned upon his heel.

'Insolent rogue,' Elihu sneered, though I could read the relief on his face.

'Well, we have agreement,' I said. 'Simply because I am too exhausted to debate further with you, sir. My valuables returned to me, and not a word across my lips about Kate's betrothal. Yet you plan another, I hear. Dear Nan to marry Sir Stephen?'

I stood, began to wander away from him, so that he had to follow behind.

'She is a difficult girl,' he muttered, though I think he was still struggling to draw his attention back from Parrish. 'One objection after another,' he said. 'Poor Stephen has become quite vexed with the whole affair.'

I looked from our corner of the garden to that side of the dance floor where Streynsham was making great play of naming my daughters formally for His Grace, the Duke of Devonshire, and I could swear I almost saw a spark fly between Annie and young James Cavendish.

'I think not,' I said. Just that, and no more, remembering my promise to Nan.

'Not what, exactly?'

'That you shall broker no match between Nan and Evance.'

He stopped, pulled at the edges of his laced coat as though to straighten himself too, to regain his dignity.

'Do you presume to instruct me also on how and with whom I might broker betrothals for my own daughters? Or for dear Katherine's girls, for that matter?'

One of the Duke's servants approached, carrying a rack of pipes, the tobacco tub. Elihu took one, examined its stem, began filling the bowl.

'You had the temerity,' I said, 'to bring the Nicks girls here, though not our own Ursula.'

He lit the pipe from one of the sconces as the servant moved on.

'It would hardly be appropriate,' he said, 'to bring that little dumpling to a social gathering of this sort. You know that.'

Poor Ursi. He was correct, I supposed. She had always managed her daily mingling with the church congregations perfectly well, but in the outside world she was often lost and frightened. I must find a solution for her, though now it was other matters that crowded my own brain.

'You told Mistress Nicks I have been in Bedlam?'

'I told her the truth. That you had grown to love nothing so well as your bottle. The Sydenham's. And that you needed the cure.'

'And what else? That I had grown hair-brain'd? Crazed? Ill-natured? Oh, I can almost see you scribbling the words, Elihu.'

He made no immediate response, and I knew I could not be far from the mark. Yet he soon recovered his composure.

'I pity the poor creature,' he said, puffing once more upon the pipe. 'She despairs of ever seeing her own girls again. Wrote to me at length, though heaven knows her written English is sometimes hard to understand. But she has taken some responsibility in the care of Madam Paiva. That dear lady has been ill, did I say? And young Charles, she tells me – Don Carlos – grown into a lusty fellow.'

Another servant approached with a tray of drinks, quickly withdrew again when he heard the tone of our discourse.

'You think I care about your various by-blows?' I said, with disdain. 'Truly? I care only about my own children. And I swear, sirrah, to put every obstacle in the way of Anne's betrothal to Evance.' There, the second of the issues I had pledged to pursue. 'He may currently control my fortune,' I pressed on, 'yet I have taken steps to amend that too. But he shall not control my daughter, nor bring misery into her life.'

It was unthinkable. I had always admired Stephen Evance and I feel for the struggles that must be his daily burden, but I already knew his marriage to Annie would be nothing but a sham.

'What? You think that your sons' Chancery claim will damage him, as well as me? I have to tell you, madam, that we shall ride the storm.' Did he truly believe this was all about money? Did he understand so little about Evance's proclivities? It seemed so. 'The loyalty of Mistress Nicks as our agent in Madras,' he said.

'Her diamond trade?' I made some attempt at ironic laughter. 'You shall tell me next that it flourishes?'

'She invested a great deal in securing the diamond for Pitt. Expected some decent and speedy return, I collect. But Pitt now finds himself unable to sell and, until he does, she cannot receive her own reward. But it shall come. You will see.'

The Pitt diamond. I have used my influence to ensure its value is diminished by every dealer in London. It posed no difficulty either, for Fernão Pereira says a brilliant of that size is almost impossible to trade unless it is first cut to smaller pieces – an action Governor Pitt refuses to countenance. Katherine Nicks, of all people, should have known that.

'Such a pity,' I smiled. 'Everybody's aspirations so thwarted.'

'Not my own, though. Not at all. My own star now shines more brightly than ever. Why, did you not know I served last year as High Sheriff of Denbighshire? And next...'

'Your aspirations towards a Baron Knight? I have made sure you never see them come to fruition.' The third of my objectives met, and had I slapped him, the effect could not have been more dramatic. He followed my gaze across to the Duke of Devonshire's party, saw His Grace offer me the most respectful obeisance.

'That old wretch…' Elihu began. 'You…'

'And Katherine Nicks, Elihu?' I pressed on. 'She never told you, I think. That she was carrying your child when you married me. You chose the greed of my sweet Joseph's wealth over the young woman who truly loved you. Found herself forced to marry John Nicks even though she then lost the babe.'

There, it was said. A fourth barb that I had kept sharpened, honed, all that time in the Bethlem Hospital, stewing upon the evil of his violation.

'That is a lie,' he protested, but I noted the doubt in his eyes. 'Another figment of your wicked sickness.'

'Is it?' I said. 'Perhaps you should ask her next time you write to your coy mistress. Meanwhile, for the sake of several reputations, I say again, you must forget this nonsense of Annie's betrothal to Stephen Evance.'

'God damn you, Catherine…'

'I am certain He shall do so, sir. I can help you with this, at least, that I may be able to recommend one or two excellent housekeepers when, very soon now, you lose Mistress Bridger.'

Yes, a fifth seed that I still needed to sow.

I was returned to Bedlam. Though today just one of this morning's many visitors and with Parrish to protect me. Even so I ventured no further than the bar gate at the women's section of that familiar upper gallery.

'Impossible to now picture you here,' he murmured. 'The place seemed so barbaric when you were imprisoned. But your presence must have distracted me from the full horror. Somehow much worse now, viewing it afresh.'

'Remarkable the difference a few fine clothes can make also,' I said, for we had passed Matron Nurse Wood on the stairs and she had given me not a second glance.

Nor did I, for my part, see a single familiar face among the patients, against the grey walls. No Maudlin Mary, nor Mistress Bingley. No Judith, Dutch Dolly or Sukie. I should have enquired about their respective fates, yet I determined it was better to live in ignorance. All my old associates, I prayed, released sane and safe. Except one, that is. She noticed me, came screaming from her cell, Keeper Agnes in hot pursuit as Winifred Bridger hurled herself against the iron grille.

'Do you not pity her, even now?' said Matthew, as I took a step back, out of range from her questing claws. But I determined to guard against any threat of sentiment here too.

'God's hooks, Winifred,' I told her instead, 'they must be feeding you far too much for you still to have such aggression after so many months.'

There was more Portuguese invective. And she did indeed appear quite mad. Incarceration in a lunatick hospital can do that to a body, I suppose.

'Mistress?' said Keeper Agnes. She was plainly puzzled. 'Do I know thee?'

It was all so easy. Easier, perhaps, than my own committal to this place must have been for Winifred and Elihu. No long preparation time. No addiction to propagate. Simply the arrangement with Annie that she should seek Bridger's assistance in returning the geographical clock to my possession. So, evidence that it had been in Bridger's hands. And once I was assured she had sent it to me, only a matter of providing a modest bribe to the delivery boy in question to deny any knowledge of her. Then persuading Wadham the thief-taker to tip a croker or two for one of his less law-abiding circle, some pick-lock of his acquaintance, to tap the Queen Square house – though on this occasion for the purpose of making a deposit rather than a withdrawal. The timepiece sequestered within Winifred's room, along with certain pieces of silver. Not the precise pieces my poor old housekeeper Ellen had been accused of stealing, and thus dismissed – for I have never discovered the true circumstance of that loss – but close enough against the possibility of any affidavit I might need to make about their provenance.

'Know me?' I replied. 'I doubt you could ever do so. But this creature. Betrayed me once. To a Jacobite traitor. To a seditious assassin.'

'No,' Bridger cried. 'It is you! *Assassina*. My husband.'

'I see what you mean,' said Parrish. 'Quite mad.'

Agnes was still attempting to prise Winifred from the bars, calling for assistance, the rest of the gallery's patients baying and barking all along the landing, while Bridger herself extended a finger in Matthew's direction.

'And *he* come to my house,' she screamed at him. '*Para minha casa*. I lose my home.'

Indeed she had. Again. For Wadham had served a warrant upon her. Suspicion of theft. And there they were, in her room. The stolen goods in question. Elihu had no choice but to turn her out upon the street and, once there, it had posed no difficulty to follow my husband's own receipt. My turn now to approach the new President of the Governors' Court, Sir Samuel Dashwood, and sufficient *pishcash* from the wealth now restored to me that I might be registered as a Bethlem benefactor. Besides, there was my sworn statement to the number of times Governor Yale himself had told me that Mistress Bridger's loss of her husband had shattered her wits.

'Such a pity,' I said, leading Matthew once more towards the polished oak staircase. 'For she ate so often from my table.'

'You must release her,' Parrish insisted as we walked out along the front path. 'It is inhuman, Catherine, despite her delusions. Despite her part in your own incarceration. Perhaps because of it.'

'Not just yet,' I said.

'I fear your time here may have damaged you more than you can know, my dear.'

'She is fortunate she did not meet the felon's fate she deserves, Matthew. But I am making arrangements. In due course she will be shipped back to Madras Patnam. Her daughters too.'

'Yet there might have been,' he said, 'more justice in seeing her stand trial. And justice should be blind, where revenge is merely partial.'

'I find revenge more satisfying,' I told him, recalling the time I have spent gathering damning evidence against those of the Bethlem governors – Roberts and Jeffreys to name but two – I had convinced myself knew about my previous activities against the Jacobite banditti and had thus been complicit in my torment there. Well, I had supplied the accumulated intelligence to His Grace, the Duke of Devonshire, but on condition that he should not divulge its source to Parrish. It would not answer if Matthew believed me willing to become his intelligencer once more.

'But what on earth can she have intended?' Parrish said now, as we neared the gate. 'About you being an assassin.'

'Deluded, as you say,' I replied, thankful that I needed explain no more for, coming through the outer gate towards us, was another old enemy. 'Reverend Hoadly,' I said. 'Are you come to be Mistress Bridger's obligor also?'

I saw his fingertips reach inadvertently for the spot where my spittle had once struck.

'Mistress Yale,' he said. 'I should have liked the chance to speak with you at the wedding.'

A se'ennight past. Immediately after Easter. My Katie wed to Sir Dudley North at St. Peter-le-Poor, though Hoadly had not officiated at the ceremony. This honour, Elihu had insisted, should fall to that despicable pecksniff John Evans, now Bishop of Bangor in Wales.

'I think there is little we might usefully have discussed, sir. And I trust you will find Mistress Bridger more biddable to your preaching in there than I may have been.'

'Catherine,' said Matthew, 'Reverend Hoadly is very much in favour with Her Majesty. Very much within our faction.'

Had he so readily forgotten the attack upon him just moments after we left the church that day? I thought not. But I sensed some trace in the tone of his voice, that deeper Matthew Parrish and his schemes, so that I took his arm, urged him out towards the lane.

'I fear some simple misunderstanding between us, Mistress Yale,' Hoadly shouted after us, 'that I should have wished to correct. Though you stayed so little time at the wedding feast.'

Indeed I had. Just long enough to spend some precious and tearful time with Ursula. Seventeen already but still such a child. She longs, she says, to live with me again and I have promised that we shall be together once more as soon as that may be possible. For, with my wealth now safely out of the Stephen's clutches and deposited with Hoare's Bank, I have begun the process of seeking a new house.

'Not the best of days for me,' I called back over my shoulder, then stopped, turned to face him. 'Though I do not see how that would be any concern of yours, Reverend.'

'Truly? It seemed such a joyous occasion. Your daughter wed to a fellow of substantial means.' Three thousand pounds per annum, according to Annie. 'And a generous dowry provided by your husband.' Twenty thousand guineas, she claims – though insists that Elihu has done nothing but complain at the figure ever since agreeing the sum when somewhat in his cups. There were matters here that were privy, not to bandied about in public, and I steered Parrish back, as close to Hoadly as I could bear.

'I hope that Kate will be happy,' I said, 'though my impression of her husband is that he is something of a clown. A gentleman, of course, but when in London spending every available moment at the coffee house or the gaming table.'

I suppose it was the collection of other guests at the wedding that drove me to feel so far from comfortable in their company.

'A clown with some unfortunate connections,' said Matthew, and Hoadly nodded his agreement.

'Mister Parrish tells me you may already be acquainted with some of them,' he said. 'Perhaps the reason you left the wedding feast so promptly?'

They had been obvious enough. Young Sir Dudley's cousin, William North – Lord North and Grey, that had lost a hand at Blenheim – who I heard quite openly espousing the view that, whilst he naturally wished long life to Queen Anne, succession to Her Majesty should equally remain with the Stuart dynasty. A Jacobite succession. And many fellows around him in happy agreement.

'My daughter's choice of wedding guests concerns me not the slightest, sir,' I lied, for the very sight of such men – plotters and traitors all, I was sure – brought back memories of Seaton, his capture of poor Ursula, and the involvement of that Irish poltroon, Colonel Porter, still at large out there, somewhere in the world. Somewhere, yet such a distant threat that I long ago even gave up carrying that old pocket pistol beneath my skirts.

'You may believe me or not, as you wish, Mistress Yale,' said Hoadly, 'but I believe the presence of such sedition so openly in our society should be a concern for us all.'

'The wretch,' I said, as the hackney swung into Devonshire Street. 'How dare he!'

'Ah, you have found your tongue again,' said Parrish. 'I am unaccustomed to such long silences from you.'

It was true. I had been seething upon our encounter with Hoadly all the way down Long Lane, past Smith Field, through Cow Lane and right along Holborn. Why, Hoadly was still on my list of those against whom I had pledged to gain satisfaction. And now...

'You think I am mistaken?' I said. 'About his pompous intentions when he came to my cell? About the attack upon your person?'

'For his actions in the hospital, I can offer no assurance. Except to say that you were hardly yourself. Our interpretation of events can often be doubtful, to say the least, when we have suffered such harsh adversity. And the attack? I have had cause to speak with Hoadly many times now. Satisfied myself of his innocence, Catherine. Of his sexton, however, I am less certain. But, one way or the other,

Reverend Hoadly is now a valuable asset for us. Please tell me you have no vengeful designs upon the fellow.'

I picked at the leather of the carriage's upholstery.

'As it happens,' I replied, 'I have enough to occupy me with Elihu's latest meanderings. And my property.'

Annie tells me he has so ingratiated himself at that parish church in Wrexham – St. Giles – he has received permission to build a private gallery for himself and his family. But which family? I ask myself. And would the rector of St. Giles Church laud him so highly if they knew the paucity of his morals.

'He still supports the Nicks children?' said Matthew as we halted outside old Devonshire House.

'Supports?' I sneered. 'The word is hardly sufficient. A fortune spent maintaining the two girls. All Betty this and Betty that, according to my daughter. School fees, dancing lessons, music classes, marriage brokers. And Nan says every letter from their mother begs that they should be sent back to Madras. Though he will have none of it. Now there is the boy too. Elihu junior. Boarding fees at a French house. All the rest of it. But he has kept his promise, I collect. No more mention of Annie's betrothal to Evance. My possessions restored to me.'

More than I had expected, if I am truthful. Not simply the belongings I had demanded but my finest settle from Broad Street, and the Guilbaud cabinet. Much of my stored clothing too, the gowns supplied to me by Madame Rémond or items I had brought back from Madras. All temporarily stored in that same house, just along the street, where I had once installed Katherine Nicks. A short lease, while I determine more permanent accommodation.

'I am delighted for you,' he said, climbing from the hackney and handing me down carefully to avoid the many puddles. 'But he spoke true, you know – Hoadly, I mean. A concern for us all, indeed.'

'You shall not entice me back into your schemes, sir,' I told him, as he paid the driver. There was a fine drizzle, a rabid dog barking at us from the stinking midden on the corner of Queen Square.

'I was thinking about your journal.'

'I wish you had never seen the thing. Filled only with my foolish scribbling.'

'Hardly flattering to your inclusion of my ode to poor Queen Mary. And you never gave me the chance to judge anything further.

Yet knowing you for a scribbler you came to mind when I had cause recently to read another most interesting journal. Did you know Reverend Morrice?'

I raised my rain-napper, lifted my skirts to avoid them being soiled.

'My father spoke of him, I collect.'

'Kept the most meticulous of notes,' he said, as we reached the porch steps. 'An Entering Book now in the hands of my old friend Doctor Williams. And since his death it has kept us especially busy, for he was adept at recording each and every sign he found of Jacobite resurgence. Connections, Catherine. Connections. Great heavens, you must know that when Queen Anne dies their ambitions shall surely flare again. And if this union between England and Scotland goes forward – it looks certain it must do so – there will be many on both sides of the border driven to join the ranks of the disaffected. More bloody civil war, my dear.'

I looked back down at him from the top of the stairs, hammered on the knocker.

'You waste your breath, sir. In more ways than one. For even had I the inclination – and I do not – to use my new son-in-law as a vehicle to spy upon his cousin and Lord North's associates, my daughter Kate can barely bring herself to speak with me, let alone invite me close enough to divine useful intelligence.'

'Well,' he shouted after me, as Madam Legh's manservant ushered me inside, 'I suppose I should be pleased you have so readily grasped the role you *might* have played. In your more ambitious days.'

Sweet Jesu, have I not already lost enough? And this, now, of all things.

Joseph Junior. Taken by the cruel sea when I had thought we must somehow be resistant to its perils. All those countless miles. My father and mother enduring Mediterranean storms. Myself and dear Joseph, travelling halfway around the world. The months I had to wait for news that the boys were safe when I sent them home. My own terror-strewn journey back from Madras with the girls. I had believed our lives all charmed, blessed by the spirits of the ocean.

But I was wrong.

My eldest son has disappeared, drowned it seems along with the Spanish galleon on which he was sailing.

'With his Creator now,' said Benjamin as we read the salt-stained letter again. From their chief factor, their *agente principal*, at Amoy. 'With Papa too.'

His tears moved me almost as much as the news. Still so unreal. As though it were somebody else's grief that I observed, rather than my own.

'It is supposed to be a comfort,' I said, 'that his restless wandering is now over.'

'How can you brook it, Mama? Richard, and now Joseph.'

'Baby Walt and little David for our tally too. My parents. Your sweet father, of course. With each loss I have embraced my pains, allowed the tears to flow without restriction, shunning the advice of those who recommended stoicism, the show of strength – for the denial of grief is not strength, it is the worst of weakness.'

I studied the letter again, searching for some crumb of comfort between the lines. But it is written in poor English, would have been easier if *señor* Peredes had sent word in his native tongue. And it had arrived by a circuitous route that would presumably be followed by Joseph's belongings, the last will and testament, which Peredes promised would soon arrive also.

'I feel this need,' Benjamin murmured. 'To remain fortified in Joseph's memory. He would have so wished to see our claim settled, don't you think?'

'He will be watching its progress, I am certain. And it is some small comfort to me that he has been spared all knowledge of his mother's madness.'

My time in Bethlem Hospital, the years piled upon me by that place, the stiff and aching joints with which it has left me, the heaviness in my soul that Joseph Junior's death has so extended.

'Do you think,' Benji said, 'that I must be doomed too?'

'We are all doomed,' I reminded him. 'And God be praised we still have Elford, safe in Smyrna. Or wherever on this earth he may be.'

'How can we be certain?' he said, and I scolded him for his foolishness, assured him that we must all pray for the Almighty's protection. Yet I could not help recalling Matthew's admonition, that the biggest threat to my surviving children now is the prospect of further civil war.

His Grace, Sir William Cavendish, Duke of Devonshire, shifted un-comfortably in his wheeled wicker chair, glowered through the open stained glass of his long gallery at the gardens and parklands beyond. Outside, the afternoon was languid with the drone of honeybees.

'That infernal saw-bones,' he said, 'claims it shall not be long before I shuffle off this mortal coil, madam.'

He shared the same physician with Her Majesty since, as steward to her royal household, he dutifully also seemed to share each of her major ailments. Severe gout. Dropsy. Goodness knows what else besides.

'Your Grace looks the picture of health,' I lied, brushing my fingers along the red velour embroidery of the window seat and breathing the rich aromas wafting in from the flowerbeds. 'I am certain Doctor Sloane must exaggerate.'

The good doctor had received news of Joseph Junior's death, sent me the kindest of letters.

'You say so? Maximising his account, perhaps, with his leeches and his purgatives.'

In truth I thought Sir William's elephantine lower legs must surely burst the silk enclosure of his stockings. And the swelling beneath his eyes – horrendous.

'Her Majesty must surely miss your services, sir.'

'Ha! You should see us together, my dear. Hobbling about the court like a brace of old degenerates. Yet I did not invite you here to weary you with my woes. No indeed, if Sloane is correct there are accounts to be settled.'

It is two years since I saw the Duke – that glittering celebration of our victory at Gibraltar. Then, last summer I sent him those details of the Bethlem governors. But we did not meet at all, so that the change in him is marked indeed. And accounts to settle? What did he intend?

'Lady Mary,' I said, to give me time to think. 'Not here?'

He leered at me, a glimpse of the old Sir William Cavendish again, which now saddened my heart. The smell of his liniment, oil of wintergreen. I knew Doctor Sloane must be correct, that the Duke could not be long for this life – and I will miss his mark upon the world.

'You fro'ward wench,' he laughed, the excitement immediately causing him to cough into his snuff-stained kerchief. 'Is that what troubles you?' he gasped. 'That I might leap from this chair and compromise your considerable virtue?'

'It is perhaps the first time in our acquaintance, my lord, that I have suffered no such fear.' When he finally stopped choking on his own phlegm, his bloated features fell into the semblance of a petulant pout. 'Yet on this occasion,' I went on, 'I wish I found you well enough to make the advance.'

He raised the kerchief to his face, turned towards the windows again, pretended to observe his verdant parklands but hiding the tears I knew he shed and, for my own part, I stood to examine some of the gilt-framed portraits adorning the inner wall of the gallery, that he should not be embarrassed. A fine palace, the largest of those lining the northern and western edge of Piccadilly and Portugal Street, the Exeter road. Berkeley House, that the Duke is seeking to name afresh as New Devonshire House.

'Lady Mary,' he called at last, 'is at Chatsworth, Catherine.' I had assumed so, since it seemed unlikely she would have tolerated my presence in their London mansion had she also been in residence. 'If I can be frank,' the duke murmured, as I returned to his side, 'it was, rather, my other Mary I wished to discuss. Now, shall you drive me?'

It would be an understatement to say that I was taken aback, and it seemed politick to feign ignorance. But when the invitation had arrived she had already been on my mind to some extent, as she has been at times over the past year. For a man with so many concubines, Mary Anne Campion had stood out from the flock. Actress and songbird, she had attracted his attention when she was just fifteen, they said – when His Grace was already over sixty – delivered him a daughter after two years, then died of a hectic fever less than two years later again. The talk of the town ever since.

'I am – sorry, Your Grace. For your loss.' I grasped the handles of his chair, pushed the conveyance along the chequerboard flooring, knowing that he cared nothing for the direction of travel.

'No stranger to loss yourself, Mistress Yale.' He had sent condolences, of course. But I wondered whether he could also possibly know the significance of today's date. Foolish, I know. Why should he? The anniversary of poor Walter's awful death. 'It is why I thought of you,' he went on. 'I need somebody – well, somebody to tend her grave. I arranged for her to be buried at Latimer. Alongside others of my family. But I could not expect any in my household...'

'I understand the dilemma, Sir William, though I do not understand how I might assist.'

'Accounts to settle, my dear, as I told you. I owe you my life. Considerably in your debt. So tell me, what might you desire?'

'That debt has already been repaid several times over, My Lord. Not that any debt was ever due in the first place. But you have been kind in so many ways already.'

We had reached the farther end of the hall and I swung the contraption about, admiring the marble bust of a Cavendish ancestor before beginning the return journey.

'Still, one boon?' he said, and although he had sprung the thing upon me, my remaining ambitions are now few. My property is returned to me. Bridger and her daughters dispatched back to Madras – with just a little help from my friends. But there are still my children, those that are left to me.

'Truly?' I said. 'Then it would be to see my daughter Anne and your son James happily wed as, I collect, they both desire also.'

'I have already denied him that match. My wife has other plans for the boy.'

Outside I could see a herd of roe deer grazing happily.

'You bade me express a desire, Sir William. I have no other.'

It surprised even me that I should be so forthright, so lacking in finesse.

'It is a considerable one,' he replied. 'Your desire. Many steps further than I had intended.'

The scent of lavender from the Dutch parterres was masked now by woodsmoke, the gardeners busy somewhere with a bonfire, almost in turn overpowering the wintergreen, and I was suddenly not certain I believed him.

'Intentions that involve Latimer,' I said. 'Those are considerable too, are they not? A tidy step to Buckinghamshire, sirrah.'

'I thought to offer you a tenancy at Latimer House. More suitable accommodation than your apartments with Madam Legh. Recently endowed to young James, though he has no desire to live there. But no other desire will suffice, you say?'

I was shocked. A tenancy?

'None, My Lord,' I stammered, felt guilty that I should be so fro'ward.

'Great heavens,' he mused, 'I could be tempted. Even were it only to spite my wife. Though we may need some further garnish to settle the deal, madam.'

'My daughter's dowry?'

We had traversed the full length of the black and white gallery floor once more and he bade me halt, urged me to haul upon the bell rope that would summon his manservant.

'A matter for Governor Yale, I think,' he said. 'No, there are other concerns. National importance, Catherine. You know what is coming?'

'Parrish is convinced we are doomed to face more civil war.'

'And you? Convinced as well?'

The idea terrified me, and I had tried to shut out the images that further conflict conveyed. Easier to deny its possibility, perhaps.

'I try to avoid politicks now, Sir William.'

'A waste,' he snapped. 'First, that you have not taken that fine fellow to your bed.' I think I must have gasped, felt my face flush. 'What? He is devoted to you, for pity's sake. And, second, that you deny our nation your extensive talents. Look, you see that?' He pointed to a painting of Mary, Queen of Scots, and I was heartily pleased that we seemed to be changing the subject. 'I keep it as a reminder that she was imprisoned for so long at Chatsworth. But more, as a reminder of the centuries we have wasted in conflict with Scotland. I fear I shall never see Chatsworth again but at least I leave this legacy, the Treaty of Union between our two proud nations. A single Parliament, my dear, for this new Greater Britain.'

There, his mark upon the world again. His last enormous public service. His legacy indeed. Not only the architect of this project but its principal broker too.

'Then why this fear of conflict?' I said.

'The Scots' economy was all but ruined by the Darien adventure and many in Scotland still blame us for its failure. An endless stream of English gold pouring over the Tweed as part of the agreement.'

Sir William's steward arrived, helped him from the wheeled chair, half-carried him towards the door.

'And copious amounts of bribery also, I suppose,' I replied, following behind. 'To persuade the Scottish Parliament to vote itself out of existence.'

'That and the loss of their own currency, my dear. So, for those who already resent the loss of independence, this is all simply salt in the wounds.'

'The disaffected and their resentments all moulding themselves around the illusion that supporting the Stuarts will be an easy solution for their long-term ills.'

'The convenient lie against the complex truth. And with the French to fan the flames, how can bloodshed not follow?'

'Then my own meager involvement would be irrelevant, My Lord. It must be so.'

'Mistress Yale,' he said. 'You, of all people, should know that those actions which seem the most insignificant can sometimes be the same that change the world. So, let me be blunt, as you have been with me. It is possible we may not meet again but I am happy to grant your wish. Marriage between our children it shall be, but only if I have your sworn agreement, first, to take the Latimer lease for the purpose I have mentioned. And, second, that you shall resume whatever duties Matthew Parrish may now set for you. But for pity's sake, take the fellow to your bed.'

'Well, he is dead,' whispered Elihu. 'Dead and buried at Chatsworth, and may God rot his soul.'

I had agreed to meet him, eventually, but only on condition of neutral ground, and the quiet sanctuary of the gallery in our recently completed chapel of St. George the Martyr on Queen Square suited that purpose admirably. And a good day for privacy, as we sat there, a little apart, for the whole world, it seems, swept off to Tyburn this forenoon to see the felon Charles Moore swing for his burglary.

'A better man, a greater man, than you ever were or could be, husband,' I said, shrugging my cloak from my shoulders and recalling that last occasion upon which I had met the Duke. 'I grieve for his loss.'

There had, of course, been no invitation to attend Sir William's funeral, though Streynsham has given me a full account of that sad occasion.

'Summoned me like some lackey, some *peon* upon his estates. Informed me – yes, *informed* – that he condescended to the betrothal of my Nan to his pup.'

The chapel is presently blessed with the warm aromas of fresh paint and the resins of carved timber rising from that exquisite new reredos, rather than the cold corruption, which is so often the characteristic of our older churches. Strangely, Elihu seemed to have dressed to match the décor: his coat and breeches the same shade of brown as the varnished timber; his waistcoat and neck cloth the precise pale cream of the gallery's wall; and his periwig an equal tone to the altar screen's chestnut hues.

'If the match displeases you, I am certain Annie will accede to your wishes.'

'You know how much it will cost me?' He slammed the balled fist of his right hand into the open palm of his left. 'Six thousand. Six. Plus two more in brilliants.'

'Coincidence. Precisely the amount by which you have profited from calling in the loans you made, to poor Edisbury among others.'

Mistress Edisbury had written, begging me to intercede on her husband's behalf. It must have cost a great deal for her to do so since, from our meeting at Plas Grono so many years ago, I remember her as a lady of great dignity. Yet here they are, impoverished almost to the point of ruin by the level of interest Elihu has demanded on a line of credit extended to Edisbury that he might furnish his fine Erddig Hall.

'God's hooks, Catherine, I am heartily sick of your spying.'

He threw himself back on the seat, like a child displaying a tanterum.

'My duty as a mother, it seems. To check that my daughter's interests are protected, since her father tells me naught. So, her portion may be six thousand pounds, but eight hundred of those are held in jointure by Annie herself. And then she is appointed to the Devonshire family's lands and properties in Buckinghamshire. Everywhere from Hundridge to Dundridge.'

'Humbug to dumbug, more like. It shall cripple me. All this expense. And Kate expecting me to settle an endowment upon her boy too. You should see him. A contented little cove.'

Dudley Junior, my first grandchild. There will be more, I know, though I fear to see my own mortality reflected in these children for, even if God spares me, I cannot live long enough to see them reach their maturity.

'Chance would be a fine thing,' I said. 'Never once an invitation to Glemham. Not permitted even to visit. Your own influence, I think.'

'The madness, rather. Addiction to your bottle.'

I was startled by a sudden noise from somewhere inside the chapel, the flapping of wings, a dove so close to us that I felt the wind of its passing upon my cheek, so that I raised a tardy protective hand to my face.

'I think we have all been afflicted by your grasping avarice, Elihu. They may think you a fine fellow at the parish church of

St. Giles, though I doubt the Edisburys sing your praises quite so high. And expense? None spared though, I think, for the Nicks girls or your by-blows.'

'And have you no pity for Mistress Nicks either? Her father dead at Fort St. George. She deserves at least some sympathy.'

'From me? As much perhaps as you afforded the death of my Joseph.'

Still hollow from his loss, the most bitter of bereavements.

'How many times must I apologise? You know how long it was before the news reached me. And Katherine's girls? A temporary necessity. Until their mother comes back for them. Sweet Betty fares well enough, though the younger one still finds it hard here, looks a little – well, a little brown, if you understand me. But I shall not tolerate these calumnies about young Elihu or poor Don Carlos.'

From the one occasion I had seen them, at Devonshire House last year, Betty bears all the fair-skinned hallmarks of the Yales, while her sister, Ursula, might bear his mother's name but carries all the swarthy Portuguese blood of Katherine Nicks herself. And what of my own Ursi? When should I see her again? And as for those boys about whom he protests just too much…

'You may persist,' I snapped, 'in this foolishness that Katherine's lad is no more than your godson, though I do not believe it for a moment. Mistress Nicks herself, the whole world, it seems, acknowledges that Charles Almanza is your own.'

'I would not expect you to understand me, Catherine. You never did, in truth.'

'I understand perfectly the delusions within which you live. The lies you convince yourself to be true. Like this foolishness that Mistress Nicks will ever bring herself back to London.'

Annie tells me all – the way he still so frequently bemoans his longing for a fine *kari* sauce, for an aromatic Indian rice, and to drink the health of his dear absent friend in the so delightful company of Mistress Nicks herself.

'Sweet Jesu,' he said, waving his hands about in exasperation. 'Shall nobody deliver me from this woman's wickedness?'

'How sweetly you sing when your feathers are ruffled, sirrah. Like one of those canary birds I hear you have sent to Madras. For Governor Pitt and for your whores. Canary birds. All taught by flageolet to whistle hymns, they say. Our Lord Jesu shall, I am sure, be happy to forgive your many sins for this reverence you show Him.'

He has dispatched pipes of Tenerife Rambla and Oratava too, it seems. And on his better days he would have made a neat clench about the canary songbirds and those same Canary wines. But his sense of humour appears to have deserted him.

'Better than that. A fine painting of the Virgin for Padre Michael at St. Mary's. You remember St. Mary's, wife? You made your vows there. But honour and obedience? Is that how I came to be humiliated so, by Cavendish? You, going behind my back to broker a deal I cannot possibly refuse. Well, I may have to tolerate the betrothal, but I shall not allow History to see me neutered in this way also. No, I shall not.'

'Your daughter to be married into the Duke of Devonshire's family. To a young man she admires. You think anybody of note shall even consider the manner of its brokerage? You are a pecksniff, Elihu. You have climbed to a high place, husband, yet you forget upon whose wealth the stair was built.'

I began to pick at the ribbons of the tabby taffeta mantle that was now gathered about my waist.

'Hypocrisy, how?' he raged, then remembered where he was. 'When you have worshipped old Cavendish so devoutly. Cavendish, who protested loudly about the arbitrary rule of kings under the Stuarts, then became William's enforcer. Cavendish, freedom's champion – so long as it is not freedom for papists. But me? How?' he murmured again, almost a whisper.

'Streynsham tells me you have requested a death mask. That you may honour His Grace's memory. You – honouring the memory of the man whose soul you wish our Lord God to rot.'

The dove had taken wing again, below, as desperate to be gone from this place as myself, I think.

'How else am I to recover from this? Master Seeman – the Mennonite, who crafted that same image of the Virgin – I have commissioned him to complete another canvas for me. Myself and Cavendish in negotiation. About Nan's betrothal to his son.'

'It shall be a lie.'

'How so? Cavendish summoned me and I met him. That is what the canvas shall record.'

I could just imagine. All the painter's gilt-framed crafts employed in an effort to show this as a meeting of equals, possibly even Elihu as the dominant party.

'And that, I collect, is the reason you wanted this conclave.'

'It will make a fine gift for Nan. For her new family.'

The dove was gone, finally finding the chapel door slightly ajar.

'Copies too, I assume,' I said. 'For more public showing.'

'Perhaps.'

'Unfortunate for all concerned, therefore, should there be controversy. Questions about the authenticity of the scene it portrays.'

He puffed out his cheeks, pulled each side of that chestnut peruke to set it more squarely upon his pate.

'Precisely.'

'I have thought many times, Elihu, that ours was more a union of business rivals rather than a marital match and here we are, back at the barter.'

It took some time, though we finally arrived at yet another accord. For all possible public consumption, we will uphold the myth that it is Elihu who brokered the marriage settlement with Sir William before his death. In exchange, he promises to restore poor Ursi to me and ensure my access to little Dudley Junior. Besides that, he will bestow upon me half of those fourteen hundred gold pagodas, which – again from Nan's invaluable intelligence – I know Governor Pitt has sent him from the sale of the house, *my* house, on Middle Gate Street. For I shall need such resource if I am to provide the garnish, the *pishcash*, with which I might fulfill my oath to the Duke and meet Parrish's requirement for the turning of Dudley Junior's father to our purpose.

'It frightens me, Mama,' said Ursula. 'The house. It is so like…'

Yesterday, and I was taken back to that other chapel, my agreement brokered with Elihu, ten months ago now, which had restored my youngest to me Yet this private sanctuary, alongside Latimer itself, is so very different. An ancient place. Yew trees. An avenue of oaks.

'I know, my sweet. But Latimer is our home now. And there is nothing to harm you in the house. So back to your prayers, if you please.'

It reminded her, naturally, of Langhorn's home at Charlton, for there are many similarities. The two-storey great halls almost identical, for instance: the same strap-work ceiling; the lacquered oak of the minstrel's gallery at the level of the first floor landings; and its white marble fireplace and over-mantle the virtual twin of that behind which Vincent Seaton had hidden himself that fatal morning I walked into his trap. And now here was Ursula in her nineteenth summer, the nightmares from her torment and capture by Seaton and that wretch Colonel Porter still trouble her. But she did as I had bidden her, lifted those pretty primrose skirts and knelt upon her hassock.

'So quiet,' said Benjamin, swatting away a troublesome wasp. 'After London. But this, is it not just a little – sanctimonious?'

An inscription to Mary Anne Campion upon a white limestone plaque set into the grey chancel wall.

'Parrish would have written better,' I smiled. 'But they are the old Duke's own composition so you shall not doubt their sincerity.'

'But written for his…'

'Most beloved actress and singer,' I cut across him, still finding the need to protect Ursi's simple and innocent view of the world. 'And one of the reasons we are here, Benji. In this grand new mansion.'

Mary Anne's grave is in the burial ground and I have already ensured it is regularly garlanded with fresh flowers.

'The old Duke is dead, Ma. And I doubt his sons have any interest in their father's illicit liaisons. But is this the only duty you fulfill here? It seems so little to merit such reward.'

He looked at me with no sign of guile whatsoever. His legal training, I suppose. By then the wasp was bothering us again and we each flapped a hand at the creature.

'Just this,' I told him. 'Supplemented by the good fortune that your sister's husband prefers his other properties for their marital home.'

Actually, the same reason, Annie had confided in me. Her husband James cannot abide being confronted so publicly by Mistress Campion each time he goes to his devotions.

'When shall we see her again, Mama?' said Ursula in that child-like voice and rising from her knees. 'I pray to our Lord Jesus daily that it may be soon.'

The memory of our family all being together for once was still fresh indeed. Nan's own wedding, just this se'ennight past. St. Peter-le-Poor again, this time with Doctor Paget officiating. It hardly seemed a fitting location for the marriage of the second Duke's favourite brother, yet the wedding feast at New Devonshire House more than compensated.

'As I pray,' I reminded her, 'that no more tragedies may befall this family.'

As we crossed in front of the servants' wing, back towards the house itself, I saw that a carriage had halted at the end of the drive, young Chaplain Burrough – who also serves as rector for Chenies – in conversation with its occupant.

'Ah,' beamed Burrough, tugging at his white cravat when he saw me, 'here is the lady now.'

From the carriage window, Matthew Parrish's smiling face appeared. Smiling but, for the first time I could recall, visibly aged, wrinkles developing around his cheeks and mouth.

'Saints preserve us,' Benjamin whispered behind his hand 'you needs only mention the fellow's name and up he comes.'

'Yes, but why?' I murmured in response, trying at the same time to return the obvious delight upon Matthew's face, though unable to smother the trepidation I felt. By then he was alighting from the coach, all pale summer silks and linens, the lightest of tawny travelling cloaks, Ursula running to greet him.

'Mistress Yale,' said William Burrough, 'give you joy of this fine day and your distinguished visitor.'

He shook Parrish's hand and bade us each farewell while, for my part, I urged Benjamin to take his sister inside.

'Distinguished visitor?' I said, when they were gone.

'I had cause to provide his father with some representation,' Parrish replied. 'He seems to think that gives me some notoriety.'

'The same notoriety that brings you here? Do you not have a campaign to wage?'

The smile had slipped from his face.

'I had not quite expected the interrogation,' he said. 'But I am assured that the seat is safe. Momentous, Catherine. Though I decided not to contest it.'

I was astonished.

'A seat in the first united Parliament of England and Scotland?' I said. 'Our united kingdoms. And our faction in the ascendancy, certain of a majority. Are you mad?'

'I hope not. But the seat will be in safe hands. Lumley. And I made arrangements for a courier in Amersham to bring me word. I have enough on my hands. Back to France very soon. Another Jacobite scheme in ruins and we need to make the most of it.'

That pretender to our dear throne – Catholic James Stuart's son, James Francis Edward – had sailed earlier in the year with a French fleet and army, almost landed in the Moray Firth but driven off by that fine gentleman, Admiral Byng.

'I apologise,' I said, warming anew to his presence and taking his arm. 'It has been a difficult week and I had not expected visitors. You know you are always welcome. You will stay, of course. And such news. I hope you may be correct – about the election. But Byng's victory was months ago. You have fresh word? About the plotters?'

I prayed he brought the intelligence I had been hoping for, yet I saw the disappointment in his eyes as he slowly shook his head.

'Wait there,' he called to the coachman, while I led him to the wide steps and entrance porch. 'And I hate to disappoint you, Catherine, but we have rounded up all the Jacobite gentry we are likely to catch. They are presently in Newgate. Porter is not among them. Are you certain your son-in-law spoke true?'

'I can be certain of nothing where Dudley is concerned. But let me show you my palace, Matthew. It is so unlike my lodgings at the Bethlem Hospital.'

'Elegant in the extreme.' The good humour returned to light his lips as he admired the herringbone brickwork of the façade, its exquisite windows, as we passed through, to stand upon the black and white tiles of the grand reception salon, where my new housekeeper awaited our pleasure.

'One hundred and twenty years of elegance to be precise,' I said, and took his arm.

'You have made it your own, Catherine. Already. And I recognise those.'

One of the many manservants balanced on a chair, busily hanging some of the likenesses Joseph had drawn of the three older boys. Oh, so many years gone by. The memories. The tragedies. He moved to the wide hearth, explored the blue Delft tiles with his fingertips.

'How very fine, dear lady. At last I find you in surroundings that do you justice. Of course I shall stay – if we may accommodate my horses and you can bear my company.'

We enjoyed dinner and, during the afternoon, I showed him the grounds. He had come up through Latimer village on the way here, of course. But Ursula insisted we all follow the path down through the meadows, where skylarks took to the air almost from beneath our feet while we picked a way through the cow pats to reach the Chess, winding its lazy way through our lush wooded valley, clouds of midges humming in harmony to the water's languid lullaby. All was green. All was growing. Such promise.

I seemed to feel the years slipping from my shoulders. I was a girl again, delighting in Matthew's foolish stories, the snatches of poetry with which he entranced both myself and my poor daughter. I have generally always felt comfortable in his company but never quite so much as yesterday afternoon. Almost – like family. He span yarns for Benjamin about my dear husband Joseph, tales that I had quite forgotten. Embellished, naturally, in the way of all good storytellers. A beautiful early evening though this, of course, can offer no excuse.

For pity's sake, I am fifty-seven years old. Too advanced in age now to be embarking upon lustful infidelities. Or perhaps I should blame old Sir William for setting his blessing upon the temptation. His dying wish, after all. And yet, with supper eaten, Benjamin and Ursula retired to their rooms, a little too much Alicante consumed, I lay upon my sheets uncertain whether the intolerable heat emanated from the exceptional July weather or from inside my own body. Until, at last, I found myself creeping in my nightgown through the panelled corridors, down the grand double staircase to the first-floor guest Rose Room, to the door of Parrish's bedchamber.

This morning it was all either uncomfortable silence in the company of my children or the servants, or fumbling attempts by both of us, when alone, to assess whether we either regretted the foolishness of the previous night's passions or delighted in their recollection. And I think we concluded nothing by the time his dirt-grimed post boy arrived at noon. The last of the constituencies in this interminable two-month process finally counted and, as Parrish expected, the Whiggish majority confirmed.

'Her Majesty will oppose it, of course,' he said, when the post boy was paid and the room emptied, his bags ready for the carriage journey back to London. 'But I must go back, Catherine. The Queen summons us. We shall see. I simply hate to leave with so many things between us unresolved, I think.'

There was a new suit of clothes, more formal. His court attire, ready to meet the Queen's command, accept his diplomatic mission to Paris, but his fresh-dusted travelling mantle was neatly folded across his arm.

'Resolution, my dear,' I said, 'by definition itself requires resolve. And since neither of us was resolute about the actions of last night, I fear we may each need some time to ponder our possible futures.'

'Sathiri...' he began, but I placed a finger upon his lips.

'I am clear upon only one thing,' I said. 'That Sathiri would want nothing for you but your happiness. And perhaps mine too.'

I was certain of it, could almost hear the tone of her lyrical voice, see the glory of my dearest friend's features, the vibrant reds and yellows of her *sarees*, recalled that her name itself meant *beautiful one* in her Gentue tongue.

'I shall need to return from Paris as soon as I'm able, Catherine.'

He unfolded the thin summer cloak and swirled it around his shoulders.

'For more intelligence gathered from my son-in-law?' I smiled when I saw that my jibe had wounded him. 'If so, you shall need a better reason, for I fear Sir Dudley may be a well from which no more water can be drawn.'

It had all been somewhat sordid. I had arranged for Wadham the thief-taker to have him pursued, to discover his weaknesses. All very tedious. Gaming debts, naturally. Indiscretions overheard and recorded at the coffee house. But evidence also that he shared certain other predilections and those I had used as a means to introduce myself to the fellow as something other than merely my errant daughter's mother. There had been rage, naturally, but finally word about his cousin, Lord William North. Interesting associations with some of those same Scottish gentlemen now languishing in Newgate – though not enough to condemn Lord North and Grey himself. Not yet, for he is still considered a hero of Blenheim.

'Dudley is not the fountainhead from which I now wish to drink, my dear,' he said, then flushed crimson at his own turn of phrase.

'Then, sirrah, be on your way but return to me soon.'

How short-lived my happiness, how swift God's retribution. The brine-blemished package arrived today while I was still languishing in the memory of Matthew's caresses. A package with the old Austin Friars direction, which had somehow been crossed out and forwarded to Devonshire Street where, I assumed, Madam Legh must have made the final correction that it should eventually reach me here at Latimer. Part of me wishes it had never found us, that I had been left in blissful ignorance. It is too cruel.

'Mama,' said Benjamin, joining me in the library, and seeing my tears. 'Tell me this is not what I think.'

I recalled my words after Joseph Junior's death. '*And God be praised,*' I had said, '*we still have Elford, safe in Smyrna.*' But then I remembered Benji's response too: '*How can we be sure?*'

'How did you know?' I sobbed.

'Elford, is it not?'

'A letter from Captain Maddox, master of the *Phoenix*, dispatched from Cape Town.'

The good captain, this purveyor of pain, hoped I might forgive the manner of his writing but felt it was his duty to advise me of the death of his purser, Elford Hynmers who, he understood, was my son. Enclosed in the package, he explained, was a copy of Elford's last will and testament, recovered from his sea chest, along with the other personal effects he had dispatched separately.

'I did not know,' Benjamin said. 'My brothers, Ma...' He set both hands to his cropped hair, then dragged them down to cover his face, shoulders heaving with the sorrow of it all. 'Simply that we sometimes seem accursed. What happened?'

Accursed. Yes, we have been so ever since the *sadhu*, the Gentues' holy man, had set his evil eye upon us at Madras. I bit upon my lip to drive away the memory, to fight back the tears.

'So little,' I said, wrapped my arms about his now manly frame and held him close. 'Bare of explanation. Regrets to say that my son had been mortally wounded in a brawl in Cape Town itself while his vessel was undergoing repairs. A brawl, Benji. It cannot be, surely? But how Elford had come to be aboard, and sailing, it seems, for the East Indies, the letter does not tell.'

I have not heard from him for almost four years, despite the many times since my release from Bethlem that I have sent letters to the only direction I possessed for him. I had even sent one to Sir Richard Levett, begging him to make every effort for its safe delivery – though I never received a response from Sir Richard either. But those last pieces of news from Elford had been full of endearments and I have them with me now, read the words afresh. His ambition to soon be back in England, his fortune made, he claimed, in Turkish tobacco, in opium, and all those other trade goods. There had been two in the previous year also. His promotion as Chief Factor not only for Smyrna but for Aleppo and Constantinople also. So what had happened? His fortune lost again somehow?

Benjamin broke free of my embrace, held me at arm's length, stared deep into my soul, seeking sense and solace there.

'A brawl,' he said. 'That does not sound like him. Unless…'

I recalled a night at the Theatre Royal, when Elford had accosted Streynsham's future brother-in-law, Peter Legh, and some of his Jacobite friends.

'Unless?'

Oh, I knew what he was thinking. He would recall that frightful scene the last time we had all been together. Ten years ago. The only time Elford returned home from Smyrna. The welcome dinner I had arranged at Broad Street that had turned so sour around the confession of his gaming debts. Is there some connection here?

'Nothing,' he replied. 'Do you think we shall find out more?'

'Perhaps this is all we need to know, Benji. For now. The will shall have to be proved, after all. Chancery again. It must be for the court to decide if more details of poor Elford's death ought to be gathered.'

'How can this be?' he said. But I think I know the answer. My own wickedness, that is how.

'Too cruel,' I told him, unable to hold back my tears anymore. 'I need time alone. Shall you break the news to Ursula?'

His turn now to comfort me, drawing me close to his breast where I buried my face in the camphored cambric of his shirt.

'And have Abigail fetch you a posset?' he whispered.

'A posset? No, but you may send the girl to me anyway.'

Not the posset I needed and, once he had left me, I quickly set pen to paper. A note to Matthew Parrish. Brutal, telling him I should prefer not to see him again. That I had made a terrible mistake. For I cannot shake this sense of divine punishment and I shall not risk repeating the sin and, thereby, risking the life of my only remaining son – or, for that matter, any of the girls. It was the work of only a few moments and, all the time, there were those images of Elford: the day I had rescued him from the sea wall at Fort St. George; the look on his poor face when I told him he must be sent back to England; his cry of anguish the night Seaton had left that dead babe in our house; and the silences that had fallen between us after he sailed for Smyrna.

'You wanted me, madam?' Abigail was bobbing in the doorway, for all the world like an overfed pied wagstart.

'Yes,' I said. 'If you would be so kind, my dear. Might you go into Chesham as quickly as you may? Deliver this note to the post-master for me.' She looked none too pleased, for the walk would take her the best part of an hour. But I reached into my purse, drew out a shilling. 'This for your troubles,' I said, then thought about Benjamin's offer of the posset. I delved for a shiny silver crown. 'And take this to Apothecary Barlow,' I told her. 'Tell him that I need a bottle of Sydenham's Elixir.'

'Of course, madam.' She curtsied.

'But Abigail, that shall be just our secret. You understand?'

The laudanum bottle stood precisely where I had eventually forced myself to place it. There, in full view upon the dining room's fire mantle, as a reminder. It seems a fitting place, for this is my favourite spot in this whole enormous house, from which to contemplate both sides of my accompts. The losses, yes. But also the blessings. From there I can gaze out of the west windows to the box hedges beyond. Or north, across the herb gardens to the servants' wing.

'Must it always be Derbyshire?' I said. 'It seems so far.'

'Always, Mama?' Annie replied, picking over the bones of the meal we had shared. 'Whatever do you mean?'

She set down her fork, but I was thinking of Streynsham, of course. At Codnor. And so rarely now in London. Though I am no longer there either, so I suppose it makes little difference. I love it here at Latimer, yet it occasionally feels like I am exiled, in permanent mourning for my lost ones.

'Nothing at all, my dear. And thank heavens the weather has broken at last.'

Three bone-freezing months. Ice floes in the North Sea and the Thames Estuary. The Great Frost, to match the chill that had settled in my heart after last summer's news.

'Otherwise we should have been at Staveley after Christmas. James says he needs to be in his constituency.'

Elected unopposed to Parliament. For Derby.

'And you are recovered sufficiently for the journey?'

Why do I still fuss so? She is a woman now, full grown, of course. No great beauty perhaps, but such amiable expression, her eyes like blue Golconda diamonds to match the sheen of her Italian silk brocade.

'Are we ever recovered from the loss of a babe?' she said. 'Even one lost so early?' A mis-birth. My own mama was afflicted with so many of them and I have experienced the same myself, though I noticed she was looking at the mantle shelf. 'I'm sorry,' she said. 'That was thoughtless of me. Poor Elford.'

'It has never been opened,' I smiled, pointed at the bottle with my knife. 'Though I had to wrestle Satan himself to leave it so. The battle lasted several months, yet I beat him in the end.' I saw by the look on her face that she thought me somewhat deranged, and I believe she may be right. 'Until the queen's tragedy, which seemed to put so much in perspective.'

'It had the same effect on me,' she said. 'The loss of all those infants. And then the dear Prince.'

One of those rare occasions when our poor nation has been united. In grief, of course. For Her Majesty's consort was, I think, an ineffective but much-loved fellow.

'Seventeen children lost, my dear. All those ailments she suffers. Now this. They say it has driven her to distraction. But let me call for tea.'

I pulled the bell rope, which brought plump Abigail quicker than I had expected. And not Abigail alone, but Merrick our chief steward also, asking whether madam should care to retire.

'Truly?' Annie laughed when the girl had cleared our plates and gone to do her duty, while Merrick had helped us from the table, opened the door to the vestibule. 'You have an abigail whose name is really Abigail? La, it is too much.'

'I am sure your father would find it amusing too,' I said, as we crossed the corridor and seated ourselves more comfortably upon my old but much loved Broad Street settle in the withdrawing room.

'He becomes more insufferable by the day,' said Nan. 'Have you seen the portrait? No, I suppose you would not. James is outraged. Enormous. You would think it is Papa who is the Duke from his posture. He stares out at us, as though Chatsworth in the background might be his own. His diamond ring, his silver snuffbox, the black boy who seems to be dancing attendance upon him. And James himself depicted as some callow youth. And not simply a single version but several. One even on copper.'

It was simply as I had expected, and Elihu's audacity no longer surprised me.

'You will try again?' I said. 'For a babe?'

'Of course. And meanwhile Kate has promised to name her own in my honour, should it be a girl.' She must be due any week now. My second grandchild, though I fear it will be as difficult to see this one as it has been with little Dudley. 'But Elford's will,' she went on. 'It has been proved?'

'His entire estate left to Benjamin. To help finance the Chancery claim against your father. Not that there was much left once all was settled. Debts everywhere, it seems. But can you not stay at least for the service?'

My brother Richard – who was always especially fond of Elford, perhaps because he bore our father's name – has determined to arrange a memorial service at St. Edmund's and I shall travel back to London for it.

'Mama, you know that I cannot. We have to be at Staveley for Easter. But when you are in town, shall you catch up with old friends?'

She tried hard to make the question seem innocent, but Annie was never the best of dissemblers.

'Do you pry?' I snapped.

'Not at all,' she said. 'It was simply that Benjamin told me you have few visitors now.'

I stood, took myself to the open mullion glaze. There was a pleasant breeze upon my face, the smell of wood smoke from the gardeners' bonfires, the gentle sound of singing voices from the chapel.

'Sir William Langhorn came to stay a few days,' I said. 'Streynsham on another occasion.'

'But nothing further from Mister Parrish? James speaks with him often now he is returned from France. On the last occasion he seemed to imply that he must have done something to offend you, though he would not be drawn on the manner of it.'

It is almost directly over our heads, the guest Rose Room where I committed the crime for which God punished me so harshly.

'It is possible to simply tire of a person's company, is it not?'

I have hardened myself against him, naturally. Not sufficient to merely avoid repeating my sinful act with him, for I must drive all wanton thought from my mind also. A battle almost as bitter as that with the bottle. I even set about the burning of his correspondence, all those letters that arrived after I wrote to dismiss him, each of them still unopened when they went to the flames. Items of poetry he has sent me over the years too. All gone now, except where I have copied verses from them into these journals. Only one exception, which I could not bear to see destroyed. The coded lines he wrote to Sir William Cavendish, alerting the old duke to my perils while I lay imprisoned at the Bethlem Hospital. This one.

I find myself once more in Pauper's place,
Impov'rished poet with the Janus face.
No words nor lawyers' tricks with which to lend
Much-needed freedom to a Bedlam friend;
A saintly woman, pure and clear, I feel
Is now a martyr to another's wheel,
Unjustly prison'd by a husband's wrath,
No sin committed but the spoken troth.
And none, Nobility nor Merchant, ought
To cage our loved ones merely for their sport.
So now, for her, I sanctuary crave
In honour of the service once she gave.

Saintly? Pure and clear? I doubt he thinks so now. Yet this ode did indeed bring me my freedom, and I must cherish it.

'Like you tired of Papa, perhaps?' said Annie. It was quite sudden, a hint of acrimony.

I should probably have said something regrettable but a knock on the door heralded Abigail's return with the tea and the ceremony of its serving. And by the time we were alone again I was at least more measured.

'You feel pity for him,' I said, turning to confront her. 'I am guessing he now bemoans the fact that you and Kate are gone. Ursula here with me. Finds himself alone. Though I shall not allow you to heap upon my shoulders whatever guilt he causes you to feel for his loneliness. It simply surprises me he has not suggested moving the Nicks girls and young Elihu into Queen Square with him. Or shipping them all off – lock, stock and barrel – to Plas Grono.'

She turned her gaze from me. 'Ah, I see he has already made the suggestion.'

'Shall you never be reconciled with him?'

She sipped at her saucer.

'He betrayed me very badly, Nan.' I would have elaborated but now, since Parrish, the words, the protestations, seem somehow hollow. 'And then there was Bedlam,' I said, finding myself back on firmer ground, and resuming my seat beside her.

'He speaks so highly of the boy. A prodigy, he says. Fluent in French and dances bravely. Still insists his mother shall be proud of him when she returns to England. Mama, he talks of buying a country house for her. Where they may drink ale together. La, the shame of it. You must do something. If not a reconciliation, then — well, I know not, but...'

'Annie, my dear,' I said. 'There shall be no reconciliation. Trust me, I have already taken steps to spare you this indignity.'

My heart almost stopped dead. The shock. I had been tending Mary Anne Campion's burial stone once more, assisted by Ursula – bearing armfuls of Corn Marigold and White Marsh Mallow – while we each exchanged pleasantries with Reverend Burrough, when one of the stable boys came running to tell me.

'Governor Yale asks to beg your pardon, ma'am. But he would appreciate a word.'

'Papa!' cried Ursula.

I had to press a hand firmly against my bosom to help still the tremulous trepidation fluttering within.

'Yes, my dear, but perhaps you might finish our work here while I speak with him in private. You may see him later.'

'And I shall assist you, Ursi,' said William Burrough. I believe the chaplain has some particular fondness for her simple piety. It is a mutual affinity, it seems, for the disappointment I had caused her evaporated again at once.

But what could this mean? It vexed me all the way back to the house where I found Elihu seated in the reception hall. Unkempt, his clothes mired with filth, his periwig shabbily neglected. And he looked more abjectly miserable than I had ever seen him.

'You have done well,' he murmured, after our uncomfortable and clumsy greetings, and I had led him into my front parlour.

'I doubt you have travelled all this distance to admire my furnishings.'

His only response was to d'off the peruke, letting it fall to the Turkmen and scratching at the stubble of his head.

'Ursula is at home?'

'At the chapel. She will be here presently. But, again, she is not the purpose of your visit.'

Tears sprang in his eyes, rolled down the florid cheeks as he bit his upper lip, the entire face seeming to collapse in upon itself. I must confess that it moved me.

'No,' he spluttered. 'This.' He took from his coat pocket a letter. Two letters, in fact, and I could think of only one thing that would have distressed him so much.

'Mistress Nicks?'

He nodded his head, wiped away the tears, drew out a kerchief and blew his nose.

'My old friend Harrison has written me from Texel.' He waved one of the letters at me. 'She is gone, my dear. Last Christmas. He was there. At Fort St. George. A terrible illness. Harrison says he never saw anybody fight so. Brave, he says. To the last. But gone, Catherine. Gone.'

Despite myself, I felt almost upon the verge of weeping too. Such a contradictory relationship I had endured with Katherine Nicks. And here was Elihu, nobody else to whom he might turn in his distress except his estranged wife. For what? Sympathy and condolence upon the death of his whore?

'I am sorry for your loss, Elihu,' I said – and I meant it. 'Her affairs, they are all set in order? The children?'

'Harrison is an able fellow. He has set all to rights,' Elihu continued. 'And Katherine's sister has broken the news to the girls. To young Elihu too. I could not bear to do so. And she has provided for them admirably. Six thousand pounds to be divided between those here in England.'

'You did not venture so far as Latimer simply to break the news of her death, I collect. Nor to share the details of this inheritance.'

'I did not,' he replied, and wiped his nose once more. 'The tragedy of it, my dear. I still wrote to her from time to time, did you know?'

From time to time, indeed. I know from Annie that he penned six or seven letters to her each and every winter, dispatched upon the various outbound vessels through January and February.

'Truly?' I said, as innocently as I was able. 'And had you done so this winter past, never knowing she was already gone?'

The tears began to flow once more and I offered him refreshment. It did not surprise me that he needed something stronger than tea, so I summoned Merrick, asked him to fetch the arrack, which I know he keeps in his steward's pantry, across the reception hall.

'Cruel irony,' he said, once the glass was in his hand and the sobbing brought under control. 'But you are correct. About my main purpose here. Though I knew you should want to hear the news from me, in person.' Why on earth should he imagine so? 'No,' he continued. 'It was this.'

The second letter. I recognised it, naturally, for I had written to her early last year, several months before that visit from Annie. It would have reached her in July gone. And from what I could see, he possessed only the outer page, with one folded portion bearing the simple direction. *Mistress Katherine Nicks. Through care of the Governor. Fort St. George. Madras Patnam.*

'Did you...?' He was about to say more but instead sat with his mouth hanging open, unable to finish.

'What?'

He turned the sheet over in his hands, though gingerly, as though there was something fearsome about the vellum.

'Winifred Bridger,' he said. 'I still do not understand how you managed so easily to have her sent back to Madras.'

'She was a thief, was she not?'

'It is not entirely common for thieves to be deported. Exiled. And the circumstance, it was all so strange.'

Tears forming in his eyes again. He gritted his teeth and I saw they have begun to rot.

'I asked His Grace to intercede on her behalf,' I said. 'With the Sheriff. Clemency. That is all.'

'You know that she believed...'

'Her husband to have been poisoned? And now, dear Elihu, you think I somehow afflicted my letter in such a way as to cause Katherine's death.'

'No, that – that would be too monstrous. But the rest of it? This is all that Harrison sent me.'

'For the rest my letter merely confronted her with the lie she told me. About you not being the father of her youngest children. For I have seen the boy's likeness, Elihu. There can be no doubt about his heritage. Yet despite that, despite your passion for an heir, you have not named him so. Nor Charles Almanza either. It would have been easy, with either of them. The pretense that they are your godsons. And nothing unusual in naming a godson as heir. But it is not so

147

simple, of course. For you, an heir must carry your name. The Yale name. And arranging the adoption of your name – well, it would all be so public. And the truth? You may be very fond of Elihu Junior in one way, but you look down your nose at him just a little, do you not? The blood not quite pure enough. And Don Carlos? A Jew for his mother. It would never do, I think.'

That was indeed the substance of my correspondence to Mistress Nicks. Embellished a little, it is true. But enough, I think, to persuade her she had no future here in England – unless she chose to live here, hidden away somewhere, far from public acknowledgement.

'That is nonsense,' he raged, but I noted the shaking of his hands as he poured himself more of the arrack. 'They are indeed merely my godsons. We have had this discussion before. Always the same. I should be proud to have either of those fine boys as my heir.'

He threw back the liquor in one swallow.

'Is it, so?' I said, deliberately smoothing my matron's grey skirts. 'When I was last in town, my brother Richard put me in contact with a very interesting fellow. The new London agent for the Massachusetts Bay Company. He had been making enquiries about you and, since you were at Plas Grono with the Nicks girls, Richard arranged for me to meet him. His name is Dummer. Jeremiah Dummer.'

'How dare you!'

'I thought I might be of some use.' Such feigned innocence. 'And he told me an interesting tale. He has an associate, it seems, in New Haven, Connecticut. A certain Reverend James Pierpont, himself connected to those of your family still living in that area. It was Pierpont who had suggested that Mister Dummer might make your acquaintance. Why? Because he knows you have sent to New Haven with a view to naming one of your young New Haven relations your heir. Young David, is it not?'

'And what has this to do with Dummer? Or you, for that matter? I have made no final decision about any of this.'

He slammed the glass down so hard upon my occasional table I thought it must surely shatter.

'To me it matters nothing,' I said. 'Except to confirm the matter about which I wrote to Katherine. That her own son will never be your heir and that you consider him rather beneath you. For Dummer, he is informed that you are considering the possibility of bestowing some charity upon one of the Oxford colleges and he wishes to persuade you, instead, that you might support their new Collegiate School in Connecticut.'

I could almost smell the sweet scent of appeasement seeping from the carved oak panelling. A charming fellow, this Dummer, thirty years my junior, but the kindest and most affable features I have ever encountered.

'That at least makes some sense, I suppose,' said Elihu, settling back in his chair. 'And he will know that my Uncle Hopkins helped establish the New Haven School.'

'I remember,' I said. Indeed, it had been my first duty when he had returned from India, breaking the news of his mother's death, and that of his Aunt Hopkins – the old lady made insane through an attack by savages upon their home at New Haven itself.

'Why did this Dummer fellow not contact me directly?'

'Because you were at Plas Grono, I believe, with the Nicks girls. Risking their lives, it seems.'

His head jerked quite violently. Shock that I should know, perhaps.

'We were in no danger at Plas Grono,' he protested. 'And, besides, my standing within the Church is well known. It is Dissenters like you, Catherine, who should be fearful. Rightly so, as well.'

I have been greatly detached from it all, of course, here at Latimer. The preachings of that wretched High Church Doctor Sacheverell and his incitement to violence against all Baptists, Presbyterians, Quakers and Methodists – against anybody not strictly worshipping in the Anglican tradition. Some deluded perception that "their" England has been infected by Dissenters and that they, themselves, have been marginalised in our society. Then the failed attempts to prosecute Sacheverell for his activities, to ban him from preaching and, in response, his supporters forming mobs across the country to attack the homes and meeting houses of those they now see as their enemies. The reports from London have been terrible. But I heard the news that Wrexham has also been badly affected, riotous and brutal assaults upon individuals and their property.

'They are no better than the Jacobite banditti,' I said. 'It surprises me to find you so in sympathy with them.'

'And why not? Those Whigs in Parliament have done nothing but favour their own. Rogues like your friend Parrish. False brethren who menace both Church and State. But at least this further election has seen them rejected.'

Another General Election, a new Parliament, and the Tories now firmly back in control.

'You can hardly blame Parrish,' I said, more defensively than I had intended. 'He is returned to France, they tell me. In service to the Queen.'

Sir William Langhorn has kept me informed.

'Then pray God the Frenchies take him for a spy and send him to the gallows. And at least we now have family in Parliament to protect our interests.'

'Your meaning, sirrah?'

'Our son-in-law, Dudley. Did you not know?' I did not, and I sat mumchance as he told me of Dudley's election for Thetford. Interesting since, all that time ago when I had agreed to help Parrish turn the young man to our purpose, to provide us intelligence about his cousin, we had thought the promise of secrecy about his predilections, the occasional priming for his gaming debts, would be sufficient to keep him in our pocket. But now? Does he believe this new position will provide him alternative protection? Immunity? Perhaps.

'I did not know,' I replied, and the ghost of a smile appeared across his maudlin aspect. As though he were pleased with something.

He snatched up his periwig, stood to leave. Yet it seemed my own news had fed not only his curiosity but perhaps also his ambition.

'And this Dummer, now?' he said.

'I advised him you might, indeed, be interested in his proposition. That he should contact you at Queen Square. Or it may be that Reverend Pierpont will write you. But if I had known you would come here to accuse me of Katherine's murder, I might not have encouraged Mister Dummer quite so much.'

'I made no such accusation.'

'It sounded very much that way. But, if not, then you came here because you have no friends to whom you may turn. You have acquired such a host of folk who despise you, Elihu. Poor Edisbury at Erddig, now entirely ruined and at risk by your avarice of selling his beautiful creation, his home, for a fraction of its value. The Myddletons at Chirk. So many others. All victims of your griping usury.'

'Those who borrow know well the lender's tune,' he protested. 'And I have friends too. I do! But this at New Haven, there will be a price for Dummer and his associates to pay.'

'A price? Your name above the door?'

'Oh, much more,' he said. 'Much, much more.'

Monday 5th November 1711

The explosions almost deafened me. Heaven knows that my hearing is not so acute as it once was and I find that, as now, the onset of winter brings me frequent pain in my joints. Especially my legs. Sixty. How I hate being sixty. But that noise! Not what I had expected.

Then the dizzying colour of it all, the rockets in red and green, the silver stars, the golden rain of painted goose quills, the hissing and wriggling fizgigs. A double wonder, filling the night sky but reflected for us all at the same time in the waters of the lake with which the Staveley gardens are blessed. And that tableau of St. George and the Dragon, each charging to meet the other in a blaze of pyrotechnical delight, then retreating again, only to repeat their attacks once more, with every advance the spectacle more astounding – and the gunpowder stench of rotten eggs ever more pervasive.

'A most propitious date,' I murmured to Streynsham as we shivered upon the terrace at the rear of Staveley House, 'to mark my grandson's baptism.' Annie's son, William, just two weeks old and baptised yesterday. So, tonight, fireworks out there in the park, though I hoped these would be confined only to some local Master Gunner's artificial contrivances, rather than the confrontations I feared. Fireworks also for Gunpowder Treason Day, and to mark the anniversary of good King William's landing at Torbay.

'Shall you not come inside?' he said. 'We shall freeze to death out here. I fear my bones are grown too old for this climate now. And when you have seen one of Babington's bangers...'

'Soon,' I replied. 'There are too many gathered here that I should rather avoid. For now.'

I glanced along the lines of guests huddled against the stone balusters, saw their faces illuminated by turns in flame scarlet, or plunket blue or primrose yellow.

'Well, you are correct about the date, at least,' said Streynsham. 'Marred only by that rogue Sacheverell choosing it to rant on behalf of his High Church fanatics. And fireworks? Bonfires? I remember how many there were to celebrate his release.'

We still reel from the mobs and riots, all this time later, the country divided down the middle. Everybody choosing sides. High Church or non-conformist. Irreconcilable. Nobody making any effort, it seems, to heal our rifts. Had I still been in London I would, without doubt, have resumed my old practice of carrying that pocket pistol within my skirts as protection. But Latimer is safe enough and the weapon must still be at the bottom, I suppose, of one of those packing cases still awaiting my attention in the stables.

'One or two fanatics among these guests also,' I said, pulling the hood of my cloak tighter around my face, the warm comfort of the wolf's fur tickling my cheeks and so sheltering me from the frigid wind that I paid no heed to the opening of the terrace doors immediately behind me.

'Fanatics you say?' That voice. Elihu, of course. How I despise that voice. So much I did not even trouble to turn. 'How in the name of Sweet Jesu can adherents of our true faith be called fanatics?'

'I can think of no other word to adequately describe them,' Streynsham replied with just a tinge of sarcasm. 'The back alleys of London ruled entirely by High Church or Jacobite banditti.'

'You would deny, sir,' said Elihu, 'that the faithful of our nation's official religion now take second place to every Tom, Dick or Harry non-conformist in the land?'

With him a young man, no more than a boy.

'Of course I deny it,' said Streynsham. 'Shall we compare the finances enjoyed by the Church of England with those you claim to be its preferentially treated competitors?'

'Or the personal wealth,' I snapped, 'of its representatives.'

'You should have them all in penury, I suppose,' Elihu scoffed. 'Like mendicant friars of old.'

I studied the boy. Twelve, I surmised. He reminds me of a cupid I once saw in a painting by Master Vermeer. His own hair, though curled, powdered and pomaded, beneath a broad-brimmed hat. A russet riding coat to keep him from the cold. Fine clothes, and I noticed that Elihu, too, seemed better attired than I had seen him for a long time.

'And you, boy,' I said. 'Elihu's nephew, I collect.' I saw Elihu bristle at my presumption. His cousin's son, of course. First cousins once removed, therefore. But nephew would suffice. Yet I knew it was not the title that annoyed him. My husband began to speak but I cut across him. 'What think you, David? The Church – should it mimic papist idolatry or the more modest method of our Lord Jesu?'

More thunderclaps overhead and we were all showered with sparks.

'Every penny is a propagator of prayer,' shouted Elihu, beating at his clothes and his eyes fixed skywards for further hazards. 'We were remiss, Governor,' he told Streynsham. 'Remiss not to bring our Gentues and Mussulmen to the Bible. Remiss indeed. But we shall correct that now. Missionaries, sirrah. We shall finance missionaries.'

Annie's last letter to me before she gave birth: news of her father's subscription to the publication of a prayer book in Welsh; his newfound faith in the Society for the Propagation of the Gospel in Foreign Parts; his lavish donations to St. Giles Church in Wrexham. He is become devout, it seems.

'You did not answer me, nephew,' I said. 'Some warlock's familiar eaten your tongue? They speak of India, but before you know it, they will be sending missionaries to Massachusetts, to Connecticut and the rest. You know not your peril, boy.'

His cherubic face had suddenly adopted a look of pure contempt far beyond his years.

'Ma'am,' he said, 'I must assume you may be my uncle's estranged wife and, if so, perhaps you are not quite yourself – as he tells me is so frequently the case.' I found that my mouth was hanging open. 'You need have no fear,' he continued, as a bursting rocket overhead turned his angelic features a shade of demonic vermilion. 'We worship as we choose in Connecticut, and no end of missionaries, I reckon, is like to change things. Woe betide any who try to interfere with that, too.'

'Still,' said Elihu, 'we find puritans and papists everywhere. We shall root them out. Indeed, we shall.'

Is this the price he will demand from Dummer and his college? A matter on which I must reflect. Some condition that it must be

High Church and nothing else. Some modest revenge for the way his family was driven from the colonies by that same puritanism. And this damn'd young man – I could no longer think of him as a boy – how do I feel about him? Resentful, of course. David Yale. Here at Elihu's side in place of my own sweet little Davy. Some distorted mirror image. This rage that is never far from my reach. Davy would have been twice this lad's age. Of course, he would. But my baby is trapped behind the bars of time. Forever young. Forever lost, even if he sleeps in the Almighty's arms.

'It would have saved us all a great deal of pain,' I said, 'had you possessed such clarity of anti-papist passion where Seaton was concerned.'

He threw up his hands in exasperation.

'Again,' he shouted. 'This again?'

A wind blew up and a sulphurous fog threw a shroud around us, stung my eyes.

'And this philanthropy?' I went on. 'Some fear for your own mortality, I collect.'

It was Streynsham's aphorism, of course. Philanthropy driven by fear of the hereafter. And the generosity always springing from almost bottomless coffers, the sacrifice as artificial as those fireworks, meaningless.

'God in heaven knows,' said Elihu, 'how ill I can now afford the contribution I make in His name. Your own son, madam. He has ruined me. And I am hit so many ways.'

The Chancery decision at last. Over eight thousand pounds to be paid Benjamin – thirty years of interest upon that eight hundred Elihu had failed to grant him from dear Joseph's estate. How I had laughed. But that loss to him is almost as nothing compared to the second blow fallen upon his fortunes. The collapse of Sir Stephen Evance. The disappearance too, therefore, of the many thousands, they say, Elihu had on deposit with him. Well, he will never see a penny of it now and though it shall not cripple him – far from it – it must still be significant, for there was a bitterness settled upon his features that was more than simple reaction to the stinking smoke. And I know he must be hurting also from the other news Annie had imparted – Jeronima's boy sent by his mother to London, but fallen ill at Cape Town. Likely to die there. I could offer him no crumb of comfort, lest it disclosed Nan as the source of so much intelligence.

'Then,' I said instead, 'it must grant even greater solace to have this young man with you. And had you paid Benji his portion, as I begged you so many times...'

There was a particularly ear-splitting explosion and I pressed hands to the sides of my hood, though it did nothing to drown out his words.

'Your son shall discover, madam,' he yelled, 'that when the devil delivers, he soon takes back double as his due.'

'Traitors in waiting,' said Streynsham. 'Look at them.'

We had returned to the house, to Staveley's great hall. Merry-making musicians, drunken dancers, cascading Flemish chandeliers, circulating servants. And one particular cabal of young bucks. Something about politicians. That congeniality they pretend to exude wherever two or three are gathered together. And these were all friends of Kate's husband, Dudley's new-found parliamentary associates: Wyndham, white-wigged and silken suit to match, with his meteoric rise – Member for Somerset one moment, Master of Her Majesty's Hounds the next; foppish, toad-like Forster who, Streynsham had told me, had been representing Northumberland these past three years; and Henry St. John, with his pursed lips, his boyish face, one of the Queen's Secretaries of State and a Privy Counsellor – the hypocrite non-conformist now taken the High Church sacrament, not through piety but for his own opportunism. It was some consolation that we did not have to tolerate their company at dinner earlier, a more intimate and delicious gathering.

'Annie tells me that James had no option but to invite them,' I said. 'To this, at least. Her brother-in-law's particular request. Dudley has told him that with their assistance James might regain his seat. Or at least avoid reprisals.'

Poor James, defeated in last year's General Election, which had swept so many of these Tories into power. The price he had paid, I suppose, for voting in favour of impeachment for that rabble-rousing rogue Sacheverell. And like all defeated candidates in our elections these days, he is bound to be hounded like any vanquished foe, regardless of his brother's prominence.

'Does he wish to regain it?' said Streynsham. 'The last time we spoke he was all a plague upon Derby's electorate. To threaten him so.'

'I doubt he will stand while the Tories have such a hold.'

I lifted a cup of mulled sack from a passing manservant, began to edge around the dance floor, Streynsham at my back. An apology here, a curtsey there, as we moved through those presently admiring the steps of three couples enjoying the *Beauteous Grove*. This year, the very thing. How apt the title, graceful as a spring morning. A breeze brushed the countless candles and the dancers' shadows shimmered upon the floor's bright-polished black oak. And, goodness, this was a grand affair – a true Cavendish family display that would have made even old Sir William envious.

'And no sign of that changing while Harley is so much in the Queen's eye.'

'The nation's eye,' I sneered. Oh, I have followed Harley's rise. Defection from one faction to the other. His cousin, Abigail Masham, now Her Majesty's favourite and her influence, surely, which has made him Chancellor – the same influence that has seen Sarah Churchill dismissed from the Queen's service, and which now seems certain to also aid the downfall of John, Lord Churchill too – once Jacobite, then the nation's warrior hero and become Duke of Marlborough, now disgraced for no reason than that he has pursued our enemies with more vigour than the Tories find affordable.

'Baron Harley now,' Streynsham corrected me. 'And these cronies of his, likely to be elevated as well before long, I'm guessing. Such a pity, that we cannot turn young Dudley back to our purpose.'

We stopped to exchange pleasantries with an old Turkey merchant and his wife. A Turkey merchant like my papa, and the fellow's father had been a director of John Company – so a close friend of Streynsham's – until his death last year. Condolences, therefore, while I cast an envious eye over the wife's *robe volante*, the blue taffeta flounce with its silver threads. Sterling silver, I imagined. It made my own salmon pink mantua seem so drab by comparison, the embroidery, pearls and tassels of my stomacher just a little out of fashion. My new eardrops, I think, saved the day.

'Well, now you see the reason,' I said, once we had moved on and could observe those three Tories more closely from the adjoining dining salon. 'No problem for such as those to bail out the bilges of Dudley's gaming debts. And whatever predilections he may have, he will be safe from scandal with Harley's protection and that of Abigail Masham.'

'We are all now mere spectators in the sport, Catherine. I had not realised how much we relied on old Sir William. Our new Duke of Devonshire is a decent enough fellow, but not his father.'

No, James's brother is most definitely not his father.

'Then we must perchance look to Walpole,' I said, remembering the first time I ever heard the name. Parrish, of course, when they had both been elected to Parliament.

'Our problem, my dear, is that it would take a miracle to put our faction back in power and Walpole into any authority.'

'It is a wonder,' I replied, turning my glance once more towards Wyndham, Forster and St. John. 'You cannot blame those rogues themselves, standing for election. For they work so hard to demonstrate their own stupidity, yet the enfranchised vote for them regardless.'

I had watched them, in their cups, sidling towards the terrace doors, the chafing dish in which the spiced sack was warming, and then, giggling like infants, surreptitiously emptying a small vial into the pan. Gentlemen of a certain kind, I think, seem to find such pranks irresistible at social gatherings. But here? To celebrate a baptism?

'I sincerely hope,' said Streynsham, holding up his own glass, 'they have not so afflicted any of the earlier brews. We had best inform your son-in-law, I collect.'

Powdered licorice root and senna, or something similar, I supposed. Childish. The whole room will stink of farts within the next hour. Or worse. But Streynsham was correct and I called over one of the manservants, whispered in his ear.

'A miracle to unseat them?' I said. 'Or an unthinkable amount more of the *pishcash*, liquor, patronage or bullying bravos it seems necessary to now secure seats in our poor Parliament.'

'Parrish tells me that all the networks upon which we used to rely for intelligence are presently under Harley's direct control. Under his thumb. Those upon whom we should rely to espy the schemes of High Church plotters or Jacobite fanatics are in the pay of those who are, themselves, High Church Tories or sympathisers of the Pretender.'

There it is! Sacheverell and his seemingly countless followers still disclaiming our Glorious Revolution as a sin against God, the denial of His anointed King.

'Parrish himself?' I said, the name almost sticking in my throat.

'Matthew can do only so much as the times allow. Harley and the Tories are pressing for peace with France even if it means abandoning our allies. The popular thing to do rather than the right thing. Parrish will be forced to play his part in the negotiations. Though he has given me some hint that he may have made at least one useful connection. You have heard from him?'

Across the dance floor, a couple of grooms were carrying away the tainted chafing dish, despite the protestations of those Tory fools, now being admonished – though in the most timid of ways – by Nan's husband.

'He has written.'

Of course he has. Those now burned, unopened letters, each earlier stained with the tears of my longing, my regrets, my duty to my surviving children. And here came my only remaining son now, bearing a plate of meringues from the sideboards.

'Mama,' said Benjamin. 'And Sir Streynsham. Give you joy of this glittering occasion. Your family all well, I hope, sir?'

'Elizabeth is somewhat indisposed. A minor ague, it seems. And though we are scarce twenty miles south of here, at Codnor, the journey can be taxing for any in ill health.' He spoke the words with such honest feeling I almost believed him, as I had done when he made the same excuse to me earlier. But even in the best of health, Elizabeth would not have been here, still resents my friendship with her husband. I have always laughed at her jealousies. Until now. For, since Parrish, I find it easy to paint myself the harlot, lacking in moral fortitude. So why should Elizabeth Master think any better of me?

'But your mother,' Streynsham was saying, 'tells me you are due to abandon her.'

'Not for too long, I imagine. But there is need for a Prothonotary within the Court of Common Pleas in Lancashire. Preston, to be precise. An honour, they tell me.'

'Preston is a neat little town,' Streynsham laughed. 'I know it well – though full of Tories, of course. But those meringues look delicious.' He turned to me. 'Shall we not partake, Mistress Yale?

For I believe my system to now be restored after all that exposure to the elements.'

At least, I thought, this Preston adventure might take Benji from Elihu's reach – the threat he had made against him. Perhaps just prattle but I was glad of the contact Sir Richard Levett had made for him. Perhaps some consolation, he had said, for his lack of information about the precise manner of Elford's death. An assault by common ruffians, he had confirmed. My son simply in the wrong place at the wrong time. Nobody even brought to justice for the crime, so far as he was aware. But Elford had already long left his service. No reason given. But taken ship, he believed, to the Bight of Benin and thence to Cape Town where he seemingly hoped for service with John Company. Met only his end. Another of my sons drawn back towards Madras Patnam, perhaps? I shall never know. But it tears me apart during my own solitary hours to think of their lonely resting places – Richie in Porto, Elford at Cape Town, Joseph Junior somewhere in the depths of the China Seas. God willing, my little Walter – Davy too, I hope – has my own dear Joseph to cradle him.

'I am certain I shall survive, sir,' Benjamin smiled, as I shook away my dark visions and we crossed to the plentiful serving boards. 'But have you met stepfather's latest ward, Mama?'

'That insolent colonial pup,' I said.

'Another godson,' Benji replied.

'Another David,' I murmured, while Streynsham filled a small platter with cold meats and I fingered the locket at my throat.

'Another mouth for Governor Yale to feed,' said Streynsham, cursing as he spilled some mustard down that fine flowered waistcoat. 'He will perhaps need to spend even more time in his diamond closet to foot the bill.'

'I simply wonder how long it will last,' Benjamin replied, taking Streynsham's plate and allowing him to dab at the mustard with his kerchief. 'For he wafts this way and that with the wind. Dishonest, erratic wretch that he is.'

There he was, over in a corner, surrounded by admirers, Kate on one arm, Ursi on the other. He noticed me and scowled.

'He will simply auction some further part of his collections,' I laughed. 'For they are still considerable.' Indeed, they are: books of great value; sealed chests of tea; jewels galore; paintings by many of the Flemish masters; and much besides.

'Or perhaps,' Benjamin mused, 'he will wait for the Nicks girl, Betty, to become heavy with child, then auction her too, like some poor Yarico.'

Something else that seems on everybody's lips. Mister Addison's *Spectator*, the satirical tale of Inkle and Yarico – Mister Inkle selling his Indian maiden paramour at auction when he realises she is pregnant, his only concern being to sell her for an even higher value given the baby. Two slaves for the price of one would never answer. Precisely the sort of calculation Elihu might admire.

'Benjamin!' I said. 'To speak so, in front of your mother.'

'God's hooks, Mama, you have some strange sensibilities. But sir, have you yet spoken of Mister Parrish? She will admit almost nothing to me, pretends that all is right with her world when, plainly, there is something seriously amiss.'

I shook my head in exasperation. Or embarrassment, perhaps.

'You forget yourself, sirrah,' I snapped, though I was watching Annie and James weave their way among the guests, thanking them for their attendance, politely signalling the imminent end to the festivity. They make a fine couple, and I rely so much on Nan's intelligence for news of her father's trials and tribulations. It made me wonder...

'All the same,' said Streynsham, 'I suspect we shall soon see him home.'

I trembled at the thought. Anticipation or trepidation? Both, I know.

'Is there nothing,' Benji said, 'that can stop the Tories forcing through this peace everybody demands.'

All Marlborough's victories, at Tournai, Malplaquet and Mons. Then last year's successes at Saragossa and Port Royal. Setbacks, of course, like Brihuega. But French Louis is on the run, almost begging for terms. If we do not finish him...

'Nothing,' Streynsham frowned. 'And the Frenchies will then be free to begin their plotting afresh. Her Majesty cannot live forever and if the succession hangs in the balance, you can be certain our old enemies will exploit it to the full. And those young fools,' he pointed with a piece of forked roast beef towards Forster and friends, 'will have led us to the brink of disaster, not for the nation's best interests but for their faction's short-term gain.'

If he intended to prick my conscience, it was a masterful stroke. I had forsworn any further involvement in Parrish's dark arts, that I might better keep my family about me. But now? My older boys all gone. Two of my daughters married, become mothers themselves. And those other determinations I had made? My possessions and my freedoms recovered. My personal fortune largely restored. My revenges upon Katherine Nicks and Winifred Bridger each for their own reasons become resolved, both of them expunged from my life.

There is still Elihu, of course, and while it may have satisfied me a while to simply see him denied elevation, his violence towards me, my incarceration at the Bethlem Hospital, now seem to demand greater retribution. Besides, all this loss of our influence, his new-found devotion to his High Church Tory friends of the Society for the Propagation of the Gospel might well serve to help him become a Baron Knight even now. Perhaps a blow against Elihu also requires a blow against those same Tories.

Then, Parrish. I have forsworn further intimate involvement with him. I remember his words, how starved our faction suddenly finds itself of reliable spies. Surely it must be possible for me to serve his purpose, to serve our faction, without risking amorous entanglement and thus risking God's wrath. And in this way settling my debt to old Sir William Cavendish for granting me the luxury of Latimer.

These matters raged about my head as Nan and husband finally made their way towards us, the other guests already thinning. Now there is a man, James, I thought, with his own accompts to settle against the Tories. Yet they seek to draw him closer, to bring him within their inner circles. One of my sons-in-law may no longer be biddable to our purpose, but young James…

I could neither smell nor see anything out of the ordinary, but I knew I was in the worst of dangers. The market at Chesham, yesterday. Wednesday. Chesham, of course, with its High Street and High House too. All flint and red brick, cobbled yards, courts and comfortable passageways. Its cage, pound and stocks unmistakable. The Crown Inn. Vendors and their wares, the chaos of crowds and their bustling clamour. All so familiar. Yet something here that did not belong.

The song. Ursula's voice. Though Ursi, I knew, was at home. Latimer. A couple of miles away.

'The hero Prince of Orange came
With forty thousand men.'

'Daughter?' I cried. 'Where are you?'

But then I saw that the higglers and hucksters all offered the same item for sale. Flowers. Lily-of-the-valley, so that I knew I would see him.

He gazed at me with lascivious eyes from the cage that should have contained him, though the grille stood open. Seaton was squatting within, his shanks bare beneath some coarse belted robe and revealing the spiked metal garter we had once found in his belongings.

'And with them up the hill he went
Then also down again.'

'She sings so fine,' he said, waving a long, evil blade as though to keep time with the rhythm.

'Be gone, spirit,' I told him. 'We are done with you.'

But he laughed, leaping from the cage, his face become that of a slavering, snarling wolf.

I ran. Out past the Pond and down towards the Latimer path. I ran just as I had when merely a girl. Ran like the wind. And though Seaton was limping along, slowed by that bloody encumbrance upon his thigh, I still could not keep ahead of him.

The Chess was in view now and I followed it past the three corn mills, my chest heaving, but Seaton whispering calmly in my ear.

'I thought I should find you here,' he said. 'Chesham. Oh, Chesham. The Den of Dissenters. The Hive of Heretics.'

Then it seemed that not only Seaton was at my heels, but all those other enemies come back to haunt me too. Scarred Katherine Nicks, her wounds as open and wet as the day Seaton had cut her. Winifred Bridger's husband, John, bearing a decayed skull I could not properly distinguish. Those traitors I had helped send to the gallows. A veritable host. But I wept with joy to see Parrish on the track ahead of me.

'Stop,' he yelled. 'In the name of Her Majesty, stop!'

It made no difference. Cold hands grabbed at me, pawed and scratched at my limbs, and I knew that, this time, he could not save me. I delved beneath my skirts, found nothing.

'You should have kept it with you, witch,' Seaton howled.

'Here,' said Katherine Nicks. She pursued me no longer but stood, instead, alongside Matthew Parrish, her features young and whole again. Homely but whole, as they had been when first we met. Young Katherine Barker that I had so despised. 'Take mine,' she said, and handed me the knife with which she had stabbed Seaton at Deptford.

'Use it,' Seaton taunted me, 'and I shall take the rest of your brood.'

'Use it,' Parrish smiled, 'and play your part, Mistress Yale. Remember the wisdom of your mama.'

I took the blade, though it was a knife no more, now become that old pocket pistol. I cocked the piece, pointed at my tormentors, and the nightmare exploded into a thousand shards of shattered glass.

First light found me in the stables. An apple for Pebble, my new pony, then dragging aside the contents of all those packaging crates, with which I had not troubled myself since arriving here. Until I found it. The pocket pistol Seaton had once left, cocked and loaded, in little

Ursula's hands when he had invaded the sanctity of my home for the second time. I carried it back to the house, swearing to myself that it would never again leave my side, set it upon the table by my bed while I rummaged in the secret compartment of my old travel chest – for the bottle that has lain there these ten years or more, I suppose. The bottle of artichoke juice, which Matthew himself had left with me so long ago. Would it still answer? Might it still possess the same efficacy?

In the travel chest, too, the sheet of paper upon which Parrish had penned that poem, the only thing I had kept of the many missives he had sent me. In the centre of the plain side I wrote his direction at Duke Street then I carefully folded the blank edges to meet each other in the middle, applying the artichoke juice along their length before applying two more folds, top to bottom, and sealing wax, to conceal the simple message within.

Midsummer, Lion Tower, Noon

They say the creatures roar but, of course, they do not. Rather, a disquieting deep-throated bark. I could hear them quite plainly, as the hackney driver, who had conveyed me from my temporary lodging at brother Richard's, insisted on waiting with me on Great Tower Hill at the end of the path leading to the western extremity of the fortress.

'Lots o' strange folk about, lady,' he said, scrutinising the line of those waiting to enter the Menagerie. 'Best not to be out 'ere alone. Know what I means?'

I did not. He was a scrawny little rogue who looked like he could not fight his way out of a damp sack, and I could feel the more persuasive comfort of the pocket pistol beneath my skirts. Besides, I have taken to carrying a stick, more adornment than necessity at the moment, but with riotous rascals reportedly still upon the streets at times, it seems a reasonable affectation while I am in town. And at least I did not have to wait too long. For here came Parrish, elegant in sky blue and a chestnut periwig in a style perhaps now too young for him. So I paid the fellow his due and went to greet Matthew as he climbed down from his own carriage, a small mongrel pup beneath his arm.

'Give you joy of this new friend,' I said, and fondled the creature's ears.

'I did not expect you would truly be here,' Matthew replied, d'offing his hat in a most formal manner.

'And I doubted, sirrah, that the artichoke juice would still perform satisfactorily.'

'It has an advantage, Catherine.' There was bitterness in his voice. 'The constancy of a simple vegetable. Such a shame we higher species have such difficulty with that quality.'

'This shall be a very short reunion indeed,' I said, 'if we cannot find the peace between us for which I had hoped.'

'These days, you will find, 'tis seldom what we expect. Finding war is absurdly easy, but peace so very hard. Still, the prerequisite is normally to find some neutral ground upon which to begin discussion. The Menagerie would not have occurred to me for such purpose, yet here we are.'

'I have never been,' I said. 'But at least you have come prepared.' I scratched the pup's nose and it licked my fingers. 'And the weather so fine. Shall we begin?'

We joined the tail of visitors while I pressed him for yarns of the part he had played in the preliminary negotiations with France, here in London, last October, then at the start of the Congress in Utrecht this January gone.

'But then poor Walpole was arrested,' he said, 'and I was damn'd by association. My services no longer required. One of the reasons your invitation intrigued me, of course. I thought we might visit him while we are here.'

The Tories must have paid a fortune in handbills to make sure we all knew the story. Venality and corruption were the accusations against Walpole. Arrest. His own faction providing clear evidence of his innocence. Impeached for notorious corruption all the same, and found guilty by the Lords. Expelled from Parliament and confined here in the Tower ever since.

'They say,' I replied, as we neared the entrance gate, the smell of the beasts within now almost overpowering, 'that there is a longer file of Whig leaders awaiting their turn to see him than of visitors for the lions.'

'He is our very own king of beasts.' He handed over the puppy to the gatekeeper, who deposited the creature in one of the cages already filling with half-starved cats and dogs, and we were ushered across the drawbridge into the Lion Tower itself, and thence to the stairwell.

'I would have been more than happy to pay the thruppence,' I said, as we began to climb the spiral steps. 'The pup would have made a perfect companion for you.'

'I had rather hoped, Catherine, that today's *rendezvous* might resolve that problem for me.' He waited for my response, though I did not take his bait and merely continued hauling myself up the stair rope, a little breathless, my skirts lifted as high as I dared. 'Besides,' he eventually went on, 'it is not a question of money. My friends told me that bringing live meat for the lions is a better way of ensuring their welfare than putting pennies in the gatekeeper's purse. And the pup would, without doubt, have become rabid before too long, living on the streets.'

'And we have enough rabid dogs on the streets already, I collect. The reason I suggested this meeting.'

'That is all? The letters I wrote, do I not deserve an explanation, Catherine? You received my condolences, of course.'

'Of course,' I lied. One of those unopened letters, I suppose.

'Only – well, I had wondered. Some connection perhaps. Your news about Elford coming so soon after...'

It was easier to pretend I had not heard when, at the top, we paused for rest, then ventured to the rail from which we could look down into the circular yard below. One of the eleven great cats, a magnificent mane of darker hair framing its head, lay asleep in the summer sun, while two others – lionesses, I think – prowled without respite around the outer limits of their freedom. Another was drinking from the cistern at the yard's centre, noisily lapping up the brackish water. The smell was feral, musk and malice.

'I read that a friend of the keeper's maid,' I said, 'had her arm stripped to the bone when she tried to stroke one that had previously seemed so placid.'

'One of the females then, I would suppose,' said Parrish, in a tone that I believe was supposed to convey irony. 'But my letters... Great heavens.'

The fellow had almost walked straight into us, pushing his way back towards the stairs. The same squat and foppish Thomas Forster, Member for Northumberland, that Streynsham had pointed out at Staveley last year.

'Parrish,' Forster said, almost screaming the word. Perfectly reasonable to be surprised by their rencounter, naturally, but at the time one might have assumed he had seen a ghost. 'I had thought...'

He had dressed for the weather, a lightweight suit of creamy silk and his own hair tied back, ribboned and powdered beneath his camel-down cocked hat. There was a young woman at his side whose skirts perfectly matched the tone of his attire.

'Shall you not introduce your friends, Thomas?' she said, quite innocently, when it must have been plain to the world that there was enmity between the two men.

'No, my dear, I shall not.' Such venom in Forster's voice. He possessed that guttural speech of the north but mingled with cadences of the Scottish tone one might find, for instance, in a native of Edinburgh. Northumbrian, of course. Then he noticed me. 'And you, madam...'

He took his companion's arm, almost dragged her towards the stairwell, while the other visitors around us exchanged knowing looks, or whispered to each other – either that or made pretense of having noticed nothing untoward. In any case, Matthew edged me towards the less crowded outer portion of the roof.

'You know him?' he said. 'Forster.'

'By sight and reputation only. I suppose we shall now be the subject of gossip among his friends.'

'Or worse. An associate of mine told me only yesterday that Forster has been spreading ugly tales about my own fiscal probity while I was in service to the Crown. Probably nothing, but you should be wary of that wretch, Catherine. And gossip? Not the best of things given, I assume, some reconciliation with your husband.'

'Reconciliation?' I said, gazing over the battlements, over the moat and wharf to the river, which shimmered in today's sunshine, all its many craft lumpish and listless upon the slack tide. 'Whatever makes you think so?'

'Streynsham told me about your various family gatherings. You must have been spending much time cheek by jowl with Governor Yale. And since I had been so roundly exorcised from your life – well, it seemed the obvious explanation. Or the least painful, perhaps.'

If only he knew how much I longed to hold him at that moment, to kiss his poor distressed face. To tell him how close he had come to the truth – about how God had punished me with Elford's death. About how I would not risk Benjamin too. Yet I could not.

'Come,' I said. 'I think I have seen enough of the lions.' But I went back to the inner rail, took a final look at that sleeping male. 'He seems untroubled by his confinement, do you not think? I hope it may be so. And you also heard there was new talk of a knighthood?'

We made for the stairwell, waiting for the newest group of visitors to finish their ascent.

'But dashed now,' he said, 'by that piece in *The Spectator*, I think. Did you read it?'

'No, Matthew,' I whispered with unrestrained glee, as we began our downward journey. 'I wrote it.'

I thought he should fall, saw him clutch at the rope as he missed the step. But I had contacted Mister Addison, suggested that if he truly wished to enliven morality with wit, to temper wit with morality, then perhaps a new member of the Spectator Club – those fictitious characters through which his broadsheet so eloquently parodies Tory foibles and hypocrisy – might be added to his pages, and I attached a sheet purporting to be written by a certain Governor Elijah Snail.

'God's hooks, you jest?' He stopped and looked back up at me from the shadows of the tower's curved wall. 'No, I see you do not. That soliloquy. I had wondered about its author, never dreamed – wait, those journals, you are still filling them with your observations?'

How I had enjoyed it. Governor Snail's boasting: about the authority he wields at his Welsh church; about how he keeps the congregation in good order and allows none to sleep in the pews but himself; about his devotion to the Society for the Propagation of the Gospel; about how delighted he has been to learn that the Society recently inherited those Codrington sugarcane slave plantations in Barbados; and about how their ownership of the slaves can therefore bring such a ready and constant supply of heathens to the Bible – not to mention the dividends brought to the purses of those who hold interest in the Society itself.

'We are blocking the stairs,' I said, urging him down the rest of the steps and past those folk impatiently waiting to make the climb. 'But yes, still writing.' We were back out in the sunshine and following the moat's causeway along to those enclosures around the Middle Tower for the Menagerie's other inhabitants. 'And now,' I told him, 'my daughter Annie knows my guilty secret too. For last time she came to visit I had foolishly left the journal in full view. I refused to let her read the contents, naturally, though she was astonished to learn that I have kept up the practice all these years. And curious also to know whether I make mention of her. Or the baby. Did you know there is another on the way?'

We had arrived at the Monkey Room, where we found ourselves mingling, without any barrier between us, with the chattering, screeching occupants, swinging from the unlit hearth's fire mantle, or chasing each other around the incongruously placed furniture. I suddenly found myself feeling guilty, for it reminded me so much of the Bethlem Hospital.

'Then give you joy,' said Matthew, 'of yet another grandchild. And Governor Snail – Elihu must have read it surely. No hint, I hope, that you might be the author?'

'None. Mister Addison is very careful about his sources, but tells me that Elihu's High Church Tory associates are so anxious just now to be portrayed as hindered by prejudice against them – rather than as the pecksniffs represented by Governor Snail – they have quietly distanced themselves from him, and thus from any support for Elihu's knighthood.'

We had stopped to watch the antics of a leopard, inexplicably savaging a parasol, and I hoped the beast had not already swallowed its owner. Unlikely, of course, since it was confined within one of the caged vaults, the arched dens, within the walls.

'He must be furious, I would imagine,' he said.

'I suppose so. Though Nan tells me he is very low in any case. It seems that news arrived in January. Jeronima's boy dead at Cape Town. And Jeronima there, apparently also at death's door and determined to be buried with her son. She has sent Elihu a silver platter of great antiquity, it seems, as a remembrance.'

'A tragedy,' he said. 'This is your evidence, then, that there is no reconciliation between you. Your contact with Elihu only through word from Anne, and then your attack against him in *The Spectator*. But if not that, I find myself exiled with no obvious reason. Lured to a meeting that serves no purpose except to wound me more deeply. And listen to me, is it not pitiful?'

Yes, I pitied him, hated myself for forcing him to so expose his inner feelings. Pitied him, in part, though I would not show it. Not now.

'I had a dream,' I said, as we moved on to view a truly sad specimen, a Hudson's Bay brown bear with glazed eyes and great patches missing from its fur. 'In truth, a nightmare. An old one. Seaton come back to haunt me. To taunt me. And there you were,

Matthew, to rescue me once more. Only this time with advice that I have not been able to shake from my head. Advice that I must play my part in these dangerous times. To heed my mother's wisdom.'

We hurried past a strutting ostrich and then an evil-smelling creature like an over-sized badger that I could not name.

'How, precisely?' he said. 'And why? The war cannot end well for our allies, for the Dutch and Austrians, now that we've abandoned them by this separate peace with France. Oh, each will finally reach their own settlement, but not before more of their blood is spilled. There is this to be said for it, I suppose – that without us being at war with France, the Jacobites will themselves be neutered. The terms already require French Louis to recognise a Protestant succession when the Queen dies, God bless her. Yet that is plainly something the French would have to concede anyway, without us deserting our European friends.'

'And if they find other allies? The pope? The Spanish? We met Thomas Forster earlier. He has been paying court to my son-in-law. Not Dudley, but young James. Promising the earth. And James may not be his father, but he is no fool. I spoke with him, persuaded him that old Sir William would have expected him to do his duty. Oh, he shied at the suggestion of spying, but at least agreed it would be a betrayal of his papa's memory if he discovered anything in the nation's interest and did not disclose it. Easy enough then to convince him I might act the conduit that relays such intelligence to his father's most trusted agent, Matthew Parrish.'

We had reached the end of the enclosures, a pit with a writhing green serpent, thick as a tree trunk. Some jackals. Three dejected white-necked eagles. A brace of owls. And a tiger, all the way from India. But by then I had tired of the place and begged that we might leave.

'To me?' he said, as we began our return journey. 'Have I not explained that I no longer have influence – or interest even. I am done with it as, I recall, you were yourself.'

'I was wrong,' I told him. 'We are still in danger. My children, all I hold dear in this country, at risk. And if you are, indeed, done with it all, why do you still maintain intelligencers in Paris? Please do not bother to deny. Streynsham told me. A crucial agent, he said.'

'Sempill,' he replied. 'John Sempill, cousin to the Pretender's own agent in Paris. I had indeed determined to cast him back into the swamp. Well, we shall see. And if James does discover anything of interest I am obviously happy to receive the intelligence – though I cannot promise that we shall be in a position to take advantage. So, that is all? A business arrangement, pure and simple. Nothing more.'

'Nothing more,' I said, as we arrived back at the Lion Tower and I saw him lift a hand to his face, press the fingers into his frustration and disappointment. 'Though perhaps one thing. I had not realised how much it would distress me, to see these creatures caged so. It has brought me too close to my own imprisonment. Do you think, if it is not too late, we might purchase the pup's freedom? It might make a handsome gift, a companion, for my Ursula.'

'We may be just in time,' he replied, though without any feeling, 'for they do not feed the creatures until three o' the clock, I collect.'

He completed the transaction, though at considerable cost, and I took the small hound from him as we came once more to the drawbridge. In the brightness, I did not immediately perceive anything amiss, until I heard the cry.

'There, that is the rogue.'

Forster again. And with him a couple of equally beefy, bearded guards wearing the scarlet doublets and black bonnets of the Tower's Yeoman gaolers. Or warders, perhaps, I know not the difference. One of them began shouting about a warrant as they advanced over the bridge's timbers towards us. I saw Parrish's hand reach for the blade that normally would have hung at his side but which, thankfully, today he did not carry.

'Arrest?' he cried. 'What calumny is this? What charge, sirrah? And what jurisdiction?'

The yeomen took his arms, though with some reluctance, I thought, both turning towards Forster for reassurance, or further instruction.

'Corruption, Mister Parrish,' Forster cried. 'Corruption and conspiracy.'

I took a step towards Matthew's captors, though with no idea how to help him, yet one of the soldiers pushed me roughly aside, the small hound under my arm baring its teeth at him.

'If there is a warrant,' said Parrish, 'I would see it now. And I would see it served, also, by the Sheriff or his Constables.'

'In good time,' Forster replied. 'For now you shall find new lodging within. Perhaps near your traitorous friend Walpole. Take him!' They dragged Matthew back through the Lion Gate.

'Tell our friends, my dear,' he shouted. 'But fear not for me. I shall fare perfectly well. But tell our friends.'

I tried to follow but Forster quickly crossed the bridge, blocked my passage, caused me to recoil as he thrust an excessively large nose into my face. At close quarters his eyes iron-grey were afire with a fanatic's fury.

'And you, Mistress Yale,' he said. 'They told me your meddling days were past. That you no longer posed a threat to our purpose. I see they were wrong.'

'I see them everywhere,' I told Walpole. He stood with his wife – another Catherine – in the line ahead of me as we all waited to take our turn at congratulating Mister Addison in the Bridges Street Yard, pleasantly roofed since my previous visit, to form a temporary reception lobby for the Theatre Royal. At least it protected us from the April showers. 'Less frequently when I am at Latimer though, even there, strange fellows have been reported in the village or spying outside the gates.'

As though Forster's words had taken human form to pursue me.

'Here in London?' he said, raising his voice above the general clamour of the crowd. His full boyish face was framed by an equally replete light brown periwig, the same tone as his velvet and silver-braided justaucorps, the long jacket reaching to his garter. The same colour, in fact, as his wife's skirts.

It is indeed a long while ago that I was last there – with Elford, of course, for *The Old Bachelor.* Tonight's performance was very different. At Mister Addison's personal invitation. The first performance of his *Cato.* And the whole city must have been in attendance.

'It seems,' said Benjamin – back at my side from Preston a while following Easter last week, 'Mama can never leave my uncle's house without some rogue watching her from the neighbours' doorways, or the coffee house windows, or following her every step. Still, she tells me she has led them a merry dance all these months.'

He spoke the words lightly enough, but I know he fears for me, and I have had to restrain him several times already when he has sought to accost those watchers. Yet now we each took a glass of celebratory champagne from a green-liveried footman passing down the line. Such a crowd. Such a quantity of champagne, it must have cost Mister Addison a pretty penny.

'I have never seen the attraction,' said Mistress Bracegirdle, who stood just behind us, shuffling along with several admirers, 'of despoiling good wine by the addition of bubbles.'

Retirement seems to suit her. Though, to be fair, she can have been little more than thirty when she made her last appearance on the stage. It would have been – what, a year or so after she abetted my escape from Bedlam? But obsessed, said the gossip-mongers, with the threat of being eclipsed by her younger rival, Annie Oldfield, appearing in tonight's play as Marcia, Cato's daughter. An exaggeration, surely, for there she was, a sumptuous crimson and gold mantua, and her hair dressed so beautifully – oh, I was riddled with envy.

'We owe Mistress Bracegirdle,' I said to Walpole, 'for agreeing to come out of retirement on our friend's behalf.'

'Truly?' he said, and sipped at his glass, but I think his mind was elsewhere. Another trait of politicians, that in a crowded room they cannot conduct one conversation without searching for another that might be more to their advantage.

'There,' said his wife, 'that is Mister Cibber, is it not? So hard to tell without his face paint. So clever, the way they do that.'

Colley Cibber, indeed it was, Walpole confirmed for her benefit. Cibber, receiving adulation for his supporting role as Syphax to Barton Booth's lead as Cato.

'You owe me nothing,' said Mistress Bracegirdle, while we all advanced a few paces more, 'given the care you are taking of Mary Anne's resting place.' She had taken, I now knew, a keen interest in the short-lived career of the old Duke's beloved mistress. 'Such a waste. It would have been a merry jape. Though a cancellation fee might be due, I suppose.'

My first scheme to secure Matthew's release. A version of our previous escapade. She would seek permission to attend him in the Tower, take some lady friends with her, create confusion and then smuggle him out dressed in women's clothing. But, by then, Walpole himself had been released and a secret parliamentary committee set to investigate the allegations of corruption against Parrish. A warrant had seemingly been issued for his arrest on the very morning of our visit to the Menagerie, and Forster must have known this – hence his surprise at seeing Matthew still at liberty.

'Perhaps you should charge the cancellation fee to Harley and his Tory friends,' said Walpole, his attention now back upon the conversation. 'For it would have been his agents, Mistress Yale, who followed you to any meetings with this good lady. And it would have taken little to fathom your connection, your possible intent.'

'An outrage, all the same,' said Benji.

Well, the corruption charges against Parrish had been dropped before we could put the plan into effect, and the place of his imprisonment had been changed, after three months, confining him instead in the house of a Queen's Messenger, in Brownlow Street, the secret committee now examining a second wave of allegations – conspiracy. That would have been last September. And the grand conspiracy in question? Some ludicrous collusion, they claimed, between Matthew and the Dutch or Austrian plenipotentiaries, to thwart the peace negotiations.

'In that case,' said Mistress Bracegirdle, 'perhaps we should simply consider the contract fulfilled if, indeed, our encounters at least helped secure Mister Parrish's move to a more comfortable location. And he seems not to have suffered any lasting ill.'

There he was, ahead of us in the line, more or less free at last, pulling at my hapless heart, and surrounded by well-wishers. I asked Benjamin if he would be so gracious as to escort me to him later, and he happily agreed, though for now I could not resist a brief and whispered word with the former actress, now my friend.

'No lasting ill,' I fingered her elegant sleeve. 'I hope not. I so feared I might lose him. And it was a comfort simply to know you were so willing to help. But the wine,' I said, setting my barely touched glass upon another passing tray, 'you are quite right. My papa, who once worked in the wine trade at Alicante with the great Moscoso, would turn in his grave at the very thought of this adulteration. Bubbles indeed.'

'Simply a triumph,' I told Addison when we reached him. It looked as though he had not shaved for a week, and those thick, unkempt eyebrows beneath an equally unruly peruke while, for some reason, he wore a black banyan over his coat of imperial purple.

'Triumph, you say?' he replied, cupping a hand to his ear.

It was indeed like some riotous assembly but still I named

Benjamin, and Addison in turn introduced those of his major subscribers – Pope, Garth and Steele – each it seemed with his own subsidiary entourage and female admirers. Sir Richard Steele I already knew a little, and we had a connection of sorts. For, like Elihu, he has been persuaded by Mister Dummer to make a donation of books to that Collegiate College in Connecticut. Tonight, though, I was pleased to see him in company with Sir William Langhorn, with whom I have done some renewed business of late, assurance for cargoes, and so far we have made a comfortable profit. But this evening he was engrossed with the young woman at his side. Young – did I say young? It barely does it justice. A mere chit of a girl. Mary Aston. Part of me finds it hard to be critical. And she reminds me of somebody, though I cannot quite recall who that might be. And she has the merest hint of an accent. Dutch perhaps. Or French even. But Sir William? Married so briefly, after all, and I know he is lonely. Turned eighty now.

'Ten years in the writing, my dear,' said Addison, waving to a party of friends leaving by way of the Bridges Street alley. 'And I simply penned it for my own amusement, never thinking our poor country should be brought so low that it would resonate so greatly.'

Cato, and the tyranny of Julius Caesar. I could not help thinking of all the times Elihu had quoted from Shakespeare's telling of the tale. Yet Addison's lines are such a thinly veiled attack on the despotism of Harley's Tories.

'And to resonate,' I said, 'even though your dear Spectator Club is no more.'

I had written several more pieces as Governor Snail but *The Spectator* itself had almost been forced into closure.

'Oh, I shall revive it, I'm sure,' Addison smiled, and shook hands with Samuel Garth as he too departed.

'It rather astonished me, sirrah,' Benjamin told him, 'to hear the raucous applause of the Tories on their own side of the theatre almost drowning that of our own faction. Great heavens, are they so deluded?'

'They did not stay to offer their kind opinion,' Addison laughed, waved his arms about. 'You see? All gone.'

Was he correct? I had no idea, looked around the room but could see not a single one of the laurel leaves that Harley's Tories have taken to wearing upon their coats and hats.

'The land of self-delusion,' said Sir William Langhorn, 'is precisely the territory they inhabit. Do you not think so, pretty Mary?'

Pretty Mary nodded her head. What, in the name of Sweet Jesu, did he think he was doing? And who *was* it she favoured? Not that it mattered.

'It makes perfect sense,' Addison replied, 'that each side should see liberty as a patriotic virtue. Though how Harley's lapdogs can interpret any of their policies and practices as synonymous with liberty is quite beyond me. They will win the election, Sir William?'

'I fear they shall increase their majority again,' said Langhorn. 'And Harley filling his own coffers like Croesus. His South Sea Company now received a Royal Charter, I see.'

'I was convinced there would be reprisals,' I said. 'After the attempt on his life.'

'Attempt?' Addison gave a snort of derision. 'Total fabrication, I should say. Imagine, you wish to assassinate somebody so you fit three pistols in a hatbox, with a string tied from the triggers to the lid, so that – well, it is risible.'

'And that turncoat Swift conveniently on hand to spot the string,' Benjamin laughed. 'To save Harley's life.'

But there had been reprisals, of course. That secret parliamentary committee had turned its attention to the possible perpetrators, imaginary or otherwise – and since poor Matthew was already in confinement, he made an easy target. I had constructed another plan, naturally, to secure his escape from the house of the Queen's Messenger, to have him smuggled abroad, but when this new and equally facile investigation began, he was moved once more, this time to the home of the parliamentary sergeant-at-arms, with no guests allowed except by permission of the Speaker.

'Though Parrish,' I said. 'What now for his life? He may be free at last but his career as a diplomat...'

I almost choked on the words. Yes, the destruction of Matthew's career had been a reprisal, the price of his release. But we are in such minority now, I cannot believe the rest of us are far from danger.

'There is a storm coming, Catherine,' said Parrish, though he did not look at me. 'I simply thought you should be warned.'

He had most formally begged a few moments privacy and I had

replied that we might kill two birds with one single stone, for Benjamin was keen to explore the theatre's pit, rather than the boxes from which we had viewed the performance. And thus we observed the proprieties, breaking away from Addison's now thinning band of acolytes, heading back down the entrance passage into the theatre itself, he leaning on his walking cane, beaver hat tucked under the arm of his russet coat. And me upon my stick. Matthew and myself seated ourselves stiffly upon one of the green-covered benches, while Benji clambered onto the stage. We were just sufficiently alone that we should not be overheard, either by my son or by the fellows paid by the owners – Colley Cibber now one of them, it seems – to clean up the stinking spilled ale, the remnants of greasy mutton pies, the discarded handbills.

'And shall you weather it, my dear?' I said, for his period of confinement had left him looking wan, weakened both in body and spirit. For my own part I trembled at the recollection of those sinful hours we had spent together. The intimacies I shared with dear Joseph had always been gentle, with little adventure about them, but warm and tender for the most part. With Elihu, often fumbling and apologetic, rarely bringing us mutual satisfaction, I think. And that awful occasion of rutting violence. But Parrish – only one night, yet more harmonious excitement than I knew in all the occasions combined that I shared Governor Yale's bed.

'It would be naïve to assume that any of us might weather it,' said Matthew as I shook those thoughts away. 'If you think Harley a rogue, this Henry St. John...'

'I was in his company,' I reminded him, as he set both hat and cane upon the bench. 'At Staveley. He was there with Forster and others of their breed.'

Benjamin tested the resonating qualities of the hall, dramatically repeating some of Mister Addison's best lines. *"What a pity it is, that we can die but once to serve our country."*

'What a pity it be,' grumbled one of the cleaners, his voice just carrying to where we sat, 'you don't piss off an' let us do our work.'

'They pretend it is political difference, of course,' said Parrish, ignoring the rascal. 'But that is nonsense, is it not? More often 'tis petty jealousies, personal enmities, that cause thieves to fall out.' He caught my gaze for the first time. 'Or some private grievance nurtured by one party but of which the other remains entirely ignorant.'

'Such grievance,' I said, 'may still have firm foundation. And the bearer might remain mumchance about the matter for a thousand reasons.' I saw his reaction again, bitter disappointment that he had not been able persuade me to explanation. 'Yet,' I went on, 'St. John – I cannot bring myself to style him Bolingbroke, for it grants him too much honour – is simply a buffoon.'

Harley elevated to Earl of Oxford, of course, but St. John merely to baron and Viscount Bolingbroke. St. John stinging too because he and his Jacobite friends have had promises aplenty from Harley, it is said, but little action to ensure their success. Though, naturally, Matthew's barb was aimed closer to home.

'Mark my words, Catherine, within a year Bolingbroke's star will wax as fast as Oxford's will wane. And then those Jacobite traitors will have the Queen's ear entire. A buffoon can still be dangerous.'

The very thought fills me with dread.

'And you,' I said, 'dismissed after all you have done. Not a single charge against you proven. Every allegation swept aside.'

'Do you not care to hear my warning?' He rubbed at that left arm, which Seaton had wounded so long ago, though plainly still troubling him at times.

'I care,' I said, 'to hear how my oldest friend might deal with the calumnies against him.'

Parrish stood from the bench, turned to me, struck a pose as Colley Cibber or Barton Booth might have done before delivering some great oration. But then his gaze dropped, as though he thought better of it.

'It is the very devil,' he murmured. 'I now understand how Elihu must have felt. Allegations dropped, though no exoneration. But if they can dismiss Jack Churchill after all those victories he brought us – I invested so much in those negotiations, then not to see them brought to fruition. Though heaven knows how it shall all develop. Menorca and Gibraltar stolen from the Spanish. I fear they shall neither forgive nor forget.'

Benjamin again upon the stage: *"It is not now time to talk of aught but chains or conquest, liberty or death."*

'Or maybe time,' I heard that same cleaner, 'you just buggered off.'

'What shall you do, Matthew?'

He was silent a moment, and I gathered the impression he was struggling with a decision, or perhaps with the manner in which he might convey it.

'I doubt it shall trouble you, my dear,' he said, 'though it looks like the army. I met General Wynne in Utrecht, struck up something of a friendship with him. A gentleman of our own faction. And I suspect that is the reason his regiment is now disbanded. But he tells me there is still considerable administration to be undertaken. I am therefore to be made Adjutant to a regiment that no longer exists. But I shall be Captain Parrish again. Half-pay, of course, like the general himself but...'

The army? And a half-pay captain? A mighty fall from grace indeed for one who had risen so high.

'It troubles me a great deal,' I replied, then hurried to extinguish the spark of hope I had seen in his eyes, 'if the storm of which you speak brings more war in its wake. And you shall miss the cut and thrust of politics.'

'I shall climb again, never fear,' he said. 'And there shall be my poetry to sustain me. But what I shall truly miss,' his voice dropped to a whisper, 'is the prospect of being always at your side, madam.'

'Matthew,' I said, 'you shall be forever at my side. But I think you intend a little more. Or perhaps this warning you bring speaks of something else that might sunder our friendship?'

'My contact in France,' he replied. 'Sempill. He has heard your name mentioned. A meeting between his cousin, that agent of the Pretender, and none other than the same wretch, Porter, who carried away young Ursula.'

Carried her away, I thought, then cast her adrift upon the tide so he could save his own neck. All the fear of that dreadful chase down the Thames came back to sunder me afresh.

'And why, prithee, should I still be in Colonel Porter's thoughts?'

'It seems they understand our weakness very well. That being in such a minority robs from us our own sources of intelligence. So Sempill heard them sharing a list of those agents still at our disposal. Those few remaining from poor Captain Baker's network. My own people too. Defoe, I was surprised to learn, still included within that number. And you, also, Catherine.'

Bad enough that I should still be a target for Porter, but were there others in similar danger?

'My son-in-law?' I said. 'James.'

'Nothing. Why? Has he been useful?'

'Once only. It seems they invited him to a gathering. St. John and Forster, with William North. Several others. I have the names. Soundings taken about who might stand with them when the throne is empty once more. His views about the Pretender – the King Over the Water, as they style him. I think he was circumspect in his replies. At least, I hope so.'

'And my only hope is that you should not be at risk again,' he said. 'Or your family.' He glanced at Benjamin, who was still enjoying himself as though he were a small boy again. *"'Tis not in mortals to command success; but we'll do more, Sempronius, we'll deserve it."*

'You lot got no 'omes to go to?' yelled the floor sweeper, leaning on his besom broom.

'How can I protect him?' I said, more to myself than to Parrish. 'Has God not taken enough of my boys for my wickedness?'

It seemed that a veil was lifted from Matthew's eyes.

'God's hooks, my dear,' he said. 'Do not tell me – you cannot believe...'

'Foolish old man,' I scolded him, the deception coming so readily to my lips for, now that he had discovered me, I felt entirely ditched, strangely stupid. 'You seriously think I should be so driven by irrationality. Or that our Lord Jesu would...'

'All the same...' he began. And I could almost read his thoughts. He was remembering perhaps, as I was myself, that Gentue holy man at Fort St. George, the old *sadhu*, and the way I had been convinced by the curse he set upon us.

'All the same,' I repeated, 'you think we are in danger? I told your friend Walpole that their spies already seem to be everywhere.'

'Then the danger,' said Parrish, 'is clear and present.'

Volume Eight

They are here. This journal bears witness to the many times – both before that night at the Theatre Royal, and in the twelve-month since poor Parrish was forced to take up his half-pay service with the army – I believed them to be watching me. But now I know they are here.

At first, today, with menacing clouds gathering in the southern sky, I convinced myself it was simply the presence of that arch-Tory, William Cheyne, now Viscount Newhaven. No warning of his coming, and our May Day had simply commenced according to time-worn lore, myself and Ursula in our matching grey silk capuchins gathering with the villagers and millers at a darkling dawn, they also in their best attire, most brandishing leafy willow wands, greenery in their hats, to waken the ancient crimson-striped pole from its slumbers at the Long Barn, then bear it in reverent procession up to our chapel, singing all the way and heedless of the early drizzle.

'*Now the Season of Winter doth his power resign,*
Aye and Flora doth enter in her glory and prime.'

At the chapel, alchemy melded them with the estate workers, and also youthful Reverend Burrough. Blessings and prayers. Several of them. A hymn too.

'*Let us with a gladsome mind*
Praise the Lord, for he is kind.'

Thus were we all vouchsafed against whatever devilish heathenism had once so inveigled its way into these amaranthine celebrations that Lord Protector Cromwell had no choice but to see proscribed, just as his Long Parliament had banned Christmas because of the idolatry with which it was being observed. Yet that was all so long in the past, it seemed to me from the perspective of my three score years and three.

And now for me to play my part. Tradition. For the master or mistress of Latimer House to garland the Maypole with a mystic wreath of spring blossoms: Bluebell; Yellow Cowslip; white Wood Anemone; star-like Ramsons; and the pale pink of Lady's Smock. The slightest scent of garlic, and the warning hum of bees, also undeterred by the weather or perhaps attracted by the strangely unseasonable warmth. Ursula had gathered the flowers for me, venturing far into the wild woods with only that mongrel hound for company – the same that I had saved from being eaten by the Menagerie lions. My duty to hang the wreath since, in the absence of the Cavendish family proper, the villagers tend to see me as the lady of the manor. Something of respect for the house and its occupants, I suppose, but from our first couple of years here, there has been a kindness also, one that I value most highly. A reminder, perhaps, of the better qualities from the years at Fort St. George. Perhaps more than that, too – the almost deified maternal point of convergence for our intimate community.

'Well,' Reverend Burrough was saying as I took my place at his side for the procession back down to the green, 'one might lead a horse to the trough, but making it drink is another matter.'

He bore a large, ancient wooden cross before him and, while he may have hoped for solemnity, the villagers had already taken up *The Ballad of John Barleycorn*. Harvest song it may be, but it seems a ritual favourite for all occasions. And, despite the hour, many of the singers were already fuelled by a surfeit of strong beer.

"Whose name was Sir John Barley-Corn, he dwelt down in a dale;
And had a kinsman dwelt him nigh, they called him Tom Good-Ale."

Raucous and joyful, though not to Ursula's taste.

'May we not persuade them to another song of praise, sirrah?' she said to the clergyman, while her black and white brindled hound scampered about her legs.

'I fear the moment may be lost, my dear,' he replied, with pity in his eyes. Pity and considerable affection. I have hoped so many times that something might develop between them. She will be twenty-five very soon, after all, and I have tried to broach the subject. But in her own simple half-grown way she merely rewards me with that child-like smile and reminds me that she only cares to be wed with our Lord Jesu. And I swear that, if she only knew of the possibility, she would by now have entered a nunnery.

'We should count our blessings,' I told them both. 'For I remember the May Days of my youth. At the Haymarket. Good gracious, such behaviour. Rank debauchery for an entire se'ennight or more. Papa forbade my attendance, of course, but was finally persuaded to take me there – though only to observe the showmen, the jugglers, the bare-knuckle fighters, the women's foot races. And those competitions to see who might eat the most semolina in the fastest time.'

'And now burgeoned so large,' said the rector, 'that it must occupy its own May Fair fields.'

'As I discovered when I returned from Madras Patnam. I went there with Benjamin.'

The rain was falling a little faster now, and a thoughtful manservant – Rogers, I think – ran up beside me with an umbrello, one that I had brought back from India and which remained serviceable, a more ample protection than my hood alone. And in this way we descended the gentle hill.

'And your son, Mistress Yale – Benjamin, he is well, I hope?'

The estate's village clusters about the sloping three-cornered green – an arrowhead pointing west towards Latimer House itself, and the chapel. The green, with its pair of young elms, is bordered along its northern edge by some fine half-timbered houses, their brickwork painted white, and along its eastern flank by the cluster of the village proper, with its forge, its alehouse, its Long Barn, its cordwainer's shop, its pimping shed. From that eastern side of the green also, the Chesham lane runs south down to the ford and the handrail footbridge connecting us to the world beyond. But everybody's attention today was turned to the green itself, and the pit dug at its centre.

'Still in Preston,' said Ursi, as a team of village stalwarts set the May Pole's foot in the edge of the pit, then raised it, hand over hand, the tallest fellows lending their strength and reach to the task's final effort. It stands as high as eight men and, though it is slender, its weight must be considerable. As usual, a great cheer went up as it pointed skyward, erect, the village blacksmith coming forward to hammer huge wedges in place, keeping it upright. It is a symbol, of course. I am no fool. And I am blessed that Ursula has no reason to make the connection, still firmly believes it serves no purpose except to point our way to heaven.

'Benjamin,' I said, 'expects his work there to last another year. Two at the most. Then he will be back with us, I trust.'

'Let us hope so,' Burrough replied. 'For much may happen in a year. And especially in this tormented world.'

Tormented indeed, but with those haunted words he carried his wooden cross through the ranks now forming about the green, carried the crucifix to the May Pole itself, gave one more blessing before tabor, flute and fiddle struck up the opening notes of *Robin Goodfellow's Misrule* so that, in ones and twos, then greater numbers, husbands and wives, sons and their sweethearts, friends and neighbours, joined hands in a tighter, inner ring, dancing and cavorting in the round, their screams and laughter fit to drive every storm cloud from the heavens. Well, they tried, but the heat was still oppressive, threatening, and Reverend Burrough persuaded us to take comfort in the large campaign tent erected at the green's northern margin.

'It has seen better days,' I said, studying the patches of mildew staining its corners, and accepting a cup of small beer from George Salom, the alehouse keeper.

'A relic of the wars, I think,' said the rector, and set the holy cross carefully against the tent wall.

Parliament's wars, of course. For the men of Latimer served so loyally in Lord Protector Cromwell's armies.

'But you, Mistress Ursula,' Burrough went on, 'shall you be chosen, perhaps, as this year's Queen of the May?'

'I shall not, sirrah,' she snapped. 'For, despite your blessings, that practice is still a heresy. Ruling the crops until harvest time is God's own work, and not a matter for such witchcraft. And not the only sign of the devil's work. Did you not see the fires of hell last evening?'

How could any of us miss them? From the upstairs windows they could be seen scattered across the hillsides. Distant, but a reminder of the satanic forces lurking just beyond the fringes of our modern enlightenment. Ursula has a point, but I suspect her strength of feeling also has much to do with the years when her views were more innocent – and she was never then chosen.

'And who presides over the ceremony this year, Rector?' I said, not without some trepidation.

'It seems,' he replied, 'we are also to be blessed. By the presence of Viscount Newhaven himself.'

'Mistress Yale,' said Cheyne – Viscount Newhaven, as he is become – interrupting my exchange with Master Stride, the village's aptly named cordwainer.

The rain had stopped but the sky was still stained with blue-black ink that seemed reflected in Cheyne's parchment-like skin. He is a man gone early to seed, his fine lavender suit, his waxed riding coat and his periwig all just too small for his corpulent frame. Beneath the coat, however, he was sporting a finely embroidered baldrick, stitched with gold thread like an elaborate chain of office.

'Sir,' I replied. 'I had thought you should have been gone by now, your announcement made.'

His steward, as though he were some potentate's high chamberlain, had made great ceremony of praying silence for his employer and Cheyne made his speech, a half-dozen scurvy rascals at his back. Now made Lord Lieutenant of Buckinghamshire, he had informed us – though perhaps warned us might be more accurate. By the grace of Her Majesty, Queen Anne. The second time this honour bestowed upon him, but now in England's hour of great need.

'The announcement,' he said, staring into the space just above my head, 'simply one reason to bring me here.'

'The entertainment then?' I replied, trying without success to meet his eye.

'Reminds you of India, I collect.' He turned towards our troupe of white-robed Moorish Men, with their blackened faces and clashing scimitars. Ursula had begged leave to see them at closer quarters and I could see her, clapping hands in excitement, beneath another rain-napper held over her by Reverend Burrough, the dog sniffing around the grass for sign of conies.

'The heat perhaps,' I said, leaning a little more heavily upon my stick. 'Oppressive, do you find?'

'A storm brewing, madam. We all know it, I think. Not a good time to find oneself exposed to the elements. To be discovered *in flagrante delicto*.'

We were almost alone in the tent now, as Cheyne nodded his head towards a young couple gaily coming up the path from the water meadows. Grass-stained. Bold as brass. No concern for the bawdy comments that greeted this return from their obvious tryst. For this was May Day, though I dreaded to think how Ursula might react to that public lack of morality. I looked for Reverend Burrough, exchanged a glance of mutual understanding with him, and he immediately tilted the umbrello in the necessary direction, drew my daughter's attention towards a red kite, wheeling and mewing above the village – and away from the scandalous couple.

'There are times,' I said to Cheyne, 'when the season demands we must wear heart upon sleeve. To boldly go out into the world and brave its trials. To create harmony from its chaos.'

The Moorish Men gave a further flourish of their flexible blades, brought them ringing together as they pranced some final circling steps and the lead dancer raised their small miracle aloft, the swords meshed tightly together in a single patterned, glittering roundel.

'Well,' said Cheyne, above the applause, 'you at least have the advantage of knowing you are observed. A comfort, I suppose, to know that little or no evil may befall when you are so closely guarded.'

Unless, of course, I thought, I am more at risk from the watchers than any other source.

'At least,' I tried my best to smile, 'I rarely feel alone these days, sirrah. Am I truly such a threat? To you? To Forster? To Harley?'

In truth I felt far from secure. I believed the villagers, the estate workers, would protect me – but those henchmen of his...

And so much distraction. Some of the crowd returning to the tent for more ale, others – Ursula, Burrough and the hound among them – making their way across towards the smithy.

'Harley, says you?' He laughed. 'Oh, Harley is yesterday's man now. But threat?' Cheyne scanned the crowd, it seemed, for his ruffians.

And there they were, some of them, at least, down towards the forge from which the Chess Mummers were emerging with their hobbyhorse, their flower-strewn attire, their bells and bladders. But no sign of amusement from Cheyne's men at the merrymaking these players intended to engender. No, the bravos looked about them fitfully, on guard, fingering the cudgels hanging from their belts.

'It must be pleasant to be so popular,' I said, nodding towards his retainers. 'Or do your friends have no May Day frolics to entertain them in – from whence *do* they come, by the way? Some sour-faced village, it must be.'

The Latimer House gardeners gave me a hearty salute with their pitchers of beer, but Cheyne chose to ignore my jibe, watched the mummers gather near the May Pole, the crowd closing about them, their narrator loudly proclaiming this year's pantomime. *The Lost Loves of Latimer*, he named it.

'You know, Mistress Yale,' said Cheyne, 'that Latimer should more properly be in my care than your own?'

His mother, of course. Lady Jane – a Cavendish, before her marriage. Poet and playwright. Rabid royalist supporter of the Stuarts. Many years dead now, but she would, I suppose, have been great-aunt to my son-in-law James.

'If you wish to explore any time,' I said, 'you have only to ask. But there, just one more reason for your visit.'

I left him smiling, a sardonic smile. I left him and the shelter of the campaign tent, collected my umbrello and raised it against another thin downpour, made my way towards the crimson and white stripes of the tall spar, stopped at a small hummock from which I might see a little better. Cheyne may have smiled, though I knew it would not be for long. I have been enough years here to know there is little originality in the Chess Mummers' May Day performances. Different from their Christmas offerings, of course, these are thinly veiled parodies on Latimer's many characters. So here we all were: black-robed Father Bug-Rug; Hammershaft the Smith with his over-sized codpiece, sprouting wood anemones; Mad Mistress Yell – myself, of course; and Lord Loppy-Links, a rotund little fellow with the face of a pompous pug. Had the players known Cheyne would be present beforehand? I doubt it, for their skill lies in fast wit and improvisation, and Cheyne's pointless declaration would have been too much for them to resist. So here they were, in harsh and mercurial, hastily prepared imitation of his speech.

'Is this not precisely the problem?' I had not heard Cheyne follow me to my vantage point. 'This lack of respect for authority.'

He tried to pull the waxed riding coat more tightly around his girth but failed miserably.

'I believe it may not be the office that attracts their mockery, sir. And I learned in my first months here to accept the mummers' attentions with a good grace. It is expected, I collect. That on this one day of the year none of us may be above a small amount of mild misrepresentation.'

I saw the tallest of his henchmen raise his head above those of the other spectators, turn a querying glance towards the Lord Lieutenant, and Cheyne responded with a curt nod of the head.

'Yes, respect,' he said, still speaking into thin air. 'And I do not believe, madam, an invitation to be necessary. To visit Latimer. The point, is it not? That as Lord Lieutenant of this fair county I am empowered to investigate any who may be a threat to the realm's security.'

'Me?' I said, feigning incredulity at his implied accusation. 'Perhaps you are insufficiently informed to know, My Lord, that my loyalty to the Crown, my actions in that regard, are beyond question.'

I would have said more, much more, but a scuffle had broken out at the edge of the crowd, a scuffle that was spilling over into the space occupied by the mummers, their performance disrupted. Oh, they tried to continue, their lines shouted for a few moments above the tumult. Then a cudgel rose and fell, rose and fell. There was a loud crack – somebody's pate being broken. And I had no doubt the victim would have been the mummer playing the part of Lord Loppy-Links.

'Stop them,' I yelled. 'Stop them.'

'God's hooks,' he said. 'You have some unruly neighbours, Mistress Yale. A blessing my men are here to restore order. And the culprits shall be brought to justice. You may rely upon it.'

'Is this the Crown you pretend to represent?' I was raging, while Cheyne's ruffians were calmly extricating themselves as though they had played no part in the uproar. But the crowd was not so forgiving. Some were helping the injured, but others were shouting abuse at Cheyne's men, and I knew that I must intercede, either to prevent more bloodshed or to also offer succour to the mummers. Yet Cheyne took hold of my wrist.

'The Crown,' he mused. 'But he or she who wears the crown may change, Mistress. And when it passes, as pass it must, to Her Majesty's natural and hereditary successor in the eyes of God, shall your loyalties remain intact? Those close to you tell us you have tried to involve them in spying upon gentlemen whose loyalty to that successor are, indeed, beyond question.'

James? I wondered. But no, this would be Dudley and my efforts to gather intelligence from him about William North, his cousin Lord North and Grey, that openly avid follower of the Pretender. I was certain that would be it, and I tried to free my arm, enraged but frightened also. What did he mean by 'us'?

'You shall release me, My Lord. You have no right. And I do not follow your drift. Her Majesty's natural and hereditary successor is already named. Has been so these many years past.'

So many years. Since I emerged from one of my addictions and Nan there to fill the news I had missed. The crown to pass to Sophia, Electress of Hanover. More importantly, Sophia, granddaughter to James the First. Stuart blood in her veins. Beyond Sophia, to her Hanoverian descendants. But many High Church Tories, and the Jacobites to whose coat tails they now cling – scoundrels like Cheyne, Forster and St. John, Viscount Bolingbroke – make little secret that they can secure a Stuart succession far more easily by handing the throne to the Pretender himself. So, another bitter smile from Cheyne.

'I believe, madam, you follow my drift perfectly well.'

I finally pulled myself from his grasp, while Cheyne's men, four of them, were backing away from the May Pole, cudgels at the ready and ugly enough to keep the angry villagers at bay.

'Do I, indeed?' I said. 'Then this is some form of warning.'

'Warning, no. You have already seen how a simple word in the correct ear can bring a fall from grace, a spell in the Tower, perhaps. And, as I said, not a time to find oneself caught *in flagrante delicto*.'

The workings of my brain are certainly less efficient than they might have been in my lesser years. But they generally arrive, sooner or later, at a conclusion. Besides, there was plenty to distract me.

Yet here he was, seeking evidence of my continued efforts for the faction he so despises; emphasising his authority over me; his absurd implications that I might be caught in some treasonable act; his jibe that he requires no invitation to visit Latimer; and those rogues he had brought with him. Why? And where were the others? At least two of them I could no longer see.

'Lord Jesu preserve us,' I spat at him. 'The house!'

I should have gathered assistance. Of course, I should. Hindsight, naturally. But then I was seized by my old impetuosity, and those I might readily have summoned to my side were all now embroiled, one way or the other, in the growing confusion of the day. So – Cheyne's warnings against interference with his duties ringing in my ears – I turned upon my heel, stick in one hand, rain-napper raised in the other, and hastened to protect my home from whatever incursion I might discover there.

I crossed the green and took the lane back towards the house, but after a hundred paces or so I swung left through the trees, taking the path that gave a more direct route back to my destination. In the woods, of course, the umbrello was more hindrance than help among the new undergrowth but I struggled to close it, finally threw it down, gathering up the hem of cloak and skirt so they should not encumber me too greatly. And I cursed myself for a fool that those same skirts did not today conceal the pocket pistol. This was May Day, for pity's sake. Why in heaven's name should I have needed it? In my own village, too. I faced danger on friendly ground too many times in the past to have been so stupid. No shame in admitting our mistakes but shame indeed to repeat the same mistake afresh, and beyond shame to replicate the thing more than once. Yes, shame. And anger. Trembling with each step, alone, in the face of unknown hazard, and only the walking cane to steady me.

Though not entirely alone for, by the time I rejoined the jumble-gut roadway, Mister Stride's fashionable black pattens crunching across the gravel beyond the arched gate towards the front porch, that hound of Ursula's came bounding up behind me. For an instant I thought my daughter must have followed my return, since the beast is never far from her side. But no, just the dog, though I thanked our Lord Jesu for sending me at least this much protection. In truth, it has never shown me the least gratitude for its rescue, nor even a modicum of affection. Though beggars, as they say, should be no choosers.

'Hello?' I yelled, as I passed into the tiled reception salon, where I would normally have removed Mister Stride's iron-shod footwear though, today, I cast custom and decorum both aside, paused to allow my beating heart to still, threw back my hood, straining my ears for any sound of intrusion.

Nothing, except the ticking of the Maysmore. The clock, the whisper of silk as I slipped the damp cloak from my shoulders, and – the hound's head cocked to one side, an almost imperceptible growl. Was it possible that one or more of the servants had decided not to avail themselves of this holiday? I thought not. And the dog might, I supposed, have simply been infected by my own trepidation.

The door to the steward's lodge and pantry, to my left, stood open, and the rooms beyond all silent, secure, so I made my move, clattered across the chequerboard to the front parlour, spotted no sign of disturbance – except perhaps the slightest hint of alien odours cutting the usual warm embrace of beeswax. Yet when I passed through into the red withdrawing room, I saw that one of the compartments in my lacquered Chinese cabinet was slightly ajar, and I could not recall having left it that way. Imagination? I could not be certain, though the hound seemed to have no doubt, its snout pointing like a spear towards the doorway leading to Latimer's heart, the grand central staircase. The creature's ears twitched and there was now a continuous low rumble at the back of its throat.

I almost could not bring myself to set my fingers to the brass handle and now I believed that I, too, could discern unfamiliar noises elsewhere in the house. But where? Turning the knob with care, and gripping the walking stick tight, I peered around the edge of the door and along the broad expanse of Flemish carpet at the foot of the equally broad flight of stairs. Nobody, though some of my papers from an occasional table in the nearer alcove lay strewn across the runner. But that foreign smell – hemp and a hint of tobacco – stronger here. And as I ventured to the bottom of the stairs, set my hand upon the crenellated newel, I could now distinctly hear the sounds of groaning floorboards and creaking hinges. Somebody above, shifting around.

'Who's there?' I shouted. 'The constables are sent for. And I shall set the dogs upon you, Cheyne's man or no.'

Constables? Who was I fooling? The nearest would be at Amersham – and under Cheyne's control as Lord Lieutenant. Yet there was no response anyway, simply a troubled silence as the shafts of olive, lemon and amber light poured through the coloured glass of the first landing's windows, picked up motes of dust in the open space rising to the carved ceiling bosses, two floors above.

The hound padded quietly up to the turn in the stairs, the nearer of the twin flights leading to the first floor, and I followed.

'I am armed also,' I cried, though fear my voice quavered before I might finish the threat. But how to proceed? Around to my right, the minstrel's gallery of the great hall, another withdrawing room. But all there was perfectly silent. To my left also, the guest rooms – five of them, including that in which I had shared my night of sinful debauchery with Parrish – and the passageway to the servants' quarters.

No. I knew I should find my intruder somewhere in the family rooms, or the long gallery perhaps, on the top floor. And the proximity made me all the more afraid, the stair here more narrow and the landings too, their windows unadorned. I stood with my back pressed to the mullions, saw the dog's hackles rise as it set to barking.

'You see?' I said. 'This creature shall rip you limb from limb. Is it worth the price your master pays you?'

I edged around the final flight of stairs, my own bedchamber above and ahead of me, the door wide open, as I have never left it. My room full of documents that Cheyne might value. And then there was my travel chest to consider. Its secret compartment. But secret enough to foil a concerted search?

A sound. An unmistakable sound. Of a pistol's hammer ratcheted back, first to the half-cock, then fully cocked.

Sweet Lord Jesus, I had thought Cheyne's ruffians only to be armed with cudgels. And the noise had set the hound to barking again, bounding up the remaining treads as, to my horror, the sound was repeated. A second pistol.

'No, dog!' I screamed. 'Here. To me.'

Too late, it had skittered around the newel post, roaring its defiance along the landing and leaping through my bedroom door as a new sound came to my ears. A low and melodious sibilance, followed by – silence.

'Now, lady,' said a voice, a loud Irish voice, 'shall you not join me? Or must I shoot you where you stand?'

I stared, stupefied, into twin pits of blackness, the muzzles of the largest horse pistols I think I have ever seen.

'Porter,' I said, forcing myself to look instead at the devil himself. It has been many years – sixteen, I collect – and while he is considerably aged, there could be no mistaking him, the marks of the pox upon his face, the shaved head, though now showing a thin bristle to match his jowls. And yes, he did indeed stink of stale tobacco and wet hemp, like a damp dog. Like the docile perfidious hound that now lay, compliant to Porter's whistled enchantment, at the foot of my bed. Ursula's dog. What had Porter called her again? That day at Charlton, when he had taken her as surety against my own complicity in assisting Seaton's plan to kill Sir William. And the Czar of Muscovy. A feather-brained little bitch, he had said. An insult for which, I have promised myself many times, he would one day pay.

'Where are they, witch?' he spat.

The contents of my dresser, of my writing slope, of my travel box, were scattered all about, but no sign of my journals. A moment of relief, for it seemed he had not the wit to discover the chest's secret. And I could see the pocket pistol, thrown carelessly onto the bed. Yet I tried not to look that way, instead stirring the papers strewn across the floor with the steel ferrule at the cane's tip.

'You wretch,' I said. 'I should have guessed.' But should I? High Church Tories like Cheyne may see me as a thorn in their side, may know of my previous covert actions against their faction, against their discredited friends among the directors of the equally discredited old East India Company. And those damn'd Jacobites who contrived in my incarceration at the Bethlem Hospital may know of my work in bringing so many of their kind to the cells or to the gallows. Yet did I truly expect to find such representatives of our government – men like Cheyne, Harley, Bolingbroke and Forster – so openly in alliance with members of the Pretender's inner circle such as Colonel John Porter? Porter, who had already escaped the Tower once, and then conspired to raise a force of English rebels to aid a French invasion. No, I could not have guessed that. 'And what is it,' I asked him, 'that Cheyne seeks, precisely?'

He gestured with the pistols for me to move further into the room and, as I did so, my pattens drumming on the oaken floorboards, he edged around me to the door, risked a quick glance down the stairs – too quick for me to seize my own gun.

'Cheyne?' he said, and almost convinced me of his sincerity.

'Bravo,' I scoffed. 'A masterful performance.'

He managed to maintain some feigned appearance of being confused, shrugged his shoulders.

'There'll be copies of reports, I'm guessing,' he called back to me. 'Code books. Lists of the agents you'd be required to contact. Not Parrish now though, I'm thinking. Others maybe.'

'You may go to hell, Porter – you and the rest of your Jacobite scum. And yes, you may take me with you. By some remarkable chance I have already survived to see three score years and three. There are few left now who would mourn my passing.'

I had manoeuvred myself past the windows, almost to the nearest of the tall bedposts, set my fingers against the deep engraving.

'It would be a shame to shoot you, sure,' he said. 'Oh, and that little dainty of yours,' he pointed one of his weapons at the pocket pistol, 'I took the trouble to blow the powder from the pan.'

The glimmer of hope I had nurtured was suddenly snuffed out also.

'Disappointment for us both, then, sirrah. For the items you seek do not exist. Ten years ago, perhaps. But now all you see is all I am. My days of spying are well behind me.'

He was back inside the room now, one eye on myself while, at the same time, surveying the blues and greys of the tapestry, the dark oak of my dresser, the white lace of my bed drapes and canopy, seemingly seeking places of concealment he might not yet have discovered.

'My associates,' he said, 'tell a different tale. Northern friends, as you might say. And then I have a personal interest too, as you might have guessed. I'd hardly call Vincent Seaton a friend but his death certainly warrants some revenge. Do you not agree? And then there was all that inconvenience you caused me. All that wasted planning.

All the time I had to spend in France, building afresh. You took my time. You took much more besides. And now 'tis time to take my due. But first, your papers. Your private papers.'

Much more besides? What did that mean? I turned back to the window, looked down into the coach yard and stalls. There was a tethered bay mare at the water trough, saddled. Porter's mount, I assumed. And I saw I had been mistaken about the estate workers, for the beast was being examined by one of the stable boys, young Israel, a lad who took his responsibility for Latimer's horses – and especially for my own dear pony, Pebble – most seriously. He carefully untethered the mare, led her off towards the stables and, at the same time, looked up at the house. I knew he would be thinking it strange – that we had a guest and nobody had thought to make sure the mount was cared for. Israel might not have noticed me but it would be easy to attract his attention – yet I knew this would be impossible for me. The memories: the innocent young man, Thornton, who had served as my coachman and been slain for his pains at Charlton House – by this very wretch, Porter; and at Fort St. George, the Roundsmen's attack, poor Sathiri – and Yaj, the *pankah* boy, who had mercifully survived, though only just. Too many innocents suffered in my service already.

No, there had to be another way. The walking cane perhaps. The thought had barely flitted through my brain when the heavy tread of Porter's riding boots at my back caused me to turn, just as he snatched the stick from my fingers – an action that at least broke Ursi's hound from his witchcraft, its hackles rising once more and its fangs bared.

'Courteous,' I sneered, then glanced again towards the window. 'I am guessing you hoped to leave the mare ready for a speedy escape,' I said.

Porter pushed me aside, caused the dog to stand now. A menacing growl that Porter chose to ignore, peered out of the window himself and cursed, while I seized the only chance I might be given. His momentary distraction, at least one pistol hand encumbered with my walking stick.

My joints might be a little stiff these days but I am still capable of dancing a pretty step or two, to kick up my heels – or, here, to strike out with the iron cladding of my trusty pattens. A hearty kick to the back of his left knee so that he collapsed forward, his head striking the leaded glass and one of the pistols – the left one, I am thinking – exploded in his hand.

Porter screamed, clutched at his thigh, all colour draining from his face as he twisted about, landing on his arse, upon the floor, which drew from him another cry of pain, blood seeping through his fingers and spreading across his breeches.

I backed away as swiftly as I was able. Towards the door, while Porter tossed my cane to one side, almost lost his grip on the remaining pistol in the process, recovered the weapon, raised it towards me. Yet the hand was shaking so badly I doubted he could harm me even if he pulled the trigger. I continued my retreat to the stairs.

'Come, dog,' I called to the hound. 'To me, boy.'

Wednesday 20th October 1714

Such a difference a single death might make. Though not just one, in truth.

First, early in June, news that Sophia, Electress of Hanover, had been taken by an ague at the age of eighty-three. And the world held its breath. For this meant the succession must pass to her son George. German George, as he now seems to be universally known.

Yet some voices exclaimed that the relevant Act had been passed thirteen years earlier – and much had changed in the interim. Exiled James Stuart was also dead and his own son, the Pretender James Francis Edward, was a different kettle of fish from his father. Well, so they said. It became impossible to know the precise strength of those voices. They were strident, certainly claimed they spoke – or screamed – for the entire country. For a more directly British monarch. But, as we know, the true majority is often disquietingly silent and there was no way to be certain whether there was genuinely popular support for a Stuart, and Catholic, return to the throne.

The optimists advised that we should not worry, for Queen Anne was still in excellent health and, therefore, plenty of time to reconsider the succession. True, she had been unwell at Christmas. But now? Why, there had been great ceremony when she had performed the customary royal touching for sufferers of scrofula, the King's Evil. Then general acclaim when Harley himself fell from Her Majesty's grace – though only to be replaced by still more fanatical practitioners of High Church Toryism.

Excellent health indeed! Rendered unable to speak by an apoplexy at the end of July and dead two days later. Sweet and merciful release, some said, from the pains and tragedies she had endured during her brief forty-nine years. And Parliament, for once, moved with swift decision. The Queen is dead, long live the King! The double-barrelled announcement. And the crowds of mourners who gathered outside Kensington Palace for the three weeks until her funeral seemed to have come fully equipped with small red flags bearing the white horse of Hanover, and clergymen of various Low Church denominations mingling freely in their midst to pronounce God's grace upon both our deceased former monarch and our blessed King George the First.

August, that had been, and August turned to September, all those weeks dragging past with rumour after rumour arising from His Majesty's repeated failure to leave his native German state. But at last he arrived, in the middle of the month, and the nation, it seemed, exhaled a collective sigh of relief. In England, at least. Scotland, we were told, might not be so easy to convince. Yet today he was finally crowned King of Greater Britain and Ireland.

I stood, of course, in the rain with Ursula and brother Richard among the crowds lining the route to Westminster, somewhat dismayed by the way in which opinion upon the streets seemed to have decayed since the announcement of the Hanoverian succession. Now it seemed to be all *Down with the German*. Or, *Down with the Turnip King*. Once again, it was difficult to discern how much these quarrelsome protestors represented true opinion. In any case, I was not about to allow my good humour to be diminished, for had I not received that unexpected invitation? A hurried return to the George Yard: Ursula left in my brother's care; a change of attire and my hair dressed afresh; then a hackney back to Westminster Hall for my numbered seat in the viewing galleries to observe the coronation banquet – though now I wondered whether it was quite the marvel I had first believed.

'There must have been some mistake,' I said to the equerry when I finally found my way to the correct section of the tightly packed balconies and leaned for temporary relief upon my stick.

'Mistress Yale?' he said, checking his lists. 'The wife of Governor Yale? Then there is no mistake, madam. Your seat is down there,' he pointed to the front row, where I had already made out Elihu's bulk, his full-bodied peruke, 'with the Governor and his party.'

I had little chance to argue since there was a press of folk at my back, forcing me down the red-carpeted steps towards my husband.

'The invitation,' I barked at him, as he stammered some excuse for a greeting. 'Your doing, sirrah?'

'Astonished, truly,' he said. 'Delighted. I had no idea. Nan,' he turned to our daughter, seated just along from him with her husband, James, 'did you know?'

Motherhood suits her. She was very much in looks, beautiful in the deepest of blue silks and pearl teardrops at her ears and bodice.

'Papa,' she replied, 'I was surprised enough that *you* were invited. Though with all these other fine gentlemen of John Company...'

I followed the sweep of her gesture and, gracious, she was correct. No less than three other Fort St. George governors in their bobbing periwigs: a sad, thin smile from grey-garbed Streynsham Master; an effusive wave of the hand from old Sir William Langhorn, accompanied by that oddly familiar painted child he had married only a week ago; and a barely polite acknowledgement from dark-browed Thomas Pitt. Around these were more of the same stamp. Former governors of other East India Company outposts, I guessed, or directors of the current establishment. Their ladies too, of course, in emerald greens and ambers, in autumnal yellows and tawny reds. Diamonds and rubies galore.

'It was all very sudden,' Elihu told me. 'But our duty to attend. And shall you not sit, my dear. Please sit.'

Sweetness and light, but I took my place all the same.

'I see that Dudley and Kate do not share that sense of duty,' I said. For there had been plenty of rumours. The numbers who had refused to attend the coronation and, I supposed, this banquet also.

'Business elsewhere, I understand, Catherine. But you never answered my letters. I was concerned. Most concerned.'

I looked over the parapet of the long balcony stretching the entire length of Westminster Hall's cavernous interior, with its arcades, its great overhead flying hammer-beams of polished oak, and its similar gallery filling the opposite side, just beneath the leaded glass arches. From below, the music of His Majesty's minstrels drifted up to us, though almost drowned by the clash and clatter of serving dishes, the clamour of those seated at the two wide and silver-laden tables, sixty or more to each of the four sides and, at the farthest southern end, upon a dais under the great window, the high table, the King himself at its centre, though from where I sat he looked very small indeed.

'I suspect,' I said, 'that the other business detaining Dudley will be similar to that which has kept so many of the realm's peers cowering in their castles. Or, indeed, those that brought that devil Porter to invade my home. Treasonous duties, sir.'

'A long and distressing story, my sweet dove,' Sir William was explaining to young Mary, who had quite suddenly lifted her head, as if noticing my presence for the first time.

They were few in number to whom I had told it. What would be the point? For those in authority, I assumed, were either responsible for Porter's actions or would not care for my distress. I had managed to get myself down the stairs with the dog. Sounds of Porter above. In the entrance hall I had almost collided with Israel the stable boy, come running after he heard the shot. But I had led him away, told him it was nothing to concern him, persuaded him to escort me back to the village green. No sign of Cheyne or his henchman. So it was a swift return to the house with a *posse comitatus* of villagers and estate workers. Porter gone, of course, leaving nothing except the blood he had shed. Then missives to Streynsham Master, to Langhorn, both of them responding with an offer of armed guards – which I politely declined. And another note to Nan, begging her to say nothing to Benjamin but suggesting she should advise James.

'Treasonous?' Elihu thumped his fist against the plum sheen of his breeches. 'Your daughter's husband? Really, my dear...'

He would have said more, but he was interrupted by the young man sitting at the far side of my other son-in-law. I had not noticed him earlier.

'I think, uncle,' he said, 'that we have had the same discussion. There's a saying in Connecticut – show me the friends and I will show you the man. There is dangerous company among Sir Dudley's associates, if you will forgive me for saying so. Dangerous. And Aunt Catherine,' he smiled at me, 'give you joy of our reunion.'

David Yale no longer looks like one of Master Vermeer's cupids. He is grown tall, now in his fifteenth year, though still finely clothed in solemn grey and sporting only his own hair, powdered and curled. I offered him a polite enough greeting, given that I felt no affection for him.

'My boy,' said Elihu, 'you have much to learn. And I cannot help thinking, Catherine, there must be more to this tale of Colonel Porter than you allow.'

'Of course,' I said. 'You would assume I must have brought the whole thing down upon my own head. And greetings to you – David.'

I struggled to speak his name but he bowed his head graciously enough in response. It was interesting though. The lad seemed to vex his uncle. And I chewed on this revelation, ignoring Elihu's bumbling response while, below, there was even greater commotion as the hall's doors were thrust open to admit the Champion of England in his brightly burnished armour. This bold paladin trotted inside, flanked by two equally caparisoned companions, and riding proudly to the first of the tables, occupied by the lowliest of those sufficiently favoured to be invited to dine. For all things are relative. So here they sat, mere viscounts, barons and those principal ministers of King George's new government, since he had dispensed with the services of the old Tory administration, replaced it almost entirely with loyal Whigs. Yes, the difference a death makes.

'Such spectacle,' cried young Master Yale.

'That one, the King's Champion,' James explained to him. 'And those, the Lord High Constable and the Earl Marshal. The custom at coronation banquets. It has always been. Since the days of – well, forever.'

The Champion had removed a golden gauntlet, cast it down between the tables – narrowly missing some poor wretch trying to carry bread on a platter – while a herald read out a lengthy proclamation from an ornate and ancient scroll, challenging any to fight who might be foolish enough to deny His Majesty. Silence and, after a few moments, Champion Dymoke, twenty-third Lord of Scrivelsby – according to the wisdom of last Saturday's *Gazette* – received the spurned gauntlet from the herald and spurred his destrier to a point halfway towards the dais.

'How many are missing?' I called to Streynsham. He seemed morose, downcast, and I did not know the reason.

'Enough.' he replied, without enthusiasm. 'No Bolingbroke. No Harley. Many others. Much of the Scottish nobility absent.'

'Please, Catherine,' Elihu was murmuring, 'I had not expected to see you but now you are here, I wonder whether we might reconcile our differences.'

'Is this what you intended, daughter?' I said to Nan, looking straight past him. 'That with so many of his High Church Tory friends missing from the feast, it is a surprise to find your papa here?'

The King's Champion had just hurled down his own gauntlet for the second time, now for the benefit of those mightiest in the realm, the dukes, the marquesses, the earls and their ladies.

'I believe Papa was truly concerned for your welfare. Can you not at least allow him to say so?'

'How many do we have?' said David Yale. 'Peers of the realm, I mean.'

'My brother,' James Cavendish replied, nodding his head towards that same section of the tables where William Cavendish the Younger, Duke of Devonshire, must be seated, 'says we are blessed with over eight hundred peers of the realm. They could not all have been accommodated here, even had they wished to attend. And beyond those, baronets without number – though they are not strictly part of the peerage.'

I glanced at Elihu, saw the flicker of disappointment cross his heavy features, for he had never achieved his ambition for knighthood, of course. And now, with his Tory associates hurled into the political wilderness, it is an issue with which, I believe, I need not concern myself further.

'Perhaps you might permit me to call upon you?' Elihu was biting at his lip, staring up at those fine roofing beams. It was pitiable. Katherine Nicks dead. Jeronima de Paiva dead too, as had been expected, in Cape Town. So now he expects reconciliation with me?

'William tells me,' James laughed, 'the poor fellow barely understood a word of the coronation – apart from those sections for which they were forced to use Latin so there would be at least *some* common language between the clergy and the King.'

The Champion's challenge had naturally gone unheeded by the high nobility too, and he was now at the dais itself, performing his duty for the benefit of those closest to His Majesty upon the high table.

'I never saw a man so reluctant to become king,' I heard Sir William Langhorn say.

'Well at least he had the good sense to lock up his wife for adultery,' said Thomas Pitt, authority and wealth stitched into every yellow satin thread of his vest, every piece of gold lace trimming the fashionably deep rounded cuffs of the scarlet coat.

I am delighted with the succession. Of course I am. Better this, by far, than the Catholic Stuarts back upon the throne. Yet, whether I have any respect for our new monarch as a man – well, that may be another matter. And I should never have expressed my views in public bating my newfound affinity with His Majesty's wife, Sophia Dorothea, a certain fellow feeling.

'He already possessed two mistresses himself, did he not?' I said, and saw Pitt recoil, the lady at his side – gracious, the most elegant French robe I have ever seen – raising an oriental fan to spare her blushes. 'Is it not possible that her own meandering might not simply have been reprisal for his own?' The shudder that went through Elihu's corpulence shook my own chair also. But I was not finished with him yet. 'And the broadsheets,' I went on. 'I know they are wont to cast aspersions upon him on behalf of the Jacobite banditti, but all the same, the number of by-blows they attribute to him. Though to incarcerate one's own wife. Sirrah!'

I have no idea whether they speak truly about much of this, but it is certain that Sophia Dorothea is still imprisoned in Ahlden Castle and is likely to remain there until her death. But King George has brought one of the mistresses with him, and possibly two.

'I hoped that matter might be behind us,' I heard Elihu mutter. 'And with the recurrence of our wedding date coming up in just two weeks, I had thought – well, they say it is a Teutonic custom to mark certain milestones in a marriage.'

I must allow he surprised me.

'Thirty-four years,' I said. 'What manner of milestone might that be, Elihu?'

Marry in haste, repent at leisure. Is that not the saying? I wished I had a draught of Sathiri's *soma*, or even Doctor Sydenham's elixir to soothe me at that moment, for I found myself fighting back tears, though with no true idea of their cause.

'Why...' Elihu began and turned in his seat.

'Here, Mama,' cried my daughter, in a plain effort to halt the drift of this discussion, and reached across her father to clutch my sleeve.

'The list of dishes.' She passed me a printed handbill. 'The equerry was kind enough to provide them when we arrived. Certainly a German flavour, do you not think?'

'My brother William says he is quite irascible, sir,' her husband said to Elihu, forcing himself to laugh. Another attempt at distraction that plainly did not answer, for Elihu was half-standing now, glowering at me. 'Entirely insisted,' James pressed on, 'that the food should be a symbol of unity between nations.'

From the dais the Archbishop of Canterbury was saying as much, I collect. A blessing upon the feast.

'Then perhaps he might have shared some of it with the galleries,' I said aloud, then whispered more urgently to Elihu. 'Shall you not be seated, sirrah? There is such a thing as protesting too much.'

'I shall pursue this later, all the same,' said Elihu and collapsed back into the seat, gritting teeth that, I noted, continue to rot badly, his breath turned foetid.

'It is a strange custom indeed,' I said, as gaily as I could manage, 'that invites guests to observe a feast though not partake of the food. Lord Jesu be praised I was able to enjoy my brother's hospitality before setting out.'

'Do our thirty-four years of marriage,' Elihu murmured, 'not entitle me to moderately less sarcasm when you say so? Is thirty-four years of marriage not sufficient a milestone in itself? And, my dear, you surely cannot compare the King's incarceration of his wife with the care I ensured was lavished upon you at the hospital?'

'I believe I was thinking, rather, about the brace of mistresses.'

'He will win few hearts,' James was saying, 'but William is certain he is no fool.'

'His Majesty,' said David Yale with a wisdom beyond his years, 'may be presented as a champion of Anglicanism, but is he not raised in the Lutheran tradition and therefore more Low Church than High?'

'I sometimes think,' Elihu growled at me, 'that the boy is more Dissenter even than you. I fear that Connecticut must be sorely afflicted that way.' But then he lowered his voice, whispered in my ear. That breath again. 'My dear, you say the wife may have meandered as reprisal for the husband's infidelities, yet might the husband not also have had cause for straying? Some need for affection, perhaps?'

'You think a breach of marital vows, made before God, can be excused as mere tip for tap, a response to some pitiable need for lust?'

I had paid little further attention to Thomas Pitt since I arrived, though I heard him keeping up a relatively one-sided discussion with Streynsham and a more heated debate with Langhorn and others about the current policies of the united East India Company. But now I saw him lean forward.

'The big question,' I heard him reply to Master Yale, 'seems to be whether His Majesty will continue to touch sufferers of the King's Evil? Does he, I ask myself, even believe in the ability of anointed kings to be God's instrument in the delivery of such miracles?'

'Can our own case then,' Elihu murmured, 'not at least be explained and understood by this tip for tap, Catherine, if not excused?'

'Perhaps, sir,' I said, 'you would do better to consider the Hanoverian case again. The wife meandering as reprisal for the husband's infidelity? You have not that excuse either. For I was always faithful to you, Elihu.'

'Always?' he snapped, and he glanced along to where Pitt was still debating the divine attributes of kings and queens with David. 'You forget that Tom Pitt shared with me the greatest betrayal of all. Those denunciations against me in your name. In my own wife's name. The ledger sheets you stole. The affidavit evidence it seems you provided for that wicked parliamentary investigation. Great heavens, faithful?'

'And your confession, Elihu, that those matters were the real reason for my incarceration. Conspiracy with that evil witch Winifred Bridger to feed me laudanum, create the semblance of madness. But tip for tap, husband? Yes, that is fair. For I took my revenges in that way, though so many years after your rutting with Katherine Nicks, so long after you took Jeronima to your bed also, that she might give you a son and heir to replace my own sweet Davy. But faithful to you in body, sir? That I always remained.'

Yet then Matthew Parrish came guiltily to mind and I could not continue this any further, called to James and asked whether he would consider exchanging our places so I might better speak with my daughter, levered myself upright with the walking cane's assistance, edged along the row to seat myself between Annie and

Master Yale. Nan sharing with me the sparse news she has of Kate at Glemham. Then her own chatter about new furnishings she has acquired at Staveley, including a canvas she has been gifted by her father – the painting by Master Seeman the Mennonite depicting the imaginary negotiation of her dowry, I suppose. Then the latest news of her children, naturally, even though there is a certain sadness in doing so – reminders of my mortality, the thought that I shall soon enough be nothing to them but false fragment of memory.

'Your grandchildren, ma'am?' said David Yale. 'What sort of future, I wonder, might our new King George gift them? What miracles might he bring? I should like to meet them,' said David. 'The little ones. I am keen to acquaint myself with as much of my family as I am able.'

For the diners, the first remove was taking place, the table linen and utensils replaced and an array of new trenchers, platters and chargers carried forth.

'I am sure your uncle shall oblige,' I said.

'And your own children, Streynsham,' I turned to our old friend. Ten years older than me, of course, but showing that advanced age more sharply now than I have ever seen. 'How are they?'

'Anne, the eldest, is due to be wed next year. To the Earl of Coventry.' He told me this without any emotion at all. 'Legh will be married soon also. Aspirations towards a life in politics. And Streynsham Junior destined for the clergy.'

'Your daughter's wedding,' I said. 'I expect that Elizabeth has stayed at Codnor to progress the planning.'

'Elizabeth,' he said slowly, 'is dying.' There has never been love lost between myself and Streynsham's wife but this was shocking news indeed. 'And not Codnor,' he went on. 'It is a cold pile. We have been living at Stanley Grange.'

'Dying?' I said.

Sir William Langhorn placed a comforting hand upon his friend's shoulder, for tears were forming in Streynsham's eyes. But little Mary's lips, I noticed, were pursed in something like annoyance.

'A malignance,' said Langhorn. 'A carcinoma, I understand.'

'I wondered,' I said, 'that she was not here. And you, Mary. You would not have met poor Elizabeth, I think.'

She shook her head, then lowered it again modestly, while

Streynsham used his neck cloth to wipe his face and it was a long time before he was able to continue. A protracted interlude during which those who had overheard, or who already knew about the tragedy, offered their condolences, or suggestions of physicians they knew who might be efficacious. It was clear from Streynsham's responses that Elizabeth's case was hopeless.

'I should not be here myself, my dear,' Streynsham eventually told me. 'Yet I can do nothing for her and she is in good hands. God's own hands, in truth. And there was duty here.'

'Duty?' I said.

'Your invitation, Catherine. The arrangement was mine – though with Elizabeth upon my mind, I omitted to send explanation.'

He lowered his voice, continued in no more than a private whisper, though I saw pretty Mary straining to follow the conversation.

'I have no words for the sorrow I feel, Streynsham. This is awful news. But the invitation – I fear I still do not grasp the reason I am here.'

'Elizabeth cannot survive this terrible illness,' said Streynsham, 'yet there is at least some chance now that our nation, this England, may survive the canker eating away at its vitals. This Jacobite threat, Catherine, is stronger now than ever before. But we have a monarch again – perhaps an unlikely one, though monarch nonetheless – who is unequivocal in his desire to see them rooted out. And good men once again at the helm of Parliament who are also steadfast in that desire. The threat is imminent, my dear. They will explain, I am sure.'

'They?'

'When these proceedings are done, they will send for you. Later. And I have no brief to say more.'

I had no doubt it would be Walpole. He had risen since I saw him last, since that performance of Addison's *Cato*, since the succession. Privy Counsellor. Paymaster to the Forces. Destined, I had seen rumoured, for still greater prominence.

'I have no part to play any more, Streynsham,' I said. 'I told that wretch Porter the same. It is perhaps Parrish they need. Save him from languishing in some half-pay captain's position.'

I thought we had been discreet, our conversations muted as best they could be while making ourselves understood above the *halla bol* – as my friend Sathiri used to name such commotion – rising from the body of the hall. The second remove.

'Forgive my intrusion,' said David Yale. 'I did not intend to eavesdrop, but did I hear you mention Parrish, ma'am? Matthew Parrish? If so, I am a great admirer of his poetry. I recently bought a copy of his latest collection and could not help noticing that your son was a subscriber. I am correct, am I not? Benjamin Hynmers would be your son?'

I felt as though I was supposed to be on a voyage, yet finding myself left behind upon the quayside with my dunnage, watching the ship sail into the distance. This conversation with Streynsham – how could I have allowed myself to be so lacking in communication with him that I had failed to hear of his distress? Then this business of politics, in which I alone seemed incapable of seeing my own path. And poor Parrish, consigned to keeping menial accounts but still writing his beautiful verses, though without me knowing his latest works while my own son subscribes to the process of bringing them before the public. Poor Parrish, craving my friendship and affection and spurned for his pains.

'Did I hear Parrish named?' huffed Thomas Pitt. 'An unhelpful fellow. I have this brilliant for sale. You may know of it.' Oh yes, we all knew of it. 'Though the very devil to find a buyer. And since Parrish was travelling abroad, I thought he might be the person to help spread the word, in Paris or The Hague. Elsewhere, perhaps. But he seemed to find the suggestion amusing.'

Forty-five carats, that diamond, if memory serves me well. From the supposedly worthless gravel-clay mine that Antonio do Porto and I had sold to Katherine Nicks and others, persuading them it still had value, believing it a revenge. Little wonder that Parrish was amused.

'He would have understood,' I said, 'that a brilliant of that size is almost impossible to trade unless it is first cut to smaller pieces. Did Mistress Nicks not advise you of that? I am certain she would have known.' I turned to Elihu. 'An interesting point, husband, is it not? If Governor Pitt finally succeeds in selling his Golconda gem, shall the Nicks estate receive that portion of its worth that she was owed? Her daughters and young Elihu would be so pleased, I imagine.'

Around me, chaos seemed to descend: Elihu's protest that I was attempting to practise calumnies against him; an admonition from my daughter that I should not taunt her father so; her husband's scolding insistence that she should hold her tongue, be less strident; David Yale's repeated pleas for forgiveness if he had caused offence by mentioning Parrish; Thomas Pitt's riposte that at least Katherine Nicks had known the mine's value; and Langhorn's futile attempts to explain all this to the infant he had wed. Yet I had done no more than speak true. As the gospels require us, even when what we say may be unpopular.

I looked over the parapet, saw a whole company of poissoniers laying out their bounty of fresh and saltwater fish, other delicacies, detailed upon my sheet: sturgeon and crayfish; baked quinces and oranges too; pickled herring; oysters in great quantity; salmon from the Rhine; stalks of asparagus; and a *Rüdesheimer* apostle wine.

Something about that word. Apostle. A recollection of a line from my Bunyan. *The Pilgrim's Progress.* "What God says is best, is best, though all the men in the world are against it."

'I think, madam,' Walpole told me, from the shadows on the far side of the table, 'you fail to understand the situation.'

Dimly lit, nothing but a small window, a single sconce to pierce the gloom of this crypt-like place buried deep within the walls of Westminster Hall.

'You are agitated, gentlemen,' I replied. The chair was uncomfortable, rocking somewhat on legs more unsteady even than my own. 'But I have told you all I know. And I do not appreciate this interrogation.'

The third person in the room had been introduced to me as James Stanhope and I knew him by reputation. Lieutenant General. Or was he a colonel? I could not recall. But now Secretary of State for the Southern Department, and replacing in that esteemed position the same Henry St. John, Viscount Bolingbroke who, as Parrish had predicted at the Theatre Royal, had risen so swiftly in Harley's place to gain Queen Anne's ear.

'Great heavens, mistress,' he cried, 'England burning as we speak. Worse to come, there can be no doubt. And your name occurring several times as we try to fathom the traitors in our midst. Still, you claim ignorance.'

I had been summoned at the precise moment when the royal pâtissiers began serving their delectable sweet treats to the diners, escorted with less courtesy than my age deserves through the labyrinthine passages by a brusque sergeant-at-arms.

'Burning, sir?'

'Figuratively, ma'am.' Secretary of State Stanhope threw up his hands in exasperation. His features were milk-soft, almost womanly, I might say. Petulant lips. Penetrating eyes. His velvet court coat was thrown carelessly upon the table, but the sober waistcoat was buttoned high to his throat. There were always rumours about Stanhope, but his service in Flanders, Portugal and Spain was remarkable.

'Post boys still arriving,' said Walpole. 'But as we speak, Mistress Yale, while we loyalists celebrate, reports coming in of riots across the south and west. Twenty incidents so far. Serious, ma'am. Secretary Stanhope might not be far from the mark. The nation may indeed be afire.'

'And we can only guess,' said Stanhope, 'what might be happening in Scotland. God's hooks, Streynsham was certain you would be biddable.'

'If you could explain more clearly that for which you seek my compliance, gentlemen, I am certain I could be persuaded to assist. Biddable, as you say.' This was disingenuous, since I had no intention of involving myself again in such affairs. Yet I continued in my role. 'But I fear,' I said, 'you suffer the same delusion as our enemies – that I am somehow in possession of intelligence which does not exist.'

'From my experience with the army, ma'am,' Stanhope said, 'it always seemed to me that those who tunnelled into the dark byways of skulking and spying were never quite able to find their way out again.'

It is a fear I have held myself this long while, though I would never have admitted so to Secretary Stanhope.

'I have been reading the reports,' said Walpole. 'Given your part in the Deptford affair, it's understandable our enemies might make the assumption.'

'From sixteen years past? And in that incident I was more tethered goat than willing agent. I may have helped thwart the attempt upon the old Duke of Devonshire – the Czar of Muscovy too – but that was more accident than design.' I thought about the geographical clock, still at Latimer, and about the war Czar Peter has been waging against the Swedes. 'And my daughter,' I went on, 'could so easily have perished in the process at Porter's hands. Since then I have been variously incarcerated with the plain collusion of

Jacobite supporters among the governors of the Bethlem Hospital; threatened by such men of power as Thomas Forster and William Cheyne. Now, gentlemen, it is chill in here and my bones begin to ache. Are we done?'

I stood from the table, eased the creases in my skirts.

'You mention Bedlam, ma'am,' said Stanhope, leaning forward to scrutinise me. 'Your husband must have played his part? An associate of those same hospital governors? A Jacobite, is he not?'

I sat again, surprised by this turn in the conversation.

'If any believed so,' I replied, 'he would not have received this invitation, I collect.'

'That provides no answer, Mistress Yale,' said Walpole, and I could see that one of the fellow's expansive eyebrows was raised in surprise. 'We could hardly have omitted your husband from the list. There are similar allegations from another former Governor of the Madras Presidency. Fraser. William Fraser. Claims that Yale was thick with the Jamesite faction upon the Fort St. George Council.'

'Fraser?' I said. Just the name was enough to anger me. A braggart, and I had no compunction in taking his gold when he had invested in that mine, along with Katherine Nicks. I always suspected that his later allegations against Elihu stemmed in some perverse way from the losses he sustained. 'A rogue of the first order. In any case, by the time my husband became Governor, there were virtually no others upon the Council except supporters of King James. Elihu was master of the Crown's Presidency there, loyal to the crown, regardless of the head upon which it sat.'

I wondered at my ability to be so effusive in his defence.

'Was there correspondence from him,' said Stanhope, 'confirming his allegiance to James Stuart? Perhaps after that despot went into exile?'

'If there had been any, it would have been treason to withhold it. Are you accusing me of treason, sirrah?' I thumped the table, frustrated at this foolish line of questioning, while Secretary Stanhope began to mutter an apology. 'But there was none,' I said. 'Nothing of relevance. And those that I received were burned.'

Walpole's turn now to stand, to pace the room.

'Streynsham tells me there were documents you supplied. Evidence against Governor Yale.'

'Concerning a variety of improprieties,' I told him. 'Though sedition not among them.'

'You must *think*, madam,' Stanhope barked. 'Truly – think.' I had taken a great dislike to this fellow. 'There must be something,' he said. 'Something important enough to set Colonel Porter on your trail.'

'Perhaps you should ask William Cheyne,' I snapped back. 'They must be associates, must they not?'

'Cheyne,' said Walpole, 'has been stripped of all position. Interrogated at length. Though there seems no connection. Not with Porter.'

'What?' I laughed. 'Coincidence? That Cheyne and his bravos should have appeared on May Day at the same time as Porter was ransacking my house – and those two things unrelated?'

Yet I recalled the surprise upon Porter's face when I had made the same association, as though he truly did not know Cheyne at all.

'Oh,' said Stanhope, 'Cheyne certainly had his men check your grounds, but we think this was more bluster, harassment, than anything else.'

And a sign of how vile things have become, that we can be confronted by these seditionists at every turn.

'Porter told me his associates still believed I was somehow a threat. His Northern friends, he said.'

Though Porter had gone much further than that. His talk of revenge against me. Of how I owed him for much more than mere frustration of his plans. But if retribution was his gold, I could surely not be the only one along the line of his shaft.

'Forster, I should think,' said Walpole. 'We have reports of them seen together. But Forster has scuttled back to Northumberland. Gone to ground.'

'Just as easily, Lord North,' Stanhope insisted. William North, Lord North and Grey. 'Your son-in-law's cousin, madam. And Dudley North well disposed towards your husband. A natural conduit between your husband and the traitors. Your husband so heavily in league with those High Church Tories and Jacobites within the Society for the Propagation of the Gospel. Do you see now? The importance of your documents?'

'For pity's sake, sir. How many times? There are no...'

'Parrish says there are journals, ma'am. Secret journals.'

I felt as though my world collapsed at that moment.

'Parrish?' I repeated the name like some lovelorn loon who just discovered her betrothed has been unfaithful.

'What, ma'am?' said Stanhope and slammed the flat of his hand upon the table. 'There are sensitivities about whatever personal trivialities of which you may keep accompt? I have no concern with those, Mistress Yale – simply any that might shed light upon your husband's possible treachery.'

As I write this, my rage at Parrish's betrayal remains unabated, feasts upon my innards. Is this some revenge of his? For my dismissal of his affections?

'He is mistaken,' I stammered, still unable to fully grasp the enormity of this latest violation of my trust. And of Stanhope's more personal affront. My beautiful journals. They span more than forty years now. Here they lie, in the hidden depths of my old travel chest. Though not for long. I must find some new place of concealment now. There are idle moments in my life when I bring them forth, skim through the volumes, relish the words I wrote about the times in which I have lived. The modest and the momentous. Simple scribblings, but important to this foolish old woman at least. 'Personal trivialities,' I said. 'Precisely that, sirrah. How could they be anything else, written as they are by a mere woman? And how could personal trivialities therefore trouble themselves with matters of such enormity as a husband's sedition? No, Mister Stanhope. I may have mentioned many times the state of Elihu's neck cloths but never the level of his political frailties.'

'There is no intention,' said Walpole, 'to cause affront, Mistress. But you must understand that we are trying here to build a network of intelligence virtually from naught. Those old circles of Captain Baker are long disbanded. Harley controlled his own intelligencers – personally controlled them. His Majesty's own informers...'

'Germans,' said Stanhope. 'Not one of them who would answer. Literally, not answer. No word of English, like the King himself.'

I had heard the stories. About Walpole. About how, like the clergy at the coronation, he and King George had established a certain rapport. In Latin, His Majesty conveying the royal imperatives to Walpole in execrable Latin and Walpole translating those imperatives to the King's ministers – making him the first minister in line to hear and act upon the monarch's wishes. The prime minister.

'And treason,' Walpole said now, 'at a level we can scarce believe. At least fifty of those currently elected to Parliament openly supportive of the Pretender. Preachers of Jacobite sedition. A parcel of High Church priests and all those who never took the oath of allegiance to King William, the non-jurors. A hundred or more rebels within the nobility. All the disaffected of this nation who have suffered at the hands of one Tory administration after another but now persuaded that each and every ill can, rather, be laid at the door of foreigners – the Dutch, the French, and now our very own German George.'

'While you, madam,' Stanhope sneered, 'sit safe at Latimer House believing yourself secure from the storm to come.'

'I had simply believed, sir, that with the succession all would change.'

He laughed so fulsomely. And I felt a fool. It is true, I suppose, that I still believed such miracles to be possible, that right will, itself, restore everything. But I know that Mama would have derided me in equal measure – that being right alone is never enough to win the day.

'It is perfectly possible,' said Stanhope, 'that Porter may be hoping to raise yet another rebel force. Perhaps more than one. And we need every possible ounce of intelligence we might gather, Mistress Yale. Anything.'

'You wish me to spy upon Elihu?'

'You have done so before, I collect.'

'Not like this, sirrah,' I said. 'Not like this.'

Indeed not. Though there was something in my husband's wish for reconciliation. Something that stoked old embers. I have never felt I truly achieved satisfaction for the wrongs he has done me. Jeronima and her boy. His violation of me. Mistress Nicks. Bethlem. But this new thing? Any port in a storm, is that not what they say? Well, damn the wretch.

'Upon your husband, yes,' said Walpole, a more gentle smile at last spreading across those boyish features. 'But upon the Norths too. And perhaps on whatever may be happening within the Gospel Society. On developments in Denbighshire even. Every little may help.'

'And little it may be,' I replied, almost without realising that, by saying so, I talked myself into their schemes. But I knew in my heart they were right, that we are all at risk from these traitors. Besides, there was a glimmer of inspiration tempting me. Elihu would not trust me with any confidences. The Gospel Society was closed to me too. Katie's husband, Dudley North also. But there was one who might open those doors for me. One who could certainly act as my means to an end.

So here I am, back in my old world of intrigue and deception, though perhaps able to fashion a difference after all. Yes, the difference a death makes.

Friday 22nd April 1715

Today the sun was simply snuffed out.

"'*And the sun*,'" Ursula intoned, clinging to me in terror as day turned instantly to darkest night, "'*became black like sackcloth of hair, and the moon became as blood.*'"

'Revelations, my dear,' Reverend Burrough smiled at her, an attempt at reassurance, though his voice trembled a little.

Revelations, yes. The opening of the Sixth Seal, was it not? I wondered whether the same thought was going through the mind of our young guest, David Yale, as he crouched there in the courtyard, cradling the head of Ursula's whimpering hound.

'It is a natural thing, my dear,' I told her, waved my copy of Moore's Almanack, his *Vox Stellarum*, in Ursi's face, though with less confidence than I should have liked. The broadsheets have been full of it for many weeks, Mister Halley's prediction. Yet at Latimer, surrounded by our entire team of estate workers, some of the villagers too, the young girls weeping pitifully, this did indeed feel like the crack of doom. Bating the silence beyond those tears. A silence so pitiless it caused my soul to quake, the birdsong fallen quiet many moments earlier, even the wind ceasing to breathe. The stillness of eternity.

And when the light began to return it was sickly, unnatural, harbouring the same menace as the eclipse itself had done. How long did it last? Hours, it seemed, while we all clung together. Time aplenty to reflect upon whatever omens and metaphors we each attached to this bizarre phenomenon. Like the way the new dawn that should have cheered us after the elections had been subsumed by the gloom that followed in their wake.

They have run throughout February, promised to give us all hope, for the Tories had been soundly defeated – will not recover for a generation or more, some say – so that they are purged entirely from all levels of government, loyal Whigs taking their place. The leaders of the most dangerous faction among the Tories, the most vocal of the Jacobite banditti, like Bolingbroke, fled to France to join the Pretender.

They seem like the Hydra of legend, that multiplicity of evil. With every head lost, two more appear upon the streets and even at Chesham there are reports of rogues heard in one or other of the taverns, humming or whistling that accursed tune they hold so dear. *When the King Enjoys his Own Again.* And there has been affray too. In the West Country, even worse.

Darkness, like that which stayed even as that insipid second daybreak spewed over us and, Reverend Burrough bestowing God's blessing on those gathered in the yard, my own words of reassurance offered to any who needed them. We crept back into the reception hall – astonished to hear, from the Maysmore, that no more than five minutes had elapsed, it just striking the quarter hour before ten o' the clock.

'We must trust in the Lord, Mama,' said Ursula, in the slow drawl that has hardly changed since she was small. Twenty-six years old and still little more than a child. A child of God, perhaps. A child all the same. And there, a debt. It may have been Seaton who damaged her – but Seaton acting for those traitors. Ursula taking my hand. 'Trust in the Lord,' she said, 'to deliver us from the darkness still to come.'

'The very thing,' David Yale smiled, as we sat at table in the servants' hall, 'to bring the sunlight back.'

I had asked the kitchen to prepare some Hatted Kit, my favourite among syllabubs, the milk frothed directly into the amber wine and bark-brown nutmeg, then allowed to ferment before the currants are added – though Ursula will partake of no strong beverage, so that cook must produce a receipt in which plum juice and cherry syrup replace the wine. And where better to sample this dainty today than with the servants themselves?

'The syllabub must suffice for the nonce, David,' I said. 'But I fear it may need a different receipt entirely to drive away the nation's gloom.'

I stroked Ursula's hair as she sipped at her cup.

'I cannot avoid the feeling, ma'am,' he said, 'that something of that kind might have been behind this generous invitation. It was kind, but...'

'Is it so strange that I might wish us to know each other better?' I said. 'Really? You are likely to be named my husband's heir, after all, I collect.' The words almost choked me, for it should have been my own dear Davy. 'And nobody forced you to come, my boy. Yet I should relish the chance of news from Wrexham. A long time since I was there and I had a certain fondness for the place. For your uncle's mama. The old aunt too.'

He knew I lied, I think, for he regarded me with a quizzical eye, then smiled.

'A strange town, all the same,' he told me at last. 'The Dissenters there – Presbyterians, Quakers – seen hard times. The New Meeting House is very fine but those who attend are often shunned by many who should know better. And there have been meetings. Some Jacobite society supported by the wealthiest merchants. A fellow called Williams. His father a baronet. Oswestry, I think, though he always seems to be around – taking stock of their tenants and businesses in town. Desires upon Denbighshire's seat in Parliament, I collect.'

I was shocked. There was more intelligence here than I could possibly have expected, and that portion of my report to Stanhope is already penned in artichoke juice, waiting for me to add my comments and questions upon the tragedy that crashed upon me later in the forenoon. And Williams, father a baronet. Might the father not be the same Sir William Williams who had so peremptorily terminated Benjamin's career in their London chambers?

'How can you know all this?' I scoffed.

'How could I not?' he replied. 'Those who attend the chapel, and Mister Kenrick, the pastor, speak of little else. And Uncle Elihu seems to believe the years separating me from my majority must make me mumchance about matters that seem so mightily to inflate him.'

I stood to reach for the jugs, refilled his bowl and Ursula's cup. She has taken to wearing black almost permanently. And a coif, too. Yellow Dutch silk, embroidered, but a coif all the same, like some Puritan penitent. The hound naturally asleep at her feet beneath the bench.

'We must see Papa again,' she said. 'I prayed for him. When the darkness came. You prayed for him too, Mama?'

'How long shall Queen Square be graced by his presence?' I asked David, stepping aside from the absurdity of Ursi's question.

David rode here from London two days ago, a tardy response to the invitation sent him in November after my reluctant commitment to Stanhope. I remembered the way he seemed to annoy Elihu, his open criticism of Dudley North's associates and it had seemed to me that he might be useful. Nothing more than that, though since his arrival he had made a more positive impression upon me. He had been not the least troubled, for instance, by making the journey alone, laughed as he reminded me of the far greater perils he would have faced making a trip of similar duration back in Massachusetts.

'Another meeting with Mister Dummer this coming Monday,' he sighed. 'And then back to Plas Grono, I collect.'

I had almost forgotten about Dummer.

'Mister Dummer,' I frowned, 'has still not fathomed the interest Governor Yale might exact for whatever beneficence he may bestow upon their Connecticut college.'

'College?' said Ursula, wiping a syllabub froth from her upper lip. 'Papa's last letter says he works with the Gospel Society. That he will help them restore the true faith among the colonies.'

'There, David,' I said. 'Interest.'

'Uncle Elihu has shipped thirty-two books,' he replied, 'to help the library there.'

'Generous,' I laughed. 'Thirty-two books. Great heavens, how can he afford so much?'

'Papa,' Ursi scolded me, 'says he will give no more while the college preaches only heresy.'

'Your family in Massachusetts,' I said to David. 'Dissenters, are they not? Does your uncle view *them* as heretics too? Or you, boy?'

'He has been kind to me, ma'am. And Massachusetts is not Connecticut. Not at all. I think when they meet on Monday, Uncle Elihu will agree to gift Mister Dummer more.'

'You believe so?' I said. And when he told me yes, that was indeed what he believed, I called cook and upbraided her for inserting too much of Alicante's finest tawny in the Hatted Kit.

*

The post boy clattered into the yard and brought a letter to remind me the darkness had not yet been fully dispersed.

From Streynsham. News that his wife Elizabeth finally lost her long battle against that malignant carcinoma and lies buried at her family's chapel in Macclesfield. Poor woman. We were far from close but a valiant lady. Her struggle and her death humble me. Codnor sold, meanwhile, and Streynsham himself gone to live with his son at a property recently purchased at New Hall, in Lancashire. He begs me to join him there, if I am able. It would be some small consolation, he says. Poor Streynsham. All these years I have known him, counted him a friend, and those precious moments when I thought he might possibly have become more than just a friend.

I read his note in the library, then tucked it inside the writing slope to keep company with the other letters still awaiting my attention and response. One from Annie with word of her husband, her children and her sister Katie – the latter still at Glemham. It reminds me that, since I now have almost no contact with my older daughter, if I wish to track the activities of son-in-law Dudley North – and thence those of his treacherous cousin, Lord North and Grey – I must find some way to turn David Yale still further to my purpose.

A second letter, from Benjamin. Still anxious for my safety following the word I sent him, my belated confession about Porter's invasion of the house – though I have made no mention of Stanhope. Benji settled in Preston, he says, still working within the Court of Common Pleas, but the town a hotbed of sedition.

I fingered the sad missive from Streynsham again, then searched the shelves until I found the section that boasted Saxton's *Atlas*, Norden's *Guide* and that precious copy of the *Thesaurus Geographicus*. Alongside them, the tome I needed, Ogilby's *Britannia*. I swung the ladder to the proper location and climbed three of its rungs so I might pull down this superb collection of three hundred itineraries, opened it upon the table. No larger than one of my journals, the perfect companion for any traveller upon our post roads, and I soon found Amersham, traced my finger laboriously up each of the scroll-fashioned routes, page to page, until I found the destination I sought. New Hall. In the district of Makerfield. Near Wigan, I could see. And Wigan? No more than twenty miles from Preston and Benjamin.

This library has become more home to me than any other of Latimer's fine rooms, for it is here that my journals are now sequestered, and here that I sit on so many evenings – as I do presently – to compose the latest entries. It took some time to discover new lodgings for them, but this is a house of considerable history. They say that, during the two years when the first Charles Stuart, that miscreant king, was held under arrest by Parliament before his execution, one of the very many houses in which he was accommodated – albeit only for a single night – was here, at Latimer, slept in the very chamber that now serves as my withdrawing room. Incredible. And I had suspected that a house once occupied by royalist Christiana Cavendish – who would have entertained many prominent Catholics here – must have its share of priest holes or similar hiding places.

My searches had been in vain, until I considered the cabinet in the recess beneath the library window. Flemish ebony and prince's wood, inlaid ivory stringing, but it had occurred to me many times that it shared all the characteristics of an altar. Inside, deep drawers, though I had eventually come to realise that some were shorter than others. And upon further exploration I found that the frames in which those sat could be removed too, each with a secret compartment attached to the rear. Compartments that, I assumed, would once have hidden Romish missals, reliquaries, papist vestments perhaps. Modest spaces, but answering perfectly to my own needs.

The various volumes were tucked safely away in their secret niches, however, and myself back upon the ladder, returning the Ogilby to its allotted place when Merrick knocked upon the door to announce a visitor. The window of the library only faces south, of course, out onto the meadows and the Chess Valley, so that the courtyard is hidden from view. It lends the room a sense of peaceful communion with God's finest invention, of cushioning against worldly intrusion. Yet here was intrusion indeed.

'Parrish, you say?' I descended the rungs, carefully weighing my choices. Perhaps simply to shun him, require Merrick to insist that I was receiving no visitors. But I suspected that his presence would already be known to Ursula, to David Yale, to the whole household – and the explanation I might be required to offer them for sending him away so harshly seemed potentially as troublesome as the bother of confronting him.

'Catherine,' he said, standing in the doorway from the central hall, toying uncomfortably with lace-trimmed hat between his hands, and it struck me that he now seemed just a little too old to be wearing the King's uniform. 'I bring news.'

I had composed myself somewhat while Merrick fetched him, placed myself at that cabinet in the window's recess.

'Elizabeth Master,' I said, determined to be stern. 'Streynsham has already written.'

'Not Elizabeth,' he replied. 'Something other.'

His scarlet coat, his buff vest and breeches, dark with damp patches where he had ridden so hard that he had not stopped upon the road even to put on his riding cloak, despite the rain. His long boots and once white stocking tops spattered with mud. Something more urgent than Streynsham's sad notice therefore.

'You could not send a post boy, sirrah?'

'I am on my way to Bedford. General Wynne is charged with raising his dragoons again. The Jacobite threat is real, I fear.'

'Always the Jacobite threat,' I snapped. 'Your reason for being here, I suppose. As it was your reason for breaking my trust, my confidences.'

'How? Great heavens, Catherine, I find it impossible to count the ways I offend you.'

He marched unbidden into the room, boot studs drumming on my fine polished floor, tossed the black beaver and his riding gloves onto the chair I had so recently occupied, then turned his back to the wide stone fireplace as though to warm himself, even though there was no blaze lit.

'You shall find little warmth here, Captain Parrish. I fear you must needs turn to your friend, Secretary Stanhope, if you seek succour.'

'Riddles, madam,' he said, turning his back to me and resting both hands high on the mantle shelf. 'And no time for any such like. I have long since given up hope of more. Simply word. About Sir William.'

'Langhorn?'

'The same.' He span around. 'Dead, Mistress Yale, though I fear your frigid heart will be shut to any sentiment at the news.'

'I collect it was your own cold-blooded desire to bring him

down as governor at Fort St. George that first dragged me into this web of spies.'

He flushed as red as his coat, though whether with rage or embarrassment I could not tell.

'Poor innocent Catherine Hynmers,' he said. 'Yes, I recall your reluctance, madam.'

Damn the fellow.

'Still, we grew to be close, Sir William and myself,' I retorted. 'I admired him, and not simply as a business associate. Even despite being practised upon so wickedly to trap Seaton. To bring that devil Porter down upon myself and my daughter.'

Close, yes, we had certainly become that.

'And you could not bring yourself to tell me Porter still torments you, Catherine. Threatened your life, even here at Latimer. Without Stanhope I would be none the wiser.'

'Yet Porter may not have done so, sirrah, had there been less common gossip about my journals. You betrayed that confidence to Secretary Stanhope. How many others?'

My chance now to turn from him, to run my fingers along the gleaming golden-brown marquetry.

'No others,' he said. 'And Stanhope only after he told me of the attack. Mere accident that I knew about your journals at all. It simply occurred to me there might possibly have been other unintended sightings. That somehow your enemies – Katherine Nicks, perhaps, almost anybody – might have shared that knowledge. And that Porter, mindful of your other secret activities, might assume that your private writings were significant. Anyway, Secretary Stanhope agreed with me.'

What nonsense, I thought, gazing out upon the misty drizzle. There was nobody, of course. Well, almost nobody, but certainly none among my enemies.

'More than just a captain of dragoons then?' I said, looked around at him for a response, caught a momentarily unguarded look of total dejection. But it took a mere instant for his mask of indifference to settle again. 'No longer on half-pay, I assume. Active in Stanhope's circle of spies.'

'It suits Walpole's purpose to make it seem I am still out of favour. Beyond that, I am sworn to secrecy.'

I moved towards the table, made some pretense of my own at tidying away the mottled porcupine quill I had been using earlier.

'But still, news of Elizabeth Master or poor Sir William. Where is the difference? A post boy would still have sufficed.'

'No, it would not. I spoke with Sir William's physician. His death – there are questions.'

'God's hooks, sirrah. He was eighty-five. Just married to that chit, merely a fifth of that number. Is it any wonder?'

He did not smile, avoided my eye entirely, patting at the dampness of his sleeves, the deep military cuffs.

'The physician believed poison. Subtle. Almost impossible to detect with any certainty. Yet there were signs, he says.'

I thought he must jest, though he was deadly serious and it shook me. Old fears. Old foes.

'The girl?' I said, unsure whether I was enquiring after her safety or questioning her possible complicity. For I could no longer even picture her face.

'Mary has vanished without trace.'

'She inherits?'

'There is no will, Catherine. None found.'

It was selfish, I know, but it made me wonder – as I had occasionally done before – about Elihu's own will, though I almost dreaded to think.

'You have added darkness to a day already drenched in sable, Captain Parrish. But I suppose I owe you for making the journey. I shall ask cook to prepare food. Arrange to dry your coat.'

I had not even offered a beverage, and there was steam rising from the scarlet wool as he moved towards the table as well. I foolishly thought he might attempt to embrace me.

'I have no time. Bound for Bedford. And from there to Lancashire. We assist Sir Henry Hoghton to raise the county militia there. Other duties besides. But it should be obvious that if this fate has befallen Sir William – and given Porter's attack here...'

I recalled Porter's words, as I had repeated them in my interrogation by Walpole and Stanhope. A personal interest, he had said. Revenge for the inconvenience I had caused him. For Seaton's death. But for much more besides – whatever that meant. Time to take his due.

'It had occurred to me,' I said, more to remind myself than to impart the thought to Parrish, 'that if retribution was his gold, I could not be the only one. Sir William…'

'Yes,' he said, with intense sadness in his voice. 'Sir William.'

I weakened, decided to press him, beg him to stay at least a while. But too late. He had already retrieved his hat and, with the slightest of bows, he was gone, though his step more gentle than when he arrived. Might I have called him back? Naturally. Yet I merely wiped a tear from my cheek, turned back to the shelves. Ogilby's itineraries. Did all roads suddenly lead to Lancashire, then?

So, here I sit, trying to make sense of all this as I write. Sir William Langhorn snuffed out, like this morning's sun. Another light gone from my world. And myself, it seems, in peril again.

Volume Nine

'Ma'am,' said David Yale, 'you should not be here.'

He was plainly distressed. Extremely distressed.

I had just arrived. A long time since I last made this interminable journey to Wrexham. Five days, Israel the stable boy driving me on Tuesday, thirty-three miles to the Woolsack at Woburn. There, on Wednesday, I joined the London to Chester rattler, which took me to the Red Lion in Hillmorton. Thursday, a short twenty-six miles to the Lamb in Coleshill – Birmingham, of course – and some blessed respite. Yesterday, another full forty-five miles to the Swan in Wellington. And then, today, the final stretch towards Chester, though I alighted at the Whitchurch stop, hired a private carriage to convey me the last miles into Wrexham. To the George, where I had lodged previously until Elihu's mama insisted I should stay with her.

'But your note, boy,' I said, tapping the ferrule of the cane impatiently on the sandstone flags. 'It seemed urgent.'

It was late. Warm evening. There was a stench of stale tobacco, of rancid ale, that was not dissipated by the open window. But I was famished, my travel chest still blocking the low and oak-beamed busy entrance, though I had been here an hour already, in my room, and a message dispatched to Plas Grono to alert David – and Elihu too, I supposed – of my arrival.

'Urgent? Great heavens, I did not intend to give that impression.'

He almost stumbled as the innkeeper's boy, having finally arrived on the scene, clumsily hauled the case past him towards the stairs. David had merely told me that my husband was suffering with an ague. Three weeks past, but it had provided an excuse for my visit.

'You did not intend...? Why, do you know the state of the roads out there? Deplorable. It is England's peril. Lack of forward planning.

Fools saying there are too many carts and carriages upon the road. But what did they expect? And you, Master Yale – what impression *did* you intend to impart with word of your uncle's illness? What point advising me at all unless he was just short of death's door?'

'My apologies, ma'am. Sincerely. Have you dined?'

He stared about him, still uneasy.

'No, I have not,' I said. 'But what troubles you, boy? Not simply my presence, surely. Has there been disturbance here too?'

'You know?' he replied, as the innkeeper came to show me his smoke-fugged dining room.

'You shall join me for supper, naturally, David.' An imperious instruction as I extended my arm, that he might escort me. 'And of course I know. There has been word of little else in each of the establishments at which we stopped.'

It had been going on for weeks, since Bolingbroke was impeached in his absence, still in France with the Pretender. Then Harley imprisoned for his questionable part in the French peace process. Their supporters – Jacobite banditti – in riotous assembly. Dissenter chapels destroyed in Manchester and Monton. A Meeting House destroyed at Shrewsbury. Mobs on the streets of London. Quakers attacked in Holborn.

'I never thought to see it here,' he said, while the innkeeper showed us to a table at one of the two windows looking out upon Wrexham's High Street. Twilight still not descended upon the town, yet the houses and business establishments already had lights showing, or lanthorns gleaming from their doors.

'Forced to illuminate?' I asked. They were becoming all too familiar, the raiders who came after dark to attack any property failing to display support by blazing all night long. And the fellows at the next table, the other window, were more volubly raging about the same matter, one of them protesting that they should send for the Denbigh militia.

'They did not come so far as Plas Grono,' said David. 'But Uncle Elihu's manservant Griffith was collecting supplies.' He fell into a whisper, looking about once more to ensure none there might hear – though it seemed something of a redundancy, given the outrage so openly expressed by our neighbours. 'Came back with tales of rampaging all around,' he went on, 'a parcel of miscreants warning folk to be lit or to be damn'd – begging your pardon, ma'am. Then, this morning, word of last night's damage. The New Meeting House attacked. Pulpit all smashed. Pews thrown out upon the yard.'

The landlord was back at the table, offering us a mess of potage, bread, small beer, all of which we accepted most heartily – though I was not certain the landlord had heard us fully, he being distracted by the arrival of more customers. They were dressed well enough, yet they seemed already somewhat in their cups and nettled both by the lack of space to accommodate them, and then by the loyal toast being proposed at the second window table. There was a brief exchange of insults before the innkeeper finally forced them back into the entrance hallway and thence onto the street.

'Young men, I suppose,' I said, as our neighbours cried havoc upon such lack of respect for the King, and I caught David's eye to make the point. 'Young men. So easy to impress, are they not?'

If he took the jibe personally, he certainly succeeded in rising above it.

'According to Griffith, I regret to say,' he replied, 'those impressed to this particular mischief were almost entirely fellows who pursue reputable trade in the town, some of its most prominent citizens. Like those who just left, I suppose. Hardly ruffians or ignorant farm hands, I collect.'

'The Pretender has such a hold here?'

How things must have changed, I thought, and recalled a conversation between myself, Madam Yale and poor Mister Edisbury – whom Elihu had ruined in his greed. A conversation I had, at the time, reported to Parrish for Captain Baker. To reassure him that the level of potential insurrection in Wales was not as bad as they had feared. Simply a few foolish remarks, Edisbury had said, from the town's young men. And those young men, Elihu's mama had confirmed, rarely conscious of the true cause for their grievances. But this – this was something entirely different. Or perhaps those same young men had now taken their foolishness into maturity.

'Not principally Jacobites, I think,' said David, then paused as the food and drink arrived. 'My uncle says these are simply loyal believers in the Church of England. Feeling betrayed by the Whiggish faction. Betrayed by those who refuse to follow the High Church and such Dissenters thus become the scapegoat for all their ills.'

He did not say Dissenters like ourselves, but it must have been in his mind, as it was in mine. I spooned aside some of the grease from the surface of the stew, dipped my bread into the broth, sniffed at the dripping crust, trying to fathom whether the heaviness of seasoning might mask something questionable about the other ingredients.

'Folk injured?' I said.

'None so far. Unless you count Mister Lloyd. My master at the Grammar School. Died during the night – though it seems of an apoplexy and little connected to the riot.'

'Your uncle, I suppose,' I said, after we had each made some further innocuous responses, 'has sympathy for the mob – these being High Church fanaticals.'

'He will not condemn them, certainly. Says he has given generously to this parish, and that if those within the parish suffer by choice of the Dissenters' path, this is a matter that God must attend, for he cannot.'

I almost choked upon the gobbet of lamb I was attempting to chew.

'Great heavens,' I said. 'I heard him utter almost the same words about the Gentue and Mussulman slaves from which he made such profit.'

'Slaves?' he said. 'Surely...'

'They do not exist in Connecticut, sirrah?'

'Too few to tax, ma'am. And those of our beliefs shun the practice.'

'Well, I suppose your uncle would not speak of it,' I said. 'But that is how he made much of his wealth. That and my first husband's own fortune as his marriage portion.'

Oh, Joseph. How simple was my life when shared with your own dear soul.

'He says diamonds,' David protested. 'And his position as Governor, of course.'

'Of course. Though, as Governor, he was richly rewarded for his oversight of John Company's trade in Indian flesh and blood.'

He dropped his own spoon, splashing gravy onto the table's timbers and the pale green of his summer topcoat.

'His philanthropy...'

'Philanthropy, Master Yale, as an old friend frequently reminded me, is so often driven by fear of the Hereafter. By those who have more, in any case, than they could possibly spend in a dozen lifetimes. It is a lesson you would do well to learn.'

'A harsh view of the world, I collect.'

'Did it never occur to you, boy, that the breath of so many old folk smells foul simply because of the quantity of ordure they are forced to digest during their lives?'

He stared at me a long time and I wondered what was in his mind. This old maid across the table from him. Modesty cap. Still in my charcoal-grey travel clothes. I must have looked like somebody's widow – as I am, of course. Joseph's widow, all this time. But I had needed to shock him.

'Something must have wounded you greatly,' he finally said. 'Most of us who set ourselves among Dissent must share, I think, those portions of the gospels that most call for tolerance, forgiveness – understanding, even, of those who see themselves as our foes. But if you will forgive me saying so...'

The innkeeper again, clearing our bowls and offering us a sample of his fine plum pudding, perhaps a glass of raisin wine, all the way from Spain, he said. A delight, I replied, informed them that I, too, had originated in the Levant, born there in Alicante. David was surprised, asked me to recount the circumstance and I did so, still speaking of Papa when our desserts arrived.

'Perhaps something of this reason,' I said, 'that I tend more towards the eye for eye, tooth for tooth. We are each different. Is this not true in all things? There are papists – I know this – who practise their faith quietly and with threat to none, yet others who would see us burn at the stake unless we bow the knee to Rome. And there are Dissenters, you must believe, boy, who will turn to violence in pursuit of their more extreme beliefs. Levellers were so called for a reason. The Diggers too. My father was a friend of Winstanley. *"All things in common."* He saw the need to take action against injustice. And my father schooled me well in that tendency, I fear. And wounded? Your uncle has betrayed me in more ways than I can count, though it is in his slavish following of the High Church – and probably their Jacobite allies too – that has wounded me most.'

'Betrayal?' he said. 'You mean the letters, I collect. He has told you?'

I had no idea what he meant, called for the raisin wine we had been promised, then offered David a shrug of my shoulders.

'They shock you, boy – those letters?'

'So many,' he replied. 'Arriving in a great bundle like that. All the way from Fort St. George.'

No more than a moment's calculation to know the truth. Or I hoped the truth.

'His correspondence with Mistress Nicks,' I said. 'Natural he would want them returned. Now stored safely with her letters to him, I suppose.'

Anxiety, while I waited to see whether I had calculated correctly, relief flooding through me as he barely paused for breath.

'That I would not know.' He frowned, used a napkin to wipe some suet crumbs from the corner of his mouth. 'They were business associates, he says. Though he speaks of her with such fondness. And then her children?'

He searched my face. Wondering, I think, whether he had spoken too much.

'More devoted to them than his own,' I said. 'Unless, of course, you take the view...'

He threw up his hand.

'Please,' he hissed. 'No more. I am not so lacking in years that I require tuition in the ways of the world.'

Two small glasses of the sweet wine were set upon the table before the innkeeper moved on to deliver a dish of cheeses to our increasingly rowdy neighbours.

'They must be of import to you,' I said. 'Those letters. Their implication. As his heir, I expect you are entitled to know his intentions, the bequests within his will.'

'You mistake me, ma'am. I have no interest in inheritance.'

'We must all eat, boy. And Mister Dummer, for one, would pay a fine price to know the content of those letters. They would give him – leverage, I think, is the word. Or perhaps knowledge of the will would benefit you both.'

The spoon stopped, frozen in time, just short of his lips, the purple plum juice dripping back into the bowl.

'You surely cannot suggest that I would do so. It would be a betrayal of his kindness to me.'

'Sometimes one must needs set Satan himself to quench the Lake of Fire, sirrah. And betrayal? Your uncle's treachery towards me may simply hint towards wider sedition. This nation needs to know its enemies, boy. The letters may assist the good folk of Connecticut to develop the college they so deserve. Yet intelligence about High Church Jacobites, about Dudley North's family – those may be invaluable to the Crown itself.'

The spoon fell back upon the pudding and the light of understanding dawned in his eyes.

'Great heavens, you are not here through concern at all.'

'It was you, David,' I said. 'The Coronation Feast. That most astute observation that if one observes his friends, the man himself shall be revealed. The danger of Dudley's associations also. It made its mark upon me.'

'But he plans to call upon you. My uncle. He asked me to let you know. Tomorrow forenoon, I collect. Touched by your visit, he said.'

'Upon Lord's Day. Perfect. And I shall receive him with all courtesy, never fear.'

'He believes you may still be reconciled.'

'Then he is more the fool than I had thought. Yet I am stranded here until Tuesday, it seems. So, should you have anything for me before that time...'

'You truly expect that I should spy for you?'

There was genuine rage in his young voice. Dismay, perhaps. But then, through the half-open window, I saw the lit lanthorns, the blazing brands – though it was still not dark – borne aloft by a procession marching towards us from the High Street's farther end. Sinister, of course, when folk see fit to brandish fire when they have need of neither light nor warmth. And it seemed to me that David Yale's rage and dismay had somehow immediately infected all those others there in the dining room of the George. For the rioters were back about their business.

'Coming here?' I said, realising that the name of the inn was perhaps enough in itself to inflame their passions, regardless of the painted sign hanging upon the wall outside so plainly declaring that there had once also been a dragon associated with this particular George.

'More likely the Meeting Houses again,' said David.

We could hear them now. Chanting. *Down with the Rump. Down with the German.* Or *High Church and Sacheverell.* Or *Long live the Chevalier.*

'Well, that could not be more clear,' I said. Sacheverell again, still haunting us. And Chevalier, indeed. That same pretender who already threatened our shores seven years ago, who as a babe had been substituted for Mary of Modena's still-born infant. Great heavens, how long must we tolerate this nonsense?

They had the appearance of working men, with scythes, reaping hooks and clubs. Hardly the traders David had described. There was a fellow at their head, a wild rogue bearing a firkin raised upon a long pole and, within the small barrel, more fire. He began to lead them in song, and from the several other inns along the street, more folk came out to join them, almost a carnival atmosphere. That damn'd tune once more. *When the King enjoys his own again.*

I found myself clutching the locket at my throat, Davy and little Walter. For, despite their apparent gaiety, that mob made me afraid. Others too, it seemed, as the room began to empty. But the diners at that neighbouring table sat defiantly at their cheese, one of them beginning to hum *The Valiant Soldier*, making light of the rioters – until the window's glazing bars were smashed, splinters of wood and slivers of glass raining down upon them, a large cobblestone crashing down to skitter and thump across the flagged floor.

'Lord Jesus protect us!' David yelled and leapt from his seat.

Arms were raised to protect faces. Screams and shouts of anguish from within, laughter and mockery from the marching mob outside, now turning the corner into the lane for Chester.

'And the Almighty be praised,' I said, my voice quaking, 'that none were killed by that rock.'

But injuries there were. A gentleman clutching at his cheek, blood trickling between his fingers. Another with a piece of glass embedded in the back of his hand, and his sobbing wife doing her best to remove it. Other fellows shaking particles of the stuff from their wigs and the innkeeper out upon the pavement, screaming profanities at the procession.

'I believe I should be going now,' said David, perhaps recalling the anger he had shown before it was rudely disrupted. 'If you are safe, ma'am.' He was stiff, formal.

'Safe enough,' I replied, and brandished my cane. 'Just let those devils come near me.' A poor attempt at levity that left him still with a face like thunder. It had not gone as I had hoped. 'But remember my words, boy. Here until Tuesday. Now, get you gone. They shall not trouble me, those wretches.'

But as the candle gutters upon the table in my room and I dip the nib into my ink, I can hear them through the clear summer night's air, my own open window. The shouting. The disquiet of destruction.

That rabble. And all the night long, or so it seemed. This morning my determination to see for myself, and possibly provide a report for Stanhope. The disorder was one thing, the apparent failure of any authority to quell such pillage, quite another. This town is near to rebellion already.

'God's hooks, you are safe.' Elihu, waiting for me at the foot of the stairs, precisely as David Yale had done. Hat in hand. Unalloyed joy spread across his features. Not precisely the crack of dawn but early, all the same. 'And come all this way for me,' he said. 'My dear, I am deeply moved. Though we must carry you at once to Plas Grono. Whatever were you thinking?'

'Give you joy of this fine morning, Elihu.' A fine morning, though I had not slept well for the riotous commotion and, from first light, a carpenter working to replace that shattered window. 'But I am perfectly comfortable here at the inn.'

His joy turned instantly to plainly displayed sorrow.

'It wounds me, Catherine, that you should spurn my hospital-ity so.'

'I was told you were seriously infirmed,' I lied. 'My duty to my children that I should ensure their interests are protected. And here I find you the picture of health. I fear I have been practised upon.'

He did, in fact, seem very well. His face, still somewhat grey about the edges, less rotund than when I saw him last October, his attire now almost as fine as when we first met on the strand at Fort St. George, his flowing peruke carefully curled, breeches and lightweight coat in peacock blue. A walking cane with ivory handle I recognised from the house on Middle Gate Street. My house. Mine and Joseph's.

'I cannot think how you should believe so,' he said. 'As you see, I am well, indeed. A minor ague last month, nothing more.' Then his eyes brightened as he took note of my cloak. 'At least you were on your way to visit? David said you would do so. Great heavens,' he laughed, 'we might have passed each other on the road.'

'Simply a turn about the streets,' I told him. 'To see for myself the ruin your High Church friends have wreaked upon this poor town.'

'Alone, Catherine?' he said, his voice immediately full of concern.

I edged past him, while he exchanged distracted greetings with the innkeeper, and I stepped out upon the street.

'Lord's Day,' I called back to him through the doorway. 'I thought I should see whether those devils have left anywhere to worship.'

He followed me outside, set the hat back upon his head.

'My dear, they are no friends of mine. How could you imagine such a thing? And I had thought – well, there is my private gallery at St. Giles. But if you insist on this venture you must at least allow me to escort you.'

I was hardly enthusiastic about having his company yet nor did I relish risking these seditious streets without protection – though I had remembered to pack the pocket pistol. So I tolerated his prattle all the way along Chester Street. There was a grand house to my right and, on the left, a small crowd gathering – men, women and children, all about the task of clearing timbers, lath and bricks, from around a gateway. Over the low wall I could see the buildings beyond, almost entirely demolished.

'This?' I said.

'The New Meeting House, my dear. Must have been last night, I collect.'

I made towards the nearest of the women, busy with a shovel and clearing rubble. But Elihu held me back.

'Wait, Catherine,' he said. 'If you please. There is something I should say while there is a chance to do so.'

'You think I shall be affronted by whatever lies within?'

The woman with the shovel – her dark smock spattered with mud – wiped sweat from the brow beneath her white linen bonnet, and she regarded Elihu with something I could only interpret as pity.

'Not at all,' he replied, barely noticing her. 'But it has plagued me. That occasion when I called upon you at Latimer. I must have seemed such a piteous wretch. And I should have offered contrition when we sat together at Westminster Hall but...'

'Your allegation that I had somehow managed to cause the death of Mistress Nicks.'

Black crows wheeled, screeching and cackling, above our heads, and the stink of burning timbers scratched at my nostrils.

'There was never any such implication, Catherine. None at all. Simply a moment – well, I misspoke. And I would not have such a foolish error stand in the way of our being reconciled. I have still not given up hope.'

I held his gaze, trying to frame my answer. He was smiling at me. Optimistic expectation, despite these most inappropriate surroundings in which, it seemed, he truly wished to court me. Astonishing, even for him. Though the effect was spoiled still further by the dark decay of his teeth and no, I thought, I may often suffer loneliness to the depths of my soul, but this as an alternative? Yet as I opened my lips to speak, that same woman called across to him.

'A burden upon thy spirit, sir?' she said, and gestured towards the ruin around her.

'Mistress Urian,' he replied, assuming once more that haughty air I knew so well. 'As Master Shakespeare might say, "The silence often of pure innocence persuades when speaking fails." I am sorry to see any place of Christian worship brought so low, but these awful deeds place no burden upon me for I have no hand in them. Though it seems you are not alone in believing otherwise. Still, you should have a greater care where you cast aspersions.' He made a small gesture towards me with the handle of his cane. 'Yet allow me to name my spouse, madam. It seems you have much in common.'

'Give thee joy of this Lord's Day, Mistress Yale,' she said, with a hint of sarcasm, 'despite all this.' Her accent was heavy with Welsh dialect and I suspected she would be more at home in that tongue.

'Thou art a Friend of the Society?' I said, and she studied me more carefully. 'My father knew Fox very well,' I explained. 'They were buried on the same day. It seems my family's fortunes have always been closely woven with those of the Society.'

'And heaven be praised,' said Elihu, 'that your own Meeting House has been spared the attentions of those barbarians.'

Mistress Urian stabbed with the tip of the shovel's blade against one of the larger stones, looked several times from Elihu to myself, as though she could not quite understand how we came to be together. A fair conundrum.

'Should thee care to see the extent of it?' she asked me at last, and when I said that yes, I would appreciate it greatly, she set down the shovel and led us inside. There were many others here, folk weeping openly as they tried to salvage some meager remnants from the wreckage. And I must confess it caused me to weep also, though Elihu seemed hardly moved.

It transpired that this New Meeting House had been attacked on Friday evening too. But the pastor, Mister Kenrick, in this case at least, eventually persuaded them to desist.

Last night they were back, as I had seen and heard, and no amount of argument could now dissuade them. Kenrick and many of his flock forced to watch as the doors were ripped away, windows shattered, the roof torn apart and even the walls hacked to shreds – and all the substance of that rapine tossed onto the street or into the town's Great Pool immediately behind the chapel and its modest schoolroom. Mistress Urian led us through the rear entrance so we might see for ourselves – the whole green-slimed pond filled to overflowing with the debris.

'No hand in this?' she said at last to Elihu. 'I could name thee those tradesmen responsible for this and say which are thy friends, sir.'

I felt no need to defend him, though I recalled that mob from last night, the breaking of the George's window.

'They did not look like traders,' I said.

'No,' she replied. 'It is more often the traders who simply incite all this. The one perpetual truth, is it not? That those with least are always persuaded by those with most – the ones who have truly exploited them since time began – that the poor wretches in betwixt are the enemies of both.'

I have frequently expounded the same thought myself. Always those who suffer true disaffection, and always those who simply use the disaffected for their own ends.

'I fear,' said Elihu, 'that they are, rather, inflamed by the chatter-mongers, by their broadsides and penny ballad sheets, those harbingers of malice that take a vice in one town and extol it as virtue, so that the disaffected in some other place might ape the deed in their ignorance, believing it is expected of them. The curse of our society.'

I thanked Mistress Urian – a flax dresser, I now understood, with a shop on Town Hill – for her patience, hoped we might meet again under happier circumstance.

'Well,' I said to Elihu as we walked back towards the George, 'it seems I must, after all, accept your offer of prayers at this St. Giles.'

The bells had been ringing for some time, calling the faithful to worship, yet I heard in their tone some gleeful note that seemed to relish rather than mourn the vile destruction I had just seen. The High Church can so often, I have found, entirely misappropriate our Lord Jesu's teachings.

'Then I suggest, my dear, that we take a different route – that I might show you just a little more of the town. Its more pleasant aspect.'

He was pleased with himself, I could tell. But, for myself, I knew that if I wished to identify those who might be the leaders of such unrest I should only find them among the High Church congregations of St. Giles.

David Yale's face still wore the same harsh mask as when we parted yesterday evening. But his words – as we stood together at the top of the grassy slope in the burial ground outside the church at the service's end – were at least more gentle. He carried a small linen-wrapped package too, turned it over in his hands.

'You have seen the devastation for yourself?' he said.

'I thought about nothing else all through Canon Price's sermon,' I confessed.

The rector was still at the double doorway bestowing farewells and blessings upon his parishioners – including Elihu. And many of those folk regarded me with curiosity, whispered exchanges, as they had done when I was first spotted inside.

'Then you might wish to open this later,' said David, and passed me the package. He saw the surprise on my face and hastened to explain. 'The latest collection by your friend Matthew Parrish. I told you, I think. Your son, Benjamin, one of the subscribers. Though I gathered you do not have a copy yourself. I was almost halfway through before I realised – only because I have come to know you better, I collect – that his verses are so plainly meant for all of us who fear this darkness. But for you, directly, Aunt Catherine, are they not?'

I could feel the flush of warm scarlet rising up my neck and into my cheeks, used the package for a fan.

'I have not read them,' I said, then glowered at some stunted crone who had stopped upon the pathway, only an arm's length away to examine me more intimately. 'But I am certain you must be mistaken,' I went on when she had finally crept away. 'Meant for me? How might that be?'

He had said nothing to me beyond polite greeting all through the Matins, the Litany, the Communion and the sermon itself. A solemn affair, as you might expect, a dozen of us – Elihu's household – in that ornate wooden gallery my husband has financed and ordered built for the privacy of his worship, the statement of his self-importance. It looked down – literally and figuratively – upon the other worshippers, and also upon that fine white marble plaque, which marks the family vault and carved with the names of his father, mother, brothers David and Thomas, as well as that crazed old aunt, Mistress Hopkins, all at rest until the Last Day when they – all of us – shall stand before Lord Jesus to be judged.

'I suppose you must read them,' he murmured, as Elihu looked around for us, summoned us to his side.

'Give you joy of this fine church, rector,' I said, as we joined them and a third gentleman just inside the porch. But Canon Price failed to acknowledge me, so I added, 'And at least you must feel safe from the ravages of the mob here.'

'My dear,' said Elihu, cutting across my words, while Canon Price spat out some incomprehensible riposte, 'please allow me to name Justice Mellor, our most recently appointed magistrate. And a most welcome addition to our town.'

Fifty, I supposed. Slim and elegant in light chestnut attire to match his periwig. A fine-looking fellow, outwardly brimming with good humour – though perhaps I might test the depths of that façade.

'A Justice?' I said, as Mellor kissed my fingers. 'Whose peace do you protect here, sirrah? Certainly not that of those poor wretches at the Old and New Meeting Houses.'

The smile never faltered, while Elihu, for his own part, attempted to bluster some apology and Canon Price expressed open outrage.

'Gentlemen,' said Mellor, 'there is no offence taken on my part and Mistress Yale has the matter quite correct. We had all expected this unrest to pass with far less impact. I avow myself a Justice who has judged badly.'

Smooth as silk, I thought.

'And Mister Mellor,' said Elihu, in some haste, 'is almost an acquaintance of your own, Catherine.' Mellor seemed puzzled, and with good reason. 'My wife's most prized possession,' Elihu explained. 'A fine Maysmore clock that once graced your own property, sir.'

'Erddig Hall?' I said. 'You purchased Mister Edisbury's house?'

'You know it, ma'am,' Mellor beamed. 'It needs work. Some extension, perhaps. But it was an opportunity too good to miss.'

'We are privileged indeed, wife,' said Elihu. 'Justice Mellor is also Master of Chancery.'

It took no more than a moment.

'And when Edisbury lost everything,' I said, 'the house fell into Chancery's hands for disposal. To settle his debts. Great heavens, Mister Mellor, an opportunity indeed. How prime to be in the right place at the right time.'

I intended irony, naturally. Yet that look of feigned innocence upon Elihu's face that I knew so well. How much, I wondered, had he himself gained from this transaction? Was it not enough to simply ruin poor Edisbury without, I assumed, also having to benefit twice from the misfortune?

'Indeed,' said Mellor. 'A double opportunity perhaps. For I have gained a new home, my time to be divided between the Courts of Chancery and my magistrate's duties here in Wrexham.'

'Here, yes,' I said. 'And knowing you have misjudged, what now? Action, I hope, to prevent further rapine.'

It had so far been a fine morning but the sky was presently darkening, growing ominous. Quiet, except for the clatter of a horse and cart on the otherwise deserted cobbles leading from church to High Street.

'There shall be no more trouble,' he told me. 'I am certain of it. And I have already begun to speak with associates about providing some relief, help for those who have suffered most.'

'You must surely send for the militia, Mister Mellor.' It was David Yale, once more in advance of his years. 'Lest you be wrong.'

'Oh, I think we are not at that stage, young man.'

'I hate to say so,' said Elihu, 'but I fear my nephew may be correct.'

It was hardly a ringing endorsement, and Elihu seemed almost embarrassed, but he had at least taken sides. He gave me a weak smile, as though acknowledging that he made this stand because he believed it would appease me. But by then another fellow had approached and, upon seeing him, Canon Price hastily ushered us out of the porch, upon the pretense that he must prepare for the evening service – and slammed the doors behind us.

'Great heavens,' I said. 'How rude.'

Yet this other rogue had joined us. He had been lingering close to us for some little while and, unless my memory played tricks, he was the same man I had seen last evening, bearing aloft that flaming firkin, leading the mob.

'Militia?' he yelled. 'Did I hear you speak of fetching the militia? If you do so, Mister Magistrate, there shall be more than rubble upon these streets. Death to Dissenters, says I. A plague upon them all.'

His eyes, as they say, shot poniards at me. Am I so marked?

'I may not hear such talk, Mister Hughes,' said Mellor.

'I care not whether you hears or not, see?' shouted Hughes. 'I'm just telling you, like.'

I did not know it then, but David told me later that Edward Hughes is renowned as the town's trouble-monger. Five years ago, he had learned, Hughes organised similar mobs following Sacheverell's release, to rampage through the streets, smash the windows of all they believed lukewarm towards the High Church. And Hughes it was who had organised the crowds that flocked to hear Sacheverell speak here the following year. But this morning he stormed off to the gates, joined another group of folk, men and women, gathered there in heated discussion.

'I have to warn you, Mister Hughes...' Mellor shouted after him, even now the voice of reason. But I had heard enough, fury rising in my gorge.

'I have rarely seen such ambivalence,' I snapped, 'from the forces of law and order towards the victims of such heinous crime. I have to tell you, Mister Mellor, that if you do not send to Denbigh and the militia, I shall dispatch a galloper myself, as well as a note to Secretary Stanhope, advising him of all I have observed here.'

Our section of the burial ground fell silent, all eyes upon me, it seemed. Though yet another fellow detached himself from those at the gate, scurried towards us. That form of peruke so much in fashion with young men of his age, his tawny coat and breeches similarly in the current style and, beneath the coat, a full-length waistcoat of sky blue.

'Ah, Watkin,' said Elihu, grateful for the distraction, I think. 'I understand that congratulations are in order.'

'My marriage, sir?' he replied, and turned to glance back towards the gateway where a slender lass in drab olive skirts stood somewhat apart from the others, drumming fingers upon the missal she carried. 'Two weeks past. Joyous affair. But Edward Hughes tells me there is talk of the militia. Please say this cannot be true, gentlemen.'

'When the storm clouds gather,' I said, with a pretense of flippant gaiety, 'the intelligent man seeks shelter.'

Elihu at last thought to name me.

'I fear, Mistress Yale,' said Watkin, 'that I may not entirely have caught your drift.'

'Why, sirrah,' I replied, 'we were just discussing the fastest way to alert the High Sheriff, to seek help from Denbigh – for I have that right, do I not? I regret I am much the stranger here, but Denbigh, I think. The place from which we must seek help to sink this rebellion?'

I have seen such venom in a man's eyes once or twice in my past. Seaton. Porter. And here was a man – little more than a youth, little older than David Yale – of a similar stamp.

'Here, madam,' he said, 'you will find no rebels. Only those loyal to the true faith. And the good people of this town see their Church, their beliefs, under attack by the pompous Whigs. Blood is up, yet they hurt nobody.'

'They certainly drew blood when they smashed the window frame at the George,' I said.

'Sticks and stones alone, *Mistress* Yale. And how does the Whig-gish faction respond? With threats of a Riot Act, that those making peaceful protest might be shot for their pains. Shot by this same militia it seems you are so intent on bringing down upon our heads.'

'You presume a great deal, sir,' said Mellor, 'for a man who does not reside here.'

'And you, Justice,' Watkin Williams replied, 'presume a great deal for a man who has only been in Wrexham five minutes. My family has held land in this town for generations. My mines at Rhos, and the colliers who work there help feed many. And my people will not stand idly by, while the militiamen of German George trample their neighbours down.'

'God's hooks,' I said. 'A Jacobite. I should have known.'

'You speak the word as though it were a heresy, madam,' he replied, 'but James Stuart was anointed by our Church of England to rule our lands. A crime against God to deny the right of his offspring to succeed, to allow one usurper after the next to wear the crown instead.'

'The point, I think,' said Mellor, his voice still dripping honey, 'is that – while I may be High Church, and certainly a Tory by persuasion – I am able to see that King George is also our anointed monarch, while my oath as a lawyer, as Justice of the Peace, does not permit me to hear sedition spoken, to see its deeds upon our streets, I am bound to act. I am not without sympathy for the feelings of the town, but I had hoped that common sense might return once their spleen had been vented. Bound to act, sir.'

Watkin Williams, however, seemed to be thinking of something entirely different while, for my own part, I began to realise who this dreadful young man might be.

'And you say, madam,' he mused, 'that you should have known? A riddle, I think.'

'My husband failed to mention that we may already be indirectly known to each other. A history of betrayal that he has conveniently forgotten.' Now, Elihu's turn for confusion. 'You must be the son of Sir William Williams, I collect. Oswestry?' I saw my husband begin to understand.

'Indeed,' said this Watkin. 'But...'

'And your father, the son of that Sir William Williams, who was Speaker in Parliament.'

'Of course.'

'My dear,' Elihu stammered, 'perhaps we should discuss this later.'

But by then I had already informed Watkin Williams how I owed the grandfather a great deal for providing my son Benjamin with a place in his London Chambers but how, sadly, I owed Watkin's sire – and my husband too, for that matter – a very different debt, for having stripped Benji of that very same opportunity.

'Biddable,' I said. 'I think that was the word Governor Yale used to describe your father's willingness in that calumny. I assume that you also are biddable, Mister Williams, though to a different cause.'

'I see I have been entirely deluded,' said Elihu, having pursued me back to the George – though I would not allow him to accompany me inside, insisting that I needed rest. 'You bear such grievances,' he went on. 'Such bitterness.'

It had all broken apart rapidly, the protests from Watkin Williams ringing in my ears and Mellor taking the opportunity to make his own escape – but whether to send for the militia or not I did not know.

'Deluded, yes. You truly believed reconciliation might be possible after all that has transpired.' I saw from the shattered look upon his face that he did indeed harbour such absurd illusion. 'Extraordinary,' I said.

'Then why?' he almost sobbed. 'Here?' And then he thought about it more deeply. 'Wait,' he murmured. 'You mentioned Stanhope. Secretary Stanhope? This with Watkin Williams. You came here for no other purpose than to spy.' He truly seemed astonished. 'Upon me? What – will this be another of your damn'd denunciations, wife? My husband used his vague acquaintance with Sir William Williams, Baron Knight, to deprive my ingrate son of a profession in which he could never have survived anyway and, as must be well-known, Sir William's own son and heir is a self-confessed Jacobite, so that my husband, by association, must similarly be a seditionist too. Is that it, Catherine?'

'A little more complex than that, I fear,' I snapped.

'You swore to me, that you would not endanger our children further. You swore. No more politicks. And you cannot believe I have any involvement with treason. You cannot,' he raged. 'God's hooks, I refuse to believe this. In the matter of treason, I find I am more sinned against than sinning.'

'Your pardon, sirrah?' I said. 'What do you imply?'

It was my own guilt, I know. Thoughts of Parrish, other things, but I saw him bite his lip. He had said too much. But how?

'Young David,' he replied, perhaps a little too quickly. 'I have invested a great deal in the boy, hoped he might bring some High Church persuasion to Connecticut – though I find he is too much the Dissenter after all.'

I am certain that might be the truth, but it was plainly not the thing he intended.

'Well,' I said, 'I doubt we shall meet again before I return to Latimer and I have things to do.'

'Matters to set down in writing, I suppose,' he said, as I turned my back to enter the inn.

I span about, but he was already gone and since I came back to my room, began to write up these recollections, I have wondered constantly whether he could possibly know. But surely not. And I tried to distract myself instead with this volume of Matthew's verses. Each in the form of an epigram, in every sense of the word. Parrish to the core. Yet I had no sooner begun to do so than, almost as a counterpoint to his words, those riotous banditti commenced their terrible cacophony afresh in the distance. This poor town.

It all gives such poignancy, such precision, such predictability to his poetry. His *Progress of Our Nation* would have been terrifying enough, with its irony, its images of division, its accusations against those charlatans who hide behind patriotism simply for their own profit. And this.

You that survive and read this tale, take care
For this most certain exit to prepare
For only the actions of the just
Smell sweet and blossom in the silent dust.

An exhortation towards not merely being on the right side, but acting for justice too. Though did he intend this for me also? I say so not through any vanity, I hope, but rather because David Yale seems to be correct. I can read the entire volume as an open letter to myself. References here, so many of them. And some open enough to have allowed David to make his assumption. But others – words that Matthew and myself have shared shaping most of his lines. And the closing poem? *To a Lady of Quality.* Such lyrical account of our night together at Latimer, though naturally without the most intimate details. I have wronged him so badly I find and so soon as I am able I shall find a direction to which I might write him, begin to set things finally straight between us though, for the nonce, I will heed his parting couplet.

> *War is seldom just, it threatens each and every stride.*
> *So justice seek and, when war comes, with caution choose your side.*

I saw no more of Elihu yesterday, though Justice Mellor was back in town and I have since been forced to consider him somewhat more favourably. It was just after noon and I was eating dinner at the inn when word reached us – I know not how – that the Denbighshire militiamen were indeed upon the road. Thank goodness, for it has troubled my conscience that I did not fulfill the promise I made – threat, I suppose – to send for them myself. Though, by the time I finished eating, another crowd had gathered upon the High Street, worked to a frenzy, plainly intent on contesting their arrival.

'Colliers,' I told David Yale this morning when he came to see me safely on my way here, to Whitchurch.

'Watkin's men?' he said, helping the inn's boy load my travel chests aboard the yellow-painted carriage out in the yard. And I told him yes, that was precisely the innkeeper's opinion.

'But then Mister Mellor arrived. Several others with him. His retainers, I collect. And soon after, while the miners were still rampaging around town, we saw him send those retainers off in all directions so that, within the hour, they came to the George with that same Jacobite rascal in tow. Oh, young Watkin protested strongly, it seems. Swore that Mellor had no right to summon him this way. And many other forms of blather.'

'The nature of the beast, I imagine,' said David. 'Blather, as you say.'

The horses were being brought from the stables by another lad, their hooves echoing in the closed space, and I wondered whether David too might still be harnessed to my needs.

'Bold enough when he has those miners at his back,' I said. 'But alone? Whatever Mellor said to him was enough. I have never seen anybody so contrite, turning his hat over and over in his hands like some charity boy caught stealing apples. And when that other rogue Edward Hughes came to fan the flames, our friend Watkin Williams meekly told him the colliers must disperse. Hughes was furious, as you might imagine.'

'That fellow stands watching.'

There were no other travellers and I was pleased to have the coach to myself, though I shall not be so lucky with the onward journey from here to Woburn, and thence back to Amersham.

'And who, precisely, David, will perform the task?'

He handed me up inside, saw that I was carrying Parrish's tome.

'I had not realised just how near to rebellion we have come,' he said. 'You read them?'

'Mister Parrish has seen the dark clouds gathering these many years. And, like others among us, he has paid a price for his vigilance. But now it seems the storm is about to break upon us in all its fury.'

'Still, my uncle's correspondence – immoral as it may be – is still his private concern. I shall not use them as you wished.'

I settled myself upon my seat, plumped up the pair of cushions I had persuaded the innkeeper to provide for my additional comfort.

'I should probably have thought less of you had you spoken otherwise.' Damn me, I find that I like the young man. 'But you were wrong,' I said. 'About me not being here through concern. The truth? I should not have been here for anything less. Concern for my country, of course, more than anything. No foolish nonsense about loyalty to one crown or another – simply a care that my children, my grandchildren, should be allowed to live without threat from those who would curse them so constantly with bloody war.'

'Yet no care for Uncle Elihu, I collect,' he smiled.

'Even there, boy, you are wrong. I may loathe him. But I have learned this much at least. That you cannot spend thirty-five years as anybody's spouse without you both becoming two sides of the same single coin.'

The carriage began its slow turn through the inn's gate, hauled the few yards up the slope from the swine market before it might turn along the High Street. The conveyance was barely moving, the horses snorting and straining at their traces, and I wondered whether the poor beasts could drag us that far. But David's hand was still upon the open window as he walked alongside, almost pushing us on our way.

'I am pleased to hear you say so, Aunt,' he said. 'And the rest – well, I shall help if I am able. Anything about Dudley North's connections, everything I gather here in Wrexham – Edward Hughes or more – and I shall write post-haste.'

A strange path that brings me north again – though now to Streynsham's present direction at New Hall, Makerfield, near Wigan. The house must have stood here two hundred years, a true jumble of differing styles all mingled together and forming a pleasant whole, surrounded by the trees in all their autumnal morning glory I can see now from my window. Streynsham's son, Legh, gained the property through his marriage to Margaret Launder. They both seem so desperately young – and Streynsham the aged parent, now in their care.

But from that path of which I speak, let me not be distracted. The first steps, the week early last month, in September, during which there was momentous news. French Louis dead. Gangrene. So much time a-dying. They say that three times he bade farewell to Madame de Maintenon, his secret wife, and twice to the Court. But such an unexpected impact on us all. He has been part of my life for as long as I can remember, like a second shadow. More than seventy years upon the old enemy's throne. More than all my years on this earth. And enemy? Yes, of course. But one fixed point in our world that has otherwise changed beyond recognition. And there had been relief, I suppose – the belief that, with Louis dead and France in a state of flux, any threat of imminent rebellion by these Jacobite devils – normally so dependent upon French support – might be dispelled. But no, to the contrary, word trickled down to us that Scotland's John Erskine, the Earl of Mar, had declared for the Pretender, raised James Stuart's standard at Braemar and, since then, has taken several Scottish towns with an army many thousands strong. And so it begins, the road to war once again.

Second, the promised letter from David Yale. Polite preliminaries, his delight at having secured a scholarship at Pembroke College,

Cambridge, then evidence that he has, indeed, determined to set himself within "the actions of the just." I have brought the letters to show Streynsham, over dinner in an hour from now.

Our Justice of the Peace, Mister Mellor, he writes, *required me to bear witness at the Great Sessions in Ruthin. Thirty-one stood accused of either petty larceny or simple grand larceny, but though I was able to precisely relate all I had seen when we dined together at the George, some of my testimony was dismissed as hearsay, for I was unable to specifically identify any of those present in the dock. And those that I could have identified – Edward Hughes among them – seem to have evaded capture. But there were witnesses aplenty without me, it seems – Mister Kenrick and others – to ensure that some of the perpetrators received their appropriate rewards. Some branded upon their thumbs and given Benefit of Clergy. Others pilloried. A few sent to the House of Correction and sentenced to hard labour. And three transported to our American colonies, at their own expense, naturally. Yet, needless to say, none of those punished were from among the Tory merchant gentlemen of Wrexham who had so fanned the flames.*

Of course not. There is a hierarchy in these things that we all understand. Those among the powerful and wealthy with a vested interest in changing society for their personal gain enlist a tier of rogues – fellows with whom they would not normally even pass the time of day, except for this purpose. Fellows, however, who have that unique ability to whip the emotions of those they need most, the poor devils who, without understanding the way they are manipulated, will swell the ranks, sacrifice all, while the wretches at the top remain unscathed, regardless of the outcome. It is some of those, I collect, we have helped to bring down in the past – and I pray to Our Lord we may do so again.

Yet I did subsequently hear, says David, *something more about Hughes. It came to me indirectly, a conversation I overheard between Uncle Elihu and Griffith, his manservant. It seems that Griffith had been imbibing – as is his wont – at the Lion in town and there, just before the Sessions, Hughes had been openly boasting about his need to be out of Wrexham. And threats, that all Dissenters, all followers of German George, would soon be swept away. He himself, he claimed, would be an instrument of the Almighty's vengeance. But, for the nonce, to distance himself from the militiamen, from the court's constables, he was away to a part of the world where there existed none but those who share his ambitions. None but those ready to lay down their lives for the King Over the Water. Folk mocked him, naturally, demanded to know where this magical place might be. Paris? They said. Rome? But no, he replied. Only Lancashire. And specifically, Preston.*

Preston, there. Benjamin has told me so many times. His letters, his occasional visits. A town full of attorneys and proctors. Notaries by the hundred. The courts, naturally. And outside that circle, he claims, almost impossible to find anybody except High Church Tories or openly worshipping papists, the Pretender unashamedly adored. As it happens, David's first letter arrived within weeks of my return to Latimer. My daughter Kate and her husband Dudley had arrived at Plas Grono from Glemham for a visit and repeated some interesting comments about that cousin of his, William North – who has for some time been Governor of Portsmouth, where he rules with a garrison of Scots Guards. And Dudley seemingly thought it a huge amusement that, according to North himself, each day they collectively drank the Pretender's health. I had passed the intelligence to Stanhope – with the almost immediate effect that Lord North has been relieved of his duties.

But David's mention of Preston persuaded me, in part, that I should at least make the pilgrimage to these parts. Visit Benjamin. Perhaps assess the situation for myself. Maybe to track down Parrish. That and the invitation from Streynsham himself, of course.

'I feel,' said Streynsham, 'that half of me is missing. It is most peculiar.'

A tear trickled down his face and I think I have never seen him so dishevelled, wrapped in a moth-eaten emerald banyan, his head crowned with a soot-stained turban, his otherwise imperial features now somewhat decayed, those once limpid eyes become rheumy. He smells none too fresh either.

'Two sides of the same coin,' I said, as I had so recently spoken the words to David Yale. 'And all that useless advice we are given. About being strong. About time being the healer. About the bounty of the Lord Jesus and the life hereafter. In truth, only those who have suffered such loss can fathom its true depths – that there is nothing except the emptiness, the passage of one lonely day after the next.'

Dinner was a simple affair of roasted beef and thin potatoes, but at least we were alone. For I have the sense that young Legh Master and his new wife do not entirely find me to their taste.

'I fear you may be right,' he replied. 'Lonely indeed. Still cannot believe she is dead. Poor Elizabeth. Bless her soul. Though heaven knows we had our disagreements.'

We each sat in silence for some while, pushing the remnants of our food around the plates until I finally broached the reason, I believed, he had sent for me.

'About me, Streynsham?' I said quietly.

'I think Elizabeth saw something in our friendship that she exaggerated. Or misunderstood perhaps.'

'Did you never wonder, old friend, whether it was not, rather, you and I who chose to misunderstand it?'

'And too late now,' he said, 'to explore that avenue afresh? A way to fill our respective emptiness?'

I glanced around the New Hall dining room, at the dark-varnished wainscot, the polished rubbing rails, the grey and rose-tinted tapestries above that hung from the intricate ceiling.

'Too late,' I smiled. 'Yet I am somewhat flattered you even thought to raise the matter. Though I doubt I was the only cause of discord in your life with Elizabeth. Peter, perhaps?'

'She loved her brother dearly. Would never hear a word against him, even when he went to the Tower.'

'And now where does he stand? This latest sedition.'

'Transformed, I collect. I know his sympathies remain firmly in favour of the Pretender, though he seems to have learned the futility of that enterprise. He claims to have cautioned his friends in the Cheshire and Lancashire Jacobite Clubs against making the same mistake as those devils in the West Country.'

The third step, perhaps. At the end of September and early this month, a whole batch of arrests across Cornwall, Devon and Somerset of those Jacobite plotters who had planned the capture of Bristol, Exeter and Plymouth in the Pretender's name. As usual, though, it is principally the intercessors who are arrested, while many of those who designed the sedition – that same Henry St. John I had first seen at the baptism of Annie's boy, William, four years ago, and St. John's associate James Butler – have escaped justice through their self-imposed exile on the Continent. St. John will lose his Bolingbroke titles through a bill of attainder, naturally, as Butler has already lost the Ormonde dukedom. Still, I wish we had seen them on the gallows and that such will be the fate of those ringleaders who have been taken, like Sir William Wyndham, now held in the Tower.

'You mean your brother-in-law has learned not to be caught,' I said.

'A little more than that, at least. You know it was Stanhope's network that infiltrated the plot? Yes, of course. But you may not know Thomas Wybergh. A useful fellow, a dragoon captain of my acquaintance who sometimes serves as an intelligencer. I privately arranged for Wybergh to apprehend Peter. It was enough. A night in the gaol, memories of his previous incarceration. As a result, we now know that French Louis had promised weapons, ships and men, but with his death – well, it seems this has taken the wind from the sails of Peter's friends. Most of them have heeded his warning, though there are those here in Lancashire who most certainly have not.'

'Preston,' I said.

'You have lost none of your edge, Catherine,' he smiled, then waited while a manservant came to remove the dishes and I took the opportunity to show him David's letter.

'You see the part?' I said. 'Where he talks about one of the riot's instigators – this wretch Edward Hughes – making his way to Preston also, in search of fellow rebels there?'

'It makes sense,' said Streynsham. 'You know, of course, about the rising in Northumberland too.'

We had the news a few days before I set out upon the road, yet it seemed of no consequence. A rabble, according to the broadsides, likely intent on joining up with the Earl of Mar's army and, therefore, equally likely to be crushed by the King's men dispatched for that purpose.

'They pose a threat, suddenly?'

'Difficult to say. There are reports of them from Kelso and other places, though all is confusion. General Carpenter chases them hither and thither but seems mostly intent on keeping them from attacking Newcastle. You know who leads them?'

'The Earl of Derwentwater,' I said. 'So said the last report I read.'

'Not any more, my dear. Now they are firmly under the command of a certain Sir Thomas Forster.'

I could scarce believe my ears. Toad-like Forster, who had tried to turn my son-in-law James to his cause. Forster who I had also seen at Staveley. Forster, who had accosted myself and Parrish at the Menagerie, then arranged Matthew's arrest. Forster, who had threatened me personally. Forster, the interview I had with Walpole – the rogue seen in company with that wretch Colonel Porter. Forster gone to ground in Northumberland.

'And Porter?' I said. 'Is there word of him too?'

'They ride together, I think.'

'Ride?'

'Indeed. Forster has been leading them to and fro. To Newcastle, though he found that too strongly defended for his liking. Then back to Kelso. Disappeared into the fastness of the border country for a while.'

'From what I saw of the wretch,' I said, 'Forster would not be sensible to the fact that rebellion requires vigour rather than meandering procrastination.'

'He would not, though Derwentwater might have done. But now it seems they have been sent reinforcements. Two thousand wild Scotsmen. And Old Mackintosh to strengthen his backbone.'

'Presently, where are they?'

'We don't know.'

'But Preston a possibility?'

'For anybody who might sum two and two, yes. I think so.'

'And the King's forces?'

'Too thinly stretched. The Tories so desperate to cut taxes after that so-called peace with the French that the army's flensed to the bone. Major General Wills on his way to Manchester. Otherwise, we have only Sir Henry Hoghton's county militia.'

The blood almost froze in my veins.

'Hoghton,' I said. 'The last time I saw Matthew, he was bound for Bedford. And then here to Lancashire to help raise that very force. Though can it be true – that war shall come to us here?'

Terrible images. So many of those I love embroiled if this threat of bloodshed visits itself upon Lancashire. Benjamin, of course. Matthew too. And even dear Streynsham. My friend of so many years was smiling at me. The old Streynsham.

'Damn your eyes, Catherine,' he said. 'When you responded so quickly to my invitation, I almost thought – well, no fool like an old fool, as they say. It is Parrish, is it not, has brought you all this way?'

He tried to rise from the table, but groaned terribly in the process. 'Would you mind?' he said, flopping back down upon the chair. 'My pipe?'

It was there upon the mantle shelf with his tobacco jar and his tasseled silver tinder box.

'The old knees,' I said, eased myself up with the help of my stick, crossed the room to fetch them for him. 'I have the same trouble, especially when the weather is damp. But Parrish? Only one of the spurs that drives me here. Do you know where they are, these Lancashire militiamen?'

'I have no idea, Catherine. But if they are not already at Preston, I think you can be certain they will be there before too long. Yet you should think long and hard before you make that journey, my dear. For if there is fighting, you shall be greatly at risk.'

Nobody, it seemed, wanted to run the risk of bringing me here. So, hardly the most prestigious of arrivals in this Proud Preston last Thursday. Little better than a high-sided Fly Wagon that myself and one other passenger were forced to share with the carter's casks of salted pork, some noxious hides, and bales of Manchester fabrics. Only a mildewed tarpawling to shelter us from this winter's first flurries of snow as we jolted and bounced our way from Wigan on the route that may style itself the King's High Road through Preston town to Scotland, but certainly does not merit any regal appellation.

And it took me several days more than I had intended with Streynsham to arrange even this modest form of transport. Legh Master and his wife, it seems, suddenly found themselves called away from New Hall and in desperate need of their own carriage. Their neighbours too, and poor Streynsham beside himself with frustration that he could no longer command assistance for me. But there I was, finally upon the lane from Wigan as it shook us down onto the Ribble Bridge from which I caught my first glance of the town upon the ridge above us.

'Here since the Romans, they say,' said the gentleman merchant in the opposite corner, shifting the canvas slightly so he could look down upon the parapet.

'Does it always stink like this, sirrah?'

'Exceptionally low tide, I collect. The mud, you know. Almost dried out.'

Preston certainly seemed pleasant enough apart from this stench, for it spread out along the higher ground, perhaps a mile distant and running almost perfectly from east to west, right to left, with its church tower dominating the buildings at this nearer end. But it soon disappeared from view again as we trundled into the sunken thoroughfare – with high bare hedges above us atop its steep banks – connecting the bridge to the town's outskirts.

'And how long shall you remain?' I asked.

'As little time as my business permits, madam. The market on Wednesday and, after that, I shall be away from here like the devil was at my tail. Those damn'd Jacobites...'

He stopped, his face aghast, though this mumchance not brought about, I realised, by his lapse of polite education, his mild blasphemy. No, there was something of fear in his eyes.

'Yes, sir,' I said. 'You should have a care.'

An idea had been forming in my mind since we left Wigan. A provisional plan, should one be needed.

'I have nothing against King Jamie, Mistress. Nothing, you understand – if that is where your loyalties lie.'

'My loyalties are my own,' I snapped, and lifted the canvas again, finding that we were passing some alms houses and a five-barred gate opened to allow our entrance to the town proper.

It is, they say, as large as Liverpool or Manchester, though without the industry of those towns. For, according to both Streynsham and Benjamin, only linen is manufactured here and all the rest is agriculture, for the three weekly markets, and all the trade revolving about the courts.

I found myself fingering the locket hidden at my bosom by the heavy yellow neckerchief wrapped about me inside the cold-weather cape. But perhaps he mistook the gesture for something else – something with religious connotation.

'More good, honest Roman Catholics in these parts than almost anywhere else in England, ma'am,' he said with feigned glee. 'Why, you knows the origin of the town's name, I collect. Priests' Town,' he insisted. 'Yes, indeed. Priests' Town.'

We passed the parish church and some very grand houses, myself left wondering whether the rogue was practicing upon me. Yet I decided to let it pass, grateful for the comforting wafts of wood smoke that soon muted the malodorous atmosphere within the wagon.

'It reminds me somewhat of London in my childhood. Before the Great Fire,' I told him. And that was true. 'When our rulers were perhaps more kindly towards those of my faith.' A pretty enough piece of dissembling, I thought.

'London,' said the merchant, 'I have never been so far. What a joy it must be. The very centre of things. Fresh news every day.'

'Whereas here, I imagine, it is always stale.' I could not help a sniffle as the odour of those hides caught in my nostrils.

'Always. Why,' he said, forcing a smile, 'we shall have no word of King Jamie's loyal followers until they are almost at the Friargate Bar.'

'Nothing from the north, sirrah?'

'Rumours, dear lady. Rumours and nothing more. Carlisle, I heard. Though likely nothing but some rascal's lies. Their march impeded by the militia. A *posse comitatus* of local citizens too. Hanoverian rogues, what? Do you not say so, ma'am? Yet no sooner had I heard that version than I was also told the selfsame *posse* and militia are routed at Penrith. Who knows which, if either, may be true?'

I said nothing, for here this east-west street turned sharply right, around the outside of a market square with inns aplenty and a grand structure, four storeys high, that must surely be the Town Hall, then swung west once more and north. And there, just beyond the junction, we drew into a coaching yard. The road itself, I could see, from here descended the ridge again, on its other side and now down towards Lancaster, past further wealthy dwellings. But here I was – at my destination.

'And what can possibly go wrong?' I said to Benjamin. 'We simply need to remain slightly circumspect about my true loyalties.'

It was dark as we left the White Horse. Still, I marvelled that this upper stretch of the street I now knew to be Friargate was lit by oil lamps hoisted upon iron poles – as fine as any I might have seen on Broad Street or High Holborn. There had been an interminable row since I met him during the afternoon, of course. Yes, he had received my note to say that I would visit but said he had foolishly believed it was some maternal instinct that brought me there – as, of course, it was. Well, originally, at least.

'What do you think, Mama – that Preston will raise a *posse* to oppose the banditti here? In your dreams, perhaps. And mark my words, you shall be putting yourself at risk with this masquerade. To what end, precisely?'

He has begun speaking to me, at times, as though I am already in my dotage. But I had persuaded him to show me his lodgings. At the house of Mister Winckley Junior, a barrister-at-law, further down the hill from the mansion of his apparently more famous father, lawyer Thomas Winckley. I am worried about Benjamin, however, for he has lost the colour from his cheeks, grown so terribly thin. He says it is nothing, some recent fever from which he is now recovered, but it troubles me, all the same.

'Is it so unlikely?' I said. 'This whole town stands upon a ridge. And is there not some military axiom about defending the high ground? How difficult can that be?'

'Not difficult at all,' Benjamin smiled and took my arm, steered me around a midden as we crossed the street still busy with carts illuminated by their own lanthorns. 'If only you could find sufficient fellows here in this wasp's nest of Jacobites with the will to make it so.'

'If it is be so dangerous, you should not have allowed me to come,' I snapped, and he threw up his hands in despair. As though he could have stopped me. 'And papists, you intend, surely. Yet does their faith automatically bend them to the Pretender's cause?'

'It happens there are more Catholics in these parts than anywhere else in England.'

We passed another inn, the Boar's Head, yellow light spilling in opaque diamonds out across the street.

'So I have recently been told,' I said, recalling the merchant in the Fly Wagon.

'This county therefore feels itself more penalised by anti-Catholic laws than most others. Citizens believe themselves the dispossessed, the downtrodden, the wretched, the victims of gross injustice.'

I paid close attention to the elegant gables all around me, to the neat attire of those upon the street.

'You believe that nonsense?' I said.

'I have come to understand it, even though I might not accept its veracity. Why, not far from here, in Burnley, the Towneleys openly boast of being able to raise twenty thousand for the Jacobites. It is foolish grandiloquence though that matters not. Sometimes a staunch superstition is more powerful than a fistful of facts.'

'Are all those laws upheld? Their chapels still stand, do they not?

And did you meet no Catholic scholars at Oxford? Of course you did. These are false grievances, Benjamin. False.'

'Not the point, Mama. The laws exist. That's the thing. I had only arrived here when they tried to indict a whole group of Lancashire men as recusants.'

'Tried? And therefore failed, did they not? And we Dissenters, are we not disadvantaged too? Though it does not drive us to become Jacobites and traitors.' We turned into a darkened lane on the right, no oil lamps here, though I could still see that the house before which we halted was both fashionable and substantial. 'And this?' I said. 'Your lodgings, I collect. But before we go inside, this barrister, Mister Winckley – he is a loyalist?'

'You will find few in Preston that fit such description, Mama. Not the mayor, nor the magistrates, nor yet many of the burgesses. They may not be outright Jacobites but they have no love for German George either.'

That was a rare lack of respect from Benjamin but in the gloom, as we climbed the front steps to the front door, and his face muffled in the collar of his coat, I could not divine whether it was the result of too long spent in this place or perhaps simple irony.

'And you, Benjamin – where stand you now?'

'How can you ask?' he snapped. 'It is simply a fact that the only notable in town who might willingly make a stand is Reverend Peploe. But I remain a lowly prothonotary here at the courts. A need to maintain at least an air of neutrality.'

'How fortunate for you,' I said. 'But a luxury I cannot afford, boy. Though not such a bad thing, I suppose – that the neutral son might indeed have a partisan mother. So when we meet Mister Winckley, I will thank you to follow my lead. For tonight I may have to profess just enough ambiguity in my loyalties. You can feign a certain distance from me if you prefer. And to what end, you say? Do I need to explain? I can see it in your face even in this gloom, Benjamin. At my age, you are thinking. *Foolish old woman*, I suppose.'

He rapped on the knocker.

'The only foolish thing,' he said, 'is that you should think so. I have a duty too, Mama. A duty of care when you risk putting yourself in harm's way.'

*

The same night, last Thursday, I was back at the White Horse after another disagreeable discussion with Benjamin. This time disagreeable for another reason, for it had only been an innocent enquiry from Mister Winckley to my son, concerning the health of his sweetheart, that had alerted me to Benjamin's newfound liaison here in Preston and about which, of course, he had himself told me nothing. I was vexed that he should see fit to keep such a thing from me and we parted on less than amicable terms. My time with Mister and Mistress Winckley, on the other hand, had been fruitful enough and I hope I have sowed sufficient subtleties that they might take me for at least a passive supporter of the Pretender – as, I gathered, they are too.

I mulled the evening's events with a mixture of annoyance and satisfaction while I prepared to settle for the night with a cup of warm milk prepared for me by the elderly innkeeper, Sumners – or, more correctly, by the even more venerable Mother Sumners. The rooms are well appointed though the floors slope rather, some subsidence of the foundations, I suppose. Yet there was great comfort from the fire still blazing in the hearth. But as I sipped at my beverage, thought about setting nib to parchment, above the other noises of the establishment I heard the first beatings of a mournful drum in the distance, though coming steadily closer.

I went to the window in my night gown and bed bonnet, peered through the quarry glass and could just make out the outline of folk gathering near the corner of that market square away to the right. There was a hard frost already but I knew I must open the casement to better see what was happening, but it was stuck fast and I wrestled with the catches for some moments before I was finally able to free the thing and lean out over the street, a blast of freezing air fanning sparks in the fireplace.

By then the drummer boy was almost immediately below, tapping out a beat that might have been an execution march, and disordered ranks of militiamen plodding up the hill behind. There were a few horses, scarlet-coated officers scattered hither and thither, but for the most part they were foot, with military muskets and equipment but a hodge-podge of civilian attire. Their heads were hung in sullen silence. No noise except the scrape and rasp of boots and clogs upon the cobbles, a weary army, perhaps four hundred strong in total. But if their morale was already low, they must have been dejected indeed by a civic reception more frigid even than the November weather could bring.

A silent and meagre gathering of townsfolk. None of the joy I have so often observed that is sometimes engendered by the spectacle of military parades. Here simply a mutual sullenness. At least until most of the militiamen had turned the corner, passing from my view into the market square and its Cheapside. And then there were just a few desultory cries. *Down with the Rump. To hell with German George.* But they were muted, less enthusiastic than the taunts I had heard so much upon the streets of Wrexham.

Finally, at the tail of the column, as I began to close the window once more, came a string of wagons and, beyond those again, a small troop of mounted soldiers, riding capes over their uniform coats and breeches, short muskets – *carabines*, I collect – at the ready. Leading them, an officer I knew well. Matthew Parrish.

He had seen me, though I could not fathom the expression on his face as he rode past, turning in his saddle to keep me in view all the way until he also disappeared around the corner. But to where? They must surely stop in town for the night, must they not? And I spent the subsequent hours sleeping only fitfully, almost certain he would return. I started awake with every creak of the old place, imagining him upon the stairs with each noise, and it was long before dawn when I finally ventured below, found Mother Sumners early at her kitchen.

'Those brazen rogues last evening,' I said, 'they will be long gone by now, I trust.'

I picked up her besom and began sweeping the floor, to which she raised no objection.

'Call the'selves Lancashire men,' she said, and spat upon the flagstones, lifted a kettle from the hearth. 'God damn their eyes.'

Hoghton's militia, she confirmed. Likely encamped somewhere near the Patten place.

'And where might that be?' I said. 'Will the real men of this town not burn it to the ground about their ears?'

It seems I must have passed the house on my way into town, on Churchgate, this side of the bars. She found it hard to believe I could have missed it. A considerable mansion belonging to the

Earl of Derby. Here she spat again, then added that since his bloody lordship had no love for poor Preston – it bein' beneath him an' all – it is leased to Sir Henry Hoghton as his town house and now, she believed, would serve as his headquarters, though she was certain they would run like dogs as soon as Jack Highlander arrives here.

I accepted a bowl of gruel from her, endured some questions about my reasons for being in town, about how long I would stay, and about whether King Jamie would be welcomed back in whatever part of the country I hailed from – some fine place, she imagined, and how honoured she was to have me lodge with them. Sickening stuff, really, but it gave me time to think.

Benjamin must act for me, of course, for there was nobody else I knew here and therefore none I could trust. So, back in my room, I took the artichoke juice from my writing slope and penned a short message on one side of a small piece of parchment, watched as it dried and vanished from sight.

Tonight. Ten. Disguise. Outside Inn.

On the other side, a short shopping list in plain ink.

Artichokes.
Eggs.
Flour.
Alicante.

Later, when the town was astir, I determined to make my way to that Town Hall I had seen the previous day – for that, Benji had told me, also housed the courts and thus the prothonotary's office. So, in my heaviest winter cloak, and with my trusty cane to steady me on the rhimed paving of the square, I stopped to admire the market cross, and came to that building. Still, it surprised me with its grandeur. Half-timbered, mainly red brick, four storeys, each tier projecting out above the one below, and a bell tower at this end, like a black and white buttress, the walls covered in ivy with only a few russet leaves left upon the stems.

The ground floor was all shops, of course – eight in total, I think, with the serving hatches of a shoemaker, tailor and hook-vendor already open for business, the tradesmen crying their wares – and on the far side a flight of stairs to the first level, busy with the burgesses of the town, a veritable swarm of them, an angry gathering, I collected, in response to last night's arrival of the Lancashire Militia. They were crowded above, in the antechamber to the meeting hall also, shouting their shared disloyalties or sharing speculation about the proximity of Derwentwater's army.

'God bless the true King, gentlemen,' I said on a couple of occasions, 'but for pity's sake let an old woman pass.' And in this way I finally succeeded in forcing my way to the spiral staircase leading to the two upper floors, where I soon found Benji's own chamber. Hardly commodious despite the importance of his office.

'I came to apologise,' I said, easing myself into the chair on the nearer side of his scroll-laden desk, and gazed in wonder at the tumble of other documents piled so high that the walls could hardly be seen.

'You, Mama?' he replied. 'I am guessing you have some devious scheme in which you seek my interference.'

'No, truly. This young woman with whom Mister Winckley says you are smitten – I should wish to meet her.'

'Then you shall be disappointed. For she is struck down with an ague and I have not seen her this se'ennight past. In truth I may have inflicted the thing upon her, for that fever I mentioned to you – it seems my recovery has come at the cost of Mary's own debilitation.'

'Should I attend upon her, perhaps?'

'Mama, please.' His voice dropped to a whisper. 'I do not believe in coincidence. You made your intention in visiting Preston very clear. And then the Lancashire Militia arrive here. Hours later you are sitting at my desk…'

'Is it not possible I might be here equally through concern for my only surviving son.'

'I hate it so when you do that.'

'Then through sincere interest in his future happiness.' He shook his head, wrapped fingers around his mouth and blew between them in exasperation. 'And yes,' I added, 'through whatever modest part I might play against sedition.'

'I shall be sure to pass your best wishes to Mary as soon as I am able,' he said, and I was pleased to at least have a name I could put to whoever this chit might be. 'But, for now, it would be easier if you tell me whatever it is you want from me.'

He gestured around the chamber at his mounds of outstanding work while I delved inside my cloak and then within my skirts, found the piece of parchment folded against the pocket pistol – for I would not be abroad in this nest of banditti vipers without its protection.

'Here,' I said. 'You know the Patten House, I suppose? I need this delivered securely. Might you have cause for business there?'

'Artichokes?' said Benjamin. 'At this time of year?'

'Yes, artichokes.'

'And who, precisely,' he whispered again, 'might you expect to fill your basket with these purchases, Mama – Sir Henry Hoghton perhaps?'

'Of course not, boy. But Sir Henry will have his own adjutant. You must make sure the fellow knows the urgency of putting this into the hands of nobody but Matthew Parrish.'

I was certain he would not come, spent the whole evening like some foolish girl rather than the desiccated old hen I have become. And I alternated between recollections of Benjamin's mixture of astonishment at Matthew's presence – all that renewed and suspicious interrogation again about my true motivation in being here – and images of Parrish in all the many guises within which I had known him over these past forty-five years. Including – well, including that night at Latimer.

A bell in town tolled the hour of ten, though I could barely hear it for the noise below. Lusty singing of *The Loyal Lass* from some of the militiamen, I gathered, plainly having decided that the White Horse might be a safe haven for them, since the sign above the door does, after all, represent the Hanoverian emblem – though, given her beliefs, it astonishes me that Mother Sumners has not seen fit to name the place anew.

"Some news of my love to learn," I softly sang along.

Then the night watch calling the half-hour and, by eleven, I had almost given up on my fantasies when, through the window glass, I thought I saw a flicker of light below. It was a cold night, but clear, and I opened the casement once more, fetched my own candle. At first I could see nothing. But then a deeper shadow within the darkness just across Friargate. There were folk on the street too and, when they had all moved on, that shadow ebbed out onto the cobbles, a pale orb appearing at its centre as Parrish's familiar face turned up towards me.

'Alone?' he whispered.

'Of course.'

'Then wait.'

And the blackness swallowed him again.

Now what? How did I expect matters to proceed? That Parrish is a fellow of some ingenuity, I knew very well. And at least he had answered my summons. But all I could hear was the coarse noise of those singers below, even louder now. *The Fifth of November.* As good a loyalist tune as ever I heard and apt too, we now being in the early hours of that very date. Then the sound of something smashed, a bottle perhaps. Raised voices, shouting rather than in song. More breakages. The shattering of furniture. A scream. Oaths. A chorus of chaos such as I have not heard since my time at the Bethlem Hospital. Finally, through it all, an urgent tapping at my door and my heart beating so hard I thought it must burst asunder.

'Praise the Lord I had the room aright,' Parrish hissed, almost falling across the threshold as I heaved the door ajar.

'I take it old Mother Sumners will have you to thank for the ruination of her establishment?' I laughed and helped steady him as he set down upon my table the pocket candle lanthorn he had been carrying and shook off his midnight blue riding cape, revealed the entirety of the sombre garb beneath, even down to the stockings.

'They're good fellows. Those below, at least. And lusting for something to sharpen them again after all their retreats. Believe me, Catherine, there's naught worse – even for a part-time soldier.'

'You were not seen,' I said.

'With all that mayhem? No, my dear. Your virtue is intact.'

And the mayhem continued. More cries, the sounds of fighting. But Parrish took the cloak from me, delved in the deep pockets, produced a pipe and pouch from one, a brandy-wine flask from the other.

'The liquor is welcome on this cold night,' I said. 'But the weed-smoke might be difficult for me to explain.' He pushed everything but the flask back into the pockets with a grimace of regret, threw the cloak upon the bed. 'And my virtue,' I went on, 'in tatters rather, since...'

He had sat himself in the chair by the window, peered through the glass while, from outside, more men running towards the inn.

'Since you received the news of Elford's death,' he hastily finished my sentence, 'the day after I left you at Latimer. And you determined that our liaison had brought this misfortune upon you. It took me longer than I should have liked to smoke that thing. And you said I accused you of irrationality last time we spoke of it. After Addison's celebration, you remember? Yet I got there in the end, for it is the only explanation, is it not?'

I turned to the fireplace, stretched out my hands for warmth so I should not have to look at him.

'You flatter yourself, sirrah. The more simple explanation is that you simply did not live up to expectation. That you were a disappointment.'

He laughed, then remembered himself I think, for as I swung about to reproach him, he had clamped a hand over his lips. Though, with the other hand, he tapped the lid of the pocket lantern.

'Then you should not have responded to my light, I think.'

'I responded because I am in Stanhope's service and I have no other conduit for intelligence.'

I sat upon the edge of the bed, smoothed the amber silk of my skirts as he offered me the pewter flask. Downstairs, the commotion seemed to be abating.

'It is intelligence you lack, Mistress Yale, if you expect me to believe that. A scheme – here?'

I took a hearty swig, waited while it burned down into my innards, passed back the brandy-wine.

'The seeds already sown, Captain Parrish. Some good folk of this town already persuaded of my loyalties to their Chevalier.'

He sprang to his feet.

'I thought you were here for young Benjamin. And there was a note – from Streynsham, which finally reached me at Lancaster. You were with him. Safe, I thought. Catherine, you cannot mean this. God's hooks, this is no game. This makes Seaton seem a mere nuisance. It is war, my dear one.'

'It has always been war. For me, at least. And please be seated, Matthew. You are too old to be pacing the room. But will they fight here, your militiamen?'

The liquor, the warmth of the fire, had brought a flush to my brow and I tugged at the edge of my linen cap to wipe away the dampness as, to my surprise, he sat beside me. There were a few final shouts from the ground floor, then out upon the streets, boots upon the cobbles, something or somebody being dragged away. The town constables, as I pictured them, taking Matthew's decoys into custody. Presumably he would arrange their release upon the morrow.

'Great heavens, no. We almost left Lancaster at the run, though they must have been several days behind us. No will among the townsfolk to put the place at risk or to fight. There were six cannon aboard a merchantman and Hoghton might have used them but again the threat of damage to their property weighed heavily on the citizens. So Hoghton ordered the skipper to at least set sail and put them out of the rebels' reach. Yet he didn't do so and I fear the rebels will soon find themselves six artillery pieces the richer. Sir Henry hoped for reinforcement but nobody came. And now he has word of Stanhope's Dragoons upon the road. Even then we're too few in number to stop them.'

'A rabble, surely.'

I held out my hand again for the flask.

'Forster's Northumbrians perhaps. And how I owe that scoundrel. But the Scots they have with them, Highlanders and Lowlanders alike – no, Catherine, those are fearsome. We heard today that Wills is somewhere to the south with a goodly force of our regulars. The rest of my own regiment will be with him. But even then, I doubt we can hold them. We have so few who've seen active service. And if these Preston men, or the banditti's supporters in Manchester...'

He had mistaken my gesture, I found. Deliberately or not. For instead of passing me the brandy-wine he had taken hold of my fingers while, downstairs, we could hear Mother Sumners shouting instructions for the mess to be cleared up. I could have pulled my hand free, of course. Admonished him for being fro'ward. But I did not.

'There,' I said, knowing that my voice trembled and I heard those imagined words again. *Foolish old woman.* 'That is the very point.' I looked deep into his eyes, saw the passion in them. The years. The love, I think. 'Who else do you have?' I asked him, knowing full well that he might be confused by the question. 'To pass intelligence about their true numbers? For I collect you will not be here long.'

'Long enough to liaise with Stanhope – if he arrives.' He squeezed my fingers. 'But no, we have to find Wills, muster as much force as we're able.'

I half-turned, set my free hand on top of his. And finally the inn had fallen silent.

'Perhaps it shall not be as black as you paint it, my dear,' I said. 'After all, participation in armed uprising carries huge risk. Remember Monmouth. And it seems to me these Proud Preston folk may hum a pretty enough tune but have much to lose if it does not go their way.'

'And you, sweet one, what about your own risk?' He lifted our joined hands. 'This? No further fear of consequences?'

'Matthew,' I told him, and watched the years and wrinkles fall from his face, 'I am just so sick of being alone.'

In the early hours of the morning. That was Saturday, of course. The Fifth of November. And I repeated the previous day's routine. Down before dawn, looking as prim and proper as I was able, ensuring there was nobody else about other than Mother Sumners, then calling down curses upon those wretches from last night and insisting she should show me the harm they had done. To be fair, Matthew's men had wreaked considerable damage within the hostelry and I managed to make an amount of noise myself, helping her drag tables and chairs back to their usual locations and clanging together some of the pots in the fireplace. But all that time the blood was pulsing in my veins, a hammering in my chest and especially at the moment when she paused in our labours, thought she heard the outer door, went to check but, Lord Jesu be praised, found nothing untoward.

I spent the rest of that interminable forenoon like a cat on hot coals, praying I would see him again but knowing in the depths of my despair that I would not. It had become plain that we are both too old for prolonged passion but we spent hours in each other's arms whispering might-have-beens and foolishness about whatever future may be left to us. Yet the only matter we resolved, I think, was his reluctant acceptance that I shall remain here to perform whatever duty I am able – though with my strict promise to be supremely cautious. He has, among the militiamen he helped train, he says, a reliable Penwortham man – from just across the Ribble, to the west.

A Dissenter, it seems. A fellow called Walker. And Matthew would persuade Sir Henry Hoghton to post Walker at the ferry house, just below Penwortham village, and within my easy reach should I have need of a messenger.

But by midday, word was spread about town that more of the King's men had arrived. I threw on my cloak, pulled up the hood and followed the sullen crowds, past the market square and Town Hall, across Cheapside, then around the Shambles into Churchgate and along to the lychgate into the winter-bare burial ground of St. John's. There was a stone trough, and horse-holders in military capes waiting their turn, each with three or four mounts, to water the beasts once they had cooled from their recent ride. The rest of the soldiers, in their thigh-length riding boots, were mostly at their ease, smoking, or folding the grey cloaks they hoped might not be needed for the afternoon, or shouting coarsely, one to the other, though always with half an eye to those of us who were silent spectators.

For the most part silent, anyway. Except for an excited young boy who ran up to the trough, asked a young dragoon what regiment they might be. Stanhope's, of course, as I guessed from what Matthew had told me. The regiment commanded by Secretary Stanhope's cousin William. And how many? A hundred, I calculated. Showing no sign they intended a defence here either. But I was proud of them, all the same. These were the boys, I reminded myself, who would stop the banditti in their tracks. Some place. Or give their lives trying.

Gunpowder Treason Day. The day, too, on which each year in London and elsewhere we had celebrated King William's landing at Torbay. I felt like singing, as those rogues of Matthew's had sung last night.

Let's always remember the fifth of November,
When Papists and tyrants did twice meet their doom.

A day for burning effigies of the pope. Though not here, it seemed. For, from beyond the market square, from the street they call Fishergate – the one that leads west from St. John's towards the marsh, towards the fords and ferry – came another procession, this one led by a black-robed priest. But the straw-filled scarecrow at its head, hanging by its neck from a makeshift gibbet, had a crown upon its head. German George.

The tune they were singing was *All For Our Rightful King* and I had only heard it as a mournful Irish lament – though here they stamped out the thing boldly enough as a marching tune.

Well, they had bottom, these wretches, that much was certain, for there were soldiers making towards their mounts now, fingering the buckles of leather harnesses that held their *carabines*. Though the officers screamed at their men to desist, to clear the road. And they reluctantly obeyed, heaving at bridles, slapping rumps to haul the creatures into the side lanes around and opposite the church, or towards the ground of a grand mansion I could now see through the trees beyond.

A woman at my side was weeping, crossing herself in the way of papists, and muttering some prayer, also in the Romish tongue. And here came Mister and Mistress Winckley, so that I quickly threw my arm around my neighbour's shoulders, spoke some false words of consolation.

'Such a day of shame for this dear town,' I said to the Winckleys. 'To be so assailed by these fellows.'

'Indeed, Mistress Yale,' said Barrister Winckley. 'Infamous.'

'And my son? I have not seen him abroad this morning.'

'I fear he is taken to his bed once more. A return of that fever. Some delirium.'

'A fever of the heart, I collect,' said Mistress Winckley. 'A single visit from that young woman last night and now he is smitten once more.'

I promised to visit him later, satisfied by their assurance that it could be nothing serious and more preoccupied, I think, by those fanaticals here around me. Those in the procession had halted in the road, chanting now. *Parce, Domine, parce populo tuo.* Spare, Lord – spare Thy people. Their purpose seemingly achieved, for Stanhope's dragoons had received orders to mount. And if they were on the march again...

I excused myself, pushed a way through those gathered along the front wall of the church, past one grand house to my right, and almost opposite that even more enormous dwelling on the opposite side of Churchgate, the one I had noticed earlier from further back along the street. The Patten House, I surmised. There, upon the road, Hoghton's Lancashire Militia forming their ranks, filling the lane all the way past the bar-gate, past another inn, the Crown, and along to the alms houses at that point where the highway divides, the southern fork leading downhill to the Hollow Way and Ribble Bridge – the route by which I had arrived – and the other branch marked by a stone, an arrow pointing east, the towns of Ribbleton and Blackburn carved also into the granite block.

There were fewer onlookers here and I did my best to saunter among them, exchanging an odd comment hither and thither with the disgruntled townsfolk, doing my best to seem as sour as they until, at last, I reached the column's head and saw there, as I had expected, those few other mounted troopers, a senior officer I took to be Sir Henry Hoghton and, at his side, Captain Matthew Parrish.

But he had not seen me and though he glanced often back along Churchgate, I kept myself concealed behind the bole of an ancient ash growing at the roadside. It would not answer, I knew. We had said our farewells already, sworn to find each other again as soon as this evil is done. And I suppose it may also be true that I did not wish any sign of familiarity now to betray my intentions among the townsfolk.

Find each other again? Where? As I write this, three days later, I still have no idea of his whereabouts. My intelligence from Mister Walker is no more than guesswork on his part. That there must needs be a battle seems certain. At least, one battle or more. For, far to the north, as I now know, our loyal Duke of Argyll is also sent to find and engage those still greater Jacobite forces led by the Earl of Mar in Scotland. How long shall it all continue, and how many of us will survive?

I watched him go, to rejoin his own regiment I suppose, that dear man I have wronged so often and so sorely – watched him trot away towards the hedgerows of the Hollow Way, the militiamen's drummer tapping out a regulation rhythm and some subaltern urging the first company to pick up the pace. I watched Matthew go, taking my heart with him, for I needed then to still my sentiments, to steel myself for the task at hand.

Oh, I did not dismiss him from my thoughts quite so readily as I wandered back, shivering, towards the market place, for there was my guilt with which to contend, naturally – my further infidelity, more than a mere passing thought for Elihu and his absurd desire for reconciliation. But mainly it was Matthew's poetry that preoccupied me. We had whispered about the verses at length, about David Yale's perception that they were written for me, for me alone, and Parrish's reluctant confession that the lad was correct.

So, the passing tramp, tramp, tramp of Hoghton's other companies – their heads held just a little higher now, I thought, than when they arrived. Then the jingle and leather creak of horse harness, the clatter and chime of horseshoes on cobblestone, the spitting and cursing of the troopers as Stanhope's Dragoons plodded past – all this I noted only with the fringes of my mind. And I paid equally small measure to those gathered at St. John's with their effigies of Lancashire's Catholic Martyrs, though their boldness had also increased. *Down with the German*, they yelled. *God speed ye all to hell.* Much besides, so that I saw some of the dragoons staring hard at the more prominent protestors, as though recording their faces for some future purpose.

Yet as I returned to Cheapside, the hood of my cloak pulled still tighter about my face against the chill, there was another horseman. Alone, intent upon the road ahead. Thankfully so intent that he did not even notice me. A man whose features were also burned into the hatred of my memory.

I spent the rest of the day in my room at the White Horse, simply sending a note with a boy to the Winckley's house enquiring after Benjamin's health and telling him that I, too, felt somewhat indisposed.

But the truth? I imagined myself unable to leave the inn without encountering that same Colonel Porter. It had never occurred to me that I should find him here. But how could it not be so? Where else would the rogue be?

So I was pleased when my son responded with a note of his own. Feeling somewhat improved, he said, certain he would be sufficiently recovered to attend prayers at St. John's on the following morning. And thus I spent the rest of Saturday afternoon hidden away, food brought to me by Mother Sumners herself, and then one of the longest nights of my life. Sleep was impossible and though I tried to recapture the joys of the previous one, every image I summoned was defiled by Porter's presence.

On Sunday morning I tried my best to look somewhat less dishevelled and met Benjamin below – though he appeared far worse than I had imagined from his positive note. Difficulty standing, stomach pains, and when he spoke he almost seemed cupped. But with my hood up around my face once more, we made for the church, with me fussing about his liverish complexion, scolding him for his foolishness in venturing out of doors. And I caught him dozing several times during Reverend Peploe's stern sermon against affray and disorder, the need to render unto Caesar and such like. It was bold stuff, considering his congregation. But it gave me plenty of opportunity for introspection: first, that pleasurable guilt again; second, my attempts to calculate how long it might take for that Penwortham fellow to be released by Hoghton and then arrive at the ferry house; third, how I, myself, might even contemplate meeting him there; fourth, about what might become of those armies currently being deployed, probing each other, like pieces upon a chess board; and, finally, my concern again for Benji's condition.

'My son,' I said, as we waited our turn to leave the pew, the service at an end, 'I fear you may need a physician. So pale. So…'

'It is the pain in my innards that troubles me most,' he replied. 'The flux, which accompanies these attacks. The very devil.'

'No better?' said Mister Winckley from just behind us, and Benjamin steadied himself, said that no, he was not. 'Then we shall certainly send Master Broadbent to attend you, as your mama suggests. And you, Mistress Yale, how did you find Reverend Peploe's sermon?'

'I fear, sir, that the reverend gentleman confuses his scripture. For in rendering unto Caesar that which is Caesar's, and unto God that which is God's we are reminded only that all government is divinely ordained, that it is God's gift to determine who should be king and not man's. How can any person of intellect like Peploe gainsay the divine right of King Jamie to rule? And not these Dutchies and Germans foisted upon us these past twenty-five years and more.'

'Well said, ma'am,' said Winckley, though Benjamin had collapsed back upon the pew, now suffering a terrible fit of coughing that seemed to have little in common with his other symptoms. 'And

I expect,' Winckley went on, 'the same forces of our justice to be here with us very soon. Cannot be precise but some time this coming week if my information is correct. Plans already in hand for a great reception to celebrate their arrival – our liberation, as you might say. I have taken steps to include you upon the guest list, ma'am. For I fear your son has been modest and I regret that I did not associate the name. But wife to the famous Governor Yale – great heavens, I believe the Earl of Derwentwater, General Forster too, will be delighted to meet you.'

Of Porter I have seen nothing more and must assume he is in pursuit of Hoghton's column. But the Jacobite army I now know to be at Lancaster. The town here is full of it, several news-mongers having galloped into Preston today with word of their misdeeds: the ship's cannon that Matthew mentioned, seized and mounted now on carriages; a loyalist spy captured; a mass of miscreants released from the gaol there to help swell their ranks – those previously apprehended at Manchester and elsewhere in the county for their part in the earlier riots against Dissenter meeting houses and the like; and the rebels' coffers supplemented too through stealing the taxes already gathered by the Government's collectors. They say that the good people of Lancaster did not mind this latter action one little bit – for it seems that nobody cares if somebody steals hard-earned silver that's already been taken from you by somebody else.

So, with the enemies of the state barely more than twenty miles away, within a long day's march, I have a decision to make. The safest thing will be for me to leave Preston immediately – and thus avoid any possible rencounter with Porter – or, indeed, with Forster. Or I might feign illness – the same as still afflicts Benjamin – and thus excuse myself from this civic reception the burgesses are preparing for the banditti leadership. Yes, perhaps that, since it gives me the opportunity for further observation, to see whether the small scheme I set in train yesterday might come to fruition.

Yesterday. For the decision I had already made was to attempt contact with Mister Walker, the Penwortham man – or at least to test the manner by which I might do so. And it was that decision which led me to Polk's Livery at this upper end of Fishergate. I would need a mount, for Benji had made plain to me that the track leading to the Ribble fords, and to the modest ferry, would not sustain even the smallest carriage. But might I find a creature as biddable, as docile, as Pebble back at Latimer? Papa had taught me well, but it is many years since I have handled a more substantial beast – not since Fort St. George in fact and, even then, restrictions upon our movements beyond the limits of White Town and Black Town made riding rather an irrelevance. And in London, entirely so.

But Polk proudly showed me a stocky little piebald fell pony. Just over thirteen hands, that I could mount or dismount with relative ease so long as there might be a convenient block in the vicinity, or at least a gentleman willing to cup my foot. There was a side saddle too, heavily quilted, a rail to support my aged back and a wide double footrest in place of a stirrup, on which I could comfortably settle both feet if necessary. A padded leaping horn should I be foolishly inclined to travel beyond simple walking speed or to brace my thigh without bruising myself too badly. The seat gently curved into an almost flat cantle and a perfect fit for my spreading aged rump. One shilling and sixpence to hire by the day, for pony and saddle both. A decent price. And Polk, douce fellow, waived the guinea deposit against their safe return.

Of course, I should not have been seen dead in yesterday's attire under any other circumstance. I have an elegant riding habit at home in Latimer but here my heavy russet skirts must suffice. And I persuaded Sumners, a tiny fellow, to lend me a coat and his least-infested beaver hat. A neck cloth, of course, my warmest gloves, and my travelling cloak. Polk also provided, *gratis*, the essential whip – though he assured me that the pony, Henrietta, knew the local lanes and byways so well that she would need no cue at all.

And with Polk's mounting block and his cupped hands to help me, we soon set off down Fishergate. I have to own that, once settled against the back rail, riding this piebald was no less pleasant than sitting upon my most comfortable dining chair. She is a true willing-tit, has a smooth gait and a light mouth. So, with a watery winter sun rising at our backs, we began our descent of the ridge: down past another elegant four-storey property; down past the Holy Lamb and the Wheat Sheaf; down past the black-garbed notaries, backs bent against the uphill climb for their work in town; down past the blacksmith working his bellows to fire up the furnace;

down past the boys carrying buckets for the conduit and the milk-maids returning from their deliveries; down past cart and packhorse; down past all that hubbub, the mingling wood smoke, bakery and excrement essence of a town shrugging into its early morning duties; down past the western bar-gate and alms houses; down past a shepherd with his bleating flock; and finally to the flatter fields of pasture and stubble that, after only a few hundred yards, gave way to the wetlands, beyond which I could see – and smell – the river. But I saw that here the track divided, one branch turning left between two meadows and the other tending more towards the Ribble itself along a raised causeway. Thus I touched the pony gently with the whip upon its right shoulder and soon came to the river's bank.

A rotting jetty, another on the opposite side, along with a brace of bleak half-ruined cottages beyond, and a boat – the ferry, I supposed – tethered to a mooring post but resting now upon the hard. I cursed myself for not checking the tides for, between, the only water, filthy brown, ran in a narrow channel meandering through the mud. But was this also the ford? Well, there were withies planted here and there, perhaps to mark the path. Polk had not mentioned these, though he had cautioned me at length about the treachery of the slime below the causeway when it is exposed and the lives it has claimed. He had, in truth, been somewhat bemused by my claim to be a student of ornithology, brought here in part by the fame of those feathered creatures frequenting the Ribble and its estuary. But Henrietta, I decided, was too wise a creature to allow herself willingly to be led into disaster. So I cautiously urged her forward towards the first stick – and felt the bed firm enough beneath her hooves. I only needed to press my right knee gently against the leaping horn as she skipped over the ebbing stream. It was slow, but we reached the farther shore without mishap and made for those dilapidated ferry houses, from one of which a brawny, stubbled fellow came running, wiping a hand across his mouth.

'Mistress Yale,' he cried in that Lancastrian drawl that is now so familiar.

'God's hooks,' I said, 'are you some sorcerer, sir?'

He laughed, scratched at the silver bristles on his cheeks.

'Captain gave a reet good description, ma'am. A way wi' words, as tha' knows.'

I was curious to learn how Parrish might have described me but I did not truly need to be told. I was here, after all, and I doubted there were too many other old women, unaccompanied, who made the Ribble crossing this way. In any case, by then we had exchanged more formal introductions and he had offered me a small beer, perhaps some bread and cheese that he had with him inside the ferry house. It was more snug within than it had appeared from across the river and he named his cousin, who dwelt there and was presently stoking a welcome blaze in the hearth – the cousin who, it seems, plies his oars back and forth across the waters whenever there is a call upon his services. And that elicited a reminder, naturally, that if I wished to return the same way there was now less than an hour until the ford became impassible once more and I should have to make the journey around by the Ribble Bridge – though that was not especially onerous either. Walker asked his cousin to give us some privacy, to care for the pony, and once I was perched upon a stool by the fireplace, he served me with ale, bread and cheese.

'And where might Captain Parrish be, at this moment, Mister Walker?' I asked, shaking out the hat and scratching at the vermin it had passed to my scalp.

'When I left t' column, we was on t' road for Wigan. But how long tha'll be theer...'

I explained that, in that case, the first thing we must ensure was to keep open a permanent line of communication with Parrish and his superiors.

'Do you know how we might do so, Mister Walker?'

'I 'as friends, ma'am. Chorley way, an' all.' He could be there in an hour, he said, back in two.

'And Captain Parrish told me they had to find General Wills. Do you know where the general may be?'

'E'll be in Chester, 'appen. Or Manchester.'

'Manchester,' I repeated. 'Matthew – Captain Parrish – thought the banditti would head that way too. Join up with more traitors.'

'Now't we can do about that though.'

'I have thought about this a great deal, sirrah. If the Jacobites arrive here and are free to leave again – well, I am no general, Mister Walker. But you were in Lancaster, were you not? Folk there unwilling to see fighting on their own streets, damage to their wealth.

And might it not be the same here? If they arrive and we can bring up the army swiftly enough, might the townsfolk themselves not send the traitors on their way? Retreat again? And if forced to retreat, perhaps they shall simply disband – can be apprehended piecemeal.'

He plainly thought I was quite mad, reminded me I had not included the Jacobite army in Scotland within my calculations. But he had news, at least. The traitor Earl of Mar had already taken Inverness, Aberdeen and Dundee. All the lands above the Firth of Forth except Stirling Castle. And the latest word put Mar now leading his forces to that very place, the Duke of Argyll hoping to intercept him. Hopeless, Walker believed, for Argyll had only one-third of the Jacobite numbers.

Walker shrugged.

'Yo' mun creep first an' then well go.'

'And what does that mean, Mister Walker? That we must walk before we can run?' He smiled at me. 'Then have we no allies of our own that we can call upon to assist us? A *posse comitatus* perhaps. Loyal folk who might be willing to show some force here, help to pin this Jacobite rabble in Preston, so they might pose no threat further to the south? Allow the regular army to close with its enemies.'

He said something in that dialect of his that I could not follow. Yet I saw that I had given him pause for thought. And he explained more slowly that yes, he had Dissenter friends at Atherton, not far from Wigan itself. There was a minister there, Mister Wood. And the last time Walker heard him speak, the fellow had boasted that he could raise four hundred men. At least four hundred. Men who would fight. Fight against High Church and papist tyranny. It was music to my ears and I suggested he should send word to Mister Wood, then. To begin raising his force and be prepared to march.

They shall surely run, I thought. These Jacobites. When they are confronted they shall run. And the treasonous citizens of Preston will do nothing to risk their town.

But now, as I write, word has just arrived here at the White Horse also. Forster's army, they say, will begin its march on the morrow. And there seems nothing but fervour at the prospect of their arrival, regardless of the consequence. I am reminded that Preston town has been a battlefield in the recent past – the last time only three years before I was born, when our Lord Protector Cromwell smashed Langdale's Cavaliers and an army of Scottish Covenanters here.

But where is our Cromwell now? I do not know General Wills. Nor General Carpenter. But neither, I think, is a Cromwell. The fate of my sweet Parrish – the fate of us all – is in their hands.

Sunday 13th November 1715

The horrors and bloodshed of these past five days. More difficult to record than any since I first set myself to writing these journals. And it began thus.

On the following morning, last Wednesday, it rained. Market day. And though I borrowed an umbrello – another helpful device to keep my face hidden against an unexpected return by Porter – there was little to see. More stray scavenging dogs on the streets than people, it seemed, and the vendors crying their wares with little enthusiasm, though I bought some of the local cheeses to which I have become attached, thinking they might bring some cheer to Benjamin.

I found him little improved and just being bled by the physician, Broadbent, who Mister Winckley had mentioned.

'Well, sir?' I said, and wondered that Preston might not have anybody younger to serve its medical needs. I have seen healthier-looking skeletons.

'I can find little obvious, ma'am,' he shouted, as though it were myself who might be deaf. 'Though the distended abdomen, the blood within the flux, the delirium, might suggest Mister Hynmers has ingested something disagreeable to his humours.'

Mister Hynmers. How these words took me back.

'I believe I might have been capable of such prognosis without the benefit of your training and experience, Mister Broadbent. You have nothing more?'

I think he was too old, too faulty of hearing, to take offence at my rudeness and, as he carefully removed the leeches, he merely went on to prescribe doses of a Jesuit's Bark corrective, an emetic twice each day to induce vomiting and help cleanse the system, and warm broth.

'He means well,' Benjamin murmured. 'And I simply need to build my strength. I tried to do some work this morning but the stench from the new Shambles was too much for me. I was back here by midday.'

'Sick again?'

'Several times. And the pains, when they come – I cannot bear them.'

I was recalling the early days of my Joseph's illness, of course, when Benjamin had been barely more two years old. All so horribly familiar. The dear man's bouts of retching and his confinement to our bed, his insistence that he was improved and must return to his duties. Each relapse worse than the last until…

The physician collected the tools of his trade, his glass jars, his voluminous bag, and bade us farewell as I sat on the edge of the bed and took hold of my son's cold fingers.

'This disagreeable thing you may have eaten,' I said, determined to drive away the images crowding upon me. 'Something you may have shared with this girl – this Mary? And how can it be that I have still not been afforded the chance to meet her, Benji? Am I so terrible that you must keep her from me?'

'She is merely timorous, Mama. And not quite herself yet, either.'

'I do not even know where she resides, for pity's sake.'

'She has a position at the Patten House, as it happens.'

'A maidservant?' I snapped, instantly regretted the tone I knew must have sounded like awful hauteur, and I pressed on, hoping to repair that damage. 'Well,' I smiled, 'I hope that we may soon be acquainted, boy.'

By early evening, as darkness began to gather and the oil lamps were lit on Friargate, many of the houses also illuminated in excited expectation of the Jacobites' advance guard – their horse, naturally, as well as a few light carts from their baggage train. The Town Hall bell was rung to announce the first arrivals, trotting up the hill towards the market square. The rain had eased by now, though most of the riders remained cloaked, and this initial troop – seventy-two of them, I counted – could easily have been our own dragoons. Military bearing, though with a variety of muskets slung at their backs or protruding from beneath their capes. And they might be distinguished from our own by the blue and white cockades worn in their hats though, as they passed beneath my window and I could inspect them at closer quarters, I saw that even their headgear varied from one rider to the next, giving me cause to believe there would be nothing uniform about their coats either.

Next, their officers, with a small escort of fellows in finer military attire. And I edged back behind the drapes a little as I saw Thomas Forster at their head. He is little changed from that day at the Menagerie, that absurd nose, and his wide mouth fixed in a bizarre oblong, like a frog about to swallow a fly, his hand flopping about in some foppish imitation of a royal wave to those braving the weather to watch them from the roadside. He looked little like a leader of fighting men, despite the sword he sported, and even his mount seemed too large for him.

Yet that was not the case with the fellow at his side. A handsome young man, still not thirty – perhaps considerably younger. And the crowd seemed to know him well. *God bless Lord James*, they yelled. Or just *Derwentwater! Derwentwater!* I have read about him, naturally, as have we all. James Radclyffe. By blood, they say, he is a grandson of the second Charles Stuart, by one of the King's many concubines, and raised at the Pretender's court in Saint-Germain, though settled back in Northumberland for a few years now. A renowned Jacobite, however, so that when the first whispers of armed insurrection began to spread, Secretary Stanhope ordered his arrest. But he had evaded the warrant and joined Forster when that wretch raised the banditti's standard.

This Earl of Derwentwater, I guessed, had been tutored to lead, though he was soon gone around the corner into the market square, to be followed at some distance by the rearguard. These I counted at just above two hundred. A dozen or so more than that figure. Somewhat similar to those who had led the column but here with cockades of white and red, rather than blue. Some of those bedraggled objects had suffered badly from the rain and I knew there were women in town – Mother Sumners one of them – working hard to fashion new cockades. White and blue for the Scots then, white and red for their English traitor allies. For these must be the Northumbrians raised by Forster himself and by Derwentwater. Yet I have seen better armed and mounted fellows among the Chesham Hunt. Indeed, many of them seemed equipped with hunting saddles – the gentlemen among them – while greater than half were riding poor specimens of ponies and these, I supposed, must be the gentlemen's retainers – pressed to a service for which they seem eminently unsuited. Towards the rear, one more rogue I recognised, and wrote the name carefully on the sheet I was preparing. That same Edward Hughes I had seen leading the rabble in Wrexham.

I persuaded Mother Sumners to cook an especially wholesome broth that I might convey in a carrying pot for Benjamin's supper. I was certain the Winckleys would have attempted to feed him but I know how stubborn he can be. I was still worried about him and had sent a note with a boy to say he should expect me. I wrapped myself warmly and set off down Friargate, lit for most of its way, naturally, though I carried in my other hand the pocket lanthorn Parrish had left in my room. The candle guttered inside even though its shutters were all closed but I thought it might be necessary when I arrived at the lower reaches, to which the oil lamps did not extend.

Thus, I was standing at the corner of that lane in which the Winckley's house may be found – Back Lane, it is named – and had set down the broth pot so I might open one of its sides to light my way, when I was almost knocked down. Some cloaked young girl by her build, hurrying around the corner in the opposite direction. And as can sometimes be the way of these things, I found myself stammering the beginning of an apology to her before the thought struck that it was she, and not I, who had caused the collision. Besides, as she banged into me, I kicked the pot and almost lost its contents, stooped quickly to steady it. Still, the drab uttered not a word and I caught nothing but a glance at her eyes from deep within her hood before she ran on. What was it I had seen there? Something, but by the time I had stood, rubbed at the arm she had struck, straightened the aged back with its twinges of pain from having bent so quickly, the thought had fled along with the girl.

'Am I correct in thinking,' I said to Benjamin when I was settled in his room soon afterwards, 'you have just received a visit from that young woman?'

He was propped up in bed, weak and pale, in his sleeping gown, a turban upon his head and one of his law books open on the coverlet.

'How did you know?'

'She left this?' I picked up from his table another covered pot, smaller than my own but still warm to the touch. Next to it was my note.

'Indeed, but then recalled her duties at Patten House. Insisted the broth would help restore me, though. Perhaps I shall eat it later?'

He was looking at the pot I had set down beside it.

'No, you shall not,' I said, and bent at the foot of his bed, retrieved the chamber pot before opening whatever she may have brought him and pouring the contents into his piss. He yelled a protest, retched a little when he saw the stew, while I reminded him that his mama knew best how to treat this ailment. 'And whatever this chit may have brought you,' I told him, 'well, Mister Winckley may dispose of it at his leisure.'

'Mama, she is no chit.' He had become liverish again, sank back into his pillows.

'How old then? You have not even told me that much and I believe the damn'd girl almost felled me back along the street.'

'Mary?' he said. 'You met her then.'

'Hardly the description I would have used, but...'

There was a hammering at the door below and I heard one of the servants call to Mistress Winckley. The conversation that followed was brusque but, from what I could hear, it was a Jacobite quartermaster demanding to know how many rooms, how much space, might be available to accommodate billets for their men There were protests, Mister Winckley himself summoned for assistance, then his placatory barrister's responses, his wife's voice raised in anger and, finally, the quartermaster's triumphant summary. Twenty men and all their accoutrements. To be fed at the household's expense and the cost reclaimed through fully itemised invoice submitted to General Forster's headquarters at the Eyres House, to the office of Paymaster Tunstall.

'Poor Mistress Winckley,' said Benjamin. 'She cannot have expected to pay this price for her affiliation. And, Mama, your head – is the White Horse less than clean?'

I fear I had stopped noticing the itch.

'Eyres House?' I said. 'Is that even more grand than the place your dear Mary is employed then?'

'It is not. Not quite. Though it rivals the Patten House in elegance. And sits immediately alongside the church.'

He clutched at his stomach, winced with the griping pain, and I touched my hand to his brow.

'Almost opposite the Patten House too? Yes, I remember it now.' I had passed the place on Saturday as I sought my final glimpse of Matthew before he rode away. 'Interesting that Forster should have chosen that for his base.'

Benjamin took a few deep breaths, some colour returning to his cheeks as the pain subsided.

'Mistress Winckley,' he murmured, 'believes the Patten House will be all gaiety and music. That they will make it so simply to spite both its owner and its occupier – the Earl of Derby and Sir Henry Hoghton respectively being their sworn enemies, and this almost a chance to spit upon their boots. The Eyres House they will keep for more sombre business.'

Yes, I could not imagine Forster as the pantaloon of anybody's social calendar.

'But who, I wonder,' I said, 'shall they install now at St. John's?'

'Peploe is gone?'

'He was at evening prayers, it seems, when the banditti rode in. But took to his heels almost before any could say *amen*. So much for his Sunday sermon, my boy.'

And, perhaps, so much for my fear of Mister Winckley's insistence on my inclusion upon their guest list for whatever grand reception they were planning. Surely in a place so palatial as the Patten House, and Forster possibly engaged elsewhere, there must be plenty of scope for me to at least observe them at close quarters without, myself, being revealed. Surely.

On frosty Thursday morning, quite early, the rest of them began to arrive in town. They must have been on the road before daybreak, those Jack Highlanders who came marching in ahead of the rest. I could hear and feel them, of course, long before they could be seen, the skirl of bagpipes and drumming too, and a slight trembling in the floor and walls of my room, in the casement's frame as I opened it. Then several resplendent gentlemen urging their horses up Friargate, the gentle jingle of their harness and an upright elderly fellow at their head, fist and leather gauntlet resting proudly upon his hip, heavy coat and breeches all in chequered scarlet and green, his long boots of fine leather and, upon the rogue's head, a bonnet bedecked with feathers.

Then the first of the Scottish foot regiments – if regiment is the correct term for those wild fellows. Two hundred and ninety-seven of them, I counted, including their banner-bearer – holding aloft a small standard emblazoned with an image of some cat-like creature – and their pipers. For the most part they were decked out in drab-patterned plaids belted at the waist, their shanks bare, but the upper parts shawled about their bodies, or rolled and slung across chest and shoulder, or rolled in a great bulge around their stomachs if they also wore sleeved jackets. Bearded youths or old fellows with white hair streaming from their bonnets, some armed with broadsword and studded wooden shield, but the majority bearing muskets.

I was impatient for them to pass, for I was bound to relay their numbers to Walker and, while I could wait for the afternoon's high tide and the ferry, I knew I would be better served repeating Monday's passage of the ford – which today I could effect just before noon. I had slipped a couple of pennies to one of the inn's stable boys that he might alert Polk of my need for Henrietta once more and to have her saddled, ready, for eleven o' the clock onwards.

And I tallied. Unit by unit. Thirty-six in one group of Highlanders. One hundred and twenty-two in another company of more conventionally attired though still sporting cockades of Scottish blue. On and on. Then similar units of men marked as English – though it pains my heart to honour them with that description. Yet I could hear from their chatter as they passed below, or by their songs, that they hailed mainly from these northern parts. There was a stench about them too, sweat and pissed breeks, stale food.

My running total? In round figures, a little over thirteen hundred Scotsmen and somewhat fewer than seven hundred English traitors. All to be added, naturally, to yesterday evening's horsemen. And at the very rear, baggage wagons and carts with, dragged behind them, a few sorry prisoners, then a tail of further riders, like gentlemen at their leisure, and their artillery train: two small wheeled pieces dragged by mules; then six more carts, each with a cannon barrel lashed tightly to its bed – the sort of gun I knew so well from my various voyages, ship's cannon and doubtless seized from that merchantman in Lancaster.

I was already wrapped securely in my cloak and that verminous hat long before the column's end had passed the White Horse and I had completed my notes, was out upon the street in time to follow them around into Cheapside, where the wagons and guns were halted, and from which their men seemed to be spread in every direction, along each main thoroughfare and passageway – or weind as these Lancastrians name them here – settling themselves upon whatever satchels or packs they might have been carrying, receiving refreshment from the townsfolk, smoking their pipes, taking instruction from their quartermasters whenever a billet was allocated for them, or generally basking in the adulation of those who had come out to greet them.

And, of course, they paid no heed at all to the affable old lady who picked her cautious way among them on her way to Polk's Livery, where she even received assistance from an eminently handsome young Highland gentleman who chatted to her amicably in his own melodious barbarian's tongue as he helped her mount the pony. He waved to her and, she imagined, bade her God speed or similar while she, for her part, set off down Fishergate on an expedition, she hoped, would send him and his kind directly to hell.

I made the crossing of the Ribble almost precisely as before, found Mister Walker waiting at the ferry house and delivered to him the report I had prepared for General Wills – preferably, I said, to be passed through the hands of our mutual acquaintance Captain Parrish, presumably now serving with Wynne's Dragoons once more. But, if not, then to General Wills himself, or whoever might presently be in command. Meanwhile, perhaps a summons to that Dissenter Reverend Wood and his followers at Atherton, that they should come with all possible haste but to gather there, upon the Penwortham shore, with great fanfare, though not too plainly visible so that their strength, and their ability as a fighting force, might not be too obvious. But a display, for example, of union flags or anything else that might make them seem like regulars.

For I had gleaned from Benjamin this much, at least – that Cromwell may have won his battle here, but only at considerable cost in forcing a passage across the Ribble Bridge and then near disaster as his troops were ambushed in the narrow confines of the Hollow Way.

Walker understood perfectly, pledged he would ride at once and, this time, undertake the entire journey himself, try to ensure that Wood's *posse comitatus* should be here at the earliest possible hour upon the morrow.

And thus, feeling pleased with myself, I set Henrietta to retracing our steps across the stinking mire, noting as she jumped the channel again that the tide had turned and was flooding faster than I might have expected.

No danger, however. Not then.

But the sky was lowering, and the morning's cold clarity was turning to foul weather, a damp and chilly wind following the stream inland from the Irish Sea. I recall thinking it strange that the dunlins, oyster catchers and lapwings that had been everywhere on my outward crossing had now all but disappeared. Yet as the breeze brought with it thoughts of that Ireland from which it may have sprung, and Henrietta set her hooves once more on firmer ground, it was almost as though the Irish wind itself spoke to me.

'Of all the pathways in all the world, sirrah,' he said.

Porter. His mount and himself sequestered from sight in that lane between the meadows where the raised path across the marsh divides. There was a long scarf of woollen cloth tied about his head and he wore a full-length blue riding coat, limped out in front of me, pistol in his hand and grabbed Henrietta's bridle before I could turn her.

'It troubles you still, wretch' I said, knowing this was not the time to antagonise him, but unable to help myself. 'The leg, I see.'

How had he come there, and had he divined my mission? Was Walker in danger too? I knew not, though from my previous encounter with this devil it was plain he would not hesitate to kill me.

'One more debt you owe me, Mistress Spy. Now, get down.'

I have been afraid many times in my life though there, upon those lonely wetlands, I think terror reached fresh levels. Defiance in me too. Tremulous – but defiance all the same.

'I left the blood you shed at Latimer upon the floor of my bedchamber for several days before I had the servants scrub the boards clean. It gave me a certain satisfaction.'

'Old bitch,' he snarled. 'Just get down.'

'Does it matter whether you shoot me up here or down there?' I laughed, though the fear turned the laughter to a strange half-strangled cackle. 'For I have no inclination to take instruction from you, sirrah.'

He moved around the pony's neck, dragging that left leg behind him, fondling Henrietta's forehead as he went. But then he quickly lifted the pistol, pulled back the hammer and pressed the muzzle to my own thigh where it was couched against the leaping horn – and I almost retched.

'You see, woman, it's this way. It would give me satisfaction as well – blowing a hole in this leg of yours, sure. And then drag you back to town by your hair so they can hang you alongside the other spying prickeen we took in Lancaster. But then you might just bleed to death on the way – and I promised my Mary we should both see you dance.'

I could feel Henrietta's nervousness as she began pawing at the ground, her ears flicking back and forth.

'Your…' I began, but by then he had taken my arm and tried to drag me from the saddle. Yet I still had Polk's short whip and I brought it down with all my strength against his face – the sudden movement causing the pony to lurch sideways. But for an old man Porter still had speed and caught my wrist before the goad could harm him, wrenched it from my hand and threw it aside.

Henrietta was snorting now, her head raised high and swinging from one side to the other, shying away from Porter who was cursing, reaching for me again while I pulled aside my cloak, fumbled within my skirts for the pocket pistol, felt it slip from my fingers and tumble against Henrietta's left flank.

Porter saw it too and a grin spread across his pox'd face. But the blow had caused the pony to swing towards him, caught the Irishman somewhat off-balance.

He took a backward step, encumbered by those long coat skirts, his own damaged leg unsteady.

Another step and he was off the path entirely, slipped a little way down the bank's sparse grass until one of his boots caught in cloying brown mud and, as he tried to free himself, his other foot became stuck ankle-deep also. He reached for a handful of thin reeds at the base of the slope and they came away in his hands.

'Sweet Mary, Mother of God,' he yelled, while I gentled the pony, steadied her as best I could.

Porter was floundering, heaving at the tops of his right boot in an effort to pull it from the mire. And he succeeded – only to lose his balance again and have to set the foot down once more, this time even further from the path and dropping the weapon. He was now some yards away, almost with his back to me – for he had twisted and turned so much in his efforts to escape – and considerably further below the level of the causeway.

'Sweet Mary?' I said, the words bringing something strangely to mind. And I gripped the leaping horn, eased myself to the ground, recovered the pocket pistol and cocked the piece. 'You were saying – you promised your Mary. What has this to do with her? Who is she, Porter?'

But by then I thought I knew – though, of course, I only had the half of it.

'Help me out of here, Mistress, and we may speak of it.'

His pistol was back in his hand now but as he checked the frizzen we both knew the priming was gone.

I went to Henrietta's head, stroked the fine bristle of her cheek, whispered some soothing nonsense to her, though all the while watching Porter tiring himself down there on the marsh.

'This Mary,' I said. 'And my son...'

He looked to his mount, still tethered in the lane, his powder in the saddle bags, I guessed.

'You thought I knew you was here – what, by magic, maybe?' His turn to laugh now, though it was almost as feeble an effort as my own had been. He was looking around him, seeking some means to help him escape, testing more reeds to see if they would give him purchase.

'Look,' I said. 'See how the water's now spilling out of its channel?' It was true. That stream, which Henrietta had jumped with such ease, was already impossible to cross. 'When the tide floods at full spate, your feet will still be held firm, but its force shall knock you backwards, no matter how hard you try to stay standing.'

'Then fetch help, woman. And maybe I'll speak for you.'

'With those banditti rebels you follow? Within two days they will all be dead or in a dungeon.'

'Because you've sent some rider with word of our numbers?' Now he laughed more heartily. 'By tomorrow our Manchester friends will have joined us in their hundreds. Towneley from Burnley. And Wills is a fainthearted old fool. We'll catch him dithering at Wigan or at Chester and wipe him from the face of the earth. Him and your dear friend Parrish. That'll be most of my scores settled at least.'

There was spittle around his lips.

'Most?' I said.

'That boy seems to have a charmed life, I'll say that for him.'

'Poison?' I raged, and the anger filled me. I lifted the pocket pistol, tried to aim it, but then I was uncertain whether, with my hands quaking so, it would answer, even at this close range.

'Stupid girl forgot to scour her own fingers. Or tasted the muck, more like. Made herself sick too. As much a dull-swift as her mother, that one. I suppose you'll think that's some kind of justice.'

'What did she use?'

'Does it matter? Just fetch help, woman. Blast your eyes, you know you can't just watch me die. And here.' He unfastened the woollen scarf, looked back at me over his shoulder. 'Just lead that beast down the slope. Tie one end of this...'

'You murdered my coachman – young Thornton. He was a good boy. And you thought to use my daughter. Kidnapping, I think, is how you rogues cant it.'

'I saved her, did I not? I could have simply thrown her overboard. The result would have been the same. But I put her in the boat, dammit! In the boat. Look.' And he clumsily tossed his pistol so it landed on the lower part of the slope. 'There's powder with the horse. Prime it afresh and...'

He managed to move one more time but the effort exhausted him and he bent over gripped his knees, gasping for breath, rubbing at that troublesome left leg.

'*Most* of your scores,' I said again. 'You cannot simply have intended Benjamin. Who else?'

'The old fool, of course. Langhorn.'

'Wait. Mary – that chit of a girl who married Sir William. Mary Aston?'

There, the thing that had been eluding me and I could see that child's face as plain as day, remembered how scornful we had been about his infatuation, mocked him for it when, as his friends, we should have stopped him.

'Her damn'd mother's name. Too dangerous to bear my own. Neat. But now, the scarf?'

There was a sucking sound and his left leg sank suddenly deeper into the oozing slime, water bubbling up around the knee of his boot.

'What were you planning?' I said. 'For me, Porter.'

'Blind me, I told you. All that trouble you caused me. And then poor Mary's ma. She might have been a dullard, but still...'

'Riddles, sirrah. What in the name of our Lord Jesu have I to do with your wife?' But I recalled his words at Latimer. Much more besides, he had said. 'And now you shall speak for me, though – wait, this is a private thing, is it not? Between me and you?'

If it was not so, I thought, I should already have been taken, surely. Or at least discerned some sign of mistrust from Winckley or one of the others. It was possible, I supposed, that I had been allowed rope, sufficient with which to hang myself. But that did not quite seem to fit.

'You owe me a life, Mistress Yale. Me. And my Mary. A life or maybe two. But help me now and maybe we'll see that debt as paid. Now, the scarf.'

He flicked one end of the thing towards me. I had no idea how any of this might concern his wife and I was no longer sure I cared greatly. No, the thing that vexed me more was the uncertainty of whether he was acting here alone – alone, that is, apart from his chit of a daughter, damn that evil little witch.

'The scarf?' I said, struggling to bring my thoughts back to the present. He was still twisted around, holding out the end of that grey woollen lifeline and I knew he was correct, began to lead Henrietta down the slope though ignoring the pistol he had thrown to me.

'God will bless you,' said Porter. 'Sure, He shall. And you may have my parole, Mistress Yale. Old Porter will just ride away and we shall call ourselves quits, forget all this. No other may ever need to know.'

Somewhere out on the marshlands a lonely curlew cried.

'Thornton,' I murmured. 'And Sir William. Benjamin...'

How much had the poison left lasting damage? What was it she had used? I thought about poor John Bridger, who had died all those years afterwards from my attempt to kill his treacherous wife, and

I wondered at this divine retribution. If it were so, I must do the right thing now. Of course I must. I struggled to keep my own balance, though Henrietta helped to steady me down the causeway's lip, then stood like a bulwark on the firmest ground she could find.

'That's the way,' Porter laughed. He was perhaps six feet into the mud, no more, though it was difficult for him, at that angle, to fully outstretch his arm, but even so I could easily catch hold of the scarf's loose end he flicked towards me once more. Just long enough, as well, to tie around the saddle's leaping horn. A half hitch, I think that is how a sailor might describe it. Then I waited until he took his eyes from me. He began to wrap the other end of the scarf securely about one his wrists, then gripped the section between himself and the pony as tightly as he was able. 'Now!' he yelled, 'pull me free – and keep pulling until I'm clear, woman.' I clicked my tongue near Henrietta's ear, pulled gently on her bridle so she might begin to clamber the slope. Porter at first fell backwards, of course – well, more on his right side, in truth. It knocked the wind from him, but he still shouted. 'Keep going, sure.'

But that is the beauty of a half hitch. It is supremely secure, but beautifully easy to unfasten again. And I did so, leaving him like a beetle stranded upon its carapace, his legs firmly anchored in the marsh, clutching the scarf as it snaked uselessly across the space between us.

'I was thinking about divine intervention, Porter,' I said. 'For I am not certain which of us may be the most wicked. So, I shall let our Lord Jesu decide whether you live or die – and whether I, for my part, may yet find redemption.'

Polk told me the river claims a life every seventh year at this spot but I never had the wit to ask him where we might be in that strange cycle. But as Henrietta helped me regain the causeway, and Porter continued to shout some of the vilest oaths I have ever heard in all my sixty-four years, I knew I had taken a great risk in leaving matters thus in God's hands. For these marshes are frequented often enough by cattlemen, shepherds and fisherfolk. And there was Porter's mount to consider. Was it safe to leave her tethered there in the lane? Well, I could think of nothing else to do, at least for now. Yes, a great risk. Though one I was prepared to endure for the period it would take me to complete my next duty.

By the time I returned the pony, apologised to Polk for the smears of mud upon the pony and saddle, explained that I had foolishly strayed from the path and slipped, myself, upon the marsh – for I was grimed in the stuff too – and brushed aside his expressions of concern, it was too late for me to witness the gathering that had taken place in the market square. Forster and Derwentwater had seemingly instructed the town's crier to read a prepared statement proclaiming James the Third as rightful King of England and the rest. I fully expected that they might also have issued a warrant for my arrest and my innards twisted and churned with that fear permanently, even as Mister Winckley later ushered me into the great hall of the Patten House.

'It was a moment of such joy,' he said. 'Such pride. And such a delight you were able to attend this evening. Young Benjamin, I think, is somewhat restored.'

He was indeed – marginally so, at least. And not the slightest sign that Winckley was dissembling. I had taken the time to visit Benji, asked him to at least describe his dear Mary for me and, yes, she could easily be a match for Sir William Langhorn's young widow. And then there had been the invitation to consider, images of walking directly into Thomas Forster. Or, worse, the mud-drenched figure of Porter turning up to confront me in that feast full of Jacobite rebels who would, indeed, be happy to see me hang. But I had come too far to stop now, and I spent some time maximising the odds in my favour, searching through my two travel chests for attire that might make me less readily recognisable.

Though I had one other task, once the light began to fade and before the chair – which Winckley had arranged for me – came to deliver me to the grandeur of the Patten House. I stole a blanket from the inn's linen closet and crept out to the town square, awaited my moment and, when there was nobody else about, I ventured over to the pillory where the rogues had secured the most prominent of their prisoners – the spy, Thomas Wybergh. The White Horse had been alive with the news all afternoon and it had taken me some time to recall how I knew the name. Streynsham, of course, I remembered at last. Another captain of dragoons, was he not? This was the fellow he had instructed to apprehend his brother-in-law Peter Legh and thus help garner prior intelligence of these rebellions. And even with the blanket, I doubted the poor man should survive this November night that promised another hard frost.

'A gift from Sir Streynsham Master,' I whispered in his ear. 'And I only wish it could be more.'

He thanked me but bade me leave, lest I should be taken too. I did so, though I feared it was only a matter of time before I should share his fate anyway.

'Restored, yes,' I told Mister Winckley, just two hours later. 'And I think your physician may have been correct. Something he ate – though not through your household, sirrah, I hasten to add.'

There was a piper, fingers dancing upon his chanter, the reeds wailing out a rapacious reel, and some of his countrymen impressing the guests with their footwork.

'I thank you for saying so, ma'am,' he replied. 'And might I compliment you on your attire?'

I smiled, thanked him for his courtesy. For in truth I had taken some trouble. I had with me only a few items that might have been suitable, yet I had done my best. My hair I had shaped into ringlets, a cushion too, stiffened with sugar-water, and over this confection I had pinned a veil – one that had originally belonged to my friend Sathiri and which often travels with me more for sentimental purpose than any desire for modesty. But it is simple, diaphanous and deep olive, arranged so that it masked my eyes at least. And a match for the lighter shade in the bizarre-patterned brocade of my mantua. Autumnal orange-red and fern green, the pleats of the train bunched fashionably at my waist and the small of my back almost in imitation of the way so many of these young Highland gentlemen sported their plaids. Indeed, the whole effect of the mantua's style and colour gave me the look, I now realised, of the tartans worn by a few of the officers. The longer edges of the veil, meanwhile, were draped to cover neck and bodice, secured with a brooch of amber at the ruffles of my shoulder. I had developed something of a stoop too, leaned upon my cane perhaps a little more than usual but enough, I hoped, to avoid either Forster or Hughes – or Mary Aston, for that matter – from instantly identifying me.

'I hope it will answer,' I said. 'In my wildest dreams I had not thought to be in such esteemed society. Yet my husband would think it amiss were I to be seen abroad less than discreetly in the company of so many gentlemen.'

'Indeed, Mistress Yale,' beamed Winckley. 'Propriety, of course. Though please allow me to name Lord Derwentwater.'

Was this the moment then? Perhaps Porter had only told his superiors about me – and Derwentwater, or Forster, seeing me here, would know something had gone wrong with their plans, order me taken. I hardly know how I kept my old legs from betraying me entirely as Winckley led me around the edges of the hall, past those Highland dancers, towards that gathering of fellows who almost needed no introduction.

'I do not see General Forster here,' I said.

'You are already acquainted then?'

'We met once or twice, though only in passing.'

'Then I hope your acquaintance may be renewed later, ma'am. For I understand he will join us, once his duties across the road are done.'

I murmured some nonsense about how much I should relish the reunion, tried to mask my sigh of relief. Though by now I had sighted that Wrexham rogue, Edward Hughes, on the farther side of the room – though he was plainly busy at his cups. In any case, we had reached Derwentwater's party and Winckley made great play of my identity.

'Truly, Mistress Yale,' said this young popinjay, with a jarring accent that was both Northumberland and France at the same time. 'His Majesty King James will be delighted. He has great ambitions for the East India Company, ma'am. And he has told me many times that he needs somebody upon whom he can rely to become its new loyal President. Your husband, perhaps.'

So he knew the name. And why should he not? Elihu is not entirely unknown, of course. Though there was no hint of any other form of recognition between us, no sign of any enmity towards me. My fame as a Whig intelligencer, therefore, not so spread abroad as I might have thought, even by Porter and Forster. And the relief swept through me like the flux, so much that I feared my bowels might betray me.

'It is wonderful to hear such confidence in our enterprise,' I smiled, and carefully avoided any response in relation to Elihu – for there was a piece of dissembling I might not be able to carry off. Besides, I hoped that, with all this other business to occupy him, curtailing the conversation might be the best way of ensuring he did not mention it in passing to Forster. 'And you think the way now open for our forces. To London perhaps?'

'I think we have little to fear, ma'am. A couple of enemy units at Wigan, so we are told. Nothing more. We shall take them there, unless I am much mistook.'

'Or here,' said the unsteady old fellow at his side. All grey silk, short powdered periwig, too much liquor. Shuttleworth, Winckley had named him. A local Member of Parliament, if I had heard him correctly. 'And if so I hope to see Preston's streets running with heretics' blood.'

'God's hooks, sir.' It was that same haughty Highlander I had seen leading their forces into town. William Mackintosh. Laird of Borlum – wherever that might be – and some prominence in his tribe, or clan, as he calls it. 'Curb your tongue, will ye?'

'The lady is one of us, is she not?' cried Shuttleworth, the despicable wretch. He leered at me. 'And seen the world, has she not? Mingled with Moor and Gentue. Heard worse, madam, I warrant?'

Worse indeed, Mister Shuttleworth, I thought. But if fighting comes to pass, the blood shed upon these streets shall not be by loyal Englishmen alone. I relished the prospect of seeing him, at least, upon the scaffold. Yet my optimism waned as swiftly as it had been excited by Derwentwater's erroneous assumption about the forces facing them. For, as the piper's jig whined to its end and those Jack Highlanders finished their wild fling, a brace of fiddlers struck up a more genteel rhythm and, at that moment, the doors were thrown open with a great huzzah. Several travel-grimed men burst into the room, brandishing their swords aloft and crying out *God bless King James*, or similar nonsense. Towneley arrived from Burnley and Sydall from Manchester, Mister Winckley explained. Stout fellows, he said.

'And how many do they bring to our cause, sir?'

'We expect perhaps a thousand between those two towns,' he replied, and my heart sank. A thousand? And I had not thought to include such numbers in my tally.

Derwentwater, meanwhile, was attentive, polite, escorted me to the tables set with refreshments, and there I accepted a glass of sack, engaged in conversation, listened to the fiddlers, kept my ears open. And thus I noted the subtle changes in the tone of discourse, the waves of chatter. Towneley, it seemed, had brought no more than sixty men, and Sydall none at all from Manchester. Why? Because General Wills had arrived there two days earlier and though his force was not great it was seemingly enough to dampen the ardour of the Manchester banditti. There was this too. That, while the snatches I overheard were full of praise for Derwentwater, they contained nothing but scorn for Forster. Tom Fool, they called him quite openly. Ditherer, they said. There was division here, and I stored that intelligence in my memory. If I was able to send another report...

But it was then I saw the chit. To be honest, it was Derwentwater who led me to her, for I happened to turn and catch his gaze, a look of such longing and adoration that I felt drawn to discover the object of his fascination. And there she was, exactly as I recalled her from those occasions I had seen her at poor Sir William's side. But here was not some serving girl, as Benjamin had implied.

'I see you recognise another of our guests, Mistress Yale.' Shuttleworth, behind me and I had not noticed him approach.

'Your pardon, sir?' I said, glad of the chance to turn my back on Mary Aston.

'Colonel Porter's daughter, ma'am. You know her, I collect?'

'That young woman? I have not had the pleasure, I fear. I was simply admiring that shade of emerald she wears so well.'

He was swaying from the effects of the drink he had imbibed.

'Owe her a great deal,' he said. 'Served us well, posing as a maidservant in Hoghton's household. This very house. Intelligence, ma'am. That is what she brought us. Though would you believe it? Young woman like that, a spy?'

'A woman spy?' I was astonished, naturally, at the very idea.

'Yet you must allow me to name her, perhaps,' he went on. But I demurred. Later, I told him, and begged to be excused for I needed a word with Mister Winckley – though, in truth, if I needed to renew my acquaintance with that drab, that murderous little whore, it would be upon my own terms. So I mingled amiably, as she also seemed to be doing between dances.

In India I had many times refused the opportunity to observe a hunt – once for a tiger that had been bringing terror to the local villages. But I understood the principles well enough. Patience. Infinite patience. Keeping to the cover. Closing slowly with one's quarry. Remaining always upwind. Silence, utter silence, in the approach. Until, finally, I had my back to her and no more than a foot distant, so I could hear her foolish prattle in that reed-like voice with more than a hint of French in the accent – a voice I had barely heard when she was so briefly Lady Langhorn.

Just then, however, it seemed I must wait still longer. For one of the Scotsmen had invited her to step out with him in an allemande. And yes, she said, she would be delighted. But then a hesitation. Though perhaps, I heard her say, some cordial first. Of course, said the swain and, in the instant he left her side, I took his place. One swift movement in which I slipped the pocket pistol from the bunched brocade at my waist and jammed it into her ribs. She gave a small cry of pain, glanced down at the weapon, then up at my face. Confusion in her eyes.

'Mary, my dear!' I exclaimed, and held her tight, pressing my walking cane against her other side. '*Quelle surprise.* A pleasure to see you here.' Then whispered in her ear, still with a smile fixed upon my lips. 'One of those moments,' I said. 'A crossroads in one's life. Scream and you die. I get taken, but you die. Or you can live. Quick, choose.'

'You?' She seemed genuinely surprised.

'We shall exit,' I told her, and linked her arm with one hand still holding the stick, keeping the weapon firmly in place with the other. 'The entrance hall, I think.'

I glanced back, through the veil's gossamer distortions, saw her Highlander standing where we had been moments earlier, holding two glasses in his hands and looking about for the girl but not seeing her as I guided her into a thicket of guests.

'Mistress Yale,' cried Mister Winckley as he and his wife appeared before us. 'And this, unless I am much mistaken...'

'Mary, yes,' I said. 'We are off to a quiet corner so I may reassure her of Benjamin's improved condition. The poor girl has been beside herself. Have you not, Mary?' I pushed the muzzle just a little deeper into her sparse flesh, caused her to wince, steered her a little to the left – straight into Edward Hughes. He saw me, that was plain, but he seemed to be struggling with a lack of focus, a problem of recognition, his body perfectly upright but the head swilling back and forth on the tide of wine he must have thrown down his throat. He opened his mouth to speak but by then I had pushed Mary past him too.

Several of the gentlemen bowed to us as we reached the doors, hoped that we would soon return to their company – the sort of stupidities that men so often spout when they think they are being gallant. But I pulled her swiftly aside when I saw Forster coming in through the vestibule, past the doorkeeper's pantry. Could it be that Porter answered to Forster and not to Derwentwater? Well, it mattered little at this point.

'How far do you think we might get, Mistress Yale?' the girl asked after the Northumbrian toad waddled past us into the hall without a second glance in our direction. He looked far from happy in his command.

'Where is it?' I said. 'Whatever you used to poison my son? Kitchens or your room?'

'I have no idea what you mean,' she murmured, then winced as I gave her a further prod.

'You must have a fine new room, Mary, now you no longer have to play the maid.'

'I was never that,' she spat. 'Hoghton employed me on his accompts, his books.'

Clever, I thought. An ideal position from which to observe his movements.

'But the servants' quarters all the same,' I said. 'Though not presently, I think. Derwentwater will have found a more suitable lodging for you. And not too far from his own quarters unless I read him entirely wrong.'

'You know nothing, Mistress Yale.' She almost spat my name upon the flags of the entrance hall. 'And when Dada...'

'I know this much, girl – that your father is taken. He poses no further threat to me. Now, the stairs,' I said. Of course, I knew no such thing and trembled at the thought he might, even now, be at large once more. I thought for a moment she might refuse and I was grateful there was so much activity here, folk coming and going, messengers arriving or leaving with dispatches. But then she set a hand upon the blackened-oak newel post and started up the wide treads.

'Taken? How can that be?'

'He set out to follow me. He told you that much, I am certain. But friends of mine ambushed him in his stead. You see, Mary? Even here I am not without friends.'

'And where is he now?'

'All in good time, you wretch,' I said. 'First, your room, so I may see exactly how and why you planned to kill my son.'

We reached the landing, turned up the second flight of stairs to the first floor. There were still guests, a couple of the Scottish officers, heading up or down, but nobody paid us much heed apart from the occasional polite acknowledgement, and I kept a ready smile pasted upon my face, the pocket pistol firmly at Mary's ribcage.

'Along here,' she murmured and led us down a carpeted sconce-lit corridor with rooms on each side.

'If you try to trick me, Mary, you shall surely die,' I told her. 'This is the thing. That you knew I was here. Your pa too. And he clearly suspected my reason for being here – else why should he follow me? A good intelligencer, is he not? Knew precisely what I am about. Though told nobody. Nor yet did you.' She had stopped in front of a door at the very back of the house, though still she said nothing. 'Open,' I instructed her, and she obligingly delved within those emerald-green skirts to produce a key.

'I shall tell you nothing,' she said, unlocking the door and allowing me to push her inside, 'unless you can provide a token to prove Dada is taken – and still alive.'

I was simply pleased at the chance to release her from my grip, for my hands had grown quite numb. Still, I kept the pistol trained upon her.

'Lock it,' I said, and she obeyed. 'Now, show me. Whatever it was you used to poison my boy. You still have it?'

Her face was contorted in anger, that hot and heavy state of passion I have lately heard named a tanterum, and in that humour she stamped to the room's garde-robe. I caught a strong waft of camphor as she threw open a drawer and took out a brass-bound box, set it down upon the table near her bed. At my instruction she lifted the lid and there, inside, were the remains of a few Turban Head mushrooms, those morels that have always reminded me of sheep's brains, but here their customary beetroot colour faded to an insipid brown. And now, for the first time, Mary showed fear in her eyes.

'What now?' she said.

'Now? You tell me why this feud. Is it truly no more than my own and Sir William Langhorn's part in thwarting your father's treason?'

'You call it treason but my Dada answers only to God and King James. Is that not enough cause for us to want you dead? But then there is this. That I was only a small girl when you and your friends drove my father into exile. He sent for us, of course. At Clontarf. And we set out to join him. But my mother became so very sick on the crossing. It killed her. *You* killed her.'

'What stuff,' I said. 'Your father's sedition killed her, perhaps. But I? All of this because...'

'Oh, you are guilty, madam. I had many years to think on it. And Our Lady guided my hand, caused our housekeeper at Saint-Germain to teach me the use of herbs and wild plants. And these, she said,' Mary pointed at the morels, 'are deadly.'

'Deadly indeed,' I laughed. 'Though she did not school you well enough to know you must cleanse your hands after touching them. Fie, how prime! To inflict some of the poison upon yourself.'

'And I need no schooling from the witch who killed my ma,' she spat.

Her anger had turned to pure venom now, so that I finally saw before me, revealed, the serpent beneath the guise of sweet and innocent childhood. Here was a woman weaned on pure bile. The father's daughter indeed.

'Your pa reasoned that you could both exact your revenge on Sir William, on my family, on me, without being gainsaid – and then claim credit when this rebellion is won for bringing yet more enemy spies to justice. Or at least have his crimes overlooked in the general upheaval.'

'Who would even have known?' she sneered. 'That lecherous old goat Langhorn already buried and none the wiser. Your son – that impotent, mewling fool – would not even have been missed. And you, Mistress Yale? My father would indeed have seen you hanged. And perhaps may still do so. You truly think your friends can hold him?'

My friends, the Ribble marshlands? I thought. Yes, I believed them capable of performing the task. I prayed so, at least.

'Your father has been taken south,' I lied, 'to the house of another old associate, Sir Streynsham Master.'

'Streynsham...' she began, and I saw the recognition in her eyes.

'Yes, the same. You know him already. You need not tell him about your scheme to murder Sir William.' As it happened, I already doubted her foul plan had succeeded, though I was not about to tell her so. 'He has instructions to hold Porter until he knows I am safe. But if there is any indication I may be otherwise, it will be your father you shall see hanged. Whether in victory or defeat, Streynsham will see the task done.'

'And me?'

I unfastened the amber brooch from my shoulder.

'You will take this to Streynsham Master's house, near Wigan. If you fetch me ink and paper, I will write the direction. Take the brooch so he will know you come from me. He will hold you too, of course. Because his orders are clear – to see Colonel Porter kept secure for the next seven days. If I return safely then we shall discuss your fates, with some consideration for your good faith. If I do not...'

But I could see what she was thinking. She could go straight from here to Tom Forster. Or to Lord James Radclyffe, her handsome Earl of Derwentwater. They could easily send men to have her father freed, once I supplied the direction. And then there would be a reckoning with me, regardless.

'Very well,' she said, the sweetness and light, the child's simpering, returning to her voice.

'But there is one last thing,' I said. 'Two things, I suppose. That the direction I shall give will take you to Sir Streynsham Master – though sadly not to your papa. For Streynsham's orders were for him to be sent immediately onwards to Chester Castle. Whatever else may happen, Mary, your friends here cannot rescue him from that prison.'

Her features crumpled once more.

'And the second thing?' she snapped.

'Before I parted company with your father, we had an interesting conversation about divine intervention. For you may be right about my part – though an inadvertent one – in the death of your mama, which I regret deeply. No child should be left, Mary, without its mother. Though your father and his friend Seaton would gladly have seen my own daughters and my son deprived of their own. And you too would have seen my son poisoned, had you only had the wit to do it properly.'

Impotent, mewling fool. Was that how this creature had thought of my dearest boy, whispering words of affection to him while she plotted his murder?

'The wit...?' she murmured, as I moved towards her, pressed the pocket pistol into her belly, pushed her back against the table.

'Divine intervention, as I say,' I hissed into her face. 'For whether you survive the ride to Wigan matters not one jot to me, you drab. Streynsham's orders, the fate of your father, will hold regardless. But you, Mary Aston, I leave in the hands of our Lord Jesu. For if you had known the true qualities of these beauties...' I picked up one of the Turban Heads, forced it to her mouth though, of course, she tried to keep it firmly closed, to turn her face away. I cracked the pistol hard against her ribs, and when she cried out with the pain, I forced the morel between her lips. 'Now,' I said. 'Eat.'

And I repeated the exercise over and over again. For Benjamin. For the sake of Sir William Langhorn.

In God's hands. I persuaded her that, if she found a mount, rode hard, she might complete the journey to New Hall before the toxins did their work. Or she could delay here: see me taken; put her own faith in her Blessed Virgin to save her Dada; perhaps benefit from an antidote – though that housekeeper in Saint-Germain might indeed have schooled her better.

In God's hands. For I truly did not know whether Porter might already be at liberty – the chance that Mary, in the agony I was certain she must soon be suffering, could still be preparing for the journey when her treacherous father found his way back to town after a damp and windswept day hoisted upon his own petard out there on the marshes.

In God's hands. I could do nothing but take one step at a time. I had left her in that bedchamber with a reminder, pure and wicked irony, that she should wrap herself warmly against the night's chill. Then I descended the staircase, found Mister Winckley for no better purpose than to set myself in the lion's jaw, to discover sooner rather than later whether I was already exposed. And when all still seemed as before, I begged leave to return to the White Horse, using my advanced years as an excuse to seek my bed, but making sure he might advise his cook that putting my son on a diet of winter vegetables, taken with some crushed charcoal, a little salt and plenty of liquid would – I was now certain – set him back very swiftly upon his feet. For even the most incompetent of poisoners should know that the Turban Head mushroom is only at its most lethal when consumed in its raw state – or almost raw, at least. Raw and fresh. Yet cooking the morels into a stew? The dissipation of those delicious toxins? A flux, certainly. Some delirium, perhaps. But fatality? Never. So, she may indeed have helped Langhorn to his demise, though I doubt it was poison itself that killed him.

Thus, with my word to Winckley that I should visit Benjamin early in the morning, I accepted the use of his chair to carry me to my lodgings where I spent the entire night fully clothed, the pocket pistol at my side, in full expectation that, any moment, I should hear boots upon the stairs and be taken after all.

'She is gone, boy,' I said. 'That is all I can tell you.'

He was in his bed still, though looking remarkably better than at our last meeting. The Winckleys' cook – their housekeeper, as it transpired – had fed him broth last night and this morning as I suggested, and now there was a cup of warmed ale by the bedside. Alongside the cup lay the letters I had brought.

'Gone? How do you know?'

It would have been difficult to explain that, were she not gone, I most certainly would have been. And no sign of that devil Porter either. Not then, anyhow.

'Oh, I was late at the Patten House and there was chatter among the good-wives there. Some scandal between the girl and the earl – Derwentwater.'

'But she told me...'

'And I am sure at the time she meant every word, Benji. Well, perhaps not every word. For did you know that she is strong for their Jacobite cause? Even Mister Winckley seemed to know that. Working under Sir Henry's roof for no other purpose than to gather intelligence for them.'

'A spy?' He laughed, almost could not contain himself. 'Mama, I think your own activities – if such they can be called – have entirely turned your wits. Is that the best you can do? Paid her to go hence, I assume. Or threatened her, more likely. Believe that a serving maid must be beneath me. Invent this stuff and nonsense in reflection of your own foolishness.'

'You believe I would threaten her? Great heavens, Benjamin. Do you not know how that offends me?'

317

Difficult, is it not – the living of two lives at one time? For this Catherine that would see us delivered from the division and destruction of her country would not think twice to bring damnation down upon the head of that evil little chit. But another Catherine, the mother, could think of nothing more preposterous than the thought that she could ever be less than kindness itself to her son's beloved.

'And gone where?' he said, throwing back the covers and setting his stocking'd feet upon the floor.

'I know not. But from the gossip-mongers it seems she is sent hence. Perhaps on some new secret mission.'

'Mama, this is nonsense. I shall ask Mister Winckley. He will know, I'm certain.'

'Of course you must ask him,' I said. 'Indeed you must. But meanwhile I would ask you to do something for me, also.'

'The letters?' he asked, and rummaged in his clothes chest, discarding one of the linen shirts he found there but choosing another that seemed to suit him better.

'The letters, yes. It is possible I might have to leave Preston in some haste, Benjamin, and if so...'

I was finding this difficult, almost choked on my words.

'Leave in haste? Mama, is that some circumlocution for – well, you are being dramatic, surely? And, if not, you mustn't even think...'

He was biting his lip, a frown upon his face, and though I tried to smile, to reassure him it was his own imagination that practised upon him, my own doubts and fears must have shone through. After all, I had spent most of those worried waking hours drafting the contents.

One, a note to Matthew – fond memories of occasions when we had each been happy in each other's company that would, I assured him, provide comfort to me in whatever might lie ahead; my many apologies for the contemptible way in which I had treated him; those jewels I counted as most precious among my treasures, his poems; and my deepest regrets that we might not, now, be able to fulfill the dreams we had created together on our last night together.

The second – although with Streynsham's direction, and with a short note within to that other dear friend – is in truth intended for Benjamin himself, though I could not say so. For that is my last will and testament, more hastily written than I should have liked, though for now it must answer.

At Latimer I am often in company with Mister Taylor, my accountant, poring over the accompts, my statements from Hoare's Bank where my modest pile has been stored since I regained control of it from Evance. My jewels, my gold, the product of investments, of my various enterprises with Sir William, poor murthered Langhorn. A healthy balance. So, here were my bequests, after my debts and funeral expenses are settled – at least, if my fate affords me a funeral at all.

Yet I did not allow myself to dwell on such horrors, and I have settled a full one-fifth of my estate upon Benjamin, name him as my executor and administrator, in token of the special affection and natural love I feel for him – all that is left me, now, of my sweet Hynmers. A condition, naturally, that he must continue to care for Ursula and, thus, lesser amounts to Ursi, to Nan and to Kate. To my grandchildren. To my sons-in-law – yes, even Dudley. To my brothers and *their* children. To Reverend Burrough at Latimer, desiring him also to watch over Ursula. To my maidservants. To Israel the stable boy. To all the others of my household. And to young David Yale, a handsome amount I hope he might put to good use.

And to Elihu? I had thought long and hard upon it and finally settled on the very thing. The Maysmore clock, requiring him to keep it always at Plas Grono, reminding him that a bequest such as this, written in the name of God, would bring down terrible misfortune upon his head if he chose to ignore my final wishes, though wishing him to collect, with every tick of that fine timepiece, the wicked way in which he had ruined poor Mister Edisbury.

'They are simply letters, Benjamin,' I scolded him. 'But I leave them in your safekeeping in case I am stuck upon the road. If you have not heard from me to the contrary by Monday next, perhaps you would be a good boy and commit them to the post?'

Polk allowed me to hire Henrietta once more, though he was quizzical about my desire to venture forth in pursuit of my ornithological interests on such a morning of icy drizzle. But I assured him that she was such a biddable beast that I could manage both pony and rain-napper at the same time, and that if the weather turned any more distasteful, I should return forthwith.

And thus I descended Fishergate again, with all its usual bustle, despite the rain, then followed the track west to the marshes and the

Ribble. If I had wished to cross the ford today I should have needed to wait several hours more, since the waters were still ebbing, though they had already abandoned that portion below the causeway where I had left Porter. In all honesty, I am not sure exactly what I expected. I had made that threat to him about the powers of an incoming tide but that was pure invention on my part, and I had spent portions of the night wondering what I should find when I returned – presumably either Porter escaped or Porter still anchored there in the mud. In the first case, I should now be facing painful retribution and almost certain death. In the second, perhaps the possibility of turning my lies to his daughter upon their head, convincing him that it was *she* who faced a hanging unless I remained unharmed.

I was therefore somewhat surprised to find a different outcome entirely. For there, its tops protruding from the mire, was just one of the rogue's boots, though of Porter himself, no sign at all. And, in the lane, his bay mare, cold and miserable, but tethered in exactly the place I had left her. Where might he be? Still close at hand, plainly, and a shiver ran down my spine as I looked carefully around to discover his hiding place. Without success.

A dilemma, though at that moment I was more concerned about the view across the river towards the Penwortham side. For I had hoped to see there some evidence of those fellows Walker had assured me might be brought up from Atherton. Yet nothing of them either. Nothing.

What to do? Put my faith in the Almighty, I supposed, and return in haste to town as I had originally planned. Though I could not bring myself to do so without taking Porter's horse, for she seemed so much in need of care. And thus I took the mare in tow. Anyway, it might slow him down at least. No horse. Only one boot. It puzzled me all the way back to the livery where I arrived in a state of animation, part natural through my exertions with Porter's mount, and part pretense.

'I found this poor beast wandering near the marsh,' I told Polk. 'And I fear her rider may have been taken by those rogues.'

'Rogues?' he said, as he helped me dismount.

'Across the river,' I said. 'A large body of men over towards Penwortham. Though I could not make them out clearly. You think I should make a report to Patten House?' But Polk thought it better that I should take myself back to the inn, dry myself and take some mulled ale against the chill, while he himself would take word to General Forster on my behalf. I thanked him but told him I should prefer that my name not be mentioned, even in confidence. Too much excitement at my age, I explained, could prove fatal.

'Don't tha' be feart, ma'am,' he smiled. 'I'd not let 'owt put such as thee at risk. Brass comes fust, see. An' they'll send out scouts any'ow, I reckons.'

I supposed they would, which would make my efforts somewhat less productive than I had hoped. But I accepted his suggestion, returned to the White Horse, and saw on my way that the pillory was now empty. Had Wybergh perished, after all? It would not have surprised me, but when I made a casual enquiry with Mother Sumners, about whether the wretch was dead, she told me no, simply removed to the House of Correction, the old friary. But there would be a decision that night, she had heard. About whether to hang him or not. A decision maybe after the festive frolic planned for that evening at the Town Hall, the event that would bid a fond farewell to Forster's army. An event that would wish Godspeed to them before they marched forth.

And the event, as it transpired, that would see such wrath brought down upon my head.

I dined alone – or as alone as might be possible at the inn's benches – listening with renewed satisfaction to the rumours carried there by regular customers of the White Horse. The whole Hanoverian army now encamped at Penwortham, they speculated. Other forces seen to the north, beyond Gallow's Hill, towards Garstang. Forster's forces surrounded. A price to be paid, some said, by poor Proud Preston. And what would become of them?

Well, I cared more that there was no hue and cry. There I sat, in plain sight. No Porter. No return of his poisonous chit of a daughter. No summons to explain how Mistress Yale might happen to be in town and reporting the presence of enemy forces that now seemed not to exist.

But as I finished my cheese and bread, feeling somewhat less anxious and determined upon an afternoon nap, Benjamin arrived to say that he was, indeed, much recovered – and bound for his duties, yet also fetching a message from the Winckleys, trusting that I might join them for the evening's festivity.

'You still seem far from fit for work,' I scolded him.

'Will you come tonight? I'm hoping you may be wrong, that Mary might have returned.'

'And Derwentwater? This liaison between them?'

'You said yourself, Mama. Gossip-mongers. The curse of this town. Of the whole country. Do you know that some lackwit,' he went on in a whisper, 'spread word this morning of Wills at Penwortham?'

Lackwit, indeed.

'Rumour only?' I said.

'Of course. Winckley tells me they sent out riders. Nothing. In any case, they've had word that Wills is actually on the road from Manchester to Wigan.'

All that work for no purpose. Damn Walker and his Atherton men. Still, nothing ventured, nothing gained. Is that not what they say?

'Then let us hope,' I told him, 'you may be correct and that Mary shall, indeed, make an appearance tonight. But you might do me one more favour, Benjamin.' My turn to whisper now. 'The fellow they were holding at the pillory. His name is Thomas Wybergh.'

'The spy they took at Lancaster?'

He spoke the words with an air of disbelief, looked about to check that nobody else could hear, shook his head at me in silent admonishment.

'Our agent,' I corrected him. 'Yes, the same. I need you to find out how he fares.'

'Mama…'

'Benjamin…'

'Very well, I shall see it done. But if ever there was a need for warnings to be sent, I fear it may be now.'

'Because?'

'Because Winckley has heard Forster now plans to hold here, instead of marching out to meet our forces. To defend the bridge. To make Wills pay for every inch of the Hollow Way. If they come, Mama, they shall be destroyed.'

*

The Town Hall was all gaiety and music – that chamber on the first floor now given over entirely to a Bacchanalian feast, which I must needs attend in almost precisely the same attire as the previous evening. And how much that vexed me. How much it added to the darkness in my heart at the thought of the slaughter that must follow. How little it seemed to matter just a few hours later.

'And you are certain?' I said to Mister Winckley, accepting a portion of suckling pig from one of the serving girls. 'Wills already at Wigan?'

'I have no idea why we were not alerted earlier,' he replied, and passed me the jug of herb-laced gravy. 'Tom Forster was only boasting this morning that we should know if any of our enemies came within forty miles. Yet now...'

I sipped at a fine red wine. French, I think. And their fiddlers were playing a merry little tune, *Around She Goes* or some such.

'General Forster is not here again, I see.' I had searched the room often enough. 'And Benjamin,' I said, 'the vegetables only, if you please. These meats simply too rich. Too rich by far.'

'The general seems to be suffering from some sort of flux too,' Mistress Winckley replied. 'Something catching perhaps.'

Now, if I had thought of that, I might have made better use of those Turban Heads but I could claim no credit for whatever may have befallen Forster just then. I was still contemplating whether I might still explore such a strategy when a Jack Highlander – it may have been the same young man who had, last night, gone to fetch Mary Aston's cordial – gently tapped my arm and politely, in his broken sibilant English, enquired whether I might spare a moment for Lord Jamie – Derwentwater, I supposed.

'Mama,' said Benjamin, 'shall I come with you?'

But I brushed his anxiety aside.

'Such a handsome request deserves to be handsomely met,' I told him, wiped my mouth with the napkin, threw it down on the table while the young Scotsman helped with my chair. 'And I am certain Lord Derwentwater will not keep me long.'

It was perhaps bravely spoken but those steps out into the vestibule were long indeed – and when I reached there, I saw that all my worst fears were well-founded. It was quite a reception.

'You told me Lord Jamie,' I said, scolding that young Highland officer, and I was rewarded at least by the guilt carved upon his face.

'My orders, ma'am,' he replied, looking suitably rebuked, for Derwentwater was not among them. Only my enemies.

'So it's true,' Thomas Forster said to me as I lifted the veil from my face. 'I thought it could not be so. Surely some other Mistress Yale. But no, Lord James assured me. Wife to Governor Yale, no less.'

Winckley had been correct too – Forster looked even worse than he had done the previous night, hand pressed against his ribs as though he might be in pain. And though I might have no means by which to poison him, as thoughts of the Turban Heads had sowed in my brain, I still had the pocket pistol within the bunched skirts at my waist. My own fate, I thought, must surely be sealed, but here was a chance to destroy their general. Yet what, then, would become of poor Benji? I knew I must stay my hand, for now, at least.

'And simply here to see my son, sirrah. He has been in Preston these two years past. Does my presence trouble you?'

I saw the Welshman, Edward Hughes, push through the entourage around Forster.

'In Wrexham too, she was. Saw her, I did. Proper little spy, she is.'

'And then,' said Forster, 'there was all that alarum this morning. Enemy forces at Penwortham. But when our scouts go out, nothing. We trace back these rumours and what do we find when Polk's tongue is finally loosened? Mistress Yale, he screams. Mistress Yale.'

'You simpering wretch,' I said. 'Polk is a decent man and I simply told him what I wished him to relay.'

'You begged him to keep his source a secret, did you not? You see now what you've done.'

'She was there last night too,' said Hughes. 'Saw her with my own eyes, I did. Spying, she was. Like now, I reckon. And then there's the Colonel…'

'Hold your tongue, man,' snapped Forster. 'We'll get to that in good time.'

'What?' I said, though I was trying to seek any means by which I might escape – though such a thing seemed entirely impossible. 'Lost somebody? And how long do you intend to keep me standing here, Mister Forster? Have you no respect for my age?'

'Very well,' he spat. 'Let's do it. Bring her.'

There was no polite invitation this time. Just two of Forster's ruffians grasping my arms and dragging me to the door, outside, then down the steps to the market square where some of their men held blazing torches aloft over a bundle sprawled upon the flagstones. The night was clear, bitterly cold, the sky ablaze with stars, the moon almost full.

'Shall nobody lend a cloak to an old lady?' I said, and that same Jack Highlander, who had escorted me from the dining table, stepped forward and pulled a shawl from one of the barbarians, threw it around my shoulders, much to Forster's disdain. I thanked him, while one of the torchbearers held his flame closer to that bundle. In the flickering light I saw a pair of legs, one booted, the other covered only by a riding sock, ripped and torn, open sores showing beneath, though no blood.

From the top of the slime-encrusted boot a crab scuttled out and one of the Highlanders stamped upon it, an awful crunching sound.

The body itself was still wrapped in that familiar riding coat though it too was now smeared with mud, green shreds of weed dangling from the skirts and shoulders.

I saw clenched hands, the face, the empty eye sockets, parts of the nose, ears and lips gone too. A blue tinge to the flesh, but the skin waxed.

'Washed up at the Ribble Bridge,' said Forster. 'Strange, don't you think? One of our patrols found him at low water this afternoon – though been dead since yesterday, it seems. Accident, they said. Porter enjoyed his liquor, of course. Did you know him?'

I stared at the remains of that face, as contemptible now as in life, and I felt no pity at whatever fate had befallen him – though I think I knew, of course. The force of that rising tide and its effects upon him not such an invention after all.

'How should I have known him?'

'I wondered, that was all. Something he may once have mentioned. About a boat on the Thames Estuary. When he was forced into exile. Your name mentioned.'

'It means nothing to me, sir.'

'And then there is his daughter, of course.'

'Saw them together, I did,' said Hughes.

'Such stuff!' I laughed.

'Really? And yet she was married for a while to a good friend of yours. Langhorn. Ah, you remember now, I see. So young to become a widow.'

'Mama!' I turned to see Benjamin upon the stairs.

'Go back inside, boy,' I shouted.

'Blind me, no,' Forster laughed. 'The very person. Young Mary has some connection to your son, they tell me. Such a web.' Forster shouted to those of his banditti also on the steps. 'Take him too.'

'Mary?' said Benjamin, struggling as they seized him. 'What is this?'

'If this is the father…' I began.

'Please, I beg of you,' shouted Forster. 'No more of this nonsense. You even returned Colonel Porter's mount to old Polk.'

'Porter,' Benjamin repeated, craning his neck to see as they held him against the wall. He had lost his periwig somewhere in the scuffle. 'You mean this is the rogue…'

He would, at some point, be able to put all the pieces together. Perhaps. But meanwhile Forster was nodding to one of his men, one of those holding a torch. 'Go on,' he said. 'Show her.'

The fellow knelt at Porter's side and carefully straightened the fingers of Porter's left hand, then turned it so that the pallid palm was upwards.

And there, etched into the dead flesh, a series of deep cuts that were now bloodless, stark, but still plain. Letters: Y; A; and L.

They had sufficient courtesy left in them to retrieve my cloak and my stick and, of course, many of the festivity's guests came out to see me marched away. Benjamin they hauled off to the House of Correction, myself to the Patten House for further questioning and yes, at some point, an interrogation by Derwentwater too, I supposed. Though it was Forster I feared. And those fanatical devils closest to him. Those screaming *Hang the spies* or worse.

'Be brave, boy,' I shouted to Benjamin as he was led off past the pillory and I towards Churchgate. He called back to me, some words of reassurance, I think, though I could not hear them clearly for the baying of the crowd.

I caught a last glimpse of the Winckleys too, the look of loathing upon their faces. I felt somewhat shamed by it, for they were decent folk, I thought. Misguided in their affiliations, though they had been kind to me. And to my son.

It was Benjamin who filled my thoughts as I was paraded in front of the church – Highlanders and Lowlanders alike stopping from their duties, building some form of blockade, to stare at me – and through those noble gates of Patten House, past the lodge I had so admired just the night before, though the previous night from the comfort of the Winckleys' sedan. But there was no link boy to light my way, just dark concern for my son in whatever hell might await him in the House of Correction he must share with Captain Wybergh, with poor Polk, and with whatever true miscreants that place might also hold.

I imagined the walls lining the avenue closing upon me and one of Forster's ruffians was forced to assist me as I mounted the many wide steps to the majestic masonry of the entrance. And I was almost in a swoon as they pressed me up flight after flight of those familiar sconce-lit stairs to the topmost floor. Somebody lit a candle and I was pushed into a room. It sat at the front of the house and would normally have been a lesser guest bedchamber, though from my quick glimpse of the interior before they took the candle away it was now packed with travel chests, with valises – many bearing their owners' names or initials – just a small part, I imagined, of the baggage from their train.

And there I was imprisoned. In the dark. The door locked from the outside. No fire in the hearth to warm me but my cloak, at least, that borrowed shawl also, and with the moonlight to help me my eyes slowly adjusted a little. Upon the walls, tapestries with designs I could not discern. In the corner a mound of riding capes. I prodded them with my cane, against the presence of vermin. For the bed was stripped bare. Nothing but the frame, the rails empty, the tester gone. And if sleep might be possible at all, they could provide some small comfort. But for now I satisfied myself with the window. There was a great deal of noise and activity within the house itself and below, just discernible, movement in the grounds. Yet out on the road there were torch flames dancing in the dark away to the left, a commotion I could hear all the way up here.

I was still standing in the same position some time later, leaning on the room's only chair, my mind a turmoil of torments, when I heard the key turned in the lock once more and Forster entered, carrying a small lanthorn. He was alone.

'You see?' he said, nodding towards the window. 'The welcome we prepare for your friends?'

I turned from the casement.

'Barricados,' I sneered. 'You plan to hide behind those tumbrils and gabions rather than face the King's forces in fair and open fight. Cowardly wretches.'

He laughed at me, though I saw him clutch at his side.

'You are confused, I think. For we *are* the King's forces. And, that being so, there are things you will tell me, madam.'

'What?' I said. 'Or the hot irons?'

'There are some among us who would not be troubled by applying such methods,' he sighed. 'Think yourself blessed I'm not one of them. But I need to know how far your spying has reached. What have you sent? And by what means?'

He moved to the lifeless hearth, set the lanthorn down upon the chimney's mantle shelf, sent shadows skipping across the tapestries.

'I have sent nothing,' I told him.

'Those same men,' he said, 'they are a certain breed. And they already demand that the fellow we took at Lancaster – well, that he should hang in the morning. I fear I may not be able to stop them. And if they take your son too...'

I shook my head in disbelief, then saw him wince again.

'You are unwell, sirrah.'

'You speak the words with such relish, madam. But will you not sit? And if you help me, I can arrange candles, a palliasse and blankets for the bed. Save your son too, I hope.'

'Your discomfort – the responsibility, I collect,' I said, hoping to hide my trepidation behind a barrier of my own, a buttress of bravado. Still, I took his suggestion and eased myself onto the seat. 'They say it can place great stress upon one's vitals. You have no experience of these things, after all.'

'I studied Caesar.'

If he thought this a strange twist to the interrogation he did not show it. And I set my face to stern impassivity, began to tap the ferule of my stick impatiently upon the floorboards.

'Governor Yale also studied Julius Caesar,' I said, 'though it would never have equipped him to lead an army.'

I picked some invasive white threads from my mantua's brocade, allowed my right hand to stray to the gathers at my waist, felt the comforting presence of the pocket pistol. And I thought how little this squat, stooped creature might resemble any other general in the world.

'Truly?' he said, taking himself to the window. 'A student of his *Commentarii de Bello Gallico*? Important, I suppose, in the defence of Fort St. George.'

'Gracious, no. A student merely of literature. Fond of quoting the words attributed to that particular dictator by Master Shakespeare.'

'You practise upon me.'

I looked out of the window as well, saw the work continuing on that defensive bulwark by the eastern bar-gate. The other I had seen back beyond the church. How might I warn our boys?

'Indeed,' I said.

'As you practised upon Colonel Porter. But, I ask myself, killed him how?'

'I left him on the marsh. He still lived when last I saw him.'

'Left him to drown, then. And the girl, Mary – she is dead too?'

'I think you will find one of your horses missing. The girl gone with it. But that chit is none of my affair.'

'Yet Porter, the marks he carved into his flesh – how terrified you must be when 'tis plain you cannot escape the tide of fate. A lesson you need to learn, lady.'

There was menace in his voice. If he tried to harm me I would certainly kill him but I was afraid all the same, fingered the blood-coloured drapes to still my shaking hands.

'You expect me to pity him?' I snapped.

'Some sign of humanity perhaps.'

'Then you mistake me, sir. Porter was the wretch who almost caused my own daughter's death. And that day at the Menagerie, you accused me of meddling. Threatened me too. Then Porter came into my life again. At Latimer. Your doing, I collect. He would have killed me – and I have no doubt again intended to kill me when our paths crossed once more here in Preston.'

'My doing?' He seemed genuinely outraged. 'Colonel Porter at Latimer? I know nothing of that. He answered to King James directly. To no other.'

Knew nothing about Porter's invasion of my home? How could I believe him?

'And you, wretch,' I said, 'do you not answer to that papist also? To your King Over The Water who is, in truth, precisely that. Here you are, and these banditti, waiting to fight and die. But him, Tom Fool? Where is he just now, while you prepare to bleed?'

'I answer to those Etherston folk who saw fit to send me to Parliament, Mistress Yale. Staunch in their faith in our Church of England. Though they are treated little better than papists themselves. All Dissenter this and Quaker that. We are the dispossessed, Mistress Yale. Thanks to you and your Whiggish friends. Still, it's true that Etherston has its share of Romish believers too. Punished daily for their pains. And no votes for them, of course. No, they pay their taxation, with no right to representation in return.'

'And I shall hang for that? Or these men you brought here all the way from Northumberland – their deaths out there on those barricados shall set matters aright?'

'Did I say you should hang?'

'Is that not the fate of spies, sir? Wybergh, I suspect, is already doomed. And for myself I shall tell you nothing.' But then, perhaps the tiredness, perhaps something else, I found I could not sustain my mask any longer. 'Yet,' I begged him, 'you must not allow them to hang my son.'

He was as good as his word, I suppose, though I had answered no more of his foolish questions. And he had entirely refused to have my travel chests brought from the White Horse, for again I feared the loss of this beautiful journal perhaps even more than I feared my own death. The rest might still be at Latimer, hidden in the secret compartment of the cabinet, but that was small consolation. Tallow candles, though, and a pewter pricket stand, a blackened striking tin too – since he had less than courteously taken the lanthorn with him when he left. A straw-filled mattress with stained and striped ticking. Threadbare grey blankets. Wash bowl and pink primrose ewer. A smelly chamber pot for good measure. How considerate of the wretch, I thought.

I slept little. My fears for Benjamin. The visions of Porter's ruined corpse and the manner of his death. Horrors of the fighting to come. My own fate and dread at the thought of how Ursula would survive without me. That shouting, clattering, hammering work out upon the barricados that continued, I think, into the early hours. Troubling about this abandoned journal. And then thoughts of escape. A blaze, perhaps, though with the amount of dunnage in the room it was likely I should be consumed before the alarum was even raised.

I was still huddled upon the bed, those blankets around me, at daybreak. Yesterday, of course. Was it only yesterday? Yes, Saturday. The window rimed with silver blossoms of frost flakes. The water from the ewer like ice too as I splashed it upon my face and I was grateful there was no glass in the room to reflect the dishevelled appearance I must have presented.

Outside, astonishingly peaceful, as though it were just an ordinary day in Proud Preston. Cattle lowing somewhere close at hand. The chime of a blacksmith's hammer. The smell of early roasting meats and wood fires. A fellow at work in the grounds below. Across Churchgate, that other large house, smaller dwellings and an inn. Between them I could see gardens beyond, enclosures running down towards the river and, further still, a meadow with more cows. And there, much less than a mile distant, the Ribble Bridge. I could not quite make out the river itself, but I saw the lie of the land rising again on the far side and I could follow those fields some way to the right, until St. John's blocked my view. Had it not done so I expect I would have needed to look only a little further to see the ford and ferry at Penwortham.

Peaceful, so it was. Though not for long. Drumbeats, and in the time that followed, perhaps a quarter of the hour, a party of Jack Highlanders – five score I counted – gathered out upon Churchgate. Then, from the Eyres House, that fine place across the street, I saw Forster appear, subordinates helping him to clumsily mount his horse and, without any sign of urgency, he led that small corps off towards the Hollow Way. A few other riders too, but heading in the opposite direction.

A manservant came to feed me just then, the door unlocked, bread, cheese and ale set down, a brace of guards beyond, at the head of the stairs, though they refused to give me news, or even find me something to read. And thus I fretted away the morning, dozed in the chair I think, until the click of the key brought me back to my senses. Forster again.

'Well,' I said, sitting upright. 'Do I hang, sirrah?'

'Not yet.' He closed the door behind him, unfastened the buttons of his crimson riding cloak to reveal the paunch within, though his belly was still constrained by the wide leather baldrick, and he tugged at the buckle, as though to make himself more comfortable.

'And my son?'

'He lives, for now. And listen.' He set his fat little toad's fingers to his ear. 'My army preparing to march.'

I glanced out of the window, could see and hear them gathering in clusters, ordered hither and thither, pipes and drums.

'Changed your mind about the barricados?' I said.

'It seems Wills has decided to skulk in Wigan. And I recalled my *Bello Gallico* after all. Attack, best form of defence. Surprise. Borlum's Highlanders hold the bridge against the offchance of their scouts probing our intentions. So you, your son, the Lancaster spy, all this,' his arm swept around the bedchamber's stored baggage, 'shall come with us.'

'And my own cases?'

I still worried about this present journal, abandoned there at the inn.

'In due course,' he said. 'Your fate to be decided after we dispose of Wills.'

'Or perhaps after Wills is done with you, Tom Forster. There is at least one other in the general's ranks who shall fight like Old Nick to see you laid low.'

The bell of St. John's tolled twelve.

'One?' he said. 'And who...?'

There were fresh cries from outside. A different tone from those gone before and, as I peered through the casement, there were fellows running in all directions, some pointing towards the river, exchanging hasty news. And away to the right, in the distance, across the Ribble, there was a dark stain sliding slowly along the skyline towards Penwortham and the fords. Closer, beyond the bridge, more smudges on the landscape – though these distinctly scarlet.

But then the view was blotted out by Forster's bulk.

'I was about to tell you,' I said. 'Matthew Parrish asked me to pass on his regards. But now it seems he may be able to do so in person.'

'Parrish – that traitor,' he murmured, though I could see he was otherwise preoccupied, the tips of those fingers now scraping at his cheek.

'Conspiracy, was it not?' I said. 'The pretext for sending him to the Tower. Parrish, of all people.'

'Did he not attempt to prevent the treaty with France? It was the will of the people, an end to war.'

'It was the will,' I said, 'of those of you who sought to gain power and money, sir. An unsatisfactory agreement.'

'You did this,' he muttered, and pointed towards the bridge. 'But how?' He did not wait for my answer, simply turned on his heel and ran from the room – as best a creature of that shape and size might be said to run.

Why did they not come? Almost two hours had passed and there had been little movement. Yet my gaolers had fed me again, at least. Broth and more bread. But I thought I knew now how things might have come to pass. Those scarlet units, it seemed obvious, must be our regulars. And yes, Parrish would be there among them, I supposed – prayed that our Lord Jesu would watch over him. But the others I had seen first, much further to the right, to the west, and now gathered somewhat closer. Surely that Dissenter force of Reverend Wood from Atherton, which Mister Walker had gone to muster. Perhaps Hoghton's militiamen too, for they made two sizeable formations and too drab, too dark, so not in uniform. Praise God! And what did this signify? Why, that all Forster's men were gathering here in the town, even those Highlanders marching back from the Ribble Bridge. The reason? That Forster could perhaps not be certain from which direction an attack might come. From the bridge? From the fords? Both? And oh, how I hoped I might have played some part in causing this consternation.

My memory of the afternoon may be faulty since I received nothing with which to scribe some notes until late in the evening and while I have no trouble recalling other details – I pride myself on the skill – I have never before had cause to record a battle, and I pray to God I may never have to do so again.

But, so far as I remember, it was this way.

First, those blocks of red moving closer to the river, then another long halt before a slender file eventually spread onto the bridge itself before disappearing from my sight, lost within the depths and still frosted hedgerows of the Hollow Way.

Below me, units of the banditti being moved about, dispatched into the brick-built houses and whitewashed cottages along Churchgate and the lanes on either side, even those beyond the barricado away to my left. A couple of those carts with the ship's iron cannon mounted, being trundled towards the barrier. And how I wished I had some means to signal our forces, for I found myself almost beating on the window panes, screaming to them that they need not be so timid, that all of Forster's men were in the town itself – that the trap was here.

In my foolish imaginings it seemed, at least, they heard me, for there followed a forward surge, troop after troop descending onto the bridge and each, in turn, vanishing into the dead dun-coloured ground below the town.

Second, without fanfare, a section of redcoats – dismounted dragoons from their long riding boots – marching precisely, deliberately, from my left towards that eastern barrier. There were two gaps in the barricado, into each of which one of those cannon carts had been pushed. And when the troopers were no more than a hundred paces away, first one of the guns, then the other, erupted in a cloud of smoke, a gout of flame, a clap of thunder. That shroud of smoke drifted away, to be replaced by another, this time from a volley of crackling musketry, which itself heralded an almost continuous enfilade of fire that seemed to last forever. And there was firing coming from here within Patten House. It seemed to be all around me, above, below, to each side. Deafening. Smoke even within this bedchamber, the stink of sulphur, of eggs gone rotten, permeating everything. And from the Eyres House as well, the whole façade of that place shrouded in its own smoke, which occasionally cleared to show me marksmen at the windows.

Third, the guns steadily fallen silent, the worst of the smoke eventually clearing and a great cheer going up from the defenders. A few Highlanders were carried or helped away, back towards the market square, but out there, in the killing ground between the dwellings and before the blockade, the street was a carpet of red, littered with fallen dragoons. A hundred? More? Sweet Lord Jesus, this was a massacre. How could any simkin have ordered a frontal attack in that way? I saw some more of the Scotsmen venture forth, cautiously examining the fallen redcoats, most left where they lay – dead, of course – but a few carried back behind the barricado, away to wherever the defenders' own wounded were taken, I hoped.

Fourth, though a lull here, as my ears cleared I could hear gunfire from further to the west. And I imagined other roadblocks or ramparts constructed at least across the other two main streets, on Friargate and Fishergate. I wondered whether the slaughter could have been as bad there. Well, of course it could. But if I was correct, and those across the river were the Atherton Dissenters and Hoghton's Lancashire Militia, I almost thanked God they still seemed to be there, not yet engaged, not part of this madness to which I may have summoned them.

Fifth, my door unlocked, and a still thicker thread of smoke wafted inside as it opened. A fellow in tartan trews, long brown coat, pistols at his chest, lantern-jawed, lank hair untied about his shoulders, powder burns on face and hands, a basket-hilted longsword in his paw.

'Beg pardon,' he said, though it sounded to my ear more like *peg parton*. And that was followed by some words that I did not follow at all. But by then he was shouting to his men outside the room, but in that same heathen tongue. A pair of Jack Highlanders – one a bearded giant, the other no more than a boy – with muskets, powder flasks and shot pouches. And that big fellow with the longest sword I have ever seen strapped to his back.

The giant ducked under the doorframe, growled at me with fang-like teeth, then moved the chair from the window but pulled the bed closer to the casement, smashed the corner posts away with his bare hands, turned frame and mattress on their sides to form a breastwork.

'Tell me,' I said, slowly, to their officer, 'those poor redcoats down there upon the road – you know which regiment they serve?'

He watched my lips as I spoke – as I myself have often done when conversing with others in language other than my own. And I had to pay as much attention to his answers, for the words were so littered with difficult pronunciations. Yet it is easier for me to record here the words I understood him to mean, rather than make some foolish mimicry of his speech.

'Those we took to the hospital were all Honeywood's,' he said. 'But please, will ye not be seated?'

'Honeywood's – you are certain?' Yes, he said, certain. 'And the hospital?' At the Bull, he told me as I settled myself once more on the chair. On Churchgate, behind the Town Hall. I have passed it many times these past few days. Larger than the White Horse. The biggest in town, I collect, but a less salubrious reputation. 'And you, sir?'

It seemed appropriate to ask though my head was full of thanks to the Almighty that they had not been from Wynne's regiment, that Parrish therefore had hopefully not fallen among them. And yes, I know it is a wicked thing to have thought so, but the idea I might be parted from him again was unbearable.

'Captain Innes, lady. Jamie Innes of Coxton, if ye please. In the service of Lord Ogilvy. At your service too, ma'am.'

'I am to be confined here now? Can there be any left out there still to be butchered like this?'

'They kept coming,' he said, his voice full of wonder. 'I had not thought – well, I have seen duty elsewhere. With the Danes. With Swedes too. But these...'

I felt an absurd flush of pride.

'They will come again?'

'I fear so. I fear they will not stop until we are all dead or driven away.'

'And if this damn'd rebellion fails, Jamie Innes, as fail it must, where then?'

'I doubt we shall fail,' he smiled. 'But my own future, in truth, t'was already determined. I have been offered a post in the Muscovite armies.'

I laughed. It was almost too rich. He thought me mad, of course, especially when I tried to persuade him that Czar Peter is a personal friend.

'We might help each other,' I said. 'If you shall fetch me pen, ink and parchment, sirrah, in return I shall write you an endorsement you may show to the Czar himself.'

He gave me a crooked grin, as though to say yes, of course I would. But then there were boots plodding up the stairs, pausing frequently with the effort until, at last, Forster lumbered through the open doorway, his scabbard clattering against the jamb, and I lifted myself from the chair.

'What is this?' Forster panted. 'Innes, is it not? But this chamber was to be kept for the prisoner.'

'Orders of Colonel Mackintosh,' said the captain. 'Every window, he said.'

'Brigadier Mackintosh? Borlum needs to learn who is in command here. Is there not a single room in this entire palace that might serve?'

'None, sir. The colonel...'

'Damn the colonel, sirrah,' Forster yelled.

'I was just asking Captain Innes for ink and paper,' I said. 'If I am to be confined in this room, might that be possible, General Forster?'

'You were correct,' he said to me, ignoring the request, and that guttural Northumbrian accent seeming even more prominent than before. 'A horse missing. The girl too. Where did she go, Mistress Yale?'

He gripped at his side again, his face pained.

'Is that the only thing that concerns you this day?' I murmured, prodded at the heaped valise. 'How many of your followers, I wonder, may not now be coming back to reclaim these things?'

'We lost a few stout fellows,' he replied. 'But, by heaven, we fought. I was there, upon the barricade.' I thought I caught a look of disbelief cross the face of Jamie Innes, but he hid it swiftly, crossed to the giant and boy, gave them further instruction. 'All push of pike for a while,' Forster went on, and he patted the blade hanging so incongruously at his side. 'Gave them hard clouts, all the same. Drove the devils off. But then your damn'd Old Mackintosh,' he shouted at Innes, 'refused to pursue them when they ran. Refused, sirrah. Borlum. Damn'd coward. Well, it shall be a court martial for that gentleman when this is all done. So it shall.'

If looks could kill, as they say, then the hurt and pure rage in Innes's eyes would have laid Forster low there and then, but outside the lull was over. I believe I heard a trumpet, then the firing in earnest once more, the boy at the window shouting and pointing.

'General,' said Innes, peering over the boy's shoulder. 'Attack from the lanes to the south. They're in the grounds of your headquarters, it seems.'

I turned, saw Forster struggle a moment with the captain's difficult English, the colour draining from that frog-like face as the words sunk home.

Then the crash of splintering wood and glass so close behind me that, I swear, it almost caused me to soil myself. The giant, using the butt of his musket to smash away the upper section of the casement. He and the boy each cranking back the hammers on their weapons and pointing the barrels out through the window's wreckage, aiming, firing, stepping back from the window to reload, the smoke thick now, choking, the noise assaulting my ears, and Forster running out onto the landing, calling down the stairs, then lumbering back into the room.

'The grounds? Eyres House?' he shouted above the clamour, for the fighting was close now. 'Then we must abandon this house too. Come, madam.' His face was stricken with fear. 'With me, if you please.'

Innes took one of his pistols, pointed it over the edge of the bedframe, aimed down towards the attackers and fired.

'I've orders to hold this place,' he said.

'Orders again?' Forster screamed. 'Orders? I just gave you an order to withdraw, Captain.'

'And if ye want me to withdraw, General,' the Scotsman replied, 'ye'd needs put yon order in writing.'

'You see?' I said. 'Had you only brought me paper and ink as I requested...'

Yet by then Forster was thumping back down the stairs, seemingly having forgotten about his prisoner.

'I must see what's happening,' he shouted back over his shoulder, though I doubt that was for my benefit. But Innes was at my side by then, gently pressing me towards the side of the chimney breast furthest from the danger.

'Perhaps I should sit, Captain, after all. My old legs...'

He brought the chair, sat me in the alcove, though I could see by the way he assessed the small corner that he had little confidence in its efficacy as a place of safety.

'Ye should not be here, lady. How came ye here?'

'By Tom Forster's hand,' I told him, and he lapsed into a stream of his Erse speech, which by its heat could only be invective. 'I take it then, sir,' I said, 'that you do not value him as a commander.'

'I was across the way earlier,' said Innes. 'The women there say he spent much of the forenoon in his bed with a sack posset, huddled before a fire. It should have been the Mackintosh leading us. For what does that Englishman know of fighting, lady?'

The boy called to him from the window. Urgent and perhaps tinged with fear. And, as Captain Innes strode over to their breast-work, I had time to ponder this divided enemy. The treacherous Northumbrians and Lancastrians I had seen at their celebrations here in the Patten House and at the Town Hall, or out upon the streets, were all unblooded gentlemen, or farmers, or servants and tradesmen. And what did they think – that the regular army would somehow simply run from them because they had taken up arms? That a body can declare war without, itself, suffering war's consequence?

These Scotsmen certainly understood, for only they had the semblance of natural warriors, and though they might have numbered in mere hundreds, given positions like this or the barricados to defend, they could surely be enough to tip the balance in their own favour – despite Forster.

Though I now saw doubt upon Innes's eyes, saw too the speed with which both boy and giant were then loading, priming, firing, grim determination etched across their faces.

'Well, Captain?' I shouted.

'Dragoons,' he called back. 'Below.'

He was looking down into the grounds, but then there was some explosion that shook the whole house, seemingly from within. And the firing that, for most of the afternoon, had plainly been directed outwards, was at once all echoing inside. Shouts and screams from downstairs, fighting inside the very confines of the house.

Innes told me to stay in the room, yelled to his two men, led them out onto the top floor landing.

I cowered there in my small corner, hands clasped to my ears in the hope of drowning out some of that hellish noise, tears flowing down my cheeks that I could not control – until some comparative order seemed to fall upon the world and Captain Innes was back at my side, begging me to follow him.

'It seems General Forster was correct after all,' he said. 'We might have to abandon the house.'

Like passing through a dream. The smoke. Stinking smoke. A dead Highlander with his mouth hanging open in the bend of the next landing down. Those fine oak balusters and wainscoting splintered by musket balls. An occasional shot from below. Somebody moaning in one of the first-floor rooms. My progress down the stairs slow, as though my legs were iron, not my own, the cane providing insufficient assistance.

And then we were descending the flight of treads up which I had forced young Mary Astor only two evenings before. Was it only two?

Innes's giant waiting for us on the lower landing. That snarl once more, his yellowing fangs bared – though now I wondered whether the creature intended it for a smile. Yelling again, on the ground floor but somewhere to the side of the house. Breaking glass. Crashing furniture. The rising crescendo of gunfire but so close now I could almost feel its heat. Highlanders appearing in the open doorway to the entrance hall, backing towards us, towards the staircase and, beyond them, scarlet coats. It was all pistols, swords hacking, steel ringing on steel. And blood. Spilled crimson blood and ruined open flesh.

The Scotsmen closest to us turned at Innes's shouted commands, leapt up the stairs and formed a tiered firing line below us, twenty of them perhaps.

Another command, and the men still holding the doorway fell back too, clustered at the foot of the stairs.

A space opened up and, for a mere moment, the dozen dragoons in the hallway paused in their attack, hesitated. To draw breath perhaps. Decide their next move maybe. But a fatal moment.

I saw their own officer then, black uniform hat in one hand, bloodied sword in the other, pushing his way to the fore.

'Take them!' I heard him yell as he bounded forward, his men charging behind. And for a single instant I believe our eyes met.

The Highlanders' muskets, Jamie Innes's pistol. The smoke and stench, and ear-shattering noise. Followed by ungodly silence, apart from a low moaning beyond the fog of war. It cleared.

Two of the redcoats were crawling away over the writhing bodies of their fallen fellows. Closest to me, the sprawled body of that officer.

That stupid, stupid man, I wept. I could hear myself screaming, as though I witnessed the scene through another's eyes and ears as I prayed. Prayed to God it should not be so. But there was no mistake.

It was Parrish.

*

They carried me away, the giant and the boy. Literally, they carried me, while I kicked and scratched and begged them, screaming, to let me stay at his side. But all that remained was a final glimpse of him, his dear pallid face staring up into oblivion, hat and periwig, fallen sword, near him on the floor, and Jamie Innes kneeling at his side, watching me as I was borne out through the vestibule – puzzling, I suppose, at why this one horror among so many should have affected me so.

Yet by then he would have been more occupied by the Highlanders and Lowlanders pouring into the Patten House to reinforce his post, or to provide the covering fire that allowed my unwanted escorts to haul me out onto Churchgate, past their second barricado and to the church.

And in St. John's I was confined with my grief, uncaring about the outcome and barely aware of anything that came to pass over the coming hour as darkness gathered. Oh, I know now that our loyal troops pressed more attacks, that Innes and his men were finally driven from Patten House and their Lord Murray from the first barricado. I know that the banditti at that lower Churchgate end of town fell back to the second barricado, to the church itself and its burial ground. I know that some Cumberland curate – Patten his name, though with no link, I believe, to the house in which I had so recently been held – brought up Jacobite reinforcements and stood atop the barricado in his robes, making some supposedly defiant gesture and sadly remained unscathed. And I know that another eight score of our redcoats died in the streets there, trying to flank the Jacobite positions. I can hear them yet, filling my memory, even as I write this, a day and more later.

I was still kneeling before the altar – the sounds of death penetrating even those solid stone walls, the clamour waxing and waning as the fighting's cycle ebbed and flowed too – when Innes came to find me. He lifted me gently to my feet and I saw, for the first time, the flickering glow of blue, green and red showing at the high windows of St. John's.

'Come,' he said. 'You must leave.'

'Leave?' I sobbed, but by then he was leading me along the aisle, towards the porch and I discovered I had been oblivious of this other thing too – the number of wounded, more regulars than rebels – being treated for their injuries at the far end of the nave.

'No more room at the Bull,' Innes told me. 'A butcher's shambles there.'

'The flames?' I murmured.

'Your friends fired the houses and barns at yonder end of town. And it seems we fired those at the other.'

'My friends,' I said, still numb with that wicked loss and not quite understanding his meaning. But then we were outside. I pulled the cloak about me against the cold and dark, against the smoke, against the constant clatter of musketry, glanced in each direction. And yes, hellish inferno leaping into the sky above the dwellings at both ends of town. 'Tell me,' I said, and pointed to the fires I could see westwards. 'There – how stands the House of Correction?'

'The prisoners?' said Innes, and then thought he understood. 'Ah, the spy.'

'No,' I said, and flinched as a stray ball whistled past my ear. 'My son.'

He seemed surprised.

'All here at the Bull,' he said.

'Thank the Lord.' The sense of relief almost swamped me. And a secondary relief that those flames were still far beyond the White Horse where, I prayed, my poor possessions, these meagre memoirs, might still be safe.

'The cellars,' said Innes. 'And your man to the doctors, sure.'

The inn was only a few paces away, now hectic with activity, but Innes stopped opposite the true Shambles across the road. He called out, and both boy and giant emerged from the blackness of the butchery's colonnades, ran to join him. What was he talking about?

'My man?'

'Is he not, then? That captain of dragoons?'

Something shifted inside me, a barrier of ice building against the heat of hope I must suppress.

'He lives?'

'Just, so.'

Jamie Innes was correct, this was more a butcher's yard than a hospital, more a meat market than the Shambles itself.

'Wait here,' he told his retainers, and left them guarding the doorway.

'Show me,' I shouted, covering my ears in a vain attempt to drown out the pitiful screaming of a fellow just inside the inn and held down as some saw-bones hacked with a cleaver at stubborn strands of final flesh still attached to an almost severed leg.

'There is a room above,' he said, 'away from this.'

'No, sirrah,' I cried. 'Parrish. And then my son.'

So much blood, the sickly-sweet scent in my nostrils, the iron taste upon my lips. And the misery. Such a morass of slashed and broken humanity, carcasses packed tight in that lanthorn-lit space that must normally serve the Bull's dinners and suppers, the tables now strewn with more unsavoury fare. At the farther end, stairs down to the cellars, wounded upon the stone steps and, below, more scenes straight from the pages of Dante.

'Here,' said Innes, and helped me step over and through the twisted agonies filling this lower circle of hell also.

'Catherine,' Parrish gasped, as a physician probed with one hand at an oozing wound in his left side, mopped at the flowing blood with a rag in the other. 'Pity's sake,' Matthew just managed. 'Go.' A yell of pure pain. 'Not here.'

His boots were gone, his shirt ripped open to expose that injury to his ribs, and the breeches cut away from his right leg, a bandage wrapped tight around his thigh, thick with dried brown muck. Another bandage encased his left hand though, again, it was soaked in his blood. Sweet Jesu, how many wounds did he have? And he was shivering so much I could hear his teeth chatter.

'Please,' I said, 'he shall freeze to death.'

'It might be the thing that saves him, lass.' The physician barely looked up from his work.

'Tell me. His chances?'

'Lost three fingers,' said the physician. 'Ball hit his thigh bone – seems to have been deflected. Much damage to the sinews, though. I've cleaned it, I think. But this? This ball has shattered ribs, stuck fast. And there are fragments of the lead, pieces of coat, vest and shirt. I doubt I can purge it fully, though I shall try.'

I had to steady myself against Captain Innes. But then Parrish opened his eyes again, and through those chattering teeth he managed a few scattered words.

'Better...the ball...than the blade.'

His head slumped to one side, his eyes closed in a dead faint. And I silently prayed yet again, touched the physician's shoulder by way of gentle encouragement.

'Well, he has that right, sure enough,' said Innes, his eyes fixed on another young dragoon, his face cut open to the bone. 'About the blade.'

'And my son?' I said.

The captain led me through the mayhem to the vaulted cellar's farthest end, where a grated door would normally protect the inn's more valuable provisions and wines but now kept three prisoners secure – poor Polk, our intelligencer Captain Wybergh, and my dear Benjamin.

Wybergh was plainly suffering from a fever, shaking and coughing most violently, and Benji knelt at his side, arm holding a blanket in place around his shoulders – though he himself seemed in little better condition than the spy. And Polk? Well, the old fellow was asleep, his head resting on a sack of oats.

'Benjamin?' I said, and he span around, relief on his face, though quickly replaced by anger.

'What have you done?' he cried, waved his arm all about. 'All this.'

'The fighting, Benji? You think I caused this?'

'Of course not,' he snapped. 'Though see how you have dragged us into this thing? And Mary. I have asked them so many times. They will tell me nothing. God's hooks, I thought we should die in that place. And is the battle lost then?'

'Calm yourself, boy,' I said. 'I will tell you all you need to know about Mary once we are out of here. But, for now, the battle…'

I turned to Innes.

'Old Mackintosh has written to the Earl of Mar,' he said. 'Riders dispatched. News of our victory here. We have triumphed, ma'am. Beaten back every attack.'

He was confident, and though I thought to dispute the thing, remind him they had lost at least one barricado, Patten House and the Eyres place, I knew it would be a waste of breath. The truth was that they still held the town, and for every Jacobite wounded here I calculated there were ten of our own.

'Then if the fighting is done,' I said, 'I might perhaps be some use, helping to tend the wounded.'

'General Forster,' said Innes, 'insisted you should be confined upstairs, madam. His orders.'

'And you are the fellow, Captain, who puts good sense above outdated orders, as I recall.' He smiled. 'Come now,' I said, 'I shall be here in plain sight, after all. It would be a kindness.'

I glanced back across the cellar to where that one physician still worked on dear Matthew. And oh, the pain of seeing him there, the unbearable weight of the danger he still faced. But there were several other chirurgeons here too, more upstairs that I had seen. The rebels' own medical corps, as well as women from the town, all of them at this blood-soaked business, yet still desperately inadequate to the scale of the task.

'Benjamin,' I turned back to the cage, 'you are, of course, correct. About dragging you into this. But I shall make amends, I promise.'

'Mama,' he said, 'I have heard them talking. They say if things – well, if things go badly – they shall hang the spies. Spies, Mama. The word they used. They mean you too?'

'Be not so foolish. Hang an old woman like me?' I hoped I sounded convincing, though I certainly did not feel secure. 'Such stuff! Nor Wybergh neither, I collect. Simply some mouthing prattle. But now I have work to do. Men here who require succour. And see, our old friend Parrish lies yonder.'

'Parrish?' he said. 'Mama...'

'He is badly hurt, Benji. Matthew and all these others. Though my first task, boy, shall be to see you gentlemen properly fed. More blankets, perhaps. And Jamie Innes,' I said to the captain, 'might you take care of that small matter for me?'

He agreed to do so and soon afterwards, as I mopped a brow here and there, or helped to bathe and cleanse wounds, I saw the boy – Callum, I had heard the captain name him – carrying down a jug of ale, some cups, a loaf of bread and an extra blanket and deliver them into Benji's hands.

By then the physician's efforts on Matthew's behalf were complete and Parrish was resting, a relatively peaceful repose. But near him was another of our officers, shot in the stomach and not long, we each knew, for this world.

'Such waste,' said Jamie Innes at my back. 'A valiant officer.'

I wiped a tear from my cheek, turned to see him make the sign of the cross.

'You are a Catholic, Jamie Innes,' I murmured, rather foolishly. It had simply never occurred to me.

'As are most of my folk,' he said. 'In Elgin. It seems so far away, now. And we were raised this way. To believe that if our own faith causes us to hate another's, simply because it is different, it is no true faith at all. But, for now Mistress, General Forster needs to speak with you. Upstairs.'

'Captain Innes tells me you've been tending the wounded,' said Forster. He tried to fill his pipe but his hands shook so badly that much of the pouch's tobacco now scattered on the floorboards.

Forster's own new lodging, of course, since Eyres House was now lost. The best, I assumed, that the Bull had to offer. Larger by far than the combined total of my room at the White Horse, of that in which I had been held at the Patten House, and of my bedchamber at Latimer. Fire in the hearth. A broad oriel with four separate casements. All things are relative, are they not? There was the finest linen upon his bed and a grand settle upon which I had slumped, exhausted from my labours.

'You know, of course,' I said, 'that Parrish lies languishing in the cellars.'

He showed no surprise, must have already been informed.

'Shall he live?'

'Do you care, Tom Forster? You were fast enough to send him to the Tower.'

We are entirely alone again, I thought. Me, and the greatest traitor I have ever encountered. And though my brocades were now soiled beyond redemption, they still concealed the pistol.

'Now he has a value,' said Forster.

And you? I wondered. What is your own life's worth? I knew I could snuff him out with not a moment's hesitation, and pay the price willingly myself. But Matthew? Benjamin?

'Indeed,' I said. 'And if you help save him, I may help save you in turn.'

He had finally managed to pack enough of the weed into the pipe's white bowl and, his hands still trembling, he took one of the candles to light it. Yet his eyes never left mine. They were riddled with fear. And the question – whether I might, indeed, be his salvation.

'Derwentwater says we must counter-attack tomorrow,' he stammered, between puffing on his pipe, that toad's mouth working like a bellows.

'It is not over then?'

I was weary, did not really care whether he believed me or not and, as he began to pace the floor, I was more preoccupied by the ache at my temples, kneaded the tips of my fingers into the sides of my eye sockets.

'I have a report,' said Forster, panic in his voice. 'General Carpenter's regiments sighted to the north.'

'And the fighting – not quite what you expected, I collect.'

He bit his lip so hard it began to bleed.

'Men already drifting away. The road to Liverpool left open. Deserters, madam.'

'Deserters?' I laughed. 'From among the victorious? Surely not.'

'I never thought it would be like this. We were promised. A show of force, they said. To bring a peaceful change. That it would all be easy.'

He rubbed at his paunch, then the ribs that still seemed to grieve him.

'Men like you, Forster,' I said, and shook my head in contempt. 'You seek to turn the world upon its head and think it may be easy? Or at least you try to persuade those foolish enough to follow you that it will be so. But I've heard them. Below. Your wounded men complaining they were abandoned. That when they needed their generals, they could not be found. That *you* could not be found.'

'I thought the whole Tory faction would come out, that we would all be in rebellion – but now…'

I managed to get to my feet, went to the oriel's windows. It was late in the evening, yet the light outside was almost like day. The fires burning at both ends of town. Nowhere near the White Horse, it seemed, but even so, were my possessions still there, still safe? And there were houses illuminated wherever I looked.

'So many windows lit,' I said.

'There,' he replied. 'Confusion. I ordered all the houses we hold to be illuminated. That we should know friend from foe. But Wills has instructed the same, it seems. Now – well, who may know the difference?'

'How truly amusing,' I said, though I had not a shred of caprice left.

'I suppose you might think so. Still, I have sent for paper and ink as you asked. But I need you to pen something for me first, in return.'

He had, it seemed, determined an answer to his question. About whether I might indeed be capable of saving his skin.

'First?' I said. 'First, I need your pledge that tomorrow, if he survives the night, Matthew Parrish shall be returned to his own lines. And my son with him.'

Another part of my bargain. That I should be permitted to spend the night below, to carry with me the remaining ink, quill and paper. And during the night six more of our regulars died. One of the Jacobites too. But Jesu be praised, not Parrish.

'He asked me to pen a note to General Wills, another to Carpenter,' I told Matthew this morning, this Lord's Day morning. I held his cold grey hand, as I perched upon the folded palliasse Captain Innes had provided to ease my vigil in the early hours – a vigil I punctuated, as well, by scribbling words and phrases to help me remember some of the past few days' events and conversations.

'Still fighting?' Parrish whispered.

I cocked my head. Yes, I could hear it too. Above the confusion here. All through the night it had continued. The moaning, the screaming, the curses. But now there was sporadic firing again, outside.

'Some skirmishing, I think. At the barricados. Nothing more though. Not like yesterday.'

'Your note?'

'Naming myself as an agent of Secretary Stanhope, advising Wills of Forster's wish to parley.'

'Trap?'

'Signing my own confession as a spy? Well,' I said, and squeezed his hand, 'might as well be hung for a sheep as a lamb, and a third piece of cake too, perhaps.'

'Take...no risk, my dear.'

He winced with the pain of trying to stir himself.

'Lie still,' I told him. 'Guard your strength until later. For I hope to see us all free of this place before too long.' I looked around to make sure we were not overheard but it was unlikely, given the hustle and bustle, the continuing groans of the wounded, prayers for the dying.

'How?' he said.

'The price Forster promised for the letters. Yet I think he shall need our intercession if he hopes for terms. His Northumbrians, these Lancashire men, they know they are all undone. Say so loudly, it seems. I heard some of them in the night. Ammunition running low. Provisions too. And Forster convinced they shall be prisoners of war. Not taken for traitors. He will seek a truce.'

'What say his men?'

I laughed.

'The army knows nothing of his plans. And Forster fears that if they know the truth they will shoot whoever he sends forth.'

'Us?'

I looked over to the cage where Benjamin stared back at me through the bars.

'Well, there is *that* risk, I suppose.'

It was dark, raining again. Thin drizzle spreading a greasy sheen across the cobbles and stable walls of the Bull's yard.

'Tell me,' said Benjamin, trying to keep a blanket about his own shoulders and, at the same time, help Captain Innes's boy Callum knot the ropes attaching Parrish's litter behind Polk's pony, Henrietta.

'I shall make sure she is returned to you swiftly, Mister Polk,' I said, keeping a watchful eye on the fractious gathering arguing at the yard's open gates, the men's blazing torches lighting up faces with flickering bitter orange.

'Never tha' mind,' Polk replied. 'I'm comin' wi' thee, ma'am. Nowt else.'

He had never once shown rancour towards me for his incarceration, though I had plainly caused his arrest by association. No, quite the contrary, he was simply effusive about my insistence on his release, went off gladly under guard to fetch the pony.

'And Benjamin,' I turned to my son. 'Best say little for now.'

349

Stanhope's other agent, Captain Wybergh, was already mounted on Henrietta's back, though only remaining in the saddle with the help of that Jack Highlander giant. The Scotsman bared his yellow fangs at me once more in the gloom and yes, I was certain now he must mean it for a smile.

'We should not delay, madam,' shouted Innes himself, running back from his investigation of the crowd at the gates. Part of my bargain with Forster, that the captain should be my escort.

'Are we safe, Captain?' I asked him.

Safe? How could anybody be safe in this chaos? Forster met me again during the afternoon. Wills had received my note, sent word he would hear Forster's proposals. One of the Jacobite officers sent secretly to open the parley, to seek terms. The reply, no terms to be offered, except one – that if the traitors decided to surrender forthwith they might avoid being summarily put to the sword. Rebels, after all, Wills had said, and could not expect to be treated otherwise.

'Not safe at all,' said Innes. 'They are back, it seems.' Two more envoys had been sent to Wills. Some nonsense from Forster that they be allowed to remain in the town twelve days and if not relieved by that time then he would indeed surrender. Yes, he had been persuaded that their other Jacobite army in Scotland would soon be sweeping south, victorious, to secure the rebellion. 'Your generals in a great rage,' Innes went on. 'No twelve days, they say. But twelve hours instead. If no surrender in twelve hours, we all die. No quarter. That twelve hours conditional upon the release of all prisoners. And Forster has sent word that this part, at least, is agreed.'

'As well we are ready to travel then,' I said, for I had already persuaded Forster he must set us free – persuaded him I had encrypted my note to Wills in such a way that he would personally undertake to see Forster hanged and quartered if anything untoward might befall me.

'I wish it were that simple, ma'am,' Innes frowned. 'But Wills has sent a drummer along Friargate, to all the houses they hold, ordering all fighting to cease.'

'The lid is off the jakes then,' I said, glanced again towards the torchlit gate.

'All is violence,' he told me. 'Fighting among our own. We are betrayed. The army betrayed. But come, we must needs move swiftly.'

He smacked the pony upon its rump and the poor beast lurched forward, Parrish's bier bouncing on the wet cobbles. Matthew gave a small cry and I laid my hand on his brow as I walked alongside until we reached the mob growing with every moment and sheltering beneath the gateway's roof. And I prayed with all my heart that the night's blackness would hide us.

Yet there was Forster, standing upon the steps of the inn's side wicket, with that Reverend Patten pressed close to him, holding up a lanthorn and waving his other arm about.

'Nothing but present death before us,' Patten was shouting, 'if we hold out longer. We have no remedy but to make terms.'

But one of the Highlanders, an officer, almost drowned out his words.

'Do not you be speaking for me, preacher. My own boys choose to die with swords in their hands like men of honour.'

'We'll not be dragged to the scaffold,' cried another, 'like common cattle thieves.'

I felt a tug at my skirts. Parrish.

'Keep moving…my dear…keep moving.'

'Listen men,' said Forster, though his voice was quaking. 'Honourable terms are already on offer. And Lord Derwentwater is parleying there now, as we speak. He is confident of good conditions. None of us shall hang.'

'You're a liar,' somebody shouted. 'No quarter, that's what we been told.'

Forster's denials only incited more anger, more men joining the throng and the whole crowd pressing forward towards Forster's platform.

'Come,' said Innes in my ear. 'Your man is right. We must get past while they're busy with this. Though I would rather be with them and have my say. But quietly, if we are able.'

We began to edge towards the gates, keeping to the shadows as best we could.

'And you.' An Englishmen shouted – a Lancastrian by his accent – and pointed at Forster. 'All flam. Cod's Head! General bloody Arseworm.'

Others picked up the cry. *You coxcomb!* Or *jackanapes!* Or *maggot!* Or *poltroon!* A whole chorus of insults. Cursing and blasphemies.

And such was their venom that none seemed to greatly heed our passing as we carefully led the pony through the rear ranks of the crowd.

Forster was weeping. Weeping. It was pitiful.

'What might I tell you?' he sobbed. 'You have it right, lads. I am lacking the capacity for this office. 'Twas thrust upon me. Still, I thought...'

We were out upon Churchgate now, but as I turned for a final view of Forster's desperate humiliation I saw a fellow with a pistol in his hand.

'We won,' he screamed. 'Victorious, but now surrendering as prisoners to those we vanquished only yesterday.'

Innes heard that too, looked back also, just as Forster turned to face the man, tears still streaming down those frog-like cheeks, yet he did not flinch even as the pistol came up, pointed at him. Straight at him.

There was a brief moment when my instinct told me I should cry out, warn him. And Captain Innes must have thought the same, launched himself towards the assailant, clawing his way through the closest of the banditti. Though it was already too late.

'Murray!' I think Forster said, but no more.

Flint hit frizzen and the pistol fired at the very instant the mob jostled forward – the ball cracking into the timber behind Forster's head.

His few friends must have pulled him down the steps for protection, though I could not see that plainly. No, I was more concerned for Innes, who was now accosted by the same hackums he had pulled aside in his efforts to stop that would-be assassination – and those men, I saw, included both the Wrexham fellow, Edward Hughes, and that elderly Member of Parliament, Shuttleworth, the same I had heard hoping to see Proud Preston's streets running red with their enemies' blood. And though he had his wish, it seemed not to satisfy him.

'The spies!' he yelled, as he saw us. 'Escaping, by God. And if no quarter for us, then none for them neither.'

But I was thinking of that other sense of *proud*, of a bitch in heat.

'Do you not think your town has been pricked enough, sirrah,' I shouted, 'without bringing more vengeance down upon its head?'

Shuttleworth spat some answer at me that I could not hear, for Innes was overpowered by then, held by several other louts.

'String them up,' shouted the Welshman. 'Give them the stretch. The same as we'll string up Wills when we get our hands on him.'

It seemed as though the whole rabble of them turned upon us, some of the rogues shouting and pointing, but some having at each other too, pushing and shoving.

Benji was at my side, a protective arm about me, though I pulled away from him, stepped over the trails at the bottom of Parrish's litter, reached inside my cloak, inside the bunches of my skirts, where I had also hidden the scrips of paper with my few sparse notes.

'Mama,' he cried as he saw the pocket pistol in my fist. 'For pity's sake, what are you doing?'

Parrish was trying to rise from his bier, but the boy, Callum, had let go the pony's bridle, unslung his musket too, pulled back the hammer, lifted the weapon to his shoulder, yelled something in their Erse tongue.

And the giant? He roared in anger, made towards Innes and his struggle – but then span around again just in time to catch Wybergh as he slumped sideways from the pony's back.

'Enough!' I screamed at the captain's attackers. 'Let him go.'

'Hang them,' cried Shuttleworth as Innes was forced to the ground.

A musket shot. Young Callum in a cloud of smoke, one of the captain's foes staggering away, falling, clutching at his ruined face.

Wybergh upon the ground, trying to rise to his knees, the giant free to launch himself into the affray, that wicked broadsword hauled from its scabbard on his back and the blade almost cleaving one of the rogues down the middle. He bellowed something over and over again, a war cry I suppose, and the Jack Highlanders in the mob began to take sides until all was brawling chaos.

I pointed the small pistol this way and that though I could now hardly tell friend from foe. I was as likely to hit the former as the latter, perhaps even wound Innes himself – and that was if the thing would even fire.

'Mama, come,' said Benjamin, now helping Wybergh to his feet and trying to get him on the pony once more.

Callum rammed home a fresh charge to his musket as the

giant finally lifted Innes, dragged him from the conflict, but with that enormous sword keeping all opposition safely at bay, both Shuttleworth and the Welshman still calling for us to be killed – yet neither of them willing to sully their own hands in the process, or to risk even my poor excuse for a pistol.

And thus we retreated into the night, no burning houses this evening. I tried to keep Matthew calm, to stave off Benjamin's foolish questions about the weapon, now restored to its normal place of concealment as we trod up through the market square – where there was more scuffling, two dead men – and thence to the White Horse.

'We stop here,' I shouted.

'No, ma'am,' said Innes. 'We keep going.'

But I insisted. My travel chests. And Innes reluctantly agreed, took charge of Wybergh himself and dispatched his giant to assist me. Just as well, too, for the inn had its share of sullen and outraged fellows, Sumners himself calling me out for a traitor and a spy. And upstairs we found Mother Sumners rummaging through my belongings – though the giant gave her short shrift in his own Jack Highlander gibberish, almost threw the old crow physically from the room. But even a cursory glance told me this journal was still safe and we had no sooner finished stuffing my effects back into the cases than I heard yelling and a great commotion from below, Innes shouting up urgently for me to hurry.

I went to the window while the giant was heaving first one chest, then the other, onto his enormous shoulders and I saw that another posse of rabble had gathered outside, around our small party. Shuttleworth and Hughes again. I followed my companion back down the stairs and onto the street.

'See?' the Welshman yelled, pointing down the street. 'We got this one too. Holding him at the Boar's Head, we were.'

From further along Friargate another group of them were dragging a young drummer, not a boy but little more either. Who was this? The man sent to beat the chamade, as I now know.

'To hell with Forster,' Shuttleworth was saying to Innes. 'Now we have something to bargain with. Either Wills lets us leave, to march north, or we hang these spies, this lobster rowdy-dow-dow too and fight on. To the death! And may God preserve us.'

'To the death!' shouted others at his back.

'I have my orders, sir,' Innes replied. 'I shall be escorting this party to General Wills. To the enemy lines.'

Shuttleworth seemed confused, perhaps by the captain's manner of speaking English, to which I had now grown so accustomed.

'Perhaps you did not understand me,' he said, turned to some of his followers. 'Seize them.'

Tonight the oil lamps on Friargate remained unlit but with so many houses illuminated they would have been redundant. There was a rattle of weapons. Shuttleworth's men closing around us, Innes pulling the pistols from the holsters at his chest, Callum edging back but his musket levelled, Benjamin looking about wildly, seeking some way to escape.

'Be steady, boy,' I told him and knelt at Parrish's side, took out the pocket pistol again, checked its priming this time.

'You will die first,' Innes told Shuttleworth, pointed both pistols at the wretch's chest and, for a moment, that fellow halted, spread his arms.

Yet there was a cry, away to our left, and when I turned it was to see the redcoat drummer break free of his captors and begin to stumble back down the street. Though he did not get far, for a shot from one of the houses brought him down before he had run six paces. And in that moment of distraction, Shuttleworth's banditti moved in, Callum's musket dragged from his hands and Innes knocked to the ground.

Hoofbeats. Riders coming fast along Cheapside, through the market square.

The giant stepping past me, swinging my cases like clubs, felling a dozen men or more with the sweep of one arm, smashing another's skull to pulp, the awful sound of a cracking nut, as he easily brought the second chest down overhand.

I saw a sword flash, some cove stabbing at the Highlander, and I raised the pistol, fired, watched the man fall, almost choked on the smoke. But as it cleared, those horsemen had reined to a stop. Against all the odds, Forster come to our rescue.

'Let them alone,' he shouted. And, to my amazement, most of them obeyed. Though not the Welshman. Not Edward Hughes. For he had run forward, past Innes's giant, snatched hold of my arm and dragged me to one side, a knife at my throat.

'No, sir,' said Hughes. 'We take this drab and we bargain with Wills. Or else...'

Forster's ball passed cleanly through Hughes's left eye, and he stood for a moment, the knife still at my throat, a look of amazement on the remains of his face that must have been matched by my own shock, by the surprise of all those present. But then the Welshman's knees buckled and he fell dead.

'But you could go free, Captain,' I said to Innes. We were standing outside the campaign tent used by General Wills for his headquarters.

'The rain has stopped,' he said, held out his hand in demonstration and looked up at the stars, now so clear between gaps in the clouds. 'It shall freeze again before morning, I think.'

'I owe you so much,' I told him, and shivered, wrapping my arms tighter about me.

'Perhaps less than you owe Forster,' he smiled. 'Who might have thought it?'

When Forster had dismounted and come to examine his handiwork, I saw that he was trembling like aspic about a sow's ear, his peruke all-askew and the horse pistol still smoking in his hand.

'You might have killed me,' I had said.

His toad's eyes were wild, the shakes affecting even his head, and I think he did not properly heed me.

'Tell Wills,' said Forster. 'You must help.'

'I can give you that much, at least,' I told him, but the curse of that debt to him had plagued me all the way out of town, down Friargate, past the northern bar and its barricado, past the many burned houses beyond to the town's limits, and the windmill around which this part of our army was encamped.

'Who, indeed!' I said to Innes now. 'And how could I ever have expected to owe that damn'd Forster for my life? All our lives, perhaps.'

'Mine may still be forfeit,' he said.

'Then get away.' I clutched at his arm, knowing that I should have been proud to number this young man among my sons. 'You and your men. Get thee gone.'

But he shook his head, looked over to where the boy and the giant warmed their bare shanks at a fire.

'My men?' said Innes. 'These are my two brothers. The youngest, Callum. And my older brother. Donald, you would name him in the English. We are the Mackintosh's men. Chief among us. When Wills sends him back in the morning, we must go with him.'

It was the latest condition set by Wills for allowing them the night to consider. Both Derwentwater and Brigadier Mackintosh surrendered as hostages.

'Brothers,' I said, and thought about my own poor boys. All of them. 'At least Wills was happy that you should go free. That bodes well. Forster's faith that there shall be terms. So, go with God, Jamie Innes of Coxton.'

'Me, a papist heretic?'

'I reserve my scorn for those who would force one faith upon another, boy. For those who whip others into the fervour of their own dogma – and care not if they should die in the process. Yet I shall take more care how I bandy about my words in future. And I shall remember your kindness, sirrah.'

'Then I shall write.' He smiled, touched my shoulder. 'When I am able.'

But something, something, as he turned his back, took himself to join his brothers. For I thought I would never see him, nor hear from him ever again.

General Wills was far from happy. There was a hint of the West Country in his words, however, lending them almost a comedic air.

'You used Secretary Stanhope's authority to summon this *posse comitatus* from Atherton? He shall hear of it. Beyond your authority, madam.'

The general's tent was sparsely furnished: a truckle bed; a folding table with a writing slope; a brace of stiff-backed chairs, upon one of which I was seated; two blue-painted travel chests, with his name picked out in gold leaf; and a palliasse for his valet – or perhaps for the brindled deerhound now licking at his hand. On the floor, a tarpawling was spread and, on the canvas, floorboards under the table and bed.

'Had I not done so, General,' I told him, 'Forster would likely have concentrated all his force into defending the Hollow Way, rather than falling back on the town.'

Wills harrumphed loudly, pushed the hound away and took an ivory snuffbox from beside his discarded peruke upon the table. He is perhaps fifty, eyes that seem too large for his face, and beak like a godwit.

'Tell me about Shuttleworth,' he said, and took a pinch up each nostril. He had already sought intelligence about several of the others I had encountered.

'There are some of them who clearly deserve to die. And Shuttleworth one of them. But others, like Forster, will give assurances. He believes himself betrayed by the hierarchy among the Tories – if he is promised mercy, I know he will reveal still more traitors.'

'They are papists and rebels, madam. You think I care for their assurances? Whatever he knows can be pressed from him regardless.'

He sneezed into his kerchief, already stained brown in so many places.

'Many of his men have been led astray. They do not deserve to hang, General.'

'I am no Turk, madam. There shall be no summary executions here. They shall stand trial and the law will deal with them.'

'Then they shall be treated mercifully? This is Lord's Day, after all, though the heathens in Preston have attended not a single prayer meeting. God would expect mercy, I believe. And to Forster I owe my life.'

My life. Captain Wybergh's life too, of course, now receiving attention from the general's personal physician. And poor Matthew, still in danger but sleeping peacefully when I left him. Benjamin, however, is a different case entirely. So full of rage against me. I have tried to explain all I now know about Mary Aston and Colonel Porter but I fear he still blames me in some way.

'It is not for me to give them terms, madam,' said the general. 'That will be for your friend, Secretary Stanhope.'

'But they shall not be harmed? And there will be protection for the townsfolk? No reprisals?'

I suppose I was thinking about the Winckleys who had shown such kindness towards Benjamin. Or old Polk, who had been almost tearful at our parting.

'Dammit all, Mistress Yale.' Wills slammed the flat of his hand upon the table. 'They deserve reprisals. That drummer. Murdering dogs. But I expect discipline among my men. So, there shall be no looting, no rapine. And mercy? Perhaps I can speak for them, if you insist. Mercy, indeed. Yet I know King George for a merciful monarch. Hopefully Forster may trust in that also.'

I believed he had listened to me, heeded my advice.

'Then I would crave one final boon, General,' I said. 'The Highlander who gave me escort here. Captain Innes and his two brothers. I know you already granted him leave to escape this place. Still, he is set upon loyalty to his clan. To Old Mackintosh. Whatever else may befall, might you ensure that he is not taken among the prisoners? Neither Innes nor his two brothers.'

'I shall see it done,' he said. 'And meanwhile I have instructed my valet to prepare a pitcher for you. There is a tent readied for yourself and your son. You have fresh linen, I collect?'

Indeed I did. And once I had allowed the pitcher to cool – for in this place I knew there was real risk of disease entering my body if the pores of my skin might be opened by the application of water that was still hot – I cleaned myself thoroughly, waited until Benjamin had settled himself to slumber, and began the daunting task of properly recording these events in Preston.

It has taken me all the night and I fear there may be much I have already omitted but now, as the sun rises – amid the smells of mildew and wood smoke, to the sound of trumpets and horse harness, of drums and shouted commands, of our redcoats on the march to occupy Proud Preston – up in the market square, with the assurances I have passed by note to Forster, the surrender of the Jacobite army shall be taking place.

Volume Ten

These six months since Preston have been outlandish, though nothing so strange as having both Matthew and Elihu under my roof at the same time.

'And this Jack Highlander,' said Elihu, during the first remove of today's dinner. 'No word?'

I rather resented the sardonic tone of his voice, resented also that Annie had so plainly shared with him those details I had told her in confidence.

'None,' I said, for I had searched, begged Stanhope to provide lists of the prisoners sent to Lancaster, Chester and Wigan, or detained at Preston itself. Benjamin had searched too, first taking food for Innes to the church where they had been incarcerated, more than a thousand of them, on the day of their surrender. Yet he had been refused access and, in the following weeks, he had used his position in the courts trying to track down the fate of Jamie and his brothers. Nothing.

'Then it seems General Wills must have kept his word,' said Parrish.

'If so,' I snapped, 'it would have been on that and naught else.'

The dining room table was set afresh for our second selection of offerings and it occurred to me we had perhaps been somewhat too lavish. We were few enough in number, after all: myself; Parrish; Reverend Burrough; Ursula; young David Yale; and the man who still calls me wife.

'You expected leniency for those rogues?' said Elihu, lifting the lid on the temperade of fricasseed fowl and sniffing appreciatively at the spices, coconut and almonds of its saffron sauce.

'He promised to speak for them,' I said. 'And I passed those assurances to Forster. I think they may only have surrendered because of that.'

'Then surely,' said David Yale, 'you rendered a great service to the nation. Spared a great deal of additional bloodshed. A Christian act.'

'For now, perhaps.' I spooned some of the *pulaka* rice and vegetables onto my plate, pleased that cook has finally mastered the skill of recreating these culinary memories of Madras. 'But executions make martyrs, as they say. And they are no way to mend this Jacobite madness. Not so many.'

They began in January. Sixteen of them upon Gallows Hill just north of Preston. Including that wretch Shuttleworth – as Benji had told me, the fellow's head spiked upon the Town Hall there. And so they had continued, by the dozen, through to the end of February when Lord James Radclyffe, that Earl of Derwentwater, along with five others among their leadership, had suffered the same fate.

'Well, London sees it differently, my dear,' Elihu smiled at me. 'Peaceful. Music in the air once more. And did I tell you? I was at Little Lincoln's Inn to hear that butter-box, Kytch, upon the hautboy. A whole season of concertos ahead of us, Parrish. When you are back at Charing Cross?'

Matthew smiled at him, recognised the enquiry for Elihu's way of demanding how long, precisely, he intended his stay at Latimer. I had taken the precaution of approaching my son-in-law, through Nan, of course, about whether he would object to Parrish convalescing at Latimer and he had shrewdly intimated that, if my husband had no objection, then he most certainly would not. And Elihu had, to my astonishment, readily agreed. Of course, he had said. Such an old friend, injured so badly in the course of defending his country. I believe he was being sarcastic, for there is only enmity between them – though I took his words literally and had converted the old front parlour to a ground floor bedchamber, that Matthew's broken body might more readily be accommodated.

'I have sold the London place, I fear,' Matthew wheezed, and sipped at his arrack. 'The proceeds from my last collection of poems, a little help from my friends. So it shall be Essex for me, Elihu. Downbury Hall. I have come to appreciate the pleasures of country life while I've been here.' He made sure Elihu was focused upon his food before, unobserved, giving me a conspiratorial grin. It still pained him to breathe, the inheritance of those shattered ribs, and he walked only with difficulty, yet his spirit was largely undimmed.

'Might we come to visit?' Ursula asked him. They have become firm friends during his three months here, the news of his intentions striking her down into a whole week of profound melancholy. And, of course, I had not been able to tell her that we, too, might be moving to Downbury once Parrish has made the necessary preparations.

'Of course, Ursi,' Matthew laughed and patted her arm with that left hand he now kept permanently gloved to disguise the missing fingers. 'Though my new duties as Commissioner of Customs may keep me busy a while.'

How he thinks he might perform them is beyond me, though he insists on seeing this post as recognition by a grateful nation for his services.

'Such a grand title,' Ursula beamed. 'Are you not proud we have him under our roof, Pa?'

I heard Elihu splutter, turned to see the frown upon his face.

'And your son,' he said, 'are you now reconciled with him?' He never speaks Benji's name, of course. Not since the Chancery settlement. 'Why,' he went on, 'I can still scarce believe it. Langhorn. Great heavens.'

I had explained the whole story, first, to Benjamin. In Preston. Such was his infatuation with Mary Aston that he still did not entirely believe me. Indeed, the more I had gone through the details, the more morose he had become. He still writes to me, but the contents are terse.

Then, when Matthew was somewhat recovered, and just before I left the town, an explanation for him too. Incredulity.

Then to New Hall, to find out from Streynsham how matters had transpired when that evil young witch had come knocking on his door seeking Porter – though she had never arrived there, and there had been no sign of her since. So perhaps the Turban Head mushrooms had been more effective than I hoped.

Back here, Nan travelling post-haste to Latimer to discover whether Benjamin's note to her was true. And she, in turn, had informed Elihu. By then, of course, we also had the news from Scotland. Against all odds, and outnumbered, our loyal Duke of Argyll had fought that other Jacobite army and the Earl of Mar to a standstill at a place they call Sheriffmuir. Prime, though not quite the end. The banditti's advances might be halted yet they were still in the field. And then, late in December – too late, by far – the Pretender himself ventured from his lair in France to finally join those poor victims of his ambition, those who had fought and bled and died, while he had soaked himself in silk at Saint-Germain. By that time, of course, with our victory at Preston, all the King's forces could be brought against them and, less than two months later, he had scuttled away again to France and his supporters fallen apart, abandoned to their fates.

'I could scarce believe it myself,' I said. 'She seemed such a timid creature when she was with Sir William. But all that time, vengeance in her heart.'

Vengeance. Yes, I understand vengeance.

'Women!' said Matthew. 'We must beware, Elihu. They have depths we cannot fathom. Mistress Yale, for example. The fracas in Preston.'

'These things can sometimes be exaggerated,' I replied, and helped David to some of the flummery.

'But Nan insists it is true,' said Elihu. 'She had heard it from your son. A pistol, she said. And that you shot some cove upon the street. Dead, she says. Shot the fellow dead!'

'And that Wrexham rogue,' said David Yale. 'Hughes was it not? Did you know him, Uncle?'

'Indeed I did not,' Elihu told him. 'Merely in passing.' But there it was again – the mixed recollection, the debt I owed Forster for slaying Hughes, saving my life, and how close his tremulous hand must have come to killing me instead.

'Well, you must tell it again, Aunt Catherine. All of it. Later perhaps.'

I had grown somewhat tired of that tale. The pocket pistol. All the way back to Vincent Seaton.

'Well, I am rid of it now,' I lied. 'Threw it from the Ribble Bridge on my way from Preston. It was a comfort to me for a while. Precious. But now...'

'But now,' said Burrough, 'we have you with us once more, ma'am. Hero of the hour. Oh, I see you shake your head. Modesty becomes you, Mistress Yale. Though there are no reeds without a little water, as they say.'

I had once had such hopes for a union between them – Burrough and Ursula. But it seems to me now that with each passing month he becomes more the buffoon while Ursi, twenty-six this year, sinks even deeper into the childhood that, in truth, she has never escaped. Not since Seaton.

'Heroes?' said Elihu, presently setting about the Florentine. Silver buckles on his shoes. Black silk stockings. Shot green and black silk collarless coat. His waistcoat of yellow silk brocaded with flowers and leaves of many colours with golden thread. The sleeves of the waistcoat long enough to be folded back over the coat cuffs. Neck cloth of Flemish lace. His teeth rotted even more than I remembered. Heavy sacks under his eyes. Yet his full-bodied peruke pure white, such that a much younger man might have sported. Purse-proud, haughty in his wealth. 'It was heroes we lacked,' he said, 'to stop those devils escaping so readily from our prisons. God's hooks, at one point I thought the streets must be full of them.'

It is almost risible. As recently as three weeks ago. The day before his trial, and Old Mackintosh, Borlum, along with several of his associates had simply knocked down the Newgate turnkey, Mister Rouse, disarmed the sentinels and walked out onto the street. That simple. And I wished that I had settled on such a plan where Forster was concerned. But naturally, being me, the confectionary I had concocted for that escape was somewhat more complex.

'It brings a whole new meaning to the phrase Scot-free,' Matthew laughed.

'And not the Scots alone,' Burrough noted. 'The *Courant* claims Forster is also escaped to France.'

'Attainted in his absence though,' I said. 'Removed from Parliament.'

'Is that what passes for punishment?' Elihu scoffed. 'And such tales. This woman who abetted his escape – his sister, truly?'

I suspect at some point these are pages I must destroy, for they might see me hanged in Forster's place. Yet I feel the need to unburden my soul.

And here is the truth of it – that if Forster had not intervened when the mob tried to detain us I have no idea how matters might have transpired. But it is at least feasible that he saved my life. No telling whether Hughes would have used that knife. And therefore the lives of Benjamin and Matthew too. On the other hand, I am now certain that Wills had deliberately given me to believe that, if Forster surrendered, his men should be allowed some clemency – as, indeed, those taken after Sheriffmuir had been. And since I had conveyed that possibility to Forster I could not rid myself of some guilt for what had followed.

Despite his promises, Wills had indeed allowed parts of the town to be pillaged and particularly those properties of notable Tories – the Winckleys included, Benjamin had written. And while Forster's soldiers had been scattered among castles and prisons across England, the nobles, the gentlemen, his clergy, were all dispatched to London, to face the King's wrath rather than his mercy.

I think I have never struggled so hard with my conscience. I might despise Forster – shall never forget the sight of the wretch weeping so pitifully upon those steps of the Bull – but I had struck a bargain with the devil. Free Parrish, spare his life, and I should repay him in kind. And then that guilt, that I had been a party to Wills's deception.

'You plan to rescue him?' Mistress Bracegirdle had barely been able to speak for laughing. 'From Newgate?'

Master Shakespeare's green-eyed monster did indeed mock me. Still so much in looks, that lady, and lured back to the stage some years past for a final farewell performance, though I had not been fortunate enough to see it. But she had agreed to help me readily enough. Even provided me with rooms, that my return to London might be entirely clandestine.

'It may perhaps,' I had said, 'be a reprise of the part you played in my own *adieu* from Bedlam.'

'Or the one from which I was cast aside in Parrish's release?'

'At least this is not the Tower,' I had told her.

No, merely Newgate. And gaining access was easy. She playing the part of Forster's sister, Dorothy. I, the sister's maid – the elderly maid, as Annie Bracegirdle kept insisting. It seemed like a safe plan, for the sister may be remembered, the maid certainly not.

We were met by the turnkey, Mister Rouse, at the doorway to the lodge, beneath the gateway's twin towers within which all of its felons had once been housed until the prison was extended considerably to the south. I had been here before, of course, passed beneath the gate many times and once came – twenty years ago, it must have been – to follow those villains and traitors Sir John Friend and Sir William Parkyns on their way to Tyburn. But I had never been inside, naturally, and the stench of the place hit me even as we passed over the necessary garnish.

'For this much,' said Rouse, 'you gets the full tour as well as a visit to 'is lordship.'

It was an offer I could easily have spurned.

'Sweet Jesu,' I murmured to Mistress Bracegirdle as we trudged through the dank barely lit passages and up treacherous stairs. 'I had not thought there could be worse than the Bethlem Hospital.'

Rouse kept up a steady commentary about the sections we passed – the Master's side for those who could pay their own way; the Common's side for those too poor; the foul disgrace of the cells for everyday felons; the Bilbows where the worst of those felons could be laid by their heels in iron fetters; and the separate wards for the women prisoners. And everywhere the stink of stale sweat, the clank of chains at each turn, the scampering of scavenging dogs, the crunch of vermin underfoot, cries and curses from the prisoners, the shiver of slime beneath my fingers every time I steadied myself against the walls.

'A good room 'e's got too. 'Is lordship. Over the Press Yard. Lots o' light.'

'It must be a delight,' I said. But we each knew what the Press Yard implied – that part of this hell on earth where uncooperative prisoners could be crushed into submission and compliance beneath a board weighted with boulders.

'And we appreciate that so much,' said Bracegirdle. 'Yet if we wished my brother moved to still more comfortable accommodation?'

'You'd 'ave to speak wi' Governor Pitts, ma'am,' the turnkey replied as we finally stopped in the gloom of a vaulted landing, outside one of the ironbound doors at the farthest extremity of the second floor. 'But it 'appens. At times. Special prisoners, if ye takes my meanin', see?'

He kicked aside a pig snuffling in the filth around the landing's shadow-encrusted corners, unlocked the door and Bracegirdle pushed past him.

'Brother!' she cried before Forster had a chance to even show surprise, while I pushed back the hood of my cloak so he might see my face. The cell had a second occupant, a fellow I had seen at Forster's back several times in Preston.

'Dorothy!' Forster answered her, and I praised the Lord he had at least that much wit.

There followed a banal conversation between them – family matters, all invention, I assumed – while Rouse grew bored and soon stepped outside with his stubby pipe and I looked about Forster's surrounding.

It did not take long. The chamber was vaulted also, with a narrow fireplace and chimney breast, a table and two chairs, a pair of storage chests, a modest bed and an even more modest truckle beneath the high grilled window. It was cold. Extremely cold. And both men, Forster and the wretch I assumed must be his manservant, were attired for the weather outside, topcoats, hats and scarves.

'I had not thought to see you here,' Forster said to me when he was certain Rouse might not hear him.

'I had not thought to be here,' I replied. 'And if the fates had decreed you should simply be left in this place to contemplate your sins and your sedition, Mister Forster, I should have been content.'

Tears started in his eyes. Pitiful excuse for a man. Still, somewhere in the depths of this Inferno, there was a scream of pain such as I have never heard before, and I saw the abject terror in Forster's eyes, the constant companion of the end that must await him.

'They intend execution, do they not?' he sobbed, and we both knew the form that execution might take.

His trial date was set for two weeks thence, the second week of April.

'There are gibbets across this nation filled with fellows far less culpable than you, sirrah,' I said.

'So much for your merciful King, madam.' He turned to the manservant perched on the edge of the table. 'Tom,' he said. 'The chairs.' And while the furniture was arranged for us, Forster dabbed at his eyes with a kerchief. 'I have wondered often,' he said, 'whether those assurances you brought me were simply a ploy.'

'You had other envoys, I collect,' I reminded him as I sat. 'Your own officers. Did they not bring you the same messages? I see they did. Of course. I do not entirely blame General Wills either. But we were duped, that much is plain. And I owe you my life – possibly the lives of others I hold dear also. So, debts to settle. A plan, Mister Forster. Though should we succeed you must understand that if, beyond its conclusion, our paths ever cross again, I shall personally ensure that you do indeed hang.'

The plan, I now realise, was perhaps a little more complex than necessary. But the governor, Mister Pitts, was certainly biddable to the transfer, at a considerable price, of Forster and his manservant, Tom Lee, from those Augean stables on the southern side of Newgate to one of the strongrooms built for special prisoners within the Governor's House, on the opposite side of the street.

Of course, we insisted on seeing the place before parting with the garnish, and while Pitts showed General Forster's anxious sister Dorothy about the premises, her elderly maidservant begged leave to rest a while below. Pitts locked the outer door behind us, careful to warn me not to touch the latch, for it was attached to an alarum bell that would, he said, set off an awful din within the house and doubtless, he laughed, disturb his poor wife. Naturally, I said, I should do no such thing, and he left me admiring the lock. It was impressive. Ornate, though not excessively so and, when I peered closely at its brasswork, bearing the simple inscription *Wilkes, Birmingham.*

I had within my skirts a piece of softened soap that I now carefully pressed into the keyhole, a task at which I was almost caught by the governor's own manservant when he came down carrying pots to the kitchen. And I even helped the fellow, holding the vessels for him while he unfastened the padlock from the door's hasp and staple.

After that it was more straightforward. Bracegirdle knew a locksmith who could produce a reasonably efficient pass key and a simple tapered iron spike. These we wrapped in lint and took them to Forster at our second visit, along with two flagons of sack – one for the prisoner and another for the governor to convey the thanks of Forster's surrogate sister.

Then we waited. And waited. What was wrong with the man?

But finally the *Courant* carried the story. Outrage. Just four days before his trial and Governor Pitts had been carousing with the prisoner, their respective servants too, in the strongroom allocated for

Thomas Forster's detention. Yet, these were hours of daylight and the premises supposedly secure from escape, the prisoner had been free to wander within the house. This being so, he excused himself with a claim that he must visit the necessary-room, on the floor above, and the suspicions of Governor Pitts were seemingly not aroused until General Forster failed to return. At that point the governor went up to look for him and, during his absence, Forster's man, Mister Lee, had suggested to the manservant that they might perhaps partake of small beer. The manservant had descended to the kitchens and Mister Lee had followed him clandestinely, locked him in the kitchens with the aid of an iron bar jammed into the door's hasp and staple. Meanwhile Forster, who had in fact concealed himself below, had jammed the outer door's latch and attached alarum bell with a substantial piece of lint, unlocked the door itself with a pass key he had somehow acquired, then secured the door again from the outside but jamming the key into the lock, thus effectively imprisoning Governor Pitts in his own prison.

It was, said the *Daily Courant*, audacious.

'All of my news, I fear,' said Secretary Stanhope, 'is bad.'

I had never been there before – that rabbit warren of chambers and apartments that presently house the Council, the Board of Trade, the Treasury, as well as the Northern and Southern Departments.

'Our enemies all defeated?' I said. I intended irony, though I think he did not see it. 'How could it all be so ill?'

I may never have been but I had connection. For it was from the same buildings – the remains of the so-called Cockpit and those around it, all those between the old royal tennis court and tilt yard, across from the Privy Gardens – that my old friend the Duke of Devonshire had so narrowly escaped the White Hall fire set by Seaton. It seems like a lifetime ago.

'You begged me discover intelligence for you,' he replied, brushing cascaded ceiling powder from the pine-green velvet sleeve of his court coat. I wanted to warn him that the same white flakes had also invaded the full-length auburn peruke but, by then, I had realised whither he was bound.

'Innes?'

'Indeed,' he said, and half-rose from his desk. 'Charles!' he yelled. 'The file, if you please. And Mistress Smart,' he said to the grey-draped necessary-woman swabbing the floors just outside the door. 'Later, if you please.'

She muttered some curse under her breath and dragged her buckets further along the corridor. There was a flurry of activity from the adjoining room, and another of Stanhope's cousins – the Assistant Under Secretary, as he had been named to me – bustled among the papers on his own table.

'Just tell me,' I said, bracing myself against the walnut arms of the chair, which reminded me so much of that birthing stool Parrish once carved for me at Fort St. George.

'Very well,' said Stanhope, waving his pipe at Cousin Charles to dismiss him again. 'It seems the gentleman was transported. Barbados. Aboard the *Africa*. July. Or was it August?'

Like a ball to my heart. All this time and I had hoped – no news, good news, as they say. I was convinced he must have returned safely to his Highland fastness. So long that I had almost forgotten my request to Secretary Stanhope.

'It cannot be,' I stammered. 'General Wills, he knew the service Innes had rendered.'

'There were so many,' said Stanhope. 'You could hardly expect somebody of the general's standing to watch over them all.'

So many. Forty-nine executions, five of them drawn and quartered. Over six hundred transportations.

'Yet so much leniency for those taken after Sheriffmuir, sirrah. How many transportations from the Earl of Mar's army?'

'You know the answer very well, Mistress Yale.'

Indeed I did. None. Not one. And simply a solitary execution – even that only for a military matter. Different jurisdictions, however. The punishments here in England under Stanhope's Southern Department, the charity in Scotland itself governed by the Secretary of State for the North, Townshend.

'His sentence?' I said.

'Innes and others of his clan are indentured as servants for a term of seven years.'

'Servants, sirrah? You mean as slaves surely.'

Here was the other difference, of course. That Stanhope's Southern Department also had responsibility for the American colonies – and how much it must have pleased the Secretary of State's friends among the colonial governors and plantation owners to be sent six hundred "servants" for whom they had to pay not a penny. How they must have shown their gratitude. But here came more interruption, another serving woman with a tray of tea, and a young man bearing the proofs for tomorrow's edition of the *Gazette*. For this was part of Stanhope's duties too – control of the official news carried to the outside world. As he had done concerning the casualties from Preston, reduced to less than half their actual numbers so that the victory might seem less pyrrhic. A lucrative part of his responsibilities, it seemed, since according to Parrish he directly enjoyed the profits from sales of our state newspaper, including the French edition.

'You seem unduly concerned, madam,' he said, as the tea was poured, 'for somebody who has spent so many of her years helping us send the country's traitors to their due rewards.'

I thought about the pride I had taken at some of them. My day at Tyburn to see Sir John Friend and Sir William Parkyn swing. I thought about it, and felt sick to my stomach.

'Yet I did not know them,' I said.

'A different imperative,' he told me, but nodding his head at the *Gazette* writer, pushing the approved proofs across his desk and dispatching the fellow back to his own offices. 'In the north,' Stanhope went on. 'Relations within Scotland to be restored. Though too much compassion, I fear.'

I accepted my saucer of tea, sipped at the dish. It was welcome, for it had tired me, wandering through this seemingly endless labyrinth of Under Secretaries, clerks and chief clerks, Office Keepers, embellishers, decipherers and the like.

'You need not,' I said. 'Fear, I mean. For the kin of Jamie Innes and his brothers are unlikely to distinguish between the treatments of one Secretary of State from another. And you may be sure, sir, that they will even now be dreaming of the day they may be avenged upon us for this harshness. If that passes for a restoration of relationships, I give you joy of it.'

'Joy I possess aplenty, madam. Popery defeated. South Sea and Bank stock risen again. And I shall not mince the matter but we are all Whigs now, it seems. Impossible to find anybody honest enough to admit they ever voted Tory. 'Tis a joy I might have expected you to share. Your own interests too. Your husband's. John Company now fully aligned to our faction, not a Tory left among the directors.'

Now I think I shall become a Trimmer, neither Whig nor Tory, though something betwixt. But at the time I merely set down my dish upon the table at my side.

'You must,' I said, 'put it down to my advanced years, or perhaps simply that I saw so much blood at Preston. So many young men sacrificed for no true purpose. Is that not the tragedy?'

'The greater tragedy that so many of those responsible for the sacrifices have escaped the drop.'

Another thing about which to feel guilty. I seem to have prepared a fashion. They were still following Forster's lead as late as August, when the Earl of Winton, sentenced to death, had merely walked free from the Tower. And such was the laxity at Newgate that poor Mister Pitts had been arrested for high treason, only acquitted months later.

'I have sympathy for some more than others,' I said.

'Forster?'

'Is that the reason you invited me here, sir?'

'How could you think so? I believed we owed you this much, at least. News, as I said. Though – well, Forster's case is particular. Did you know that the sister, Dorothy Forster, has an unshakeable plea of having been elsewhere? The governor's description seems to fit none of Forster's female associates.'

I had wondered. For our escapade at Newgate had not been without one additional episode. Myself and Mistress Bracegirdle leaving the prison after our second visit and I almost walked straight into an old acquaintance – that same Mister Edisbury who had once been the proud owner of Erddig Hall, and neighbour to Elihu's family at Plas Grono.

'Dear lady,' Edisbury had said, looking aghast at the door of the governor's house. 'I trust you have not been distressed by your visit to this terrible place.'

'You are mistaken, Mister Edisbury. I was simply here as my good friend's companion. Her brother, I fear, is wrongly imprisoned within.'

Then he smiled, a jest preparing itself upon his lips.

'A pity. I had so hoped you might tell me your husband is incarcerated in the Debtors' Ward.'

'Alas,' I replied, 'it is not so. And you, sir? What brings you to Newgate?'

'I live here. Not here, exactly, but we have rooms at the Blue Spires – merely a step from here. And might we not invite you to dine with us?'

How very low, I thought. To have been from such a fine country home to mere rooms near this Old Bailey. But sadly, I had told him, I must return at once to Latimer. And, in any case, I was travelling

376

rather *incognito*, my friend also. Innocent her brother might be, though an embarrassment all the same. I hoped he would understand. Of course, he had said. Discretion, naturally.

Yet it has been six months since that last visit to Forster in Newgate and I have lived in fear ever since, with every tick of the Maysmore in my hall, that some chance discussion might cause poor Edisbury to speak of our rencounter. For he owes me nothing. Quite the reverse, after the way Elihu helped destroy his fortunes.

Stanhope, however, did not press the issue and I merely shrugged.

'It would be easy enough, I suppose,' I said, 'for Forster's sister to protect herself that way. For myself, I am more grieved than you can know to hear about this enslavement of poor Jamie Innes. An undue concern, as you say? A sign, I suppose of my years, as you imply. Time that I bowed out from this double life I have led, do you not think?'

'I wish a grateful nation might express its thanks in a more tangible way, Mistress Yale. To you, and to Parrish also. I am tasked, it seems, with negotiating a new treaty of alliance with France, and I wish I had his abilities at my side when I do so.'

'I think you should find him unwilling,' I said. 'His last diplomatic efforts on behalf of the Crown landed him in the Tower if you recall.'

'Forster again,' he smiled. 'All roads lead to Forster, it seems. Still, Parrish has other duties now.'

Matthew has undertaken them enthusiastically, dividing his time between Downbury Hall and the Custom House Quay. Travelling is difficult for him and he is entirely reliant upon a cane to help him walk even a short distance. And though he has begged me several times, I have not yet accepted his invitation to join him in Essex. Poor Ursula has been unwell several times during the year and I decided to spend some little while repairing my relationship with Benji, now returned at last from Preston.

'Other duties,' I repeated, 'as you say. But I thank Our Lord his incapacity kept him from them at Bagley's.'

'Fortunate, yes,' he said, and pursed his lips as though uncertain whether to say more.'

'Wait,' I said. 'You said *all* your news, sirrah. Something about the explosion?'

It had been billed in the *Courant* with great fanfare. A whole collection of captured French cannon to be melted down and recast at Matthew Bagley's Moorfields foundry – the only location in all England where brass ordnance might be fashioned. Parrish had been invited but finally decided the event would be too difficult for him.

'We are still counting the dead,' said Stanhope. 'So many simply impossible to identify. Two of my own officials, Bagley himself, killed in the blast.'

'Deliberate?' I gasped. 'Sweet Jesu, they are still at their work?'

For a moment I dreaded he might tell me there was a connection to Forster. But no, it was worse than that.

'There is a suspect, Mistress Yale. A young girl.'

It was not the first time I had been shocked out of my wits while tending Mary Anne Campion's burial stone at Latimer. Last time it had been when I received word that Elihu had come to visit. But this time it was something entirely more terrifying.

Ursula often undertakes this duty but she has been unwell once more, another of those unexplained agues that so often afflict her. And with each illness we seem to have more folk making pilgrimage to our door with votive offerings towards her safe recovery – as though she is some blessed saint or holy recluse in a hillside cave. Her acts of charity among the poor have certainly made their mark in Chesham and all our surrounding farms and villages. Yet last Friday there was a marked absence of well-wishers and I took some of those floral oblations left upon the steps during the previous afternoon and used them to refresh the flowers in the chapel. Yellow Loosestrife, white Lady's Smock, and the reddish-purple of Burdock.

The sun was only just rising and the inside belly of the small church still dark, a single candle helping to light my labours. It was this cloying gloom perhaps that shaped my humour, made me think once more about that other Mary – the young witch who had tried so inexpertly to poison my Benjamin. Porter's daughter.

Since last November there have been conflicting reports following Stanhope's original intelligence she might also have been responsible for the foundry explosion. But if she *had* been guilty of that crime, to what purpose? To kill Parrish simply through our association? If so, it was fortune indeed that he had, at the eleventh hour, decided to stay away. But then a later report, also from Stanhope, that one of the wickedly burned bodies could, in fact, have been Mary Astor's.

Stanhope himself, as it happens, has also fallen from grace. Replaced in the negotiations with France and shifted to responsibility for the Northern Department – Walpole, it seems, no longer trusting him with the more important Southern Department.

But the treaty with Paris has indeed been concluded – back in February – and just one of its advantages being the end of the Pretender's sanctuary at Saint-Germain. Exiled from exile. Gone now to Rome. And Forster, we hear, gone with him. And gone, too, any risk of Mister Edisbury divulging my secret – for word also arrived that the poor gentleman has died in virtual penury at the Blue Spires.

I was saying a quiet prayer for his soul when I heard it.

A footstep, I was certain.

I turned towards the altar at the chapel's farther end but there were only slender slivers of light angling through the window glaze, insufficient to shed proper illumination on whoever might be lurking in the many shadows.

'Anybody there?' I shouted. Probably nothing but how I wished I had never given up the pocket pistol.

To my side was the small vestibule, the open outside door, and it screamed at me, begged me to use it, simply to get out.

But I could not. And there was that noise again, softer now. A scraping sound, a flurry of movement in the shadows. The air, I thought, had grown colder, the musty odours of the chapel grown heavier.

'Mary?' I whispered into the echoes, and took two cautious steps between the pews. 'Mary Astor?'

And a devil descended upon me. A blur of white. Something bursting from above. A clatter that made me cry out, smack my hip into the side of the pews.

Pigeon. A damn'd pigeon from the rafters that had, even now, flown out through the door.

My heart hammered and my hip hurt like Hades. Yet I limped back to Mary Anne Campion's memorial stone, cursed myself for a fool. I busied myself arranging the flowers in their vase and turned to think of more pleasant things. There was the invitation to consider. Elihu's half-hearted invitation. The King had planned a great celebration upon the Thames, commissioned Herr Handel to compose music to match. The *Courant* had made the announcement and suddenly the whole world, it seemed, planned to hire boats and barges of their own to enjoy the spectacle. It was too much for Elihu to ignore and he had arranged a vessel large enough to accommodate Kate and Nan, their children too, Ursula and myself as well. Not Benjamin, of course. And Elihu could not resist several jibes within the invitation about how very low it has brought him to know that I now spend so much time at Downbury, about how he should wish to discuss this if I am able to tear myself away from Essex.

But Benji had brought me a peace token, as it happens. Or, rather, one from Streynsham, who had successfully tracked down the indenture details for Jamie Innes of Coxton. Barbados, indeed. Those same Codrington plantations now in possession of the Society for the Propagation of the Gospel in Foreign Parts. Now is that not an irony? That having inherited so many heathen African slaves already, this pillar of High Church Anglicanism should now have been gifted with considerable numbers of Catholic Highlanders – literally a captive audience for their Protestant missionary zeal.

But Elihu so thick with the Society, it occurred to me that my acceptance of his invitation might serve another purpose entirely.

And there – that noise again!

A single scuffling footstep and the creak of the vestry door.

That impetuosity, which has so often brought me to the brink of disaster – though impetuosity tempered by my ability to only hobble the length of the chapel.

'Show yourself!' I was yelling, searching in vain for anything I might use as a weapon, seizing upon the only thing Reverend Burrough had failed to lock away – the polished crucifix standing upon the altar itself.

I hesitated, knowing this for a scandalous sacrilege, a hateful heresy. Still, I hefted it in my hand, pushed the vestry door fully open – and found there Ursula's useless mongrel hound, curled comfortably in the corner.

The Thames again. Of course, I should have known it for an omen. How could I not have seen it?

And today's *Courant* may have carried a pretty enough account of Wednesday night's royal procession upon the river, yet no official version shall ever reveal the truth, I collect.

I took the opportunity – on Wednesday itself, two days ago – to lodge with my brother Richard, still dutifully managing Elford's Coffee House and refusing to let us leave without a warning that we should take care – for, he insisted, such occasions attracted more than their share of rogues and cut-purses. But I had laughed at him, for what harm might befall us upon the river? What harm, indeed. And I had then taken carriage with Ursula to meet her father, her sisters and their families, at the Somerset Stairs, where Elihu greeted me with little more than a scowl as we all embarked on the converted lighter he hired. Eight young oarsmen and a gay green and white awning to provide shelter for us, should it be needed, in the ample forecastle constructed there for this very occasion.

'The master, Mister Briggs,' cried Elihu as we clambered aboard, 'begs that we should all keep to our seats as much as possible.' Eight dining chairs, in various states of disrepair, from which I chose the steadiest and best upholstered.

'But the children, Papa,' said Kate in her now customary state of anxiety. And why must she always dress in such sombre fashion? 'You promised this vessel was safe.'

No chairs for the six children, though a short bench for the two servants Elihu had insisted were necessary for our comfort. But there was little to save any of us from drowning except some low netting the barge-master was still securing to the awning posts around three sides of our crowded platform.

'Safe, ma'am?' barked Mister Briggs. 'Safer than in yer own 'ome, this be.'

Kate's husband, dubious Dudley, assured her all would be well, the waters calm and plenty of us to watch that the children came to no harm.

As it happened this was a fine evening, alive with insects and, at once, the sounds of a city in celebration. So many boats upon the waters, I could never have counted them. Wherries, skiffs, shallops, pinnaces, longboats, handsome launches, tilts, tunnies and peterboats. Small sailing yachts. The banks crowded with spectators everywhere I looked, and the clamour of their chatter, their laughter, the cries of vendors moving among them. I had forgotten how much the city is simply an embodiment of the Thames itself, every one of its half-million either employed in its trade, or dependent upon the goods carried there. All the smells of the river itself reflected in those bounteous cargoes: coal and claret barrels; fish and heady grains; tobacco and cordage; pitch and pine. The colours of the multitude in their finery and flags – the pinks, the deep greens, the blues. And we were not without a certain elegance of our own – apart from Kate, of course.

'I suppose this must remind you, my dear,' Elihu sneered, somewhat out of breath, and tugging at the edges of his bulging sky-blue waistcoat, 'of that day upon the river when we opened the Garden House?'

He had needed assistance from his sons-in-law, and from young David Yale, to bring him onto the lighter, then up onto our makeshift passenger deck, for he has been suffering attacks of gout that afflict his knees quite badly. His girth, I suppose, does not help either, and he is showing his age. But what did he intend by his comment? Strange to remind me of a time when my Joseph was still alive, when Elihu himself had been at his most boorish.

'The day,' I said, 'that ended with the earthquake, you mean? I sincerely hope this might be a happier occasion, sirrah.'

I hoped so, though it was not meant to be. Yet Ursula gave a squeal of delight, regardless.

'Mama,' she said. 'An earthquake? You was in an earthquake?'

I squeezed her arm, simply relieved that the illnesses with which she is so often plagued seem now to be abated. We have consulted Sir Hans Sloane of late, though he remains perplexed by her condition.

'I shall tell you the story later,' I said. 'But listen, can you hear?'

The King's party had commenced further upstream at White Hall and though their ultimate destination might be Chelsea they had taken advantage of slack water after the ebb, at eight o' the clock, allowing the oarsmen to first stroke easily in the opposite direction up towards the Bridge.

'You see?' said Elihu. 'He was bound to come this way first. Such an opportunity to impress the crowds.'

'I simply pray we have seen an end to it all,' I told Nan. 'The Pretender scuttled off to seek lodging from the pope, our true King here resplendent in all his victorious glory upon the Thames River. God willing the victory is indeed complete.'

An end to it? I should have known better, and in truth the

splendour at that moment was more audible than visible. But as our lightermen cast off, the strains of the orchestra came drifting to us, clear and melodic. Violins. An overture that spoke to me, to all of us, of joyous prancing fountains, of cascading waterfalls festooned with flags of red and gold and imperial purple.

'Lord Almighty,' shouted Katie, as our vessel lurched a little when we pulled away from the jetty steps, 'I trust it shall not be like this all the way.'

The children, however, seemed to think this great fun, though the master was plainly less than happy with the performance of his boatmen.

'Chop! Chop!' he yelled from his bench, beating his hands together, keeping time with each repeat of the instruction, with the pattern of those distant strings, until he finally brought them into some form of unison – though he constantly called them for wretches and worse. Yet he had assured Elihu they were all properly licensed.

'Perhaps too much liquor beforehand,' David Yale laughed as we steered out into the river itself, where we finally saw them: a naval barge gliding towards us, longer even than the vessel that fetched me back from India; a score of liveried oarsmen, their backs and their sweeps moving in graceful harmony with the music's rhythm; beyond the oars, a gilded and many-pillared pavilion with crimson roof; and beyond the pavilion a great, sweeping after-deck all festooned with flags of blue and red. None so enormous as the union flag itself.

'So many of them,' Ursula shouted. 'The King has so many friends.'

But still so many enemies, I thought. And it has been rumoured that His Majesty has instructed Herr Handel to make the music loud enough to drown out any objectors. Yet you would not have thought from this display that any could be present here tonight. For the royal barge was not alone. I could count four more similar vessels already, each crowded, I supposed, with his courtiers and ministers. The Lord Mayor's own golden barge equally impressive. And immediately behind the King, another of the elegant craft, this one even longer, entirely open, an enormous platform behind the oarsmen to carry Herr Handel and his musicians. Too far to be precise, but I guessed there must be fifty or sixty of them, enough to cause their acoustics to carry across this whole expanse of water, to each of its margents, and to the full extent of this floating progress.

'Come children,' said my other son-in-law James, gathering the six little ones to him. 'Let us count them. You can all count, can you not?'

They all readily agreed, though the smallest, Polly, hardly more than a babe, seemed to think there was nothing other than seven, eight and nine, shouted loudly, over and over again.

'Papa,' said Nan, fussing at her niece's hair and resplendent in skirts of royal blue and white, a bodice of shocking red, 'are we required to get these victuals to Chelsea ahead of the royal party?'

It would not have been Elihu had he not also seen the opportunity for profit from tonight's excursion and he had responded enthusiastically to some royal sutler's request for transport tenders listed in the *Gazette*. Hence, in the shallow belly of the lighter, beneath our platform, a cargo of lacquered chests replete, we were told, with shrimp paste pots, jugged and kippered herring, bottled salmon – though the hampers for our own midnight feast were there with us, in our own private pavilion, stowed beneath the servants' bench.

'Naturally, my dear,' said Elihu. 'We must beat those other rascals to the end.' He pointed at a considerable fleet of vessels approaching from the direction of Black Friars, with the great white rock of St. Paul's behind them, the lowering sun blazing upon its new dome. 'The sutler told me a goodly half of those boats carry cases packed with either ice or hot coals, to keep their culinary contents cold or warm. Imagine!'

The music had paused some moments earlier but now began afresh – hautboy, flute and recorders – skipping and dancing like the scales of a merry tune I once heard played by a shepherd in the meadows below Latimer. It reminded me too of the way the river burbles there, just beneath the footbridge. Delightful. Too delightful for me to remain seated, so I asked Annie to lend me her arm, kicked off my slippers.

'Mama,' she exclaimed. 'In your stocking'd feet?'

David had opened a bottle of champagne – the same shade as the brocade of my skirts. He offered me a glass, served the others likewise, though James preferred to tope from his own stingo flask. And there was the music again, effervescence of white and gold.

'I was always thus upon the *Rochester*, sweet girl,' I said, recalling the lesson that Captain Sutton had drilled into me, and gripping the upright that supported the awning. *One hand for yourself, one for the ship.* 'And upon the *Revanche*, though I suppose you would have been too young to remember.'

But I remembered – while, around the riddles of that foot-tapping pastoral melody, the King's barge came abreast of us, though some distance away. The oarsmen's blades backed on the farther side at the coxswain's command, but those at this side swept on, so that the boat swung in a graceful arc that caused the thing to come about almost in its own length. That stretch opposite Paul's Wharf. And with the Bridge, its tumble of houses, barely a half-mile to the east, she pointed smoothly back in the direction from whence the royal barge had first started. The musicians moved seamlessly into a triumphant fanfare as the first of the rising tide caught the hull, oars raised and feathered, since the flow itself was now sufficient to carry the craft onwards without their assistance. Timed to perfection, the trumpets' martial pageant heralding the true start of the promenade.

'And the barrels, Pa?' said Annie's husband, James.

'The barrels?' said Elihu, while I sipped at the glass. 'A good question, my boy. Casks of pickled oysters, I believe. What say you, little devils?' he cried to the flock of my grandchildren cavorting around the deck. 'Shall we try the oysters, or leave them for the King?'

The casks had been a late addition to the cargo, delivered to the quayside after the sutler himself had already left and the barge-master, Mister Briggs, unwilling to take responsibility for goods not included on his inventory, though Elihu had agreed to pay him extra, fearing His Majesty's wrath, he jested, should the King's passion for oysters go unassuaged and poor Governor Yale held to account. But there had been room for them, just, beneath the after-section of our temporary platform – below that same space where the young ones were making such play – behind the curtain Mister Briggs had so thoughtfully hung to conceal the chamber pot we would all need for such a lengthy excursion.

'For the King,' they shouted back. 'For the King.'

First, Kate and Dudley's brood – four of them: Dudley Junior, ten; young Anne, eight; another Elihu, now six; and Polly, just two years old.

'When shall we eat?' demanded Dudley Junior in that imperious way he has somehow inherited. Their children vex me for the most part. They want for nothing, yet the more they are given, the worse they behave. And the worse they behave, the more they receive. Except Polly, bless her, who seems not to have been infected with her siblings' unpleasantness. But Annie and James at least have raised their own offsprings somewhat better: William, just turned six; and Elizabeth, four.

'Look,' said Dudley Junior's father, as we turned the South Bank bend at King's Reach, 'you see those boats – that one with the yellow hull, and those other two, the red and the black? We shall each place a wager on which may be the first to come abreast of the Westminster palace, and the winning wager rewarded with portions of pound cake.'

Their fathers both in Parliament again. Dudley himself – still addicted to the gaming tables, naturally – has been the Member for Thetford these several years past, and James returned to Parliament for Derby since the rebellion. The children play together, after a fashion, though their fathers barely acknowledge each other, for James well recalls the threats made against him by Dudley's associates – though, naturally, like most of the population, you would now not think that any Tory thoughts had ever passed through Dudley's mind. And, of course, nobody – but nobody – speaks of Dudley's cousin, Lord North and Grey, still known for a Jacobite, though none has been able to bring proof against him of any part in the rebellion.

'You lubber-louts,' Briggs bellowed at his lightermen for they were, indeed, making a poor show, one or two of them crabbing their oars more often than seemed natural, despite the amount of liquor they may have consumed.

Meanwhile, the music had paused again, the musicians then striking up a fresh piece, more solemn, to suit the barge-master's mood perhaps. Hautboy again. horn and trumpet, though a dirge that saw us slow past the fields and marshes to our left and raise the new building taking place at White Hall on the opposite side.

'I want to eat now,' screamed young Anne, and stamped her foot. 'Now.'

'Kate,' I snapped, 'can you not control your daughter's behaviour?'

'Perhaps, Mama,' she replied, 'if you devoted less time to Essex, you might yourself behave more like a true grandmother.'

She meant less time with Parrish, of course. He is settled at Downbury now, and I have spent pleasant days there, though always taking Benjamin with me. I chose to ignore her, however, watched as Herr Handel's musicians settled into another air, a piece in which the bassoons and recorders hinted perhaps at the mystery and deep menace to come. Yet a stately dance at the same time, one that vibrated through the barge, made me wish I could cut a step or two with dear Matthew – though his crippled leg makes him less than the elegant courtier I recall so well from Madras.

'Mister Briggs,' said Elihu, 'I fear if we do not make better progress, we shall not find a mooring. We shall be crowded together like these kippered herrings we carry. Another reason to get there swiftly.'

He spoke these latter words most loudly, but that fellow simply scowled back at him, returned to scolding his rowers for their lack of skill.

'Chop! Chop!' he yelled as we came abreast of St. Peter's and the palace, Dudley Junior claiming his prize of pound cake from the hamper. 'You ninny-hammers,' Briggs cried as the rhythm was lost once more and I went below to avail myself of the Oliver.

And our destination? The shores of Chelsea Reach, the grounds of Ranelagh House there – now in the hands of the late earl's daughter, Lady Catherine, and adjoining the gardens of Chelsea's Royal Hospital.

'I read that Lady Catherine,' said Nan, 'is living on Jews' Row.'

'It is still a fine place,' I told her. 'Just the other side of the hospital. And she has Walpole for a neighbour. Besides, she prefers to use her wealth for charitable purpose, I collect.'

Lady Catherine is an admirable woman. I have met her on several occasions – though not sufficient or so formal, naturally, to secure us invitations to the midnight royal supper she would be hosting later – and once with others of her circle. Literary women. Women of influence. Elizabeth Thomas, whose poetry Matthew greatly admires. Judith Drake, who so expounds the equality of wisdom between men and women. Elstob, the astonishing linguist. Young Lady Mary Montagu, with whom I had once discussed my Elford's cure from smallpox through the practice of engrafting by a Turkish physician – one that had, at the time, smacked to me of witchcraft, but one for which Lady Mary has become such an outspoken advocate and Sir Hans Sloane become such an avid practitioner. Yes, women of influence. Women that Mama would have admired very much. Women who know that being righteous in itself is not enough, that we must all *act* in the name of right, against injustice.

'And for endless gay amusement, I daresay,' said Kate, bitterness in her voice despite the joyous sequence of dances with which we were regaled. Minuet, bourrée and hornpipe that set my feet a-tapping all afresh.

'Charity, you say?' Elihu jeered. 'Schools for girls? And the company she keeps – that creature Astell.'

'You should heed Mary Astell,' I told Nan, and repeated my favourite of Mistress Astell's aphorisms. '"*If all men are born free,*"' I said, '"*how is it that all women are born slaves?*"'

The light was beginning to fail now as we came abreast of the Horse Ferry on either bank and Lambeth Reach off to our left. And, for some reason, this seemed to trigger a regular procession of our passengers and crewmen taking turns at the chamber pot. Yet the sunset sky was daubed with crimson, violet and orange that I could almost imagine Her Handel had ordained as accompaniment to his score.

'One hundred guineas I have just gifted to the Royal Society,' said Elihu. 'That is charity. My contribution to natural philosophy.'

I looked at him then, and remembered Mary Astell's more detailed advice to young women on matrimonial choices – the need for strong reason, good education, well-tempered spirit to help them choose wisely. I had possessed all those, and *still* married Elihu.

'Lady Catherine's grandmother,' I said, 'was herself a great natural philosopher. Though seems to have expected nothing in return. Whereas your hundred guineas, Elihu, was little more than your entrance fee to the Royal Society itself – a Society from which, needless to say, as a mere woman, Lady Ranelagh would have been prohibited.'

'Mistress Drake, I hear,' my son-in-law Dudley guffawed, as Elihu dismissed me with a shake of his head, 'predicts that one day women might even be permitted a vote in our elections. Such stuff!'

He filled his pipe, helped Elihu likewise.

'Not in two hundred years,' said Elihu. 'Or ever, I collect.'

Not so long, surely, I hope.

'Sweet Jesu,' I said, 'assure me that women shall receive their due at least during little Polly's lifetime.'

'And I see you all there,' Elihu went on, 'your lady scribblers,' he almost spat the word, 'exchanging all those little snippets of secrets among yourselves. Like some coven.' He recited several lines from that Song of the Witches, that Master Shakespeare had penned, plainly thought himself jocose for having done so.

But I wondered what he meant, saw Nan look quickly up at him, all anxiety – or was it guilt? But she avoided my eye and I made a note to myself that, when we reached Chelsea, I should ask her about it. But by then, of course, that was the last thing on my mind.

I had moved away from them, to the rear of the platform, looked down upon the backs of the lightermen, and David Yale joined me there.

'Great heavens,' I said, 'they certainly make heavy weather of this.'

'Riding the flood tide too,' he replied. 'I think even the children would make a better showing.'

'We carry a great deal of cargo, I suppose. Heavily laden. It would not be your uncle had he not squeezed every opportunity for profit. But still, our *masula* boatmen at Madras would have put these rascals to shame.'

'Some of them so pitifully small too,' said David.

It was true. A couple of them looked hardly strong enough for the task. But I watched Herr Handel's violinists, crowded so tight upon that barge there was barely room for their music stands, for them to complete their bow strokes without stabbing each other. Yet they were skillfully conjuring the gentle patter of rain, of summer showers.

'Well,' I said, 'Mister Briggs insists they are all licensed. I suppose we must take his word. And matters at the Connecticut College? How do they proceed, David?'

Mister Briggs at that moment had left his seat in the stern and made his way between the lightermen, rummaging in a locker directly beneath our feet.

'The move from Saybrook,' David replied, 'is decided. To New Haven.'

'Ah,' I laughed, 'they hope to exploit the Yale connection still more.' It was, of course, the site settled by Elihu's uncle Hopkins, despite all the attacks by local savages.

The barge-master had lit a taper, climbed to our platform and opened the lanthorn hanging just next to me.

'Beggin' pardon, ma'am,' he said, shielding the taper's flame and setting it to the tallow candle. And, as if by magic, I saw each of the other craft illuminated, one by one. Fireflies that danced also, now, to the violins' summons.

'I fear,' said David, 'their hopes may be somewhat frustrated. You recall Mister Dummer? Yes, of course. But the poor fellow has been pressing Uncle Elihu for some small share of his wealth to be gifted to the establishment – though I swear he keeps his fists tightly closed about the purse.'

'Elihu's support for a Dissenter Academy? Always a lost cause, I think.'

Briggs lit a second lanthorn for us, then climbed down to his station once more.

'Yet he finds himself between two stools, Aunt Catherine. Mister Dummer playing upon his Yale heritage, the possibility of perpetual renown should his name ever adorn their gates. On the other, the Society for the Propagation of the Gospel, pressing him with the conviction they might convert the college entirely to High Church Anglicanism. Yes, two stools.'

'Though between two stools,' I said, 'one simply falls to the ground.'

My first warning that Elihu had joined us came with the cloud of tobacco smoke from his pipe.

'Did somebody mention the gospel?' he said.

'David mentioned the Society.' I turned to face him, drained the champagne from my glass. 'And it happens I wished to discuss the same with you.'

His pipe glowed red in the gathering gloom as he drew upon the stem.

'God's hooks,' Elihu replied as David politely excused himself from our company, 'shall you tell me you now support our aims?'

'It would be less than honest for me to say so, sir. But you will remember the debt I owe that young Jack Highlander, Jamie Innes?'

'For pity's sake, Catherine. These obsessions. Was he not hanged?'

His tone could almost have been a counterpoint to the triumph in the fresh hornpipe now washing over the Thames. And this *was* the King's triumph after all: his new ascendancy; his demonstration that he could excel even his errant son, the Prince of Wales, for extravagant exhibition; his determination that the spirit of our nation, already English, and having embraced the Dutch, must now firmly grasp the German.

'He was not,' I said. 'Merely sold into slavery upon the plantations of your High Church friends in Barbados. I would purchase his freedom.'

'Is that all?' he sneered.

'In truth? No, for I would purchase freedom for his brothers too. For Callum. And Donald the Giant.'

'This was your reason for being here, I collect.'

'You invited me.'

'At your daughter's insistence. And must you always,' he began to whisper, 'treat me as a bubble? You have myself and Parrish at your table. To taunt me? Knowing you intended to be his whore at Downbury?'

More horns. More trumpets. Images of gold, and fire, and war chariots. Yet I allowed them to abate before I answered.

'You have no grounds to reproach me, Mister Yale,' I hissed. 'And I came here to be with my family, sir.'

But he was already distracted. For we had pulled alongside another boat, a skiff, its own lanthorn ablaze on an upright spar.

'Girls,' Elihu cried, waving his pipe and his face likewise alight with joy. 'Oh, my good girls.'

It had been a while, but I would have known them anywhere. That other Ursula, like the ghost of her mother. She has done well. Katherine Nicks would be proud of her, married to Sir Edward Betenson, already a noted attorney. Yet he may be skillful in the practice of law, but a pitiful hand at seamanship. For as his wife shouted back greetings, her sister Betty too – the old smallpox scars more prominent in the lanthorn's glow – Betenson somehow managed to swing their boat towards us. And while three of our lightermen saw the collision coming, raised their sweeps in unison to avoid damage and pulled the shafts inboard, the fourth, one of those puny rogues, succeeded only in having his oar dragged from his grip, so that the sweep vanished momentarily under the skiff.

'You dandyprat!' bellowed Briggs as our vessels crashed together, caused us to roll and Kate to scream in anguish. 'You Judas jackanapes!' Briggs stood from his coxswain's stool, flapped a finger at the miscreant. 'Get below. Get below.'

The lad was wearing a blue Monmouth cap, several sizes too big for him, and he pulled it down, almost masking his eyes as he obeyed the instruction, scrambled from his bench, lowered his head – in shame, I thought – and disappeared from sight beneath our deck. It takes but one crab, they say, to cripple a crew.

'God in heaven,' shouted Elihu. 'Are you all safe?'

It was the Nicks girls, naturally, for whom he was concerned. There was a stammered apology from young Betenson, laughter from Betty and an assurance that yes, all was well.

'And my brother,' she shouted as Betenson shoved them clear. 'He has his appointment. With John Company. He says he will visit you. Before he sails for Pegu.'

'And you must let us know,' Betty called through cupped hands, 'when the portrait is complete.'

Then they noticed me, enmity and shadow clouding their faces as we left them astern, while the trumpets, the violins, horns, the whole ensemble, joined in the most jubilant of pieces. On it ran. On and on.

'Her brother,' I said. 'Your by-blow. And you call me whore?'

He bit his lip, and I wondered what the Nicks girls thought of me – for how much of their mother's misfortunes did they hold me accountable. I still had no idea, of course, whether that other Elihu was sired by my husband, though now he did not deny it.

'My position, Catherine. It is my position. I am proposed for membership of the Society itself. Prominence. Do you know that the government of Connecticut will make no provision for our own Church of England to send missionaries there?'

'Perhaps they fear this new High Church propensity for slave owning might spread to their colony also. Grasp their land, gift them the gospel?'

'You think there are none indentured in Connecticut already?'

'I care not,' I told him. 'Only for the release of Jamie Innes and his kin.'

'Am I not kin also, Catherine? Good Lord Almighty, how I wish you might show me even a portion of that same consideration.'

'I would perhaps think better of you, husband, if you practiced the Christian act I requested. Help me secure their release. Or at least provide the direction to which I might address my proposition.'

'I shall consider it.'

'And this portrait, of which Betty Nicks spoke?'

His face glowed with hubris and the lanthorns' gleam.

'Young Enoch Seeman,' he said. 'The Danzig fellow. Son of that same Mennonite who crafted the canvas of myself and Cavendish in negotiation about Nan's betrothal. I am sitting for him.'

'I wonder whether this shall be as much an invention as the earlier one,' I said, imagining the canvas would show a slimmer, younger version of Elihu Yale than reality deserved.

I remained there for some moments after he left me while, as the strains of that glorious hornpipe faded away, the clock from some church over around Nine Elms Reach chimed half-past the hour of ten into the comparative silence. And we began the long turn westwards for the final stretch of the journey. The moon had pierced the indigo night clouds and sent ripples of light across the river, punctuated with silver minims, crotchets and quavers reflected from a hundred floating lanthorns.

'Can we not pull harder, Mister Briggs?' said Elihu though, in truth, the lightermen were performing better now, even with only seven at the oars. The eighth? Still in disgrace, I assumed, and decided it might be an act of Christian kindness to borrow my son-in-law's pocket flask.

'We'll get there when we gets there,' said Briggs. Yet we were keeping station admirably enough, perhaps two hundred paces astern of the royal party. 'And we'll berth alongside 'Is Majesty or my name ain't Billy Briggs. The 'alf-hour, I reckons.'

That seemed to hearten Elihu and I had a notion I might help by going below, perhaps speaking with that disgraced young oarsman, engage him in ensuring the cargo was all ready for unloading. In any case, I needed to relieve myself again, so he would need to surrender his place of exile, at least temporarily.

I eased myself down the makeshift stairs, cautious in my stocking'd feet, carrying the flask and easing my brocades aside to aid my descent and to preserve my modesty from the prying eyes of Mister Briggs. But it was dark down there, the spectral grey of the rowers' backs astern, keeping a slow and steady beat to the stately progress of the musicians' minuet. *Chop*, pause. *Chop*, pause. And they might still be riding the flood but they had now been at their labours almost three hours. They must be exhausted. And that, perhaps, the reason for the puny fellow's inadequacy. Well, the stingo might bring him succour, though he must needs be instructed to give me privacy within.

Yet, as I ducked my head beneath our platform, pushed aside the curtain, I could not immediately see him. It was dark as pitch in there and perhaps the rascal was sleeping. But no, as my eyes became at least a little accustomed to the blackness, there he was. A faint glow in the dark, growing more pronounced, more red, and showing the wretch in silhouette as he blew upon the short length of cord protruding from one of the casks. A slow match? But why?

I moved forward, almost shouted out, to challenge him, but then the curtain fell behind. Deeper darkness, the glow obscured in a blur of movement and something slammed into my ribs. Something heavy. Something sharp.

I fell sideways, into the jumble of lacquered chests, cracked my head against the hull's timbers, dropped the flask.

'Help me,' I shouted, though all I could hear were the stamping feet of the children as they ran about just above me. That and the music still vibrating through the barge.

Then a hand over my mouth. A small hand, but rough. Another at my throat that squeezed and squeezed.

'Both of them,' the rogue hissed. 'This for both of them.'

The voice...

I tried to kick, to scratch at the villain's eyes, at the face, but this devil's reach was longer than mine, and every movement shot bolts of fire through my side, where the blow had landed.

I gasped for breath that would not come. My head began to feel like it must surely burst, sharp flashes of light behind my eyes – dazzling white light.

All my reason left me and I knew my struggles were becoming weaker. And I began not to care. I could hear Mister Briggs still goading his lightermen but it seemed to come from a great distance, echoed in my brain, even the agony in my side subsiding into a more benign dull ache.

That damn'd music, I thought, as the rhythms of a sarabande – I think it were so – came to carry me away. Joseph, dear Joseph, there to lead me in the dance.

But then the pain, Joseph fading away from me as I clambered up out of the abyss. A new pain, yes. I must have slammed my arm against one of the hull's ribs maybe. And I know that saved me.

Terror still gripped me, yet I stretched out that wounded arm and my fingers touched something that was porcelain smooth. A handle that I could grip, lift, though it was heavy.

My last chance, all the same. And it seemed that Joseph came back to me just then, lent me strength.

The chamber pot came off the deck, its foul contents spilling – on me, on my attacker, on everything – though with every drop it emptied, so it became easier to wield. It must have caught the wretch somewhere about the shoulder, for there was a squeal of pain and the grip on my throat eased.

I dragged in fresh breath, rolled a little, kicked as hard as my bruised body and those damp skirts allowed, so that my attacker tumbled over beside me.

Praise God the Oliver was still intact and as I scrambled to my knees I tried to call for help again. Nothing. Nothing more than a feeble croak.

But now I was angry and when the dark form of the dandyprat rose towards me I swung it with every ounce of strength I possessed.

And this time it shattered. It shattered as surely as did the skull of my attacker.

'Aunt Catherine?' David Yale, just the other side of the curtain. 'Is everything well with you?'

I held my wounded side, watched in horror as the red glow of that slow match disappeared inside the cask, tried to poke inside the bunghole with my finger. How long did I have? The only thing of which I could be certain was that the barrel contained something far more lethal than pickled oysters. There was only one purpose for a slow match. An assassination attempt, to be sure. One that would kill my family in the process. And if it was timed to coincide with our arrival at Chelsea it needed only a few inches of match cord inside the cask to burn for the next short while.

'Not well...not at all,' I croaked. 'Help...me.'

Every word created agony in my throat, in my ribs. And I was amazed he heard me, yet he pushed his head around the side of the curtain, peered into the blackness.

'Your voice,' he said. 'What is it?'

'Never...mind.'

I reached for his hand, pulled him to my side and as his own vision adjusted to the gloom, made out the fallen body, he gasped, recoiled. From the sight of the corpse, naturally, but perhaps from me too – for I must have stunk to high heaven.

'God's hooks,' he said, 'what...?'

'Forget...that. Must help me...get this...over side.' I patted the cask. Speaking was painful but I managed to spit out the words one by one. 'Long...story. Must...believe me. This barrel...petard. Set to explode...when we reach Chelsea. Slow match...burning inside... cask filled...with gunpowder. Those others...too. That is...my guess.'

'The lid,' he said, and began looking around for something he might use, picked up a length of timber – the same piece, I guessed, with which I had been struck, the blow that still caused me so much pain.

'Could be...a mechanism,' I insisted, 'inside. Trigger explosion... should we...tamper with it. Just help.'

I did not need to share with him the terror I felt should this thing explode with my family aboard.

'I shall fetch assistance.'

'No. Must do it...together. But careful.' I began to edge the cask towards the starboard side, feeling useless, pushing with one hand, clutching my ribs with the other. 'Keep the barrel...upright. Perfectly upright.'

'A petard?' he said. 'Surely...'

He glanced over his shoulder at the body.

'Just...help,' I snapped at him and, thankfully, he obeyed.

Between us we managed to lift it, rested it upon the broad strake of the gunwale, as the barge-master's voice bellowed from the stern.

'All well back there?' he shouted, and David called back that yes, all was well, that his aunt simply needed some assistance. And his aunt began to count.

'One...two...' I nodded my head. '*Three.*'

Sweet Jesu, I thought, let this work. We dropped it straight down into the water with less splash than I might have imagined, though it was hardly silent.

'What were that?' cried Briggs, and David told him some nonsense about a damaged barrel.

'Now,' I said, 'fetch...your uncle. And...a lanthorn. But no word...to anybody.' I rubbed at my throat for it hurt like fury. 'And... over there.' I pointed. 'Floor...flask.'

It took him a moment to locate it but he handed over the stingo, left me as I collapsed back against the gunwale, my head spinning so violently I thought I must retch. I tried to calm myself, to think about what we must do next, and to take a painful swallow of the liquor. Then I rummaged about among the cargo until I found a tarpawling to loosely cover the body, checked again for any signs of life, though there were none. And I had that absurd thought, prayed that none of my family should now need the chamber pot until we reached the shore. I had wished to relieve myself, and the attack had resolved that problem for me, my inner skirts and my legs soaked with my own piss, as well as the pot's contents. I did not care. I had survived, and the giddy gyrations of my brain swam into a morass of stamping feet and children's laughter, the chop of the oarsmen's blades upon the water, and the sweet dance of Herr Handel's next piece – a morass into which I allowed myself to sink.

'Catherine.' Elihu's angry voice calling me back from the swoon into which I had fallen. 'Catherine. What is this? Nan is asking for you.'

The lanthorn's light pained my eyes. And I had dropped the flask, the remains of the stingo soaked into my brocades also.

'Tell...him,' I instructed David Yale, and the young fellow told his uncle precisely how he had found me and what had transpired, though he made no mention of the body.

'A petard?' Elihu whispered. 'No, you are mistaken. What is

this? Some return of your old affliction? Some foolish attempt to discredit me?'

He could not have known how much, at that moment, I longed for a sip of Sathiri's *soma*, or a draft of Sydenham's elixir, but I merely crawled over to the tarpawling, pulled it aside as Elihu lifted the lanthorn, gasped as he saw the face, stepped back quickly and banged the back of his head on a beam.

'Great heavens, is that…?'

This for both of them. I remembered the words. The voice. Well, she would be reunited now with father and mother, the whole family of them, it seemed, dead by my doing. And, to hell with them.

'Indeed. Mary Astor. Poisoned Langhorn…then tried to poison…my son. Caused all those deaths…the explosion… Moorfields foundry.'

'But Briggs…' He glanced back towards the curtain.

'Knows…nothing, I believe. That drab…hated me…revenge… and King George…both.'

'She attacked you?'

I put a hand to my throat.

'Strangled,' I said, though with difficulty.

'You have brought this upon our family?' he stammered, regarding me with terrible venom, then he span about. 'These others?' He pointed at the remaining barrels. 'Might they not be the same?'

'Gunpowder…no doubt. But only…the one…petard, I think.'

'You think! God's hooks, we must have Briggs put them all over the side immediately.'

'For once,' I said. 'Do not be…the bubble.' Despite David's reticence, I persuaded him to help me drag the body to the space left by the missing barrel, to haul her into that gap, then cover her again with the tarpawling. And all the time Elihu paced about, scolded me, insisting he should tell Briggs. 'Do so,' I said, 'and all…shall be…lost.'

'I shall not be a part of this,' he insisted. But then there were footsteps on the stairs, Nan's voice.

'Mama? Pa, is anything amiss? What are you all doing in there?'

'You mother has had a slight fall,' Elihu shouted. 'But no harm done. You must not alarm the others. Please tell them she is well but needs a little rest and quiet.'

She argued, of course, tried to insist that she should see me, though finally she reluctantly obeyed.

'Not part of this?' I said to him when she was gone. 'And if the King…should learn…you willingly allowed this vessel…to be loaded with enough powder…to blow the entire royal party…to Kingdom Come?'

I saw the possibilities weighing upon him.

'Surely the king…' David Yale began, but Elihu stopped him, watched as I winced with the pains that still gripped me.

'You are hurt,' he said, though with no real concern in his voice. 'You fought with that girl?'

'Of course…I fought. But not now…Elihu.'

'Then what?' he implored me.

So I painfully explained. That he must garnish Mister Briggs sufficiently to win his silence. And Briggs must be clear that if he broke that silence there should be consequences.

'Consequences, Elihu – do you understand?' He nodded, and I continued. When we reached our destination, Briggs must send the lightermen ashore – to stretch their legs, or some other excuse, before unloading the cargo. The family too, naturally.

'If we are fortunate enough for our family to survive that long,' he hissed, looked up at the timbers, listened to the noise of our kin above our heads. 'God damn you, Catherine. We should put ashore at once.'

I ignored him, naturally.

'Then,' I said, 'we shall…slip this drab's body…over the stern… allow the tide…to do the rest…when it begins to ebb.' By the time we began our return journey, I told them, she would hopefully have beaten us to Nine Elms Reach or beyond.

'This is wickedness,' Elihu said, and began to beg the Almighty's forgiveness.

'Indeed,' I told him. 'But not so wicked…as the King's rage…if he discovers…your part in this.'

The lightermen would ask questions about their crewmate, naturally. But I had assumed the witch was acting alone in this, that Briggs had been duped by whatever false licence she carried. That she was unknown to the other oarsmen. Simple enough, I supposed, to claim she had come up from some farther section of the river in answer to the call that had gone out far and wide to fill tonight's excessive demand for additional watermen. We would say this eighth crewman had left the barge also. And if he had not appeared in time for the return – well, they managed without him most of the way there.

'Mister Briggs, I imagine,' said David Yale, 'shall be most biddable in being sworn to secrecy. After all, how should his reputation suffer? Bad enough to lose a lighterman but...'

'Please!' said Elihu. 'Bad enough to have my wife conspiring in this dreadful manner.'

'Yet...there are...the other casks to consider.'

'Uncle,' said David, 'you may say the King no longer requires them and allow Mister Briggs to dispose of them as he sees fit.'

The boy has promise, to be sure.

'Travel back two hours on a barge full of black powder?' said his uncle.

'Quite...safe, Elihu. Though you must...be careful...where you light...your pipes.'

Elihu was not amused.

'Or send for a coach,' said David. 'Use the excuse that the children are weary. Two further hours upon the river too much for them.'

'How might it be possible?' Elihu sighed. 'To keep all this between ourselves? And Briggs – may he be trusted?'

'Briggs is...the least...of your concerns, sirrah.'

'What do you mean, woman?' he snapped.

'Only this...that if we survive...you would not want...the King...to know. Would you, Elihu? So perhaps...you need to think afresh...about my proposition...that you should...get Innes released.'

For the rest? The *Courant* is accurate enough. The King and his party landed safely just after eleven o' the clock, dined at midnight in the grounds of Ranelagh House and Herr Handel was required to conduct his orchestra through the entire performance again – though I suspect he may have arranged the pieces rather differently so that the arrival of fresh dishes would have been greeted by one of those triumphant hornpipes, while the more gentle airs must have accompanied the feasting itself.

In any case, the supper continued until two in the morning, at which hour the royal guests took to their barges once more – as did the hundreds, perhaps thousands, who had eaten along the shores or upon their own vessels.

Meanwhile, all had proceeded as we planned. Mister Briggs brought into my husband's confidence – an embroidered version of events and an excessive quantity of garnish. Myself recovered enough to climb the stairs again, a feeble yarn about having been taken ill while using the chamber pot – yes, how embarrassing – then fallen and smashed the damn'd Oliver, cracked my ribs upon the deck and somehow damaged my throat too. The state of me. And the stink. Nan beside herself with concern. My apologies to James for having accidentally spilled his stingo flask.

'Spilled?' Kate scoffed. 'Truly?'

Hugs from sweet Polly, despite how I smelled.

The crew and my family, myself, the servants too, disembarked. Mary Astor committed to her watery grave by Briggs with Elihu and his nephew for accomplices. The King's lacquered chests collected on carts by the royal lackeys. Our own feast unloaded and prepared. And yes, I insisted, I should be well enough to join them if only I could receive a modicum of assistance. David was also kind enough to visit Ranelagh House in person, to explain my predicament – the invented one, naturally – and to bring me a change of attire and blankets.

Briggs also offered his own support by insisting he should open a couple of the other casks, to reveal only a single layer of pickled oyster bottles within, the rest of each barrel packed with deadly sacks beneath, exactly as I had supposed. But seemingly safe now, at least. It took little imagination to calculate the scale of explosion this quantity of gunpowder would have caused, the mayhem and murther it would have occasioned.

As our supper progressed, post boys dispatched to find coaches that, as David had suggested, might make for more convenient conveyance back to town.

Yet despite Annie's fevered protests and Polly's tears, I made the return journey alone, two painful hours back to the Somerset Stairs, for most of that time, when I was not asleep, serenaded by Herr Handel's musicians. For, as the *Courant* so accurately describes, our noble King had insisted on the entire performance being played, for the third time, as his barge rode the freshly ebbing tide downstream once more.

He had breathed his last between two and three o' the clock of the morning, seven days ago, his body preserved at his home in Ruscombe pending the arrangements for today's interment in the Friends' burial ground outside Chalfont St. Giles.

I would have made the journey to his funeral regardless, yet I was pleased not to travel far, a mere seven miles from my home. For that experience upon the Thames – more than a year gone already – has left me with a certain debility, a shortness of breath, a frequent aching in my bosom, even more unsteadiness upon my feet. So perhaps Mary Astor has had some revenge upon me after all.

Though I am still here, and should be thankful for it, while poor William Penn is now in the ground beside his first wife as he had wished.

'I wonder,' I said to Matthew as we waited in the green tranquility outside Old Jordan's Meeting House for the funeral cortege to arrive, 'what grief his present wife must have suffered in complying with his request.'

A warm and gentle wind stirred the tall hedgerows surrounding the grassy meadow with its neat pattern of headstones, and blackbirds sang in the trees.

'You are concerned, I suppose,' he smiled, 'at the sorrow you shall inflict upon Elihu when he discovers you wish to be buried with dear Joseph at Fort St. George.'

'A poor jest,' I scolded him, 'even for you, sir. In any case, I have no desire to spend eternity anywhere other than at Latimer.'

'I know it full well, madam. I never realised how impossible it might be to prise you away from there.'

A sore point between us. He has asked me so many times to

live with him at Downbury Hall, to renounce my wedding vows. And each refusal seems to hurt him more. I have spent much time there, though always with company, the proprieties carefully observed and our amorous liaisons entirely clandestine. Of course, I could simply have abandoned Elihu, but that would have risked Matthew being pursued in the courts for considerable quantities of adultery compensation. Elihu was never going to divorce me through a private Act of Parliament, first, due to the enormous cost and, second, because of the disgrace. It vexes me that, as a woman, of course, I have no right to pursue a divorce at all. And nor did I have a right to auction my husband, whereas he could – but would not – engage in a wife sale at any time he chooses. But that was not entirely the problem.

'You know my affection for you is boundless, Mister Parrish,' I teased him. 'But I understand I am too set in my ways now, have been so long allowed my own liberties, too selfish to ever again be able to share a home.' We leaned upon our respective walking canes – leaned away from each other, as though to put distance between ourselves and this discord. 'Besides,' I went on, 'since that business with Mary Astor, Elihu could not care less where I should be buried just so long as it happens soon.'

'Still vexed?' he said, as one of the Society's elders urged us to find a seat inside, for the crowd of mourners continued to grow. It astonished me how quickly word must have spread. The *Gazette* carried the news two days after Penn's death and we received that edition last Saturday, plenty of time to make my arrangements, to exchange word with Matthew. He had reached there before me and upon my arrival taken some time to name those mourners with whom I might not be familiar. Swift, renowned for his High Church sympathies and now Dean of St. Patrick's in Dublin, whose *Tale of a Tub* I have read. Old George Whitehead, the ancient Quaker preacher and essayist. William Dawes, Archbishop of York and William Wake, Archbishop of Canterbury. London's Chief Rabbi, Aaron Hart.

'Vexed would be an abysmal adumbration,' I told Parrish as we passed through into the close warmth of the panelled interior. It was not excessively large, wooden benches on all four sides and a long table at the centre, the floor red brick. It was already full but gave me to feel at peace, despite the numbers. 'I think he has never despised me quite so much as now.'

'Let me guess,' Matthew whispered as we took the only two remaining places on the pews. 'Furious that your duties for the Crown have put your family in such danger.'

'In truth? I think he resents me for denying him the opportunity to claim royal reward for his part in saving the King's life. It eats away at him, I collect. Denied him his entitlement yet again to become a Baron Knight.'

'And all compounded by living under the threat you might, to the contrary, betray him to the authorities – imply that he might not have been entirely innocent in allowing those barrels aboard his barge.'

I laughed – clamped a hand over my mouth when it occasioned such disapproving glances from those seated around us. Apart from those named by Parrish, there were several I knew myself. Horse-faced Daniel Defoe, his coat turned once again and now writing satirical pamphlets against his recent paymasters, the Tories. Sir Hans Sloane. Members of the local Penington clan, the family of Penn's first wife, and Friend William's son and daughter from that first marriage to Gulielma – the only two of their eleven children to have survived, the rest buried here at Jordan's too. Stanhope. And Walpole just along from him, though the two men were now bitterly divided, a schism within the Whig faction that had seen Walpole resign from his post as First Lord of the Treasury and Stanhope assuming that same position, as well as being Chancellor of the Exchequer, but now elevated to the House of Lords and sometimes serving as our nation's ambassador to Paris and Madrid.

'He never seems to have considered,' I said, 'how implausible that imagined threat might be – considering he had his entire family on board also. Or if he *has* smoked it, he had already fulfilled his promise to me.'

'The Innes brothers?'

'A letter from young Jamie last month. There was a legality to overcome. Something connected to this new Transportation Act. And the payment to secure release from his indenture with the Codrington plantations had to be made through the Treasury. Elihu has a friend there, Kirwood, who received the garnish and relayed it to the Gospel Society. Elihu had to stand as Kirwood's guarantor and then to settle the bond at once, but Innes wrote to say he expects to be back in the Highlands by Christmas.'

Elihu. And there he was, coming into the Meeting Room with David Yale at his side. I should have guessed, I suppose. Friend William went to visit him many times when my husband had been at a particularly low ebb at Queen Square, before Penn's own sequence of apoplexies over this past ten years. And today Elihu's extensive periwig seemed just too heavy for him, or perhaps it was the funereal black satins that weighed him down, for he has plainly grown considerably more feeble than when last I saw him, so evidently infirmed that several of those good folk on the benches opposite jumped up to gift him their place. He saw me then, though did not acknowledge me, and David offered me only the slightest of greetings.

But then we all heard the carriages arriving and we fell silent as the simple coffin was carried inside, draped with a green velvet pall embroidered by a tree of many branches. Behind the coffin, the solemn figure of Elijah Penington, an elder I knew from my visits to the village and, following Friend Elijah, the brave face of Hannah the widow, supporting their four young sons and only surviving daughter. She is a strong woman, I know, only recently returned from Pennsylvania where she has taken control of the colony there since her husband first fell ill. Yet she herself supported now by another woman of near my own age – and I had once met her also. Jane Fearon, that female minister of the Society who had so famously been imprisoned upon the Isle of Man for her preaching.

The coffin was set upon that central table and Penington explained, for the benefit of those unfamiliar with the practices within the Religious Society of Friends, that this meeting should provide space for silent worship to give thanks for the grace of God in the life of Friend William.

Parrish read a poem he had written for the occasion, *The Demon and the Dove: An Elegiac Tale* – that elicited tears of joy from many, and scowls of anger from my husband.

But through it all I kept my own counsel, my sacramental silence filled with memories of Friend William Penn. He had died a pauper, of course, and I had not really seen him since that feast at Devonshire

House – it would be thirteen years ago – when even then he was threatened with debtors' prison. But before that? I had first heard him speak alongside George Fox with Papa in the years before I married Joseph. And in some ways it was for Papa that I came there today. Penn had always been something of an enigma: friend to Catholic King James; friend to Protestant King William also; friend to Czar Peter of Muscovy – and I almost expected Czar Peter to be there among the mourners. Though, even if word could have reached him, I collect he is permanently occupied in his endless wars with the Swedes. Yet there, again, William Penn's dream that was Papa's dream too – a parliament of European states that would end these interminable divisions between us. And, finally, my recollections of Friend William's address at the Deptford Meeting House when I was embroiled by Seaton in his murderous designs, Penn's words in the aftermath.

'Satan quakes,' he had said, 'when the innocent take up arms.'

I had never been certain whether his aphorism was entirely in keeping with the Religious Society's teachings, but it has served me well enough, I suppose.

And when all was done, each person present shook the hand of our neighbours while the coffin was carried outside again to Friend William's final rest.

'Mistress Yale,' said Stanhope, as we gathered in the grassy meadow where Penn's grave had been so recently dug – in truth, it is rather the burial plot for so much of his first family. 'Sad occasion, is it not?'

He must be twenty years younger than me but looks now to be my senior. His once handsome features have turned sallow and bloated at the same time. He had not shaved and his dark clothes, his long black peruke, seemed more to foreshadow his own end than to mark the passing of Friend William.

'It is good to see so many here for his farewell, and from such diversity of faith or faction,' I replied. 'A goodly depository for his mortal remains too, do you not think?' And so it was, the burial ground inviting each of us to contemplate its occupants despite the thin summer shower now threatening to dampen our tranquility.

Stanhope agreed, summoning a manservant – who soon dutifully opened a rain napper over our heads – then exchanged polite words with Matthew, hoped that he had now recovered fully from his injuries at Preston.

'And you, madam,' he whispered, 'from your tribulations upon the Thames.'

I had scribbled a confidential report for him, naturally. And there had been loose ends to be tied – barge-master Briggs cleared of any involvement but the supplier of those barrels, several conspirators, silently dispatched.

'They have left their mark, lordship.' I glanced over to where Elihu was engaged in some heated debate with the Archbishop of Canterbury. 'But I hope Mary Astor's end was at least the final nail in the Jacobites' own coffin.'

'I fear,' said Matthew, 'we may never be rid of them. We might have the Frenchies for allies now, but if there is war with Spain...'

An alliance had been formed. An alliance that was edging us towards conflict with the Spanish. An alliance between France, the Dutch Republic, the Holy Roman Empire and Britain. This latter word was a distraction, the Act of Union already eleven years old and yet still so unfamiliar, so mistrusted on both sides of the Tweed.

'I shall never be used to it,' I said, 'this idea we are now somehow *Britain*.'

But both men paid scant regard to my comment.

'Of course, Parrish.' Stanhope nodded his head. 'Spain will arm the devils all over again. And those Jack Highlanders never seem to learn their lesson.'

I thought about Jamie Innes and his brothers. Surely they would not be so foolish. But by then Friend William was being lowered into the rich loam and Elijah Penington was reading words of consolation, the deceased's own words, he told us.

'Though death may be a dark passage,' he said, 'it leads to immortality. The truest end of life is to know that life never ends. And he that lives to live ever, never fears dying.'

I find I cannot quite bring myself to excessive enthusiasm for heaven and eternity, since that would have the effect of diminishing this brief mortality. I am told there are those heretics who possess no belief in the hereafter at all and, while it is impossible for me to credit that lack of faith, I rather envy them the simplicity of their existence. Only one life? How they must savour it. Whereas some of the most godly folk I have known are so obsessed with eternity they seem blind to the glories of this jewelled earth. Or like Elihu, intent on purchasing their place in paradise.

'But we owe you a great debt, Mistress Yale,' said Stanhope. 'Simply a pity we cannot recognise the debt with greater reward. Still, the whole incident must still be kept from His Majesty. For the nonce, at least. But when the time is right...'

'Your office has already rewarded me enough, sir,' I told him. 'And reward was never my intention. Yet you have, I understand, received your own good fortune.'

The circles of life are strange at times. There had been that diamond of Governor Pitt's.

'The brilliant,' said Parrish. 'Sold at last?'

I had lost interest in it after Nicks died and my Jewish friends in the trade had informed me, not two weeks past, that it was finally purchased by the French Regent, the Duke of Orléans.

'One hundred and thirty-five thousand pounds.' I spoke the words slowly, with all the awe that amount deserved.

'You are too well informed, madam,' Stanhope murmured, as Penington's reading came to an end and we were invited to the building adjoining the Meeting House, where refreshments would be served.

'Your father-in-law *did* tell you the price, I collect?' I smiled. For there was the rub, the twist in the rub. That Stanhope had, some time ago, married Pitt's daughter – Pitt presently Governor of Jamaica. 'And if there should be scope for my further reward, sirrah, it would be this. There may be an argument put forward by the estate of Katherine Nicks that the portion of the diamond's worth she was owed should be paid to her children – and I hope I may rely upon you to ensure such a calumny cannot come to pass.'

'Well,' I said to David Yale as I picked at the food, simple cold meats and cheeses, 'you have no word for me?'

He was hardly delighted to see me. But Matthew had taken up a conversation with Walpole. Elihu still hounded the Archbishop but took every opportunity to glower at me whenever he caught my eye. And David was at last alone, I did not want the day to pass without confronting him about the breach that seemed to have opened between us. I had not yet done with him.

'I came to realise I do not know you, Aunt,' he frowned. 'And that girl – great heavens, the commandment that we shall not kill...'

I could see Mary Astor's ruined face again, dim in the darkness, that gaping astonishment, the light fading from her eyes. And I imagined David Yale's turmoil as he helped Briggs heave the harlot's body over the stern of our barge.

'You did not. Kill her, I mean. I did.'

I set down my dish, smoothed the charcoal silks of my skirts, tried to summon the patience I needed for this discussion.

'And you feel no remorse at the deed?' He spat the words at me.

'I shall answer before God Almighty when the time is appropriate. But remorse? No, never that. There is evil in the world, young man, and there can be no remorse in destroying it. When your uncle was Governor of Fort St. George he understood that, at least.'

'Did he truly?' he hissed. 'Well now he is preoccupied with other matters.'

'Dummer's college, I suppose. You know not how he ensnares you, boy.'

Friend William's daughter from his marriage to Gulielma, Letitia, brought a tray with cups of fresh goat's milk.

'If it helps in your intelligence gathering, madam – for that is your trade, I collect – then you should know my uncle is more concerned with the Gospel Society. Though perhaps the two things are one. I must admit myself surprised he came here today at all, for he says he has declared war against all Dissenters.'

Hannah Penn came to us, upon the arm of Elijah Penington, her children in tow, making the rounds to thank all those who had come to honour her husband's memory.

'War against Dissenters?' I said, as she moved on, after we had exchanged a few polite words, Hannah confirming she must soon return to Pennsylvania. 'He means war against me, does he not?'

He bit his lip, troubled by our discussion, I think.

'Ensnares?' he said. 'He wishes me to choose sides. There is a representative of the Colony, Reverend Mather, who has written to Uncle Elihu. He gave me the letter to read on our journey here.'

He dug into the pocket of his coat, made certain that Elihu's gaze was averted elsewhere. And I read the contents, following David's lead and keeping my back turned as I did so. There was considerable opening flattery, reminders of the Yale connection to New Haven, where the college is now located. And then this.

And your munificence might easily obtain for you such a commemoration and perpetuation of your valuable name, which would indeed be much better than an Egyptian pyramid.

That final word tore at my heart and I touched the locket at my throat, with its images of Walter and little Davy.

'Could this Reverend Mather,' I sobbed, 'possibly know that my own sweet little David lies under his own pyramid at Madras Patnam?'

Alongside my dear Joseph, I thought, just as William Penn now lies beside his first wife here at Jordan's. No, that was a foolishness. But how this letter must have made Elihu swagger. His name upon a college? I remembered the envy in his voice when he told me the story of his father's friendship with Reverend John Harvard – how Harvard's name has now become so synonymous with the glory of God's truth and enlightenment.

'Does your distaste for me stem from my name, then?' David Yale asked me.

'In the beginning perhaps,' I said. 'But now?' I returned the letter to him as clandestinely as I was able. 'Now we are at least accomplices, I suppose. Yet he has responded? To the letter?'

'Initially only with disdain. He said that even to get his name above the door he would do nothing to help an institution so much under the thumb of Puritans and Dissenters. He is a true son of the Church of England, of course. And the son of a father driven from Boston by those same Puritans.'

Elihu burst upon us like a storm. To be more precise, he hobbled towards us but with a face like thunder.

'Puritans?' he shouted, and drew quizzical stares from those closest to us. 'New England Puritans, you say? Plague on them. But the Gospel Society has convinced me it is my duty before God to send missionaries to Connecticut.'

'And no better way to do so,' I mocked him, 'than to gain a foothold through the New Haven college. So, you have bestowed bounty upon them?'

'I see it as no concern of your own, madam,' he said, then pressed his face close to mine. His breath stank. And those teeth, now entirely rotten. His skin, at close quarters, is flaked like fish scales. 'But books,' he hissed. 'Yes, books. It amuses me to think that books – *my* books – shall help to poison Dissenter belief. A first step towards restoring all New England churches to the Anglican faith. Does that not enchant you, wife? That I shall be the weapon by which Dissenter heretics might we swept aside.'

'Heretics like me, Elihu?'

'Like you,' he spat, and stumbled away again.

'Books?' I said, and sipped again at my milk.

I think David was shocked at Elihu's vehemence.

'Not books alone,' he replied, his tone more mellow now than it had been previously. 'A cargo of muslins, calicoes, poplins, silks and camlets for sale too. Worth a considerable amount. But a collection of books for their library. Four hundred, I think. Plutarch's *Lives*; Heylyn's *Cosmographie*; Bishop Griffith's *The True Church*; and dozens of others. I cannot recall them all. But yes, it amuses him to think he crusades against the heathen.'

'Has he time? He looks too feeble.'

'That is less than Christian.'

'You know how he despises me. Wishes me dead, I collect. And, if so, I do not relish the prospect of death. Yet, of late, I have come to view it as an unwanted journey that I must plainly make before too long and for which, therefore, the expectation is more uncomfortable than the event itself is likely to be, thus making me somewhat impatient for the passage. To be reunited with my one true husband, with my sons.'

'Your losses must be a heavy burden, madam. I shall pray for you when I am at Cambridge.'

'Cambridge?'

'I commence there in January. Pembroke.'

'Then you have chosen your side already, David. Great heavens, have you no loyalty to the Colony of your birth, sirrah? You shall stand aside in Cambridge while Mister Yale helps force your friends, your family, to now conform? Become slaves to his High Church. Well, boy, shall you?'

Tuesday 2nd July 1719

He came for me. I had known it would be him when I heard the carriage wheels crunching upon the gravel, the neighing of horses. But today, of all days, and while I tried to find a moment of quiet contemplation in the chapel. Quiet and dark. For while it might be no more than a week past midsummer, yet it has felt like winter. Perhaps the ice in my heart.

'So,' Elihu cried as he eventually hobbled in from the porch, 'you are here.' I squeezed my eyes tight shut in the vain hope that I might dispel his presence. 'Damn their eyes, those scoundrels you employ refused to tell me where I might find you. Did you instruct them?'

'Had I known you intended to visit, sir, I should certainly have done so.'

I pushed myself upright, pulled my emerald shawl more tightly about my shoulders, turned to face him – he back there at the font, myself at the opposite end, the foremost pews, near the altar and vestry.

'He is gone,' Elihu raged. 'And I am sensible of your part in his – well, his parting.'

I waved my psalter at him.

'You know well he left you in spirit many months ago. You expected him to become a weapon, one that you and your High Church friends of the Gospel Society might use.'

He finally remembered to d'off his hat, scratched beneath his periwig.

'It is the duty,' he shouted, limping back and forth, 'of all good folk to help spread the word of God, no matter what form that may take. Those rogues in Connecticut – I send them another cargo of precious books, a valued portrait of the King, and how am I repaid? By David's departure.'

I had met the young man before he sailed back to the colony. He in turn had been with Jeremiah Dummer who had written to the Trustees of the Connecticut College confirming that Elihu would be honoured to allow his name to be associated with that institution. He believed the Trustees would confirm the decision later in the year, though Dummer was mindful of Elihu's clandestine purpose.

'You may have lost David, but has he not served your ends? Your name above the college door? Though I think now his return to New Haven shall allow him to give first-hand evidence of your pitiful attempts to turn their beliefs.'

I swear he stamped his foot, but I sat upon the pew once more.

'You conspired in this,' he said. 'I knew it. Well, he shall not be my heir. He shall not!'

I gazed up at the black-painted ceiling beams, ran my fingers along the polished oak of the bench, sniffed at the beeswax that lent such gleaming refinement to the wood – and I slapped my hand down upon the pew, the retort echoing around the whitewashed walls.

'You still have that by-blow,' I shouted. 'Where is he now? Pegu?' There was silence. I turned in my seat, saw the look of astonishment upon his face. But Nan had told me. His letters to Elihu Nicks, his arrangements for yet more fresh supplies of goods to be sent from that distant and mysterious lands. 'Pegu Earth Oil,' I laughed. 'You think that will cure your ailments, sir? Lubricate your gouty joints? And so it may – though you may be assured it can never smooth your way to having Nicks's son as your legitimate heir. You lost David and he may not be replaced.'

Of course, he could not. He may wish it but to acknowledge that other Elihu would be to also confess his adultery. He dragged the peruke from his head, threw it down upon the floor in frustration.

'You turned him against me. Do not deny it.'

I stood, my fists clenched in fury.

'War on Dissenters,' I said. 'Was that not what you promised? Well, I shall give you war, sirrah. War is already upon you.'

Helping deprive him of an heir was simply the beginning of my campaign yet, to my surprise, he smiled at me. As though he had scored some great victory. Then he sat himself upon the pew nearest to him, preening himself with smugness.

'And upon you, madam,' he smirked. 'Ask your precious son what he thinks.'

Benjamin. Since his return from Preston – more than two years ago now – he had been writing an account of that last rebellion. An excellent account, the completion of which had coincided with David's first announcement of his intended return to Connecticut. And when Benji sought subscribers they had been difficult to find, a significant amount of ballad sheets and pamphlets defaming the accuracy of the details. Some prominent names publicly denouncing Benji's abilities as a historian, satires written against him – Dean Swift among the worst of his detractors – and the stench of Elihu's fingers in the pie.

'You think,' I said, 'we did not know it was your gold that financed the slurs against him?'

Of course we did, and I had accordingly taken my own action – though I collect he could not presently know the scale of it.

'And war you say, Catherine? Is there never enough war to satisfy you?'

Did he truly believe I relished the mindless slaughter that men – yes, always men – inflict upon each other, upon us all? Though, sweet Jesu, he was right in part. For I had thought it was all over, should have known better.

My first inkling had been the letter from Jamie Innes, when he was about to sail home, a free man. He had assured me his brothers were well and that he had never lost faith in the prospect of freedom. *Sometimes,* he had written, *all we need is hope that escape is possible.* But then there had been some reference I did not follow. He trusted his return might be timely, he said. For what? I had wondered.

It puzzled me all through the spring and meanwhile our four-way alliance had triggered war with Spain precisely as intended. Then a visit from Parrish, still just in touch with some of Stanhope's former agents. And there was a rumour. A Scottish merchant in Spain, Pringle, trusted by the Jacobites but, in truth, loyal to King George. He sent word, Matthew had learned, of a planned Spanish invasion.

415

An intention to land in Southwest England, an army of seven thousand Spaniards to take London. A much smaller force to land in Scotland, link with Scots Jacobites there and take Edinburgh. But divine tempest meant that the seven thousand never arrived and only the smaller contingent found their way to the Highlands. Three hundred Spanish marines, two frigates, joined by William Mackenzie, Earl of Seaforth and William Murray, Lord Tullibardine, with one thousand Jack Highlanders, while a similar force of government regulars and a Highland Independent Company with artillery – mortars I think – under General Wightman, caught them at a place named by the *Courant* as Glen Shiel and defeated them. And I had prayed that Jamie Innes and his kin could not, by then, have completed their travels.

'I would wish war on nobody, sir,' I said. 'It is an abomination. Yet it seems it will now touch us no more.'

The battle may indeed have brought all Jacobite aspirations finally to an end. The leaders not even pursued. Their campaign such a disaster they have made the Jacobite cause no more than a bitter jest. And Matthew believes that this and other defeats will at least force Spain to the peace table.

'Then you will not have seen this.' He reached into the deep pocket of his cinnamon-coloured coat, pulled out a sheet of newspaper. He flung it down the aisle towards me, though it simply fluttered a few feet and he made no effort to retrieve it. But I could see it was a copy of the *Gazette*.

'I am no serving wench,' I spat, 'to pick up that which you have so carelessly discarded.'

He took a step towards me, then stopped.

'Perhaps better for your conscience, after all, to let it rest. It would not serve the virtue of dear Catherine, I suppose, to confront the repercussions of her own deeds. Naturally, that should never answer.'

Elihu bent down with great difficulty, picked up his periwig, shook it before setting it back upon his pate. I knew I was defeated, collected my cane and walked down the aisle towards him, stopped at the *Gazette* and stooped to collect it.

'What?' I snapped, this reverse side of the broadsheet contained all the normal advertisements, a notice from the Merchant Taylors' Company and two resolutions passed by the House of Commons. But Elihu carved a sneering circle in the air with his finger and

I dutifully turned the paper over to the front page. Some paragraphs from last month about Czar Peter's sea war against the Swedes – reports from St. Petersburg, from Hanover and from Copenhagen. Then the second column. The Duke of Bolton's speech to Parliament about the continuing threat of the Jacobite cause in Ireland and there, finally, Lord Carteret's latest account on the aftermath of that engagement at Glen Shiel. I peered closely at the words. The rebels, it seems, had left few of their dead or wounded behind but here was a list of those deceased Jacobite officers identified upon the field. And yes, of course, Jamie Innes of Coxton was among them.

'You see, wife?' He spat that word too. 'Without your interference he would have been safe in the King's justice and his indenture to the Codrington plantations.'

The pain pierced me, the way the ball or mortar shell fragment may have pierced the heart of that generous though ill-advised young Highlander. A lion led to a wasted demise by the architects of artifice in a dishonest cause.

'A slave you mean,' I said, slumping heavily onto the nearest pew. 'I did not know him well enough, I collect – yet sufficient to be certain he would have chosen death over enslavement by your High Church any day.'

Though I did not feel entirely sure about that. And there was no mention, naturally, of the brothers, sweet-faced Callum and Donald the giant. But here was something about which I could have no doubt – that if the body of Jamie Innes lay untended on that barren heath, it could only mean that his brothers slept beside him.

'Sympathy for those of the Romish faith after all this time, madam?'

'Perhaps I have come to wish a plague upon all our houses,' I said, though I was thinking about Thomas Forster, wondering how much that other man I had helped escape might have aided design of this latest foolish endeavour, foment the passions of their disciples. For how quickly folk may be stirred by evil eloquence to follow even unto death some mere formless notion that, in truth, will serve them not the least. But guilt and remorse? Oh yes, in abundance, sufficient to trump any blame I might heap on others.

'The plague,' he said, 'is that I simply wasted my money. I paid my due to the Treasury and Kirwood received the payment into his coffers with my bond as surety. The Gospel Society collected their due and Innes was released, Yet I did not promise to keep him alive. And heaven knows I am already bleeding sufficient money at this moment.'

But not as much as you shall do soon, if I have my way, I thought.

'You must be weeping all the way to Hoare's, sirrah,' I said. 'Annie tells me you received payment from the Sun.'

'A pittance, madam. A fraction of all I lost.'

I thought he should weep tears of rage. Two of his houses on King Street, destroyed by fire and countless quantities of his valuables – furniture, floor carpeting, bales of the finest cloth, baubles of silver and gold. All gone. And I had known it would cut him to the bone. Wadham too old now to provide the service for me, though he has associates. Reliable associates. And there was this also, that I had now received my further dividend from the enterprise I established so long ago with poor Sir William Langhorn, assurances for maritime cargoes. For that establishment had developed a little. He may have thought it was the Sun Fire Assurance Company that covered him but in truth it was an offspring of my own business.

The same arrangement, my name secretly written under the necessary contracts – in this case with a certain Elihu Yale, one contract for each of his many properties and for the goods stored therein, and the necessary premiums collected from him. The fire had simply been a way to wound him, the four thousand pounds we awarded him indeed a mere fraction against the true value of his losses and a satisfactory additional reward. Yet perhaps the greatest satisfaction came from the careful removals undertaken by Wadham's associates before the fire was set – and those beauteous objects now stored in my own godown. And my final recompense? That my own interests and stock had been transferred to the real Sun Fire Assurance, sold to my considerable additional profit.

'I wish it gave me some satisfaction, sir, this blow to your arrogance. But this news...'

I read the words one last time, then balled the broadsheet in my fist. And good Lord Almighty, yes, I know it was Thee. One more payment for my wickedness.

'I sometimes feel there is a serpent in my bed,' Elihu told me, as though I might be responsible for hiding it there. 'But this – if you had left all this in God's hands, as I counselled, perhaps Innes might still alive.'

'Was it not God that guided me? Is not this all God's will?'

'How can that be when you are a Dissenter, a heretic?'

He sought to wound me, though perhaps he acquitted me instead. And I lifted the crumpled copy of the *Gazette* towards him.

'You brought me this,' I said, 'as you once brought me the body of my boy. Too late, too stupid to save him.'

Elihu regarded me as though I should be returned to the Bethlem Hospital without delay. Yet I saw the pain fill his eyes too.

'Little Walter,' he said. 'What has this…?'

'Forty-five years ago,' I hissed. 'Forty-five years ago this very day.'

Yes, today of all days.

Saint Bartholomew, as we all know, was flayed alive. And it was in my mind today that this was the revenge I was inflicting upon Elihu, flensing not his flesh but the fortune from the now decrepit sinews of his soul.

I have not seen him since that day, more than a year ago, when he brought me news of Jamie's death. Damn him. But I have worked hard to repay the compliment. And while I have arranged to meet Annie at today's Bartholomew Fair principally to renew acquaintance with my daughter and her children, I also wished to ascertain the extent to which the blow I aimed at him has hit its mark.

'Shall we see the puppet show, Mama?' Ursula cried, and I swear she was more animated than Nan's two youngsters, or even little Polly, who was staying with her too.

'Bartholomew Fair without a puppet show, sister?' Annie laughed. 'La, what might Mister Jonson say? Yet you are such an innocent, my dear.'

Ursula smiled, took this as a considerable compliment. For innocence, she believes, is the most godly of attributes. But in truth I was looking forward to the performance myself, this year's puppetry production an adaptation by my old friend Colley Cibber, of Jonson's own *Saint Bartholomew's Fair*. How prime.

'And your papa?' I asked Nan, while William, Elizabeth, Polly – and yes, Ursi also – munched on their gingerbread.

We had all met, appropriately enough, outside Barts, which I last visited on the night Vincent Seaton so grievously wounded Katherine Nicks. But this evening it was all good humour at the stage by the hospital gate where players acted out *Sir Richard Whittington*. And from there we strolled through the booths, stalls and tents that pressed hard up against the walls of the hospital itself and spread all across the Smith Field pastures. Not too late in the evening but a twilight filled with ten thousand voices, with fiddle, fife, rattle and drum, with wood smoke smut settling upon our faces, and meat fats sizzling upon open fires.

'Well enough,' Annie replied. Her words were guarded and I could always tell when Nan was giving me only half the truth. 'A letter from the trustees of that college in Connecticut,' she told me – though she must have known I would already have that intelligence from young David. 'Now Yale College, they say. Yet he seems less delighted than I should have imagined.' I tried not to smile. 'And the other Nicks girl, Betty,' she went on, 'married – though not as well as Papa should have liked, though he will not say as much.'

'Life so full of disappointments then,' I said, as we stopped at a brazier where pork was roasting – and I chose not to press her further for the news I truly sought. Not just then.

'I have such a craving,' she told me as though it were a guilty secret. 'Goodness, you would almost think…'

'You are not…?' I said.

'Another babe?' Ursula almost jumped for joy.

'Indeed no,' Nan protested, after she handed over the tuppence for her meat and shared some of it with little William – nine already and a sweet boy. 'There shall be no more.'

The birth of Elizabeth had been "difficult" – I think that was the euphemism employed by the physicians at the time. A pity, for she is a good mother, unlike her older sister. And now she guided the three youngsters through the maze of attractions here.

'May we, Mama?' said Ursula, and the three youngsters took up her plea as we wandered into that portion of the fields where the swing-boats and merry-go-rounds had been erected. I paid their pennies and stood back with Annie while the showman worked his lever back and forth, taking them ever higher and eliciting louder and louder screams from them.

'Bless them,' I said. 'Such innocence. I only pray that now, at last, we may have peace a while.'

A treaty had been signed, at The Hague. The end of the war with Spain, thank heaven. And Nan looked about at the crowds of pleasure-seekers drifting past.

'I think, Mama,' she said, 'I have never seen so many at the fair as this.'

She had it aright, I collect. As though the whole city, for these few fleeting days, had set aside its cares, severed the chains of harsh daily reality, thrown itself into a frenzy of felicity – from much of which we must needs protect the children.

'Nor so many at their debaucheries,' I replied, averting my eyes from the couple who rutted so vigorously, with so many squeals of delight, within one of the merry-go-round carriages.

'The crisis, I suppose,' said Nan. It was the word of the month. 'Folk trying to forget.'

The nation's debt. And the value of the South Sea Company's stock – which any fool must have known could not continue to rise so substantially, to raise such income for the Crown – has of course begun to fall most sharply. Bankruptcies already. Finance houses and goldsmiths beginning to teeter. Far worse to come, I fear. Shares that Streynsham had purchased at one hundred pounds each, he wisely sold two months ago for eight times that amount, when it seemed the whole world was clamouring still to buy – a fevered scramble that infected everybody from the lowliest peasant to the mightiest lord. For myself I would not touch them. So much of the Company's gold raised through the trade in slaves. So great my suspicion of corruption in its dealings.

'And your father?' I said, as Ursula brought her nieces and nephew back to us. 'Among the winners? Or shall he join those clinging to the sinking ship, sure she will right herself once more?'

'He believes himself safe from any loss,' said Nan. 'Why do you ask?'

The children insisted on visiting the Temple of Arts with its clever moving images, ships sailing as though truly at sea, ducks swimming upon a flowing river. Oh, the wonders of this modern age, but the cupidity among our citizens it seems to carry in its wake.

'Merely that I heard a rumour,' I told her. 'Another bond he was persuaded to put up – against that friend of his. The goldsmith contracted to the Treasury. What is the fellow's name again?'

She stopped abruptly.

'Mama,' she said. 'Tell me you had no hand in this.'

Ahead of us there was a scuffle, some drunken hackum being hauled away by the constables.

'A hand?' I said, as innocently as I was able.

'Mister Kirwood,' she snapped. 'Surely you must know.'

'Kirwood, yes. Indeed. I knew the name only because it was through his bank that the payment had been made – the payment to release that unfortunate Jack Highlander who showed me such care in Preston.' The girls know only the barest details of the dangers myself and Benjamin had faced in that town. 'Kirwood. Something has happened to him?'

Sir Matthew Kirwood. No wonder the Receiver-General had demanded such surety before contracting with him more permanently to act as a banking collection point for businesses to pay revenue they owed the Treasury. It was Wadham's associates who told me how narrowly Kirwood had, only a few years earlier, escaped prosecution in relation to tickets from the state's Malt Lottery he had apparently "lost." Yet he had been knighted all the same. But now...

'Disappeared, Mama, as I'm certain you already know.'

Here were the grotesques and I tried to steer the children away from them, for this whole section reminded me too much of the Bethlem Hospital. And that recollection brought to mind that it was Elihu responsible for my incarceration there.

'Come, little ones,' I cried, though it was almost impossible to tear them away. In the end, I managed to distract them with a circle of hot sausage for us all to share.

'Absconded without trace,' said Nan. 'Along with thirteen thousand pounds of the Treasury's money.'

To be precise, thirteen thousand, seven hundred and ninety pounds. Plus eight shillings and thruppence farthing. From his premises at the sign of the Golden Fleece, on Lombard Street.

'Gracious,' I said. 'I had no idea the amount was so great. And does the Treasury pursue him?'

'They pursue Papa, who so foolishly signed another bond against Sir Matthew's good name. A bond for forty thousand pounds.'

I almost choked on the sausage. How exquisite. I knew there was a bond, but I could not have expected such an amount in my wildest dreams. Forty thousand. Great heavens, sufficient for a gentleman to live upon his entire life. He could have purchased a dozen prime properties in the most expensive sections of the city and still had sufficient change to furnish them all. It must wound him deeply. Oh, how I hope so.

'And shall the Treasury succeed in their pursuit?'

'The court has already found against him. Though he says he shall surely win upon appeal. New evidence, it seems. That Kirwood dutifully paid the money to one of the Treasury's own agents. A man called Gull. Conrad Gull.'

But Gull was, of course, that same associate of Wadham the thief-taker. And Kirwood had taken little persuasion that it would be in his best interests to vanish from the public eye a while. There had been garnish to pay, naturally, to Gull and to Kirwood, now in Amsterdam. And it would have been less than moral had I taken the balance of the Crown's gold for my personal gain. So I have invested my share in the Greenwich Blue Coat Girls' Charity School.

'Then I am sure your father's attorneys,' I said, 'will prosecute his defence most admirably. Yet Kirwood disappeared? Why, the scrub. It certainly has all the marks of a defalcation, does it not?'

'You are certain,' said Nan, 'that you have played no part?'

'I am merely shocked that you should think so,' I scolded her, then called to the children. 'See, you rascals? A pleasure wheel. Should you care to ride?'

They seemed less than certain, for it was a considerable height. But we finally settled upon myself, Ursi and little Polly in one chair, with Nan, Will and Lizzy in the other.

'What is a soiled dove, Mama?' Ursula asked me as our whole team of strong men worked the capstan that, in turn, slowly span the creaking wheel and lifted us shakily skywards.

'Soiled...' I began, then saw the sign too, illuminated by red lanthorns, in the tent below us, in the appropriately named Cock Lane. 'Oh, but see,' I pointed in the opposite direction, 'Mistress Salmon's Waxworks. We must go and see those wonders, my dear.'

And so we did, wondering especially at the chillingly realistic mechanical tableau of Charles the First's execution. Though that was later, after the display of pugilation, after we consulted the Learned Pig and had our fortunes foretold – yet before we finally arrived at the puppet show, that second performance of the evening. Cibber's adaptation kept all the riotous mayhem of the original with simple jests for the young ones and more bawdy double meanings that only the older folk in the audience might understand.

Saint Bartholomew's Fair. And when the puppet representing Justice Overdo repented in the final scene, offered forgiveness to all the play's malefactors, Nan quietly asked me whether I thought myself and her father might ever be reconciled.

'Dear Annie,' I replied, Jonson in my mind, though it were *Sejanus* rather than this present work. '"He threatens many that has injured one."'

'It says here that you are dying, Elihu,' I told him, leaning from the chair to hold that copy of the *Weekly Journal* towards him, though he was too far gone, I think, to see it properly. He was diminished, there upon his bed, the nightgown, the banyan and the turban each too large for this smaller frame into which my husband had shrunk. 'It says you lie at the point of death.'

'Not...ready...yet,' he managed to whisper.

I had never been inside his house before. I had passed the outside many times, of course, when I was lodged across the square, in Devonshire Street and I never believed I should cross the threshold, still did not wish to do so, but Nan had known I was in town and sent word that her father had suffered an apoplexy and was unlikely to survive, begged me to visit and make my peace with him before God. It had been impossible to deny her. And then, this morning, as I left Richard's, there had been this copy of the *Journal*.

'Still,' I said, as the candles flickered and the shadows deepened his sunken features still further, 'it must be true, for it says so here, in black and white.'

The bedchamber stank, of course. He had never been generous with his servants and I suspected they might now be returning the favour. The stench of his unwashed body, the foulness of his breath, the neglected Oliver.

'Getting...better,' he managed to say.

'Truly?' I said, and looked around the room. Despite the gloom, it was plain that even this inner sanctum served as a repository for his collected treasures, several travel chests stacked one upon the other and ornate picture frames leaning willy-nilly against the walls. 'Have your children been to see you like this?'

'Ursi...with you?'

'Too unwell, herself, to travel. That legacy from your friend, Seaton. You recall? But Kate – has she stirred herself away from Suffolk?'

'Don't...know.'

No, of course she had not. Too occupied with her life at Glemham, as usual.

'And have you – well, I do not wish to be abrupt, but have you left all in order?'

'Must...help. My will...Wrexham. I did...not mean...'

'Did not mean what, precisely?' I snapped. Some form of pathetic deathbed confession? Oh, where has he gone, I thought, that strutting peacock who landed in my life from the *masula* boats of Madras Patnam?

'Foolish...thing to say.' He gasped for breath, and I had to bend forward to catch his words properly. 'Foolish...but should...have allowed...me in.'

'I should have allowed you – where?'

But he was rambling now, I think.

'Baby...Walter,' he whispered. 'God has...shown me... I was wrong. Babe...not alive.'

Walt. He meant little Walt. And oh, how I prayed, as I have prayed so often before, that this foolish man had been mistaken about hearing my child's cries from the grave. The death wicked enough in itself, but the idea of that sweet infant suffering such terror...

'It is with your attorney in Wrexham?' I fought back my own sobs, that same terror too. 'The will?'

'Need...to add...'

'A little late for that, sir.'

'Always him,' he wheezed, the breath rattling in his throat. 'Hynmers...always Joseph...never me. And...your boys...'

My boys. Yes, but where are they all now?

'And you, Elihu. With you it was all about wealth. That endless pursuit of wealth.'

'God's gift...to me.'

Oh, the times I have heard the lecture.

'You wanted to be as rich as Virji Vora, did you not? I wonder how each of your tallies have ended up. And Joseph? Joseph loved me for the person into whom I had become through his adoration. He curbed the excesses that would otherwise have made me intolerable – the person that, after he was gone, I had striven to remain though, in truth, the person I miss now almost as much as I still miss Joseph himself.'

I watched a tear form in the corner of his fading eye and run down his cheek.

'Not…all bad. Our…time? Please…say it was so.'

'All bad? You ask me that? Though…'

'You could…have loved me.'

It came like a child's plea, as though an infant himself, speaking to his own mama.

'Perhaps I did,' I said. Though perhaps that was only in my mind. 'A little.'

It seemed pointless to say more and, by then, he had raised himself a little from the pillows, was pointing to the small cabinet close to his bed.

'Epitaph,' he said. 'Shall you…make sure…' I rose from the chair and went to examine the thing.

But as I did so there was a demon's howl and something shot from beneath the cabinet's legs. I screamed too, leapt back, clutched at my own heart. Scrabbling and scratching upon the floorboards. A cat. He owned a damn'd housecat. But perhaps the creature had given him some comfort.

'First…drawer,' he told me and fell back.

Inside there were many papers, and among them some lines he had written, though the script was uneven. Poetry. I lifted a candlestick, peered at the words.

Born in America, in Europe bred,
In Afric travell'd and in Asia wed,
Where long he liv'd and thriv'd; at…dead.
Much good, some ill, he did; so hope all's even,
And that his soul, through mercy's gone to heaven.

There was a space on that third line, for the place of his death to be added, I supposed.

'This?' I said.

'Epitaph…for my…tomb.'

Tomb, I thought. No simple headstone for Elihu Yale then. Such conceit. Though what else might I have expected?

'And when, precisely, did you travel in Africa, my dear? Shall you be a dissembler, even in death? For all eternity?'

'Cape...Town.'

'You stopped in Cape Town on your journey home,' I said. 'You think that qualifies?'

'You...weary me.'

He turned his head, closed his eyes.

There was something familiar about the wording, though I could not quite recall where I might have seen it. Matthew would know, I supposed, though it mattered little. It would not have been Elihu without him acting the plagiarist.

'Parrish could have done it so much better,' I said, and his eyes opened once more, his body tensed, his mouth opened and trembled. 'I may ask him to make a few improvements.'

The thought amused me. And it pleased me that mention of Parrish must hurt him so. There was just the ghost of a smile.

'Final...word.'

'You think this will be some final riposte to Matthew?' I almost choked with laughter, and something in the verse caused me to think of that last collection of Parrish's poems, another idea was conceived within me. 'Perhaps it cries out for amendment,' I smiled.

'God...damn you.'

'Oh, I think our Lord God shall be too busy with your own damnation, Elihu.'

'Served Him...all my life.'

'Truly? If, as you always told me, the creation of wealth is a gift from God – a denial of His will should you neglect to use that gift – then surely an insult to the Almighty if you later lose that wealth again so carelessly? The Almighty must surely seek to punish you.'

'Lose?' he gasped, choked a little on the word.

'Forty thousand pounds, my dear. The bond. The court case against you by the Treasury.'

'My...appeal.'

I took from my skirts the thing that had brought me to town in the first place. The judgement, at last. I unfolded the paper, held it close to his face.

'Your appeal,' I said. 'It has failed. Lost, Elihu. Forty thousand pounds, my dear. Forty...thousand.'

The noise was pitiful, a long rasping sigh.

He turned towards me, made a last gargantuan effort to raise himself from the bed, pointed one claw-like finger at me. Then he stiffened, his eyes wide with sudden fear.

And I saw the life go out of him.

Saturday 22nd July 1721

I broke my fast in the same room where I dined with young David, six years ago. The tortuous journey again. Five days. This very inn where I had also lodged on my first visit to Wrexham Regis.

'Your rooms are satisfactory, Mistress Yale?' said the innkeeper, Mister Roberts, as he served me some fresh goat's milk.

My rooms here are modest, though perfectly acceptable. The first floor of this additional wing, new-built in fine local red brick. All very much in the modern style. Spic-and-span. The table large enough to accommodate a rosewood writing slope upon which I scribble these lines – that I trust remain legible, despite the tremors that have now become a permanent companion in my seventieth year.

'I have stayed in worse,' I told him, sipping at the milk. 'Though it is all so – new.' The smoke fug somehow now suffused by fresh paint. 'And I preferred the old name. The George. I suppose your new owner was never going to retain anything that might imply his support for the House of Hanover.'

It must originally have been named for our saint, of course, but still…

'I could not say, ma'am,' he stammered, looked around in fear and the hope that anything he said to me would not be repeated to his employer.

'Could you not?' I said, loud enough for the whole room to hear. 'Watkin Williams – is he not the new owner? Or his father, at least. Though I suspect this town has a short memory. That peacock. That Jacobite peacock, sirrah. And had I known, I should have lodged elsewhere.'

In my mind I heard again the chanting from that riotous crowd. *Down with the Rump. Down with the German. High Church and*

431

Sacheverell. Long live the Chevalier. The singing: *When the King enjoys his own again.* And I saw the shattered window once more.

'Your late husband, madam. Always so generous. And with Mister Williams now bein' so highly placed, like…'

Yes, I knew this story also. How young Watkin Williams had become the Member for Denbighshire no more than a year after the riots. And then inheritance through the death of his father-in-law, so long as he added the old fellow's name, Wynn, to his own.

'Watkin Williams Wynn,' I said, moving some of my coddled eggs and hash around the plate. 'I must say it has a ring.'

'And Mister Yale's sad journey 'ere,' said Roberts, in that strong Welsh lilt. 'Can't 'ave been easy, I s'pose.'

I am suddenly sensible to the fact that I have been keeping these journals, more or less, for almost fifty years.

'I have noticed, Mister Roberts,' I said, setting down my milk and sniffing the air, 'that there is always a taste of iron upon the breeze here. The town's many metalworkers, I collect. Or is it perhaps from the blood, which I see still cakes the bull-baiting post outside. Mister Watkin Williams Wynn still savours such sanguinary sport, then?'

'He believes in the old ways bein' preserved, Mistress.'

'Preserved? Yes, I suppose. Like my husband, since you ask the question. Almost two weeks since his demise. Packed in salt, Mister Roberts, and preserved in his ice house at Queen Square while the arrangements put in place.'

In practice, he and his coffin spent last night at his other icehouse. Plas Grono. Thank heavens too that, though we had not paid excessively for the coffin, I had invested more heavily in its lead inner, its heavy waxed cerecloth winding sheet for, despite the quality and the preservatives, he has been leaking very badly. And five days since the corpse began its slow journey north, here to Wrexham. Well, at least that is long enough to know he shall not rise again. To be buried alive by mistake. Such things happen, of course, as I know so well. But that is a place to which I must not go, for that way lies a return to madness.

'Tragic, ma'am. Tragic. The Governor such a great man.'

'So said all the broadsides, and thus I suppose I must believe them,' I said.

That Tory rag, the *Post Boy* had reported extensively upon his death. And so had our own Whig faction's *Flying Post*. And last Saturday, *Applebee's Original Weekly Journal* marked Elihu's passing as a notable event – pushing many perhaps more significant events from their pages.

'A man for 'is times, like.'

I suppose that must be true also. And such times they have been. It had been here at the George – now the Spread Eagles – that six years ago I read Parrish's beautiful collection. All those verses he had dedicated to me, the masked intimacies. Though, at that moment, it was a few lines from his *Progress of Our Nation* that came to mind. But then we were joined by my maidservant, come to remind me it was time for my early appointment – with Elihu's attorney.

To my wicked wife…

That is what he wrote. Despicable fellow. His last will and testament, this Schedule in his own decaying, detestable hand that I should have known anywhere after all these decades. He did not even afford me my name. No *Catherine* even. Well, the curtness of phrase stands testimony to the man, says far more about Elihu Yale himself than any infamy it would ever cast upon one of my advanced years. Yet, beyond the phrase, there is nothing. A blank section upon the page. It cut me, and it angered me at the same time.

'Is this intended as some form of irony?' I said to the attorney. 'Some attempt at dark humour? He bequeaths me nothing, after all he owed me, and he symbolises the fact in this distasteful manner?'

There was rain whispering darkly at the small windows, a funereal gloom casting shadows upon the mysterious mounds of scrolls and documents piled ceiling-high around his establishment.

'Mistress Yale,' Mister Lloyd-Hughes attempted to correct me, 'I believe the Governor may simply have paused in the drafting.' It has always struck me as strange, that so many folk should continue to style my estranged husband as *the Governor* when he rescinded that title twenty years ago. At Fort St. George. Madras. But that is Elihu Yale for you. A long reach even in death. 'Never completed the task,' said the lawyer. 'Other clauses the same. Incomplete. Including your daughters.'

'At least he troubled to list our daughters' names,' I said. 'My only surviving son,' I went on, 'warrants not even a mention.'

'But this? Well, I must allow I never saw its likes before. This…'
He stabbed a finger at the offending line.

'A wicked wife?' I said. 'My husband was a pecksniff, sirrah. You had your own dealings with him. Well? Did you not?'

'Speak as you find, I always say. Or show me his friends and I'll tell you the man. All he's done for the town. For the church. You'll find few around here, madam, with a bad word for Elihu Yale.'

But plenty for me, I suppose. A wicked wife? Is this what was in his mind? Was this what fed those deathbed words of his? My fight for them all these years? Or was it Benjamin's court case? Or the way I hated him for each of their deaths. Five of them wasted, gone. My poor boys. Is hate too strong a word? Everybody needs someone to love, they say, and I suppose that I did love him. At times. In my fashion. But I think it is true that every one of us also needs an object for our hate – and how bizarre that, in Elihu, I seem to have found both in the one man.

If it were any of those, they were minor sins, though part of the reason that brings me here today, to set matters straight. To see him buried. But those other matters, of which I can barely write – oh, of those issues, he could hardly have known the half. The blood on my hands. The Poison Nut seeds. The traitors I have sent to the gallows. My revenge upon Elihu himself. And for those you should need to return to the beginning.

To the very beginning.

Fifty years ago, when I was still a young bride. Though not, of course, Elihu's bride. Not then.

I shall indeed read them all again, when I return to Latimer, though I know the things I shall find there. And I know too that the answer to this mystery must lie elsewhere. For Mister Lloyd-Hughes at least allowed me to scrutinise the will in more depth, and especially the Schedule of specific bequests. To Wrexham Parish for the care of their poor. To Barts Hospital. To that damn'd Gospel Society. To the Connecticut College. Other charitable amounts. And then all of those listed – including myself – with no sums confirmed.

There was a curiosity. The name of his by-blow, Charles Almanza, crossed out. But Katherine Nicks still listed. Was it simply that he could not bring himself to delete her? Or did she still live when he wrote this final testament. One other anomaly. He gives David Yale as "now in England and Wales", as though he had recently arrived. The answer was simple. That Elihu had penned this after the death of Don Carlos, but only just after David's arrival. So he had branded me his "wicked wife" eight years ago. Perhaps nine. Not "paused in the drafting" at all. By no manner of means. Why then? What was the connection? And why, in all that time, had he never completed or signed the thing? I suspect that the latter I may never discover, though I began to wonder whether the answer to the former questions might be more obvious than I initially thought.

But first there was the funeral and interment to attend.

His funeral cart was decked with flowers as it was hauled to a halt outside the inn. I had arranged it so. That the many mourners, hired and otherwise, might take a little mulled wine and biscuit before proceeding back along to the churchyard.

'We shall raise a glass,' I said, then recalled some words Elihu had spoken when he first returned from Madras. 'A parting glass.'

This time it was the bitterness of the wine that foretold a less than comforting outcome to the day, which set the tone for the afternoon. But I tried my best, forced myself to recall the words I once spoke to David Yale.

'I may loathe him,' I had said, 'but I have learned this much at least. That you cannot spend thirty-five years as anybody's spouse without you both becoming two sides of the same single coin.'

Well, it has been more than forty now, and I simply thank heaven that the time requirement for wearing widow's weeds is not incremental to the length of the marriage. Though I have to admit that when I had examined myself in the glass before descending, the ebon bombazine did seem to supplement my withered flesh quite handsomely. My linen beneath, of course, was all fringed white cambric, which matched my cap and lappets, but contrasted so elegantly – well, so I think – with the blackness of my silk shoes, my skirts and sleeves, my cane, my gloves, my paper fan and my gauze love-hood.

Gracious, a sea of blackness before me too, each of the ladies, naturally, and the gentlemen all in their weepers as well, their periwigs, silk suits, swords and buckles entirely a-match. Though there were few sorrowful countenances in evidence. It is Dean Swift,

I think, who observed that we shall often find the merriest faces in mourning carriages, and I think on this he may be correct. Some collective defence against the horror of mortality. Still, I suppose I had expected some greater measure of respect for the dead.

Yet there they were, revelling in each other's company: my girls, Kate and Annie, with their husbands and children – though not Ursula, who remains unwell at Latimer, Benjamin attending her; a host of notables and directors from John Company, with their wives; Thomas Pitt, dark-browed as ever, "Diamond" Pitt as he now seems to be universally known, presently Member for Thirsk, having surrendered his post as Governor of Jamaica – a post he served without ever having troubled to go there; Katherine Nicks's daughter Ursula, glowering at me from over in the corner, with her husband lawyer Sir Edward Betenson; and Bishop John Evans, that miscreant merchant parson, who officiated at Katie's wedding and my nephew's baptism but whose enmity I had earned long before by refusing to have the wretch marry me to Elihu.

'And to absent friends,' the Bishop cried now, as my own toast was repeated and glasses were indeed raised.

Absent friends. Oh yes. Old Langhorn gone, of course. And Streynsham having written with his condolences but incapacitated. Parrish's decision to stay away. But I thought about Sir Stephen Evance too, about how close he had been to Elihu until his financial crash. He would have been here, I think, bating his self-murther. Shot himself in the temple some years ago. And when that failed, hanged himself.

But there were many others present. And some in particular I needed to address.

'Mister Lloyd-Evans,' I said to the attorney. 'So good of you to be here.' I took his arm, walked with him, lowered my voice. 'It shall all take a long time to resolve – that he did not sign?'

'My pardon, mistress,' the lawyer replied. 'But there is the greater impediment. To a speedy resolution. The Crown's own claim against the bond that, sadly, in this case, your husband *did* sign.'

'Spilt milk, I fear.'

'Forty thousand pounds, madam – spilt milk?'

Well, I could hardly tell him the net loss to myself would be significantly less than that amount.

'Stuff!' I cursed. 'What an infernal mess.'

'All to be resolved by the Prerogative Court, I fear. Or a higher power.'

'How long, Mister Lloyd-Hughes?'

'It could be some time, see. Nothing moves rapidly through the Doctors' Commons.'

'The estate taken into trust, meanwhile?'

'Almost certainly.'

'He could have kept matters more simple. But now – I shall see him in his grave with even greater enthusiasm.'

I left him with his mouth hanging open, for here came another I should gladly have seen dead, that same Watkin Williams whose family now owned my lodgings.

'Mistress Yale,' said the young peacock. 'How sorry we were to hear of your husband's passing.'

There was a clerical fellow at his side, a rotund, more senior cove with bulging fanatical eyes.

'A tragedy, madam,' said this stranger. 'I had the honour of providing your husband's last consolation of religion, I believe. Just days before he cast off this mortal coil.'

'Indeed, sir? I fear I am not familiar...'

'Forgive me, ma'am,' said Watkin, with an insolent grin. 'Please allow me to name Doctor Sacheverell.'

It was a deliberate goad. I knew it was. I had made no bones about my distaste for Watkin's affiliations when last we met, yet here he was now, thrusting in my face this rabble-rousing sponsor of violence and rapine against Dissenters and Catholics alike. It felt as though Sacheverell had haunted my dreams forever and now here was the monster himself.

'You must feel very much at home here, sirrah,' I snarled at him. 'They say that Mister Williams – Mister Williams *Wynn*, I apologise – still hosts dinners here for his Jacobite traitor friends. Your friends too, then. In this very establishment. How proud you must be, stuffing your faces with the fruits of God's beneficence while setting ever more fatuous schemes for enticing gullible young innocents to their deaths upon battlefields that neither of you should ever deign to grace with your own blood.'

'You see, Doctor?' Watkin snapped. 'The serpent, the Eve, in Governor Yale's life.'

'And a pity, sir, that a serpent did not bite you in your crib.'

God in heaven, what made me think of that?

'They say, madam,' said Sacheverell, 'that you have the morals of a strumpet. And blood upon your own hands, though none on mine.'

'Directly?' I said. 'Only once have I taken life. At Preston, that was. And I only regret it was not the life of this town's traitor, Edward Hughes. No, that honour fell to Forster.'

The room was full of noise and bustle but, even so, I could see heads turning and, of all people, it was my son-in-law Dudley who came to my assistance.

'God blind me, gentlemen,' he said, 'have you no respect? Watkin, what is this?'

They know each other, of course. From Parliament. Perhaps other connections too – Dudley's links to the Jacobite cause through Lord North and Grey – though I think his views may be substantially more muted in the wake of the past few years.

'Hard to imagine,' said Sacheverell. 'Governor Yale such an ardent supporter of our High Church. Yet the wife...'

'My husband may have been many things. But he was no traitor. Neither Jacobite puppet-master nor puppet.'

'Declared himself a Welshman, did he not?' Sacheverell snapped.

'Factually,' I said, 'my husband was born in Massachusetts. His roots were always here, however, that's true.'

'Then, if a Welshman,' said Watkin, with disdain, 'how could he so tacitly endorse this German usurper? How not support the return of this country's true kings?'

'True kings,' I laughed. 'For pity's sake, how many times must you lose that fight?'

I turned from them, thanked Dudley for his unexpected support, but was immediately accosted by another rogue who was far from being a friend. Marshall, the rector of St. George the Martyr in Queen Square, a parsimonious little wretch who had introduced himself to me earlier.

'I hope you will not consider this inappropriate, Mistress Yale. But I must assume you have seen it – the will, I mean. And your husband such an ardent supporter of our Gospel Society...'

'Reverend Marshall,' I said, 'I have certainly seen the will. And there is indeed a bequest to your Society.' His thin face beamed.

'To help you, I collect,' I went on, all prim and proper, 'inflict your High Church missionaries on Dissenter and Quaker, as well as the innocent heathen, all across the world.'

'Madam...'

'But I have to tell you that the will is unsigned. What else might you have expected from one who was bubble enough to believe your twattle? And if you wish to await a Prerogative Court decision in your favour, sir, I must warn you that you shall see hell freeze over first.'

'Walk with me,' I instructed Annie, as the cortege prepared to move. 'Take my arm. Support me.'

The funeral-undertaker regarded me from the cart and I waved my gloved fingers at him, that he might proceed. To be fair to Mister Lloyd-Hughes, the attorney had written back as soon as I advised him of Elihu's death. No details of the will's specifics, simply confirmation that there was no named executor or administrator and therefore, as his lawful spouse, his widow, the duty fell upon me to arrange the funeral itself. And, for now, at least, I must needs stand the cost.

'This must be so difficult for you, Mama,' Annie said, wiping a tear from her cheek. Or a splash of rain perhaps. July. But showery, of course, this being the Welsh marches. So different from those other funerals. The merciless heat of Madras. My poor Joseph. Walter. And little David, God bless his soul. He would be thirty-four now. All those years. That was my grief, remembering them afresh.

'Not difficult. But I would speak with you, daughter.'

Some beadle with his staff of office took up position and, behind him, the minister and his parish clerk. Then the funeral-undertaker, and his four men lifting the coffin, draped in its heavy black pall – embroidered with the Yale coat-of-arms, white shield, red saltire cross, small wild boar above. I remember how proudly he had sported a *kurta* at Madras, patterned with tiny replicas of the same design. And I had asked James and Dudley to serve as pallbearers, so that they now came forward, straightened the cloth, then nodded their acceptance that all was in order.

'Is it Papa's will?' Annie asked as we stepped off behind the coffin, turning into the High Street while, by some splendid feat of planning, the lych bell at St. Giles tolled its first mournful summons to the funeral rights. The first of seventy-two, I had organised – and paid for – one for each year of his life.

'Indeed it is. I have told nobody else as yet. But the document – well, your father did not sign it.'

'He passed before…?'

'I wish it were so simple. No, my dear, it seems he had every opportunity. But you recall that night upon the barge? Herr Handel's music.'

'It was a strange night. Such animosity between you and then, at the end – well…'

'That night he accused me of wickedness,' I said.

'Wickedness? Why…'

'The reason does not signify. But he used the word again within his will. His wicked wife – that is how he describes me.' She gazed around, a pretext of looking for her children. 'What?' I said. 'You have no comment?'

We had processed half the length of the High Street, folk swarming in considerable numbers from the thoroughfare's many inns and shops. D'offed hats and bowed heads, and I acknowledged them all with a nod here, a sad smile there.

'Today, Mama?' said Nan. 'You choose to pursue this today? Well, I have my own questions. Many of them. Among other things, about whether you were with him when he died?'

'He still lived when I left him,' I lied. 'His servants found him next morning, did they not? But he said some strange things, Nan. And they brought to mind that night on the Thames. Something about lady scribblers. About secrets. And I saw a look upon your face. Anxiety. Or was it guilt, my dear? Had you told him, perhaps? About my journals? Other things? For the Schedule, in which he so defames me, was written some years ago. Around the time…'

'I know not what you imply, Mama.'

The death knell still tolled from St. Giles.

'Simply this. That only three people apart from myself have ever seen my journals. One of them was Vincent Seaton. Dead, of course. The second is Matthew Parrish, though he never read them, I think. And the third, my dear, was you.'

That one occasion when she came to visit and I had so foolishly left the ledger in full view. Eight years ago? Nine? Hard to say. But she had made some comment about lady scribes. About me being another Aphra Behn. About whether Nan herself received a mention. Astonishment that I had continued to fill my journals all those years.

'You expected me to keep it from him?' she snapped. 'I think it came as no surprise. Did you know – he had already smoked that it was you who wrote satires against him for the *Spectator*? I think I have never seen him so enraged?'

Perhaps Mister Addison had not, then, been as discreet as I had imagined.

'He would have blamed the articles,' I said, 'for denying him his knighthood, I suppose.'

'He did not say so,' Nan told me. 'Enraged, yet said little. Only that your journals must surely show a side of you he never saw. Never understood. Wicked, he said, that you never allowed him inside.'

Allowed him in? Ah yes, that was what he had said. Of all things, I thought, as we turned the corner into that short lane leading to the Parish Church. Of all the things I had listed in my mind as just cause for defaming me, this one had not occurred to me.

'My life,' I said, 'has been both bramble *and* its bounty, daughter. So many sleeping dogs I allowed to let lie where your papa was concerned. But the journal – I had never imagined...'

We passed through the exquisite new iron gateway – not here when I was last in the churchyard.

'Brambles, Mama?' she said. 'Was I one of them? All those years you could barely look at me, believed I had taken the very life from my brother.'

That again. After all this time.

'Strange, Annie, how we each bury resentments, brandish them from time to time whenever we need an excuse for our own bad behaviour. You betrayed me when you told him.'

'My fault then, Mama,' she taunted me, 'that my father named you a wicked wife.'

'Not really,' I said, as the death knell tolled for the final time. 'But your fault perhaps, Anne, that your papa would have shared his anger with Kate, Kate with Dudley. And then? Almost without doubt, Dudley with his cousin, William North. From Lord North, I imagine, to that devil, Colonel Porter. From Porter...'

The trail that led him to Latimer. From Porter to a cycle of death. Great heavens, such a web.

'What?' I said. 'You could not even trouble to spell his name correctly? After all he has gifted to your church?'

Reverend Jones had invited me to view the entry in the Record of Baptisms and Burials.

Eliugh, it said. *Eliugh*. Was it this fool's ignorance? He made some apology, of course, but it seemed to affect him all the way through the funeral rites, while I wondered what might have happened to Canon Price, who I had met during my last visit here. The ironies of vanity. My husband had not named me and they, on the other hand, could not be troubled to spell his correctly.

'I wondered, ma'am,' he said, as though that excuse for an apology was enough. 'As you say, Governor Yale so generous in life...'

And I laughed at his impertinence.

'A good friend of mine once reminded me, reverend,' I told him, 'that philanthropy is so often driven by fear of the Hereafter. Thus, you are a little late, perhaps. Elihu has already purchased his entrance ticket and I think he should rather resent discovering that the price has risen retrospectively.'

The coffin stood upon its trestles before the altar and the whole nave was hung with the blacks, the drapes for which I had paid so reluctantly, as well as for the mourning dress in which Elihu's Plas Grono household was all attired, and those other costs: the doles for the Poor and the Parrish; the sexton's fee for digging the grave; the burial plot itself; Reverend Jones's turgid sermon. Even the cheapest of fittings on that pine box.

But I was looking at the white marble slab on the floor – across from the wooden gallery, the one Elihu had financed for his private worship – next to the elaborate iron chancel gates he had also donated. It was the slab, leaf scrolls around the edges, marking the place beneath the floor where his family was buried: his father and mother, David and Ursula Yale; his aunt, old Mistress Hopkins; and his brothers, David Yale Junior and Thomas – Thomas who I had liked so much.

Marble. Elihu's will insists that he should have a chest tomb of marble. Black marble. Well, sometimes we must launch as linsey that we may linger as lace. So he will have to settle for decent, honest – and cheap – sandstone.

Rosemary. All those mourners at the open grave, each in turn, showering rosemary down upon the coffin. Many had not ventured inside the church. But at my side, one who might be very useful indeed. And he remembered me, this elegant fellow, still serving as a local magistrate, still living at Erddig Hall when he is not in London – when he is not at Chancery.

'I know I should not ask, Mister Mellor,' I said, 'but do you think there might be some way to expedite the procedures of the Prerogative Court?'

'Whatever did you have in mind, ma'am?' He peered at me down his long imperial nose.

'You plan to extend your property, I understand. At Erddig.'

'Already begun. One phase at a time, however. Resource permitting, as they say. Should not wish to repeat poor Edisbury's error. Indeed not.'

'His error, sir, was not to see my husband for the usurer he had become. Yet perhaps – I might be of assistance. That issue of resource, do you think?'

'We shall be neighbours?'

'I plan to sell Plas Grono as soon as may be possible. Another matter for the court, naturally.'

'And is there impediment, Mistress Yale? To the speedy settlement you desire.'

I explained the bond, made it clear I should set no obstacle to the Treasury's perfectly valid claim against the estate.

'Forty thousand,' I said, 'though sufficient remaining for our mutual benefit, I believe.'

The mourners seemed to have multiplied, an entire array of other umbrellos and rain-nappers now deployed against the downpour. Local tradesmen and the merely curious gathering around the family and Elihu's associates.

It was a more solemn and impersonal affair than the burial of Friend William Penn had been; the customary prayer from Reverend

Jones – *"for dust thou art, and unto dust shalt thou return"*; more rosemary sprigs cast into the ground; and only my son-in-law Dudley to break with tradition.

'It falls unto my lot,' he said, in a voice I barely recognised – presumably the one he reserves for parliamentary debate, 'to read the epitaph written by Governor Yale himself.'

And there was silence, bating only the soft patter of raindrops upon those same rain-nappers, including the umbrello held above Dudley's head by his manservant to protect the parchment.

'Born in America, in Europe bred,
In Afric travell'd and in Asia wed,
Where long he liv'd and thriv'd; at London dead.'

I had dutifully inserted the place of his demise, thanking the Lord he had not passed somewhere with more syllables for it should have spoiled the whole damn'd thing.

'Much good, some ill, he did; so hope all's even,
And that his soul, through mercy's gone to heaven.'

He paused a moment, blew his nose into an enormous white ker-chief. Then he proceeded, reading the final lines that only I, it seemed, knew were in truth penned by Parrish. And how pleasing now, that I had made the addition. *My wicked wife*, Elihu? Sweet revenge.

'You that survive and read this tale, take care
For this most certain exit to prepare
For only the actions of the just
Smell sweet and blossom in the silent dust.'

Those present, I think, were not quite certain how to interpret the sentiment.

'It pleases me no end, Mama,' said Kate, as departing mourners tossed handfuls of damp soil into the grave, 'that you permitted Dudley to read Papa's poem. Give you joy of it.'

It had been a minor sacrifice. After all, if I could marry Elihu for no better reason than to provide a surrogate though second-rate father for my boys, this was a comparatively easy bridge built on the road to repairing the breach with my older daughters. And there was a great deal of water flowed under that particular bridge since the days when I had been forced to see Dudley as a potential enemy. Besides, I have begun to think I may not have Ursula with me much longer.

'But those final lines,' said Dudley. 'So familiar.'

I still find it hard to tolerate the fellow, his Tory High Church principles. Though I think his ardour for the banditti has now been quenched. There were always his gaming debts and I could see he was on his best behaviour, plainly expecting Elihu's estate to hold some reward for him. But had he read Parrish's most recent collection?

'I believe,' I said, 'Elihu may have been inspired by that song. *The Glories of* – Lord, what is its name?'

'*Blood and State*,' Dudley beamed. 'Of course you are right. *The Glories of Blood and State*. I have sung it many times, have I not, my dear?'

Kate agreed.

'Though I think variations on the theme are common enough,' she said. 'And it may have been Papa's wish, but does it not diminish his achievements?'

'Well,' I said, 'his wish, as you say. And it shall soon be carved upon the side of his tomb.'

The case tomb the masons will be cutting and erecting over the coming months. The words capture him sufficiently for public consumption, I believe. And if he thought me wicked before, how much more must he despise me when he sees I have rubbed his nose in lines that Matthew Parrish scribed. And not for him!

'Bless you, Mama,' said Kate, as Nan and James joined us also.

I put my arm around Nan's shoulders to let her know that all was well between us, and she offered me a thin smile.

'Where is he now?' she wept. 'At the right hand of our Lord Jesu?'

I doubt that. But it pleases me to think he may share a pipe with my dear Joseph – who shall gently explain to him the error of his ways in handling my wayward nature – or take our little Davy in his arms once more, and at least exchange some civil discourse with my other lost boys. He remains here too. I see him in Kate and Annie, in their children. And I know it is more than just blood.

That there are so many here he has touched, shall continue to touch – myself included. This whole town, I suspect, will speak of him and keep Elihu Yale with them for all eternity. Beyond Wrexham, at Madras Patnam. And at New Haven in distant Connecticut. I hope that folk in days to come might visit his tomb, take pause to ponder the words they shall find written here. But first we needed to return to the inn. There would be food. Drink. Meats and sweets, as we say. More cost. But worth it. Another parting glass.

One more unpleasantness in store, however. That lawyer Betenson falling into step alongside me as I made my way back along the High Street. His wife, Katherine Nicks's daughter, that other Ursula, too.

'I have to assume,' he said, 'that my wife – perhaps her sisters and brother also – are named in your late husband's will.'

'Indeed they are Mister Betenson,' I said.

'Then there shall be a reading for the benefit of designated recipients? It is irregular, madam. For Governor Yale's attorney – Mister Lloyd-Hughes, I understand – not to have gathered the beneficiaries together.'

'Irregular, sir? But not legally necessary, I think.'

'We – I mean, my wife, Mistress Yale. My wife has entitlement.'

'In a will that is unsigned?' I said. 'Invalid?'

'Not...' stammered his wife.

'Unsigned,' I told her. 'And when the Prerogative Court issues a Grant of Probate you shall be entitled to see a copy. Though you should know, my dear, that you will see not a penny of my husband's estate.'

'Then we shall fight, madam. And we shall win.'

The rain had stopped, and I had halted also.

'Mister Betenson,' I said, looking him directly in the eye. 'I think you, perhaps, have not understood what has been happening here. For I have already won. I have outlived him.'

The Betensons did not join us for our meats and sweets at the inn. And nor did Watkin Williams Wynn. But there was one unexpected arrival waiting for me there. Jeremiah Dummer.

'Oh, ma'am,' he said. 'I should have been here for the service. But lost my way. Can you ever forgive me?'

'In truth, Mister Dummer, I had not expected to find you among these vultures at all.' I saw I had offended him, quickly apologised, explained to him about the will – but assured him I would try to make sure Elihu's wishes in relation to the college might be honoured. 'Five hundred pounds,' I said. 'It is considerable. And yet you, sir, have done so much more for the establishment. Inestimably more. It seems unfair.'

He laughed then.

'Oh, Mistress Yale,' he said, 'you surely did not consider that the Trustees would ever have named it Dummer College? Lord, how prime!'

He wandered off to collect a glass of wine. A fine selection of Alicantes I had ordered in honour of my own papa. And, outside, those July showers had turned to heavy rain that hammered at our windows, a wind that rattled our walls. And I could not help thinking of that day when the southwest monsoon had brought Elihu into my life. I had written that he was a most objectionable fellow, and I have often had cause to think him objectionable again over these past fifty years. A wicked wife? If he considered me thus through his hurt that I had not shared my inner thoughts with him, how much greater the hurt had I done so?

And I determined then that this shall be the last entry in my journals. I shall write no more, devoting my time to caring for my own Ursula in whatever span God grants her. I shall savour each day, my time with Matthew, dispose of Elihu's goods in preparation for the Chancery decision – perhaps appoint agents to employ auctions in the way my husband himself had done. No, I shall not write, and in that way I might rid myself of all the guilt I feel. Guilt for so many things. But I shall read. I shall visit again the pages of my *Pilgrim's Progress*, learn Mister Bunyan's instruction, remember Sathiri's lessons for dealing with my demons. I shall contemplate my own ending, and the changes I must make to my final wishes, for I think I shall require Benjamin to see that these ten volumes go with me into the grave. That seems appropriate. Oh, and perhaps the pocket pistol too. After all, one simply never knows!

The storm seemed to carry with it the voices of Madras Patnam's *masula* boatmen, their strange rhythms carrying above the surf. No more than the hubbub of Elihu's mourners in their merrymaking.

And Dudley – for whom I have never had great affection – came to stand beside me.

'Earlier,' he said, 'before the cortege, you raised a toast to Governor Yale. A parting glass – you recall?'

'I recall,' I told him.

'Excellent turn of phrase, Ma. Excellent. A stirrup cup to your husband's journey.'

It seemed to have touched him.

'There was a night,' I said, 'during that carnage at Preston. I was helping to tend the wounded.' I failed to tell him that I was slumped, exhausted, at poor Matthew's side just then. 'Our own and those of the rebels. It was the wee hours before dawn, and suddenly all the cries of those poor boys fell into silence. But one of the women began to sing. *The Parting Glass*, Dudley. She sang it so quietly. For one of those young men who had just given up the fight, in her arms. You know it, of course?'

He smiled at me as, I think, he has never done before and, without my bidding, he began to sing too.

'*O, all the money e'er I had,*
I spent it in good company.
And all the harm that ever I've done,
Alas it was to none but me.
Yet all I've done for want of wit
To mem'ry now I can't recall.
So fill to me the parting glass,
Good night and joy be with you all.'

There was, as they say, not a dry eye in the place.

Karma, I suppose, for as I joined them and raised my glass, I knew this was a stirrup cup also to my own travels, to those that have brought me here, and to that final journey upon which I must set out soon. Very soon, I think.

The End

Historical Notes and Acknowledgements

Ursula Yale died just two months after her father, in August 1721, following which Catherine remained at Latimer with her son Benjamin until her own death on 8th February 1728. By then, her eldest daughter (Katie) was also dead, for she does not appear in Catherine's will.

Streynsham Master – with whom Catherine must have been very well acquainted from their years together at Fort St. George – was also dead, in 1724.

Catherine seems to have spent her own last years in and out of the courts, either defending herself in the Betenson claim on behalf of the Nicks girls or pursuing her own claims to recover outstanding debts owed to her late husband. In truth, she also contested – successfully – that promise in the will of £500 to the Connecticut College. Meanwhile, pending the Chancery decision, Catherine needed to make arrangements for the disposal of Elihu's considerable collections. At the beginning of the 18th Century, it was usual to auction livestock, property – even a man's wife – but there is no record of "fine art and collectibles" auctions until Elihu Yale's coffee house sales just after his return from Madras. Natural then, perhaps, that Catherine would have employed the same method after his death. Seven separate auctions – the catalogues still exist – with 10,000 items in 3,600 lots for sale between December 1721 and April 1723, five of the events last six days each and one lasting four days.

Ursula and her mother were both buried at the Latimer House church, though Catherine's headstone is now lost to us.

Ursula's headstone, on the other hand, still lies next to the church door and reads as follows:

Under this stone lies the body of Ursula Yale the third and youngest daughter of Elihu Yale the sometime Governor of Fort St. George in India. She departed this life the 11th August 1721 in the 36th year of her age. Eminent for many virtues particularly her charity in which she excelled. And at her death shew'd the same by a very liberal donation to the poor.

Lady Anne (Nan) Cavendish was named as executor of Catherine's will though when Anne herself died in 1734 this duty passed to her half-brother Benjamin. The will itself was signed and dated the day before Catherine's death and allows for the settlement of her debts and funeral expenses, as well as a considerable number of bequests amounting to over £17,000 – a sum that, according to Bank of England inflation calculators, would now amount to about £3.4 million.

Benjamin lived on at Latimer, cared for by his faithful servant, Mary Hall, until his death in October 1743. Benjamin's own bequests helped to repair and "beautify" the church at Latimer where he's buried, and left a legacy of silver altar plate and chalices as well. He also left behind a charitable fund, which provided bread for the poor of the parish whenever they took communion, and also wine to be used for the communion itself.

He had been a great "subscriber" for new books too (an early form of crowd funding) so had his name listed as a financial contributor to various publications, a devout and learned man.

Benjamin was originally buried in a white marble altar tomb outside the farther end of the original church. Into the marble was carved an image of Benjamin's head, weeping cherubs and a coat-of-arms. Under the monument was a vault and, in the vault, lead coffins – Benjamin's, obviously, and almost certainly Catherine's. When the church was effectively re-built in 1841, the new south wall of the south transept divided the vault and effectively sealed off Catherine's burial place.

Next to Ursula's headstone is a more damaged memorial stone that reads:

In memory of good men being required to encourage the exercise of duty and honour in succeeding generations that it may be known that here lie the remains of Benjamin Hynmers Esq.

The rest of the inscription is difficult to decipher but talks about: *his sincerity, integrity, innocence of manner and his benevolence, distinguished by a firm attachment to the constitution of the kingdom, church and state.*

The dedication contains the names of Jonathan Wood and William Hall gentleman, probably his executors – William Hall being the brother to Benjamin's "faithful servant" Mary Hall. In addition, there is mention of his mother, Catherine Yale. William inherited portraits of Catherine and her daughters, Katherine and Anne, though the later history of these paintings is a mystery. Similarly, we have no idea what happened to Benjamin's white marble tomb.

Despite the number of grandchildren to Catherine and Elihu Yale, their line now seems to have vanished into history, with no direct descendants still surviving.

But their legacy lives on. Yale University ranks, in the history of humanity, as one of the world's greatest seats of learning, along with Kraków, Salamanca, Oxford and many others. Its name is synonymous with liberal education and greatness in the arts, regardless of any flaws there may have been in the character of the man whose name it bears. And it is therefore nonsense that the name should be changed, as some have suggested, because of Elihu Yale's involvement, as Governor of old Madras, in the Indian slave trade. The name is to be celebrated, rather than airbrushed from history, and Elihu, I think, deserves his place in history for that reason alone. This view was strongly impressed upon me when, during the writing of this third part of the trilogy I was fortunate enough to spend some time on the campus at New Haven, Connecticut, where myself and my wife Ann were treated with exceptional kindness by everybody we met, though I especially want to acknowledge the help we received from Harry Cohen at the Yale Bookstore, from Colleen at the Atticus Bookstore Café, and from Larsson, Liz and Ed at the New Haven Information Office.

Like Robert Clive, Elihu Yale is also a controversial figure in helping, through the Honourable English East India Company, to lay the foundations for the British Raj. Historians and social commentators, both in India and Britain, are still at odds about the various pros and cons of British colonisation in the Sub-Continent – often citing positive social reforms and infrastructural development on one side, but economic and political subjugation, as well as atrocities, on the other. Yet, warts and all, this was a hugely significant period in the history of both nations and, as such, Yale deserves his place there too. Indeed, I have been surprised at the extent to which he has become neglected as a notable historical character, particularly in Britain itself, and I want to thank those who have helped me understand this better.

And Part Three obviously required a lot of additional research and full details of the various resources employed over the three novels are listed on my website, www.davidebsworth.com.

The chapters set back in England and Wales were particularly difficult since, though Yale and Catherine mostly lived apart following his return to London, they remained married and must obviously have encountered each other at the many family weddings and funerals, or similar occasions. Sadly, no record now remains of those meetings. Once again, therefore, I have tried to plausibly fill the gaps while keeping my fictional back-story moving along at a decent pace and using some of the "clues" so clearly visible, for example, in the lengthy correspondence between Elihu and Katherine Nicks, now in the archives of Yale University. And a quick word about Southampton Row? This is mentioned in Yale's biographies as the location for several houses in which he stored his collections. Southampton Row seems to have been so named much later than the period in which this novel is set and is more likely to still have been known as King Street.

I have tried to create credible historical backgrounds: for Catherine's years at Latimer; for life in the Bethlem (Bedlam) Hospital; for the Wrexham riots of 1715; for the Battle of Preston in that same year; for that first performance of Handel's Water Music; for Elihu's death and funeral; and for the way that Yale helped to ruin poor Edisbury.

But there were a few more intriguing things I should share with you.

Elford's Coffee House, for example, continued to be a fine London establishment until at least 1748 and Catherine's father,

Walter Elford, is credited with the invention of a particularly clever machine for the roasting of coffee beans.

Poor Sir William Langhorn (Langhorne), on the other hand, did indeed die in 1715 at the age of 85, having only recently married his second wife, the incredibly young Mary Aston – who then disappeared entirely from the pages of history. Again, Catherine and Sir William would have known each other very well from Madras.

In the 1700s, also, an unconventional means of payment for admission to the Royal Menagerie at the Tower of London came into force. People could enter without having to pay the three halfpence fee – all they had to do was to bring some cats or dogs to feed the always-hungry lions. Apologies but I could not resist. But at least I reprieved the puppy in the end. Well, to be honest, Ann insisted on it!

And those many prisoner escapes from Newgate Prison and the Tower in 1716? All perfectly true. It made me wonder why anybody would have been stupid enough to hang around waiting for the execution!

Then the famous picture of Elihu Yale seated at table with the Duke of Devonshire and Lord James Cavendish. Yale University owns two versions of this painting, which purports to represent the betrothal of Anne (Nan) Yale to Lord James Cavendish. The artist is unknown. But in 1717 Enoch Seeman the Younger painted a famous portrait of Yale. Enoch Seeman the Elder (his father) had arrived in London in 1704 (his son was then about 10) and a member of the Danzig (Poland) Mennonite (German Anabaptists) Church and it is at least possible that Seeman the Elder painted that earlier picture. And I was taken with the often-expressed view that Yale probably commissioned the painting himself. Yale stares out of the canvas as though he is somehow the Duke of Devonshire's equal, Elihu boasting a famous diamond ring, surrounded by images of international trade – and, of course, the little black slave-boy! And hence the novel's premise that Yale invented the entire scene for his own self-promotion.

Perhaps a word about Matthew Parrish's poetry as well. Parrish is an entirely fictional character but he is based quite loosely on real-life diplomat and poet Matthew Prior, who also died in 1721. Prior's politics were very different from those of our Matthew but there are lots of parallels between their lives. So, when I needed some lines of verse, I looked for appropriate poems written by Prior and then rewrote them in a similar style but with my own words. I hope that works.

Similarly, Colonel John Porter is fictional but based on the real Jacobite colonel, John Parker.

Catherine's actress friend, Annie Bracegirdle, is buried at Westminster Abbey.

Pitt's diamond is, of course, famous too. He bought the rough stone for £20,400 (equivalent to £3,252,000 in 2018), and had it cut into a cushion brilliant of 141 carats (28.2 grams). After many thwarted attempts to sell, it was eventually purchased by the Duke of Orléans in 1717 for £135,000 (equivalent to £20 million in 2018). The involvement of Katherine Nicks and Catherine Yale in its story is entirely fictional but the true history of the stone is probably stranger anyway. It was later set into the crown of Louis XVI, then adorned one of Marie Antoinette's hats, was stolen but recovered during the French Revolution, ended up in the pommel of Napoleon Bonaparte's sword, then in the crowns of Louis XVIII, Charles X and Napoleon III, and then in a diadem for the French Empress Eugénie. Its current value is estimated at around £50 million.

Finally, here, the tale of Elihu's tomb. It stands just in front of the fine tower at St. Giles in Wrexham and the famous poem may still be read upon its side. Or, at least, a version of the poem. It reads slightly differently from the lines given at the end of the novel – although we know that these were the very words that graced the sandstone slab throughout the 18th Century and through most of the 1800s too. In addition, the script presently to be seen does not even resemble one that would have been in use during 1721. But we know that the tomb was substantially renovated by the Yale Corporation in 1874, because the original slabs were in such poor condition. Indeed, there is evidence to suggest that the Corporation's representatives were obliged to ship the original all the way back to New Haven in order to make the case. Good for them! But that original sandstone slab – where is it now? Destroyed, perhaps. Though there is a strange yarn, with some credibility, that members of one of the university's more notorious student bodies, the Skull and Bones senior class society, stole the slab and have, ever since, had it on display in their own Society Hall, also known as The Tomb, on the campus grounds. I still hope that, one day, a Bonesman may read this and kindly send me a photograph by way of evidence.

But confessions? I think I only have a few: first, that I brought forward the year of Legh Master's marriage to Margaret Launder and therefore his occupation of New Hall; second, that I am (almost) certain Catherine would not have been at Elihu's deathbed; and, third, that Elihu almost certainly wrote that epitaph for his tomb himself, though perhaps with some help from his son-in-law, Sir Dudley North, who perhaps helped him adapt those final few lines from another source. As always, however, I am sure there must be many more confessions to be made, so perhaps allow me to finish as usual with the catch-all disclaimer that, naturally, any other accidental errors in the history are entirely my own.

Last, but not least, the title. *The Parting Glass* (the song) has enjoyed something of a revival lately. Recordings by Ed Sheeran and Cara Dillon among others. And now by our daughter-in-law, Monika Evans. But I remember it as a staple of folk groups like the Dubliners, the Clancy Brothers and the Corries. It dates back at least four hundred years, the earliest printed version is from the 1770s, but there are references to it on song collections from 1615 onwards. The words also appear in a poem known as *Armstrong's Goodnight*, penned by a Border Reiver executed in 1600. And thus, though it literally celebrates the custom of offering a stirrup cup – a final hospitality drink to fortify departing guests once they were mounted – it has come to be associated with partings in general and, of course, bereavements. And since Catherine suffered so many tragic losses in her life, it seemed entirely appropriate to the story. After all, of the eight children we know about, only Nan and Benjamin survived her – and Nan only by a very few years. Benjamin therefore the only one who lived past the age of fifty. I've used here the most commonly known lyrics of the song – though Sir Dudley North (an accomplished singer, it seems) would undoubtedly have known very different lines.

In closing, I should say that setting out to write a trilogy is itself terrifying. What happens if the story dries up after Part Two? A thousand other dangers. But we got there in the end and I hope the novels have helped to bring Catherine Hynmers Yale out from the shadows of history.

David Ebsworth
Wrexham, North Wales, April 2020

A Letter to Readers and Supporters

The encouragement I've enjoyed on this journey has been especially appreciated. The writing itself has largely been completed through the tolerance of the teams at my favourite coffee houses – Lot 11 in Wrexham and Pastelería Monge in Guardamar del Segura. More of the scribbling and all the rewrites in the Reading Rooms of our wonderful Gladstone Library in Hawarden.

My thanks for the support, variously, from authors Vaseem Khan, Waheed Rabbani, Deborah Swift and Barbara Erskine; from Thomas Tharu and Thirupurasundari Sevvel at the Madras Literary Society; and from Parvez Mahmood at Pakistan's *The Friday Times*. Thanks too for the kindness shown to myself and Ann by Rosemary and John Went during our visit to Latimer church itself during the summer of 2018; by Katherine Gwyn at the Buckinghamshire County Archives, as well as Anqa Tirmazee-Kaleem at the De Vere Latimer (Catherine's home for 20 years), and the staff at the hotel there who made our stay such a pleasant one.

As usual, my deepest thanks to the regular team – Helen Hart and her publishing assistants at SilverWood Books; cover designer Cathy Helms at Avalon Graphics; editor Nicky Galliers; my ideal beta reader Ann McCall; and, of course, to all those "subscribers" to the first two parts of the trilogy who are named at the end of those novels, along with Joe Dwek and his Family Trust who helped to make the work possible – in fact, to everybody who took the trouble to read this and helped bring Catherine Hynmers Yale to life!

If you want to keep in touch, I send out regular monthly newsletters and I'm always happy to chat and answer questions.

My website is: www.davidebsworth.com. You can sign up for the newsletter there too. I'm also on Facebook (my personal page, dave. mccall.3 plus my David Ebsworth author page, @EbsworthDavid) and occasionally Twitter (@EbsworthDavid). And if you liked the books, a short review is always welcome.

Thanks again for taking the time to read all this and best wishes.

David Ebsworth
April 2020

CPSIA information can be obtained
at www.ICGtesting.com
Printed in the USA
BVHW030239090920
588367BV00001B/2